Murder at the Metropolitan Opera

Dear Jill —
We met at the Wesselis and
enjoyed Bloody Marys together.
I hope you get a chuckle out
of their literary exploits . . .
The next book is about the K.P.
garden club + why can't you be
in it? Let's talk!
Happy Reading
Joyce

J. Tracksler

Llumina
Press

Original cover design by bryce creative, kittery point, maine

This is a work of fiction, although many incidents, names and places, while real, are used fictitiously. Most historical references have been meticulously researched, however, a bit of history had been fudged here and there. For purposes of the story-line, some dates have been moved slightly, but not much. The names of many of the characters have been borrowed from friends, and these, while real, have also been used fictitiously, you lucky ducks, you.

ISBN: 978-1-60594-111-0

Printed in the United States of America by Llumina Press

Library of Congress Control Number: 2008905602

Dedication

This book is dedicated first to Ron and Sherry Leard of Forked River, New Jersey. Forgive me for my omission last time...

And to the *real* Baroness Barbara and Baron David Wessel, and their generous support of the Vermont Symphony Orchestra, and Radio Station WDEV...

And to the *real* Troy family: Alex, Dale, Ariel Sarah, Rachel, and Abby and their generous support of the DOMUS charity

And to the *real* Frank DeSarro and his family, and his support to the Seacoast/AIDS Foundation

And to the *real Angelique* - Debbie Orloff – the BEST Musetta ever...and her always generous and unflagging support of Fair Tide, Kittery, Maine

And to the *real* Carey Marvel Mabley – a true renaissance woman and a high flyer...and her always generous support of Fair Tide, Kittery, Maine

And a special GHS-59 thanks to Tom and Sue Z, for my sweatshirt which says: "Careful...or you'll end up in my novel!"

And always, to my own Captain Jack, Kathy and Adam, Jenny and Matt, Boon and Ruby...

FYI

Every evening, after supper, Death sits down to make the list of who will be taken the following day. Among those present at the table are Mother Nature and Birth. It is Birth who informs the group of how many new souls will join the living and where the new babies will be born. Based on Birth's information, Death schedules a nearly-equal number of demises. Otherwise, the World would be too burdened.

Death is fair, apportioning a certain percentage of the elderly, but also picking a few who are in their prime, and even some who are very, very young.

It is all based on actuarial tables – nothing personal – just an efficient way to keep the balance on Planet Earth. All the planets in this Universe and other Universes that harbor life work on the same principal.

Epically tragic events, such as earthquakes, tidal waves, avalanches and so forth, are handled by Mother Nature, who confers with Death a week or two beforehand, so that the count of souls on Planet Earth stays on an even keel.

It usually goes as planned, but once in a while there are some screw ups. Sometimes a person who is scheduled to die suddenly, for no reason, really, except that he or she is on Death's List, changes his or her plans and isn't in the spot where he or she should be when Death comes to collect them. Death then makes an on-the-spot decision to either take someone else along (usually someone who is nearby), or, perhaps to wait until the next day to accomplish the original task. More often, there is an unexpected death, generally caused by murder...a surprise to Death and Death's plans. When this happens, Death mutters a few choice curse words, and then... philosophically... scratches off a similarly-aged, similarly-sexed person who was to die from his list. Death really doesn't care one way or the other. It just has to balance out in the end, so to speak. How Death handles these exceptions to the otherwise smooth plan makes for interesting conversation and some spirited discussion the following evening around the table.

Greenwich, Connecticut, July 1929

*They were careless people...they smashed up things
and creatures..., F. Scott Fitzgerald, The Great Gatsby*

"Yahoo!" Ernie Soames careened the old jalopy around the corner, tires screeching protest; the entire car nearly out of control. "What a hoot!" He laughed, a hysterical cackle, and steered the car with maniacal glee left and right, veering all over the darkened street. "We're hittin' on all six!" In the inky darkness of the moonless night, the car rattled and lurched onto the sidewalk, nearly hitting a tree.

"Watch it, you sap!" Lorne Roxbury punched Ernie's shoulder. "You dope! You'll crash and we'll get pinched! We gotta' be careful!"

Ernie reached under the seat and pulled out the bottle of hooch they'd stolen from his Uncle Norman's cellar before they'd left that night. He steered the car with his elbow and uncapped the bottle. "Uncle Norm will be pretty futzed when he finds out that you stole his booze." He swallowed, then nearly choked, coughing and wheezing. The car's carburetor sputtered and almost stalled as Ernie stepped hard on the gas.

"Cut it out, Ern, you loon!" Lorne grabbed the bottle. "Just drive this fliver and don't goon around!" Lorne drank deeply, tilting the jug up. "Ahhhh! That's the cat's whiskers! Man!" His eyes watered and he coughed.

"D'ju finish it? You scag!" Ernie reached over, hoping that the bottle still held a few mouthfuls. "Gimme some a' that!" He wrestled for the bottle. Lorne held it just out of reach, jeering at him. The car, without anyone to steer, leaped the curb again, heading for a row of hedges.

"Holy Joe!" Lorne's mouth went dry. "Look out!"

"Ahhh, keep your hair on." Lightheaded with the hooch, Ernie jerked at the wheel, turning the jalopy back into the street. "I got it all under control." He raced the engine as he approached the corner that would lead them into Church Street. He took the corner on two wheels, laughing and grabbing again at the bottle. The car spun around, skidding, and Ernie took both hands off the wheel. "Yee, ha!" He grabbed the bottle and held it high, trying to see by the light of the street lamp if was empty. Again, the car bumped over the curb and climbed the sidewalk. There was a loud smacking sound and Lorne's mouth dropped as he watched the insubstantial body of Louisa Mae Sokol, who would have been seventy-nine the next day, bounce into the air, slide over the car's hood and drop to the ground on the other side. Other than the bumping noise, she didn't make a sound.

"*Christ*, Ernie! You *hit* her!" Lorne's eye bugged out. "Stop the car!"

Ernie's mouth went dry as he almost sobered, realizing what he had done. He braked for a moment, opened his door and saw the darker heap on the darkness of the ground. Panicked, he slammed his door and jerked the car forward. "I ain't stoppin'. She's a goner. The cops…the cops…if they catch us…." He floored the engine and the jalopy shuddered back over the curb and into the street.

Death was there immediately, gazing dispassionately at the crumpled body of Louisa Mae. *Pity. She wasn't on his list until December of 1934.*

THE METROPOLITAN OPERA HOUSE PRESENTS

Fall-Winter season - OPENING NIGHT SATURDAY EVENING, OCTOBER 12, 1929

LA BOHÈME

MUSIC BY GIACOMO PUCCINI --- LIBRETTO BY GIUSEPPI GIACOSA AND LUIGI ILLICA

PREMIER GUEST CONDUCTOR - MASSIMO ORSINI

Marcello, An artist ....Dante Lazzarelli

Rodolfo, A Poet ....Sergei Andreyi

Colline, A philosopher .... Josef Mercurio

Schaunard, A musician ....Claudio Vizzi

Benoit, The landlord ....Simon Forest

Mimi, A poor seamstress................................... Vivienne du Lac

Parpignol, A toy vendor...................................... Niles Samuelson

Musetta, A flirt.. Angelique Orloff

Alcindoro, A rich and infatuated old man ....Sandor Calli-Curri

Old Waiter ....Michael Merriman	Young Waitress ....Gay Ann Fay
A Vendor of Flowers .... Muriel Durgin	A Vendor of Sweets........Antonina Sabatino
A Vendor of Fruits .... Frank Antonio	A Vendor of Larks ....Joanetta Grasser
A Vendor of Clothing ...... Marcia Parmenter	A Vendor of Fish.......... Dana Foster
A Mother .... JoAnn Paradis	The Rag Woman ....Karen Heffernan
Young Male Beggar ...... Philip Perri	Female Beggar ....Sue Shigeoka
Old Male Beggar .... Ralph Bocchetta	The Flamenco Dancer ....Carlota Santana

THE CHILDREN ... Wendy Mason, Lorraine Palmer, Frances Bierel , Donna Iannuzzi, Susan Kelly, Kristin Rettino, Jeb Brethauer, James Pariello, Molly Murphy, Cheryl DeToro, Ann Perri, Angela Perri, Olga Bryant, Virginia Costaregni, Susan Brethauer, Juliana Rettino, Jason Stelman, Alyssa Stelman, Amanda Stelman

THE MOTHERS/THE FARM WOMEN...Ellen Kingsbury, Ardenia Wood, Jennifer Stevens, Ruby Stevens, Patricia Salzillo

THE SOLDIERS......George Lamonica, George Wood, James Brunetti, Curtis Neel, George Badolato, Harold Moran, Paul Giggi, Lloyd Williams, Richard Monaco, Joseph Naylor

THE TOWNSPEOPLE .... Betty Tortora, Karen Stewart, Sandra Martens, Diane Meyler, David Particelli, Don Dietrich, Craig Newhouse, Rita Parmelou, Mary De Toro

UNDERSTUDIES: PYTER OMEROSA, KOROL PETROFF, IGNATZIA VOLENTE, ZIZANNE FOND

THE METROPLITAN OPERA COMPANY

BOARD OF DIRECTORS

Baron F. David Wessel, Chairman

Alex Troy, Chief Financial Officer

Rawlins I. Cottinet

T. de Witt Hollister

Sir Dennis Staer, B.P.O.O.N.

Commodore John Carson

W. K. Vandersmythe-Winthrop

Sir Eustace Maltravers-Goffe

Chalmers Petrof

Ambassador Charles Mabley

Cornelius Marvel-Mabley

Sir Richard Dillworth D'Allee

Horatio Cooperstyne

The Honorable Athol Wolf III

EXECUTIVE STAFF

Arturo Calle, Executive General Manager

Urbano Valeria, Master Stage Manager

Sigrid Chalmers, Assistant Stage Manager

Anatole Goodman, Choral Director

Lucian Bolte, Master, Ballet Corps

Rudolph Schubin, Orchestral Assistant

Henry Wu, Make Up Director

Victor Calligari, Wig and Hair Stylist

Fausta Cleva, Costumes and Wardrobe Mistress

Forsythe Wicks, Properties

Johnston Redmond, Master Electrician

Timothy Weaver, Master Carpenter

Janet Connelly, Dresser to the Ladies

Peter Pawlowski, Prompter

METROPOLITAN OPERA CHORUS

Morgan McCurdy, Lillian Quimby,
Michael Connors, Nancy Connors,
Maria-Pia Assoluta, Charlotte Ryan,
Robyn Benson, Roque Nunez, Horz Bortel,
Patricia Flynn, Marrietta Bossie, Lorraine
Carpentier, Juliana Patten, George Patten,
Jan Lawrence, Peter Curry, Craig Newhouse,
Sandra Marks, Rita Pomerleau

METROPOLITAN ORCHESTRA

Garvin McCurdy, 1st Violin
Alice Mary McCurdy, 2nd Violin
Patricia Odams, Eileen Boyle,
Dean Armandroff, Thomas Zeranski,
Mary Frangiamore, Wendy Littman,
Kathie Hess, Arthur Littman,
Joanna Farman, Carol Barnes,
Judith Pedersen, William Ferdinand,
Harriet Grannick, Milton Bickle,
Audrey Brogden, Dorothy Jill
Cleveland, Vas Hubert Brogden,
James Fay, Leon Venedicktou,
Joy Anderson, Janet Merriman,
Marion Craig, Barbara Upton, Pat
Laulette, Virginia Gerstung, Lynn
Parker, Donna Freeland, Marlene
Littlefield, Rose Nunn, Ruth Walsh,
Jack Murphy, Elaine Neale,
Jami Uretsky.

Chapter one

*Because I could not stop for death,
his carriage stopped for me...Emily Dickenson...*

The Baroness Barbara Wessel took one last look into the mirror, checking to be sure that her lipstick wasn't smeared. The mirror reflected a slim, modish woman, wearing a dark blue charmeuse dress accented with a red and white patterned scarf. A navy cloche hat hid Barbara's blonde curls. The dress fell just below her knees in the very latest style, and Barbara's superb legs were encased in silk stockings purchased while she and David were in Paris last month. Barbara's smooth forehead creased with a doubtful frown. Might Lady Maltravers-Goffe think her dress too short? Barbara snorted to herself and spoke out loud, "Who cares about Lady Maltravers-Goffe? The stuck-up old biddy! It's none of her beeswax!" Barbara turned around and twitched her slim silhouette, secure in her own youth, wealth and loveliness, stuck her tongue out at herself and the absent Lady Maltravers-Goffe, then reached for her gloves, not knowing, of course, that she was third on Death's list for New York City for the morning of Friday, October 11, 1929. The taxicab, driven by a gentleman named Sirus Zetner, who was number two on Death's list, would be at the front portico in five minutes. According to Death's plan, Barbara and Mr. Zetner, together with four others, were to be taken in exactly eighteen minutes.

She pecked at the cheek of her husband, David, who would miss her greatly after her already pre-planned death, and then stooped to pat the wooly head of Teddy, their beloved Fox Terrier. Teddy would miss her even more than David.

Teddy whined. Some say that dogs have some extra-sensory perception, and, in Teddy's case, that particular homily appears to have some basis for truth. He was a very well-behaved doggie who would ordinarily never dream of jumping up on anyone, much less Barbara, but today...today was different. Today, Teddy was a bad doggie. He leaped upward, barking with sharp, staccato yelps and his paws landed in the vicinity of Barbara's expensively silk-clad knees. In his bout of unusual agitation, Teddy's claws ripped great holes in the cobwebby stockings, and Barbara, after administering a blistering tirade to the dog, had to change her plans and her stockings.

With Teddy in disgrace, dragged off by his collar by Barbara's maid, Carolyn, confined to the kitchen and swatted (carefully, with more noise than

1

strength...the Wessels really loved the furry creature) by David with yester-day's copy of The Herald Tribune, a slightly more stressed Barbara once more began her exit from the Wessel's Central Park West apartment.

Of course, because of all the delay, Barbara didn't appear on time at the apartment's portico. Death had already scripted the crash that was to happen and, although a bit disappointed that Barbara had inadvertently messed up the list, quickly adjusted. Ergo, as you have already figured out, Barbara wasn't in Mr. Zetner's taxicab which crashed into the horse-drawn brewery wagon three bocks north of The Metropolitan Opera House. Her seat in the taxicab... and... coincidentally, her place on Death's list ...was replaced by the well-cushioned rump of Alicia Duvall, who lived on the third floor of the Wessel's apartment complex. After dawdling over her morning coffee and toast, Mrs. Duvall had hurried to catch a taxicab to her seamstress' apartment. The Wes-sels and Teddy resided on the sixteenth floor and had a much better view of Central Park. Alicia Duvall was a widow who hated dogs, which was a mis-take on her part, as perhaps her own pup might have prevented her own early demise. Alicia Duvall and Mr. Zetner really do not impact this story any fur-ther except to show that the axiom "When your time is up, it's up" is not always necessarily true.

That evening, Death and the rest of the group had a good chuckle at it all and Barbara's name was put back into the huge receptacle that held the lottery for the next day. There were so many names in the receptacle; however, that in reality, Barbara Wessel ultimately lived to an extremely old age.

"Why is traffic so congested?" Barbara asked the taxicab driver. She was going to be late for her meeting and still harbored a bit of annoyance at Teddy's bad-boy behavior.

"Bad crash, Ma'am," the driver, a curly-haired young man named Neil Odams, informed her. "I heard that a couple of people died." He spat out of the window and shook his head.

"Oh? How awful." Barbara dismissed the tragedy. After all, it had nothing whatsoever to do with her. A policeman whistled to them and the taxicab lurched forward to the middle of the intersection before the cross-town traffic blocked it once again. "Officer?" Barbara opened her window, batting her enormous green eyes upward. "What is happening?"

Newly appointed Detective Third Class Joseph Manger, known to his friends as Buddy, approached her. *Good lookin' dame*, he noted. *Class all the way through.*

He touched his cap. "There's a very bad accident ahead, over on 37th, just a block before the Met." Barbara, although a very happily married woman, was aware of Detective Third Class Manger's blue eyes and smoothed her skirt.

"What happened, Buddy?" Neil Odams had no knowledge that Detective Third Class Manger was, in fact, sometimes called Buddy. "Anybody killed?"

Buddy looked morose. Here he was, a newly appointed detective, stopping cars and waving them on again, like a lowly traffic cop. He should be over at the scene of the accident, not here shoving buses and trucks and delivery wagons around. "I hear it was a bad crash." He looked down again at Barbara's knees, visible through the open widow. "A taxicab and a brewery wagon. A couple of people crushed and one horse dead, too. Where are you headed, Ma'am?"

"Oh, Officer!" Barbara gasped. "Actually, I'm going to a *meeting* at the Met! I should have been right at 37th about fifteen minutes ago!" She pressed her gloved hand to her mouth. "I was late today! I would have been…my dog…It might have been me!" *Indeed*, Death observed. *How true, how true.*

Detective Third Class Manger gave a suitably astonished gasp and bowed toward Barbara. He acknowledged that any such accident to her person would indeed have been a tragedy. An automobile blew its horn in frustration. A horse-drawn wagon shifted forward, a man shouted an obscenity and traffic began to creep ahead. Reluctant at leaving such an attractive diversion, Buddy Manger waved his hands at the chaos of oncoming traffic, touched the brim of his cap and yelled at the driver of the horse-drawn wagon.

"My wife works at the Met," Neil Odams spat out of the window again. He half-turned around conversationally. Odams wasn't worried, though. "My wife, Patricia, isn't due to be at the Met until noon time."

"Noon time? *Really?* Is she an opera singer?" Barbara's green eyes were wide. The name didn't resonate, but there were so many people who worked at the Met…

"Nah. She plays the organ, the piano-forte, and tonight, she'll be at the harp." Neil shrugged his shoulders. "She's an educated woman." He hunched his shoulders and said with some pride; "Learned how to play the piano and the harp and all. Not like me." He tapped the wheel. "All I can do is drive a cab. She's the star in our marriage."

"How clever," Barbara sat forward, marveling that both she and the organ-playing Mrs. Taxi-Driver had serendipitously just missed being injured. "Will she be at the rehearsal today?"

"Yeah, but she goes in later. Lucky for her and lucky that you didn't get an earlier taxi." Neil Odams stuck a cigar into his mouth and noisily shifted into second gear. His taxi swung around the hapless horse and in a few moments, he safely delivered his passenger to the corner of 39th and Broadway. Neil surprised himself by leaping out of the cab and running around to open the back door. "Here you are, lady…I, uh, I don't know what your name is…I mean, I'm gonna tell Patricia that you…I mean…"

Barbara hesitated and then spoke, "Barbara Wessel. Mrs. Wessel." She felt that she really didn't have to mention that she was a baroness. It just wasn't necessary and might sound snobbish. He was a nice man and she was still slightly unnerved to know that she just might have been in an accident if Teddy hadn't been a naughty dog.

Neil put out his hand and assisted Barbara out of the taxicab. Amused by his gallantry, she paid the fare, accompanied by a suitable tip. "I'll see if I can find your wife later on today. I'll say hello to her." Barbara was really a very nice person and certainly democratic. After all, she had come from an old and slightly impoverished family and understood that sometimes, one married taxi-drivers. Fortunately, *she* hadn't. *She'd* married darling and wealthy David. She turned back and gave Neil a slight wave, then climbed the broad steps that led to the heavily embossed gold doors. The taxi driver watched her. *Nice looking woman*, he again mused to himself. *Good legs in those silk stockings*. He grinned, happy that the new styles and recently raised hemlines allowed him this glimpse of feminine glamour. *Nice. And a good tipper to boot. Rare in a woman. I wonder if she and Patricia would meet.* Whistling, he drove off into the melee of the New York streets.

"Morning, Mrs. Wessel," Hiram Goldblatt, the elderly man who watched over the lobby and the stage door, touched his forehead. "They're all late this morning. Some terrible accident." Hiram's lugubrious face looked even more woebegone. "I don't know what will happen if more automobiles get onto the streets." He made a tsking noise. "Too many people. Too many."

Barbara gave him a nod. "Am I the first then?"

"No, Lady Maltravers-Goffe is here." Hiram's pouchy cheeks wobbled. "She's always on time," he checked his watch. "And young Miss Mabley, your friend Mrs. Miller and two or three others. They've gone up to the boardroom, too." His head tipped upward and Barbara nodded, also looking up. The lobby stretched in front of them…yards and yards of marble floor, shining from the nightly polishing done by Clemons, the elderly Negro who performed the never-ending chore and also managed to care for the cantankerous heating system in the opera house. The golden doors that led into the interior of the opera house itself were closed. The 1929 Season would start on Saturday night with *La Bohème*. Barbara grinned…she just loved the opera! Even being here early…it was *so* exciting!

"Into the fray!" Barbara grinned at Hiram and walked to the small baize door at the back of the lobby, her heels clicking on the marble floor. Clemons, as if by magic, appeared and opened the baize door for her. She gave him a genuine smile.

"Hallo, Clemons," She couldn't imagine how anyone could keep the floors looking so beautiful. Clemons might have told her. *Many, many hours of backbreaking work, that's how.* But Clemons just touched his grizzled grey hair and offered her an answering good morning. Barbara went through the door and disappeared from view. Clemons gazed mournfully at his floor. There would be at least nine or ten more ladies for this morning's meeting -

ladies who would traipse over it and mess it up again, nevermind the performers and musicians who would sneak through the lobby. He sighed.

The women were gathering at The Metropolitan Opera for an unusual meeting. Unusual in that the MOC had never before had a group of women raising funds. It had been Barbara's idea. Baron Wessel, her darling husband David, had been at the helm of fund raising for the Met for several years. "Why can't I help you, bunny?" Barbara had asked him one morning over breakfast. David had given her his special look, the one with one raised eyebrow and an expression of disdain. The expression was one he used a lot...from executive boards and chairmen to men of the Exchange. It always worked to discourage the inquirer. But Barbara wasn't looking at him. She was busy buttering a piece of toast to give to Teddy. "You need a new chandelier and the curtain is a disgrace!" She took another slice of toast for herself. "Curtains and lights. Those are women's things." David opened his mouth...then considered how he should phrase his discouragement. He had found in the years of marriage with Barbara, that, once she had an idea, she didn't pay a great deal of attention to his opinion. Before he could speak, his wife jumped up from the breakfast table and kissed him on his forehead.

"I'm so glad you think it's a good idea, darling," she whirled away to make some telephone calls to several of her wealthiest friends and the wives of the MOC Board Members.

"We'll be raising funds to replace the chandelier. Won't it be fun? What do you think?" Not surprisingly, she easily gathered a committee of fifteen women who expressed interest in invading what was formerly their husband's business. And thus, this morning, barring Death's intervention, they would gather at the Met, upstairs in a meeting room, being careful not to disturb the hundreds of employees and performers who were also converging at the huge edifice that stood on the corner of one of the busiest streets in New York to participate in the dress rehearsal for Saturday night's performance of *La Bohème*.

Barbara checked her list:

TENTATIVE LIST FOR NEWLY FORMED METROPOLITAN
OPERA WOMEN'S GUILD

Chairwoman: Baroness Barbara Wessel
Members: Lady Maltravers-Goffe
            Corintha Marvel
            Carey Marvel Mabley
            Judith Miller
            Brooks Allgood
            Helena von Vogel
            Chloe von Vogel

Clair von Vogel
Dale Troy
Lady Dorothea Staer
Anastasia Stuyvesant
Zelinda Chalmers
Susanna Nielsen Kelly
Diane Meyer
Marcia Walls

***

The huge, originally glittering, but now dull and damaged chandelier that dangled over the audience… the enormous but slightly tattered and dusty gold curtains that opened and closed over the stage. Who could imagine that a chandelier and some curtains could cost so much? Goldblatt stood outside the front door and lit a cigar, enjoying the beautiful October weather and wondered if a committee of women would be able to raise that kind of money. *Women!* He spat out some pieces of tobacco. *Silly sheep should be home taking care of their men instead of trying to gee-gaw up the Met.*

On the stairs leading to the boardroom, unaware of Goldblatt's musings, Barbara mentally outlined her plans to be presented to the committee of women, all determined to show the world, their husbands and the Executive Board that they could do as good a job, and perhaps even better, than a group of men. She muttered, practicing her speech: "I am determined, ladies, that we can not only raise the funds to replace the curtains and the chandelier, but perhaps exceed our goal and purchase new lighting for the foyer!" Barbara prayed that her enthusiasm would be catching. The dingy light in the staircase showed her reflection in the polished mirrored panels. She looked lovely, her blond curls peeping out from under the blue felt cloche hat she wore. (She'd tried on six or seven hats before she found just the right one – conveying attractiveness with feminine determination. Even David had agreed that with such a hat, few men would be able to resist her appeal for a minimum donation of five hundred dollars). She cleared her throat and opened the boardroom door.

***

Also approaching the Met that morning, down in the bowels of the Interboro Rapid Transit System from Brooklyn, was Urbano Valeria, the Stage Manager for the Metropolitan Opera Company. Sitting on the hard bench seat with him was his neighbor, Francesco DeSarro, fresh off the boat from Italy and newly-hired as a carpenter at the Met. In another car, sat Timothy Weaver, Master Carpenter in charge of scenery and all that was constructed on and off stage. Tim and Urbano had joined the Met's backstage staff eleven years before and together had risen to their places of vast importance. Tim passed the time of day reading his newspaper and talking with Janet Connelly, a young, blonde, blue-eyed woman who was the personal dresser of the female opera stars. Janet, who looked like a Dutch doll, spent the best of sixteen minutes complaining about Vivienne du Lac's temper tantrums. "I can't work with her! She's the most temperamental *diva* of them all! And, you know, I have worked with some doozies...but du Lac! She's not only mean and vicious, she's evil!" Janet's voice hissed.

Tim, a large, easy-going placid man, simply nodded. As far as he was concerned, *all* of the opera singers were pains in his ass. All he wanted to do was build a beautiful stage set – one that was sturdy and easy to move and store - and then go home. He listened patiently to Janet's anger and shrugged, "They call the tune, Janet, honey. She's the star and she gets just what she wants."

Janet reacted with fury. "She should be bitten by that flea bag dog she carries around! Bitten and get rabies and die!" Tim, his surprisingly beautiful baby-blue eyes twinkling behind the heavy eyeglasses he wore, laughed at her tirade. He patted her on the knee and told her relax.

"It will all be over by Saturday night. Then she'll go away."

"No! She's doing next week's opera, too!"

"She is? Says you? Two weeks in a row?"

Janet nodded with gloom. *"La Traviata* next week." Janet bared her teeth. *"Traviata* is just right for her, the whore!" Janet's blue eyes rolled dramatically. "She's a snake, by jingo. I can't even tell you how awful she is with the costumes! And she's driving poor Victor nutsy. He trails her around the stage, trying to get her to stand still long enough to put a wig on her head. She grabs the wig and refuses to mess up her hair with it! He's fussy enough about his wigs!" Tim chuckled at the mental picture of the short-statured, effeminate Victor Calligari brandishing his wigs ineffectually at the temperamental singer. Janet widened her eyes and waved her hands away from her face. "Keep that wig away from me!" She mimicked the *diva.* "Poor little Victor. He has no chance at all against her temper. But not just to him! Oh, no! She's loathsome to everyone!" She sniffed. "The woman should be strangled."

At the back of their car sat Forsythe Wicks, the Property Master, and Anatole Goldman, the Choral Director. Although Forsythe and Anatole shared a seat, they didn't converse. Each was immersed in the crossword puzzle in The New York Herald Tribune, racing, as they did every morning, to see which of them finished first.

In the car behind, three more stagehands read the New York Daily News, one of the pictorial rags published in the city, better known for its lurid photos than its editorial brilliance. Except for the elderly black man who had cared for the temperamental furnace at the Met and polished its never-ending floors, known only by the name of Clemons, these three men, all Negros, were the first people of color hired by the opera company. There names were Stephen Gibson, Richard Davis and Emmet Matthews and their jobs had been secured at the urging of Commodore John Carson. If Commodore Carson had not insisted, no Negros would have ever been hired as stagehands or carpenters. The other stagehands and carpenters were not pleased at this experiment in social equality. These jobs were well-paying ones, and the fact that Negros usurped jobs that white people might have had, made for tensions behind the gold curtain.

Gibson, Davis and Matthews, ever aware of the precarious nature of their job security, worked quickly and competently, a little bit faster and a little bit more cheerfully than anyone else. They wanted, above all, to cause no problems, make no waves and keep their new jobs.

Suddenly, the subway train stalled somewhere under the Hudson River and, despite the coolness of the October morning, the air in the carriages quickly began to get stuffier and hotter. Gibson, Davis and Matthews began to sweat in the sticky heat, worried that they would be late and make a bad impression. They were not the only ones.

Urbano and Francesco spoke in Italian. "What's the matter with this train? Why have we stopped?" Francesco wiped his brow and glanced nervously out at the blackness beyond the window. It was obvious that he would be late for work.

Urbano gave a futile gesture. "Who knows?"

Death knew. Up ahead on the track into the city, the prior subway train had been halted as Death watched his twelfth listing of the day make the voyage into the next stage of Man's Destiny. The body of an elderly man, checked off on Death's list as Henry MacAlroy, heart attack victim, was trundled off the carriage by two morgue attendants after being declared dead by John Dempsey, the Coroner for the Borough of Manhattan. Only then was the subway train allowed to leave the station, and only then, was the train that held Urbano and Francesco, Janet, Timothy, Forsythe and Anatole allowed to proceed.

"We're gonna be late!" Steve Gibson ran a finger along the damp collar of his blue chambray shirt. "Urbano's not gonna like it."

"Doan worry," Emmet fanned the air in front of him, "He's stuck on this damn subway too." He made a gesture with his chin. "Up in the car ahead."

"You sure?"

"Uh, huh. I seed him myself. We be late, he be late, too."

In tandem with his fellow workers, Francesco fretted.

"I will be disgraced." Francesco rolled his eyes. "For you," Francesco mourned, "they will not mind if you are late. But me, I am new here. I am ashamed that I will be late and perhaps they will not keep me." His dark eyes flashed his concern and shame.

"Please, my good friend," Urbano laid his hand on Francesco's thigh and patted him with sympathy. "Do not worry. You are with me and there is nothing anyone...not even the great Conductor Massimo Orsini himself... can do about New York traffic!"

***

The morning train from Greenwich, Connecticut to Grand Central Station also held several travelers who were impacted by Death's schedule. In the Club Car, Alexander Troy checked his gold pocket watch and muttered soft, snide comments about the inefficiency of the railroad into his wife's delectable ear. Dale Troy didn't mind the delay. She was excited to be on the train with her husband, and laughed at his irritation. "Simmer down, Alex. We'll get there." She patted her chignon and poked at the collar of her shirtwaist dress. "I hope I'm dressed like the others." She bit her lip and worried. "I don't want them to think I'm a country bumpkin."

Alex smiled down into her hazel eyes. "Sweetie-pie, you'll be the bees' knees." She giggled and the train lurched and rattled forward for fifty yards, then stopped again.

"What the hell is *wrong?*" Alex stood up and approached the conductor. "Excuse me, what's the matter here, sir?"

"Sorry, sir. Seems to be a body up ahead on the tracks." The conductor, being a sensitive man, spoke softly into Alex's ear. "Don't say anything, please, to the ladies." Alex nodded and then sat down, ghoulishly delighted to immediately tell Dale just what the trouble was. Up ahead on the tracks, Death hovered, making sure that his sixteenth listing of that morning, a bum known only as Barney, was being properly dispatched.

Barney, despite his pungent, decomposing, and ravaged body, was being escorted to an Eternity of Bliss. Barney had been a fair, honest and generous man, even though he was a railroad bum. Justice would be fair to him.

Death grinned, thinking of his next victim, an attorney named Richard Maxwell who lived in the Bronx. Maxwell, a venal, grasping man, had always professed himself to be an Atheist, believing that the spark of his identity would end at his death. *Not so fast, Maxwell,* Death chortled. *You're going to get the surprise of your Life...ah, I mean your Death. Wait until you see what will be your existence for Eternity.* Death swiftly moved to the Bronx and watched Maxwell die. Maxwell's eyes widened in horrific surprise at what awaited him. Death blinked as Maxwell's contorted body twisted in a spasm of pain. A stroke had ended his life on Earth and his spirit, still puzzled at the journey Maxwell had never expected, poised before the flames of Hell.

They can never quite believe how wrong they were, Death mused. *Silly how some humans were. God tells them and tells them, but they think they know better.* Maxwell's scream reverberated on and on...forever, as a matter of fact... in Hell. Death, his business with Mr. Maxwell finished, moved quickly away.

***

And in the less-expensive second-class cars, Antonina Sabatino's grey eyes stared blankly out of the window. She seemed oblivious to the delay. Antonina was full of the bloom of youth and her own loveliness. She had much more important things to reflect upon this morning. *La Bohème!* Her role as the Sweet Vendor; her few lines of song, the electric thrill of being – actually being – on stage at the Met! And more. Much, much more today. And last night! She grinned and lifted the heavy fall of light brown hair that cascaded over her collar. *Her hair. How Peter loved her hair!* Ah! Last night! Last night, she had finally surrendered her virginity to Peter Bovi, her boyfriend of several years. This morning, as early as she could, she had stealthily left the house before her mother, Francesca, could see her. *Mama would be able to tell.* Antonina wiggled in embarrassment on the scrufty plush seat and hunched her slender young body into a more comfortable position. *Mama knew everything!* But by tonight, Antonina would be able to cope and face the all-seeing eyes of Francesca Rosato. By tonight, Antonina would be more used to being a real woman. She'd be able to wipe the expression off her face that would give her secret away. Mama was a bit busy these days, thank goodness, buying the new building, getting her bakery up and running on Greenwich Avenue, hiring three new helpers... and her attention – usually so fine-tuned to anything unusual happening to any of her children - was elsewhere.

Antonina groaned, shifting her weight as the train curved around the reservoir in Yonkers. Her entire lower anatomy ached with pain. Who could know that something she had longed for would be so painful? She wondered if Peter felt any pain. *Probably not*, she thought. *Men always come out on top.* She giggled to herself at her terrible pun and clutched at her stomach as the train lurched again.

***

Back in Greenwich, Peter Bovi awoke late, stretching his lithe, young body and reveling in the joy of last night's lovemaking with Antonina. *Can't believe that she finally gave into me!* Peter leaped out of bed and began his stretching exercises with a loud chorus of *"You're the cream in my coffee....la, la, la in my stew!"*

Brushing his teeth, he exulted in a fine feeling of sexual energy fulfilled. *What a man I am! She just couldn't resist me! Now, she'd have to give up that stupid dream of becoming an opera star. An opera star! How silly! Now, she'd be his wife...they'd finally get married and she'd settle down to be Mrs. Peter Bovi, housewife and wife of the famous Doctor. "You will always be, my ne-ces-ci-tee. I'd be lost without you!"*

Downstairs, Giovanna, his adopted mother, smiled as she heard his voice. "Today, he's happy!"

"Ummm," Paolo, her husband, had his face stuck into the financial pages of The Greenwich Times.

"I wasn't sure," Giovanna poured hot, fragrant coffee in Paolo's cup, "When he came back from college…he didn't seem too happy."

"Too many girlfriends," Paolo sniffed, turning the page. "He'd be best to stick to Antonina and forget the rest."

"Ah, he's young," Giovanna would forgive her eldest anything. "And besides, it isn't Peter who doesn't want to get married. It's Antonina." As much as Giovanna adored Antonina, the daughter of her very best friend, Francesca, she loved her adopted son more.

"Good coffee, *cara*." Paolo drained his cup and held it out for a refill. "They're both too young anyway. Peter should finish his schooling and finish his residency before he even thinks of starting a family." Paolo thought about himself when he was Peter's age. Young, strong and eager, working in the Count's vineyard, wildly in love with Giovanna, mad with unfulfilled desire and nearly penniless.

Giovanna, after so many years of being married to Paolo, was thinking the same. "Ha! You were crazy in love with me. You lusted for me! Having no money didn't stop *you* from marrying *me!*"

"It was different then." Paolo grinned and reached out to take his wife's hand. "The children nowadays…they have few worries like we did back then in Italy." Giovanna rumpled what was left of her husband's hair.

"To be fair, Antonina has her own career. What kind of marriage would they have; him in a hospital somewhere and her touring all over goodness-knows-where in an opera company?"

Paolo shrugged, got up and kissed his wife good-bye. "Ah, who cares? These are their problems, not ours, *Dio grazie*! I don't have to worry about any of it. For some things – it is good to be old!" He patted Giovanna on her rear end. "And for some things," he pinched her bottom, "It is good not to be too old." She swatted him and blew him another kiss. "I will see you at four."

Giovanna turned on the radio. It was time for her favorite morning show, "The Life of Mary Tremont." Every morning, as she cleaned up the breakfast dishes, she listened to Mary's worries about her elderly mother and the fortune hunting man who craved Mary's mother's money.

"I think Mary should shoot the old goat!" Giovanna whirled as her best friend, Francesca, came into the kitchen without knocking. "Or," Francesca paused, "Maybe Mary should marry him herself!"

"Bella!" Giovanna hugged Francesca and offered her a fresh cup of coffee. "What are you up to today? – *Que cosa vai oggi*?" Although both women had been in America for many years and both spoke perfect English, Gio-

vanna often slipped back into the Italian dialect from their little village of San' Antonio.

"I'm headed for The Avenue. A few problems with the store. I'm meeting Simeon so that we can iron out everything. But I have six minutes to drink some coffee with you and share a bit of concern."

"What concern? A problem?"

"Mmmm, not really a problem. More of a…well…situation…" Francesca suddenly giggled. "I feel as if I were fifteen again and back in Italy gossiping with you about boys."

"Hmmm. Second time today, I have talked about the old days. First with Paolo. We talked about how young we were when we got married." Giovanna patted her hair. "And what memories are you dredging up from our childhood?"

"Ah, my best *cara amica*. Remember when all *we* could talk about was sex and boys?" Francesca rolled her eyes.

"And your crush on Signor Talerico!"

"He was the world to me in those long ago days. The first man I dreamed about! Ha! Fat old Talerico! I want to forget that part! But even before I fell for his, um, elderly charms," she giggled, "I dreamed about sex, and we always gossiped about sex."

"That's *all* we ever talked about!"

"So…"

"So?"

"So, your son and my daughter." Her chin jutted out.

"What about them?"

Francesca picked up one of Giovanna's cookies, crammed it into her mouth and started out the door. "Well, I think …last night…I think they did it!"

***

As the train neared New York City, it stopped at the Yonkers Station. Maria-Pia Assoluta and Charlotte Ryan, members of the chorus of *La Bohème,* boarded the second-to-the-last car. Death was the last thing they were thinking of; their discussions centered on the two men they had met last night. "Handsome devils, weren't they Char?" Maria-Pia rubbed a small bruise on the side of her neck. "Hope they come to the performance and meet us afterwards."

"They promised they would," Charlotte twisted her hands together in anticipation.

"Men promise anything." Maria-Pia snorted and watched the tenements whiz by the window.

Four seats behind the two women, Ernest Rattner, stagehand, massaged his temples, trying to get rid of the headache caused by a late night in a saloon. His mouth felt like a sewer; his tongue had a coat of fur sticking to it, despite the mouthwash he'd swished around. "And the bitch hadn't even come across", he grumbled. He slumped back, pissed at the delay and knowing that it was going to be a skunk-shit kind of day.

***

Many people had prayed for and dreamed of having Death come and grab Vivienne du Lac, but, as of this moment, she was unknown to Death's lists, although she traveled constantly world-wide and might have been on the lists for almost any of the large cities of the world where opera took place. On this particular day, Vivienne woke up in the arms of a young lover, yawned and called to her maid to draw her bath so as to prepare herself for the day. The young lover, a youth called Horz Bortel, also awoke, still half-drunk and wholly bemused to find himself in an empty bed, watching the wobbly haunches of the woman who was the leading opera *diva* in the world, the woman who had seduced him last night, walk away.

Vivienne was quickly immersed in scented water, a reviving cup of chocolate in hand coupled with a pony of brandy to balance the pain in her head from last night's excesses. She shook three pink and black capsules from a jar into her hand and threw them back into her throat, followed by a swallow of brandy. She closed her eyes, letting the alcohol and the drugs waft into her veins.

Last night…she reviewed the performance of what's his name….the little chorus boy. Adequate. Merely adequate. He was really too old for her. Too practiced, too experienced. She needed someone less…well, *less* experienced. A real youth. One not yet into puberty, with no hair at all and tiny, budding nipples. Much younger…a boy. She made a mental notation to give Crespi an order for tonight. She needed the jolt of smooth, soft skin. Not older than twelve or fourteen. There were so many hungry children prowling the streets of New York, seeking a bit of food and a place to bed down. Crespi would be able to find a comely child on the streets with no trouble. And if that didn't work, perhaps a young girl?

As the brandy revived her, she shuddered, dreading the rigors of the dress rehearsal. Her voice…it was failing her. In the honesty of her bath, she knew that she simply wasn't able to sing as she once did. Once she had sung better than anyone on earth, but no longer. Her throat was hoarse and raspy from too many cigarettes and too many late nights. Her lungs were soft and pulpy inside, not strong and elastic as they once were. She needed the lift of ether to sing. She needed the boost of unusual sex to be able to prance around the stage and sustain her energy. She needed all the nastiness and *sang-froid* in her repertoire to reign supreme as *la prima diva*. She needed, above all, a potion to make her young again. Alas, even Crespi couldn't conjure that up. These two roles…these would be her last. She could no longer sustain the pressure. Any more singing…ah, who was she fooling? Any more *trying* to sing…to keep entrancing the audience…impossible. She would make these two roles her last and gracefully retire before she really made a fool of herself.

But, between now and next week, Vivienne vowed, her lips ugly with disdain, she would make everyone's life hell on wheels. She would show *them!* And to begin, she snapped at Celestina, her maid, "Stupid cunt! This water is too hot!"

***

Vivienne, who cared for nothing and no one except herself, would travel in style to the Met much later in the day. Stars of her magnitude did not have to dance to the orders of anyone…nevermind the annoying instructions of the odious Stage Manager Arturo Calle, who had ordered everyone in the production to be on stage and ready by ten. Ten! Ha, she might be there at noon, or perhaps a little later. It would depend on how her toilette went. Feeling better, she languidly squeezed a sponge of soapy water over her still-handsome shoulders.

Horz, on the other hand, was merely a minion in the chorus. As the maid yelled at him in loud Parisian accents to get out, get *out*, he stumbled into his creased and tumbled clothing, hopped on each foot to put on his boots, and was escorted unceremoniously out of the door, chased by Vivienne's yapping flea-bitten dog. In horror, he realized that he was going to be late for rehearsal. He ran through the New York streets, skidding to avoid the clean-up of the terrible accident at 37th and Broadway. Panting, sweaty and needing a shave and bath, he nonetheless arrived at the stage door of the Met just as the last of the performers and stage workers filed in. He signed the sheet, shaking and almost retching. "Where the hell have you *been!*" His good friend and fellow chorus member Roque asked him. "You smell like a pisspot!"

Horz rolled his eyes. "I have barely escaped a fate worse than death!" Horz staggered into the hallway. "Wait until I tell you! You will not *believe* what happened last night!"

***

Walking to the opera house, Garvin McCurdy and his wife, Alice Mary, both violinists in the Met Orchestra, savored the crisp fall day. Thoughts of Death never crossed their minds. As they walked up Broadway, avoiding the clumps of horse manure that littered the street, they met several members of the Met Chorus: Juliana and George Patten walking briskly with Nancy and Michael Connors. Veterans of dozens of productions, they all called greetings to one another and the positions in their journey to work changed as the women lallygagged behind the men. "Come on," Garvin prodded. "We'll be late if you ladies don't get a move going." The dress rehearsal for the gala opening production of *La Bohème* started at 10:00 AM sharp, and as the members of the orchestra and chorus well knew, the wrath of Arturo Calle would descend upon them, good excuse or no excuse at all. Garvin stepped up his pace and urged the ladies to hurry.

***

Angelique Orloff and her little daughter, Anna, stepped out of their apartment on Madison Avenue. The wind was brisk and Angelique tied Anna's scarf tighter, then dropped a kiss on Anna's nose.

"Bye, Mims," the little girl hugged her mother. Angelique stood and watched, waving goodbye as the child trotted off to her school. *How much I adore her*, she mused. *I'd lay down my life for her.* As the little girl disappeared from sight, Angelique's heart melted, as it always did when she watched Anna. *Brrrr.* She shivered slightly as the sun went behind a cloud. She turned up the collar of her fur jacket. It would never do to let the wind catch at her throat. A professional always watched out for her treasure, and Angelique's treasure was her voice…pure and beautiful. She was as ready as she always was for the rigors of the dress rehearsal and her performance as Musetta tomorrow. Angelique was a consummate professional and her voice was a precious thing. Almost as precious as Anna. Almost. She walked quickly, opening up the cachet paper that held a throat lozenge from her pocket, sucking at the honey candy to ward off any chance of a throat problem.

As she walked, she heard her name shouted and turned to see Zizzane Fond calling her. Zizzane was her understudy…her cover… as it was called at the MOC. *"Bon Jour, Angelique,"* Zizzane caroled. "Are we in good voice today, *ma petite?"*

She's praying that I get laryngitis. Fat chance! Angelique smiled serenely, her lovely face taking on a Madonna-like glow. "I have never felt better, Zizzane." Companionably, for Angelique was a particularly nice woman, she tucked her arm under Zizzane's and they hurried, not daring to be late and incur Massimo Orsini's wrath. They turned the corner with ten minutes to spare and saw the huge building looming. As they approached, the sidewalk was suddenly teeming with employees – chorus members, violinists, the timpani section, the costume women, stagehands, electricians, office workers, the prompter, the organist…They rounded past the front entrances to wiggle into the crowd of other Met workers who formed themselves into a noisy line, waiting to go into the bowels of the building through the stage door.

***

At the Central Police Station for The Borough of Manhattan, Police Chief Anderson von Vogel took a telephone call from the downstairs desk. He jotted down a few notes and then went to the office of his chief detective, Pedar Pedersen. "First thing! Even before my tea. Murder in the morning, Pedar."

Pedar looked up from the newspaper he was reading. "Eh? What's up?"

"Dead woman behind the garbage down in the Bowery," his boss gestured towards the coat rack. "Let's go."

Shoot, thought Death, immediately there in the Bowery to look down on the raggedy corpse. *A murder. Unexpected. An extra one today. Name of Caroline Smythe, most likely once a pretty and vivacious woman; now, with the horrors of cocaine, alcohol and prostitution, a ravaged corpse. Ah, well, I'll fix up the numbers tomorrow.* Making a notation on the list, Death finally left New York City for the day and traveled to Boston to see to what had to be seen to. A river steamer, plying its passengers between Boston and Hull was about to sink. Death had two pages filled with the names of seventy-three passengers who would be making their last journey. Better get to the scene quickly.

Chapter Two

" 'Gainst knaves and thieves men shut their gates"
...Shakespeare – Twelfth Night

*I*t started about six months ago. There was a call at 10 PM from a Mr. Robert McCallister of 105 Putnam Park, a ritzy spot, as Cliff Gustafson remarked when he'd hung up the telephone. "Break-in. Gentleman sounded really upset...barely coherent." Cliff raised his massive bulk from the chair. "Who's comin' with me?"

"Ah, it's my turn," Mike Murphy threw down the chewed cigar stub he'd been mouthing.

"You feel like going out?" Cliff asked with the delicacy of an old friend. "You don't want to get home?"

Mike's face was a study. "I think Nora is sound asleep. It's fine." He punched his partner's shoulder with camaraderie. "And anyway, I like those posh jobs up in the country."

"How's Nora doing? Any better?"

"Nah," Mike's voice was bleak. "Damn doctors can't do anything more."

"I'm sorry, pal." Cliff sighed. "I'd give my right arm..."

"I know. Everyone is so good to her. Her sister is sitting with her to-night". Mike shrugged. "Not much else we can do but keep her out of pain and wait." The two policemen went into the soft night air and got into the patrol car. Mike drove. Cliff figured it was good for him to concentrate on the roads instead of on Nora.

The trip to the back country roads of Greenwich, past large and even larger estates, took approximately thirty minutes. Old friends, Mike and Cliff talked about the baseball scores during the ride. There wasn't much point in talking about Nora.

"Hellava place!" Mike marveled as the headlights lit up a large, gated driveway flanked by two shiny new bright electric lights. He stopped the car, but before he could get out, a man opened the gate, beckoning to them.

"Police? Thank goodness....I'm Robert McCallister. I called you."

"Good evening, Mr. McCallister," Mike touched the brim of his cap. This sort of place seemed to require his best manners. "Will you ride to the house with us?" Cliff lumbered out of the front seat and held the door for McCallister. Robert McCallister was a tall, dark-haired man, dressed in a suit-coat. He got into the front seat, Cliff crowded himself in the back and Mike put the car into gear.

17

"What happened, sir?"

"You're just not going to believe this, officer. I have no...I..." McCallister shook his head. "Just wait until you see..." The car pulled up to the front door of an imposing brick home. The lights were shining from every window and the front door was opened immediately by a woman in a rose-colored dress.

"Irene," McCallister got out of the car. "The police are here," he announced. He hurried to the woman and put his arm around her.

She beckoned to the policemen, "Come in, officers". She was an attractive woman with brownish-grey hair rolled into a chignon at her neck. Cliff took off his cap and bowed slightly. She must have been a beauty in her youth. She was lovely even now. He introduced himself and then introduced Mike. Mrs. McCallister backed into the house, motioning to the policemen to follow her. In the spacious hall, she turned. "It's in the lounge." She made a disgusted face. "I can't believe that people could....Ugh!"

Robert McCallister followed Mike and Cliff. They went through an open double door and into a large room, beautifully decorated in soft chintzes and elegant furniture. Everything was obviously expensive, but despite the antiques and munificence, the room had a warm and lived-in loveliness – that is until Mrs. McCallister pointed to the carpet in front of the fireplace and Cliff and Mike gasped and clutched at their mouths.

"Jesus, Mary and Joseph!" Murphy said involuntarily.

"Holy sh...uh, uh..." Cliff was openmouthed.

"Exactly." Robert McCallister winced. "Not only did they rob us, but *this*! His wife cringed back against him. "The *bas*tards!"

On the edge of the obviously expensive carpet was a pile of what appeared to be human excrement. The heap's odor wafted into the room, causing Mrs. McCallister to cough and put her hand over her mouth.

Mike cautiously approached the pile, his eyes bugging out, his nose outraged. "I never saw nothin' like this! *Je*sus!" He looked over at Mrs. McCallister. "'Scuse me, Ma'am." He tried not to gag at the smell. "Was it just like this when you found it?"

"It was warmer...and steaming a bit," McCallister tried to joke, but made a retching sound.

"My beautiful house!" Mrs McCallister wailed. "I just can't ...." She hid her face in her husband's shoulder. "How *could* they?"

"You say 'they'. Was there more than one person?" Mike, who had seen so many atrocities in his career, had his equilibrium back. "What happened? Uh, wait a minnit, here. Um, let's go, uh, somewhere else in, um, the house..." Mrs. McCallister nodded and drew them into the kitchen.

"Some coffee, Officers? Maybe something stronger if you're allowed?"

"Uh, coffee would be fine." Mike was dying for a drink. *Shit! Shit? That's just what it was!*

Mrs. McCallister busied herself at the stove. Her husband invited the men to sit. Cliff took out his pad and pencil and Mike began the questioning.

"We were out with friends. Our maid, Harlene, is off tonight. She's gone to visit her family in Port Chester." At Murphy's eyebrow twitch, she assured him, "Harlene has been with us for more than ten years. She would never...*never* have anything to do with anything like this!"

Her husband continued, "We came home. The house was in darkness except for the lamps at the end of the drive and the night lights. I drove the car to the entryway and we got out, opened the front door and we came in. I smelled this terrible odor and then we went into the lounge. I...I...I nearly vomited when I saw..." His wife brought four mugs of coffee to the table. She put out a sugar bowl, a pitcher of milk and a platter with a pound cake.

"Here, gentlemen." She was gracious and had a sense of humor. "We'll all feel a bit better with this in us." She cut the cake and placed a plate in front of the men. She continued the story. "I waited down in the hall while Robert went through the house. He saw that the kitchen door had the glass smashed in. He didn't touch anything, however." She smiled and touched her husband's hand. "Then he went upstairs. We were worried that perhaps there was someone still in the house. That's when we saw that we'd been robbed."

"What did they take?" Cliff held his pencil up.

"Mostly worthless junk. My jewels are in the bank. We keep a little money in Robert's dresser. Maybe a hundred dollars. That was gone. His watch was taken, and they took Aunt Millie's necklace." She paused for a moment. She and her husband looked at one another and burst into helpless laughter.

"Are you feeling well, Ma'am?" Cliff was alarmed that she was going into hysterics. "Wha...wha...?" Cliff asked. "What's so funny?" They seemed so respectable...so unflappable, telling the story. Were they both going to become unhinged?

"Oh, my!" Mrs. McCallister wheezed. "It's just that..." And she began to laugh again. "You must think we're crazy!"

"No, Ma'am. I think you've had quite a shock," Murphy was concerned. "This has been a terrible ordeal for you. Do you need a doctor? Maybe a friend or a neighbor to come and help?"

"Oh, dear, no." Robert McCallister chuckled. "You see, Irene inherited this necklace from her Aunt Millie. It was a very valuable necklace...a solid gold chain with a large pendant in the shape of a cat...with emerald eyes and a collar of diamonds," he snorted and began to wipe his eyes.... "It was the ugliest thing you could ever imagine! We both hated it!"

Mrs. McCallister chuckled. "It *is* valuable...I think it was insured for five thousand dollars..." Mike whistled under his breath..."But...I must say, I really don't care if I never see it again!" She began to laugh helplessly again. "They must be really stupid thieves with no sense of beauty!"

***

The policemen helped the McCallisters to clean up the mess, using the rubber gloves that Mrs. McCallister produced from under her kitchen sink, scooping the pile of excrement into a newspaper and wrapping it securely. "We'll bring this down to the station and give it to Doc Sullivan tomorrow," Mike grinned. "He'll be very appreciative of the gift." The two men helped to take up the dirty rug and deposited it in the back yard. "We'll be along again tomorrow to take a list of what's missing, the junk stuff and Auntie Millie's pussy cat necklace." They shook hands with both of the McCallisters. "I'm so sorry that this happened to you. You're two nice people and you don't deserve all this….um, trouble."

And at the station the next day, Chief McAndrews agreed with Mike's estimation that it had been an amateur heist. The thief or thieves had left many expensive artifacts, silver, paintings and small valuables. The necklace and the watch were the only things of value taken. The necklace was insured and the watch of negligible cost. "Looks like a couple a' mugs with no sense other than nonsense. Why the hell did they shit all over the house? To make mischief? Was it someone who hated the McCallisters?" Mike Murphy shrugged.

"It's a funny one, all right."

Doctor Sullivan did his best with the pile of evidence, holding a piece of wintergreen-soaked gauze over his nose. "Corn and peas," he muttered. "Somebody had corn and peas for supper." He washed his hands for the third time, dried them carefully, and wrote on the report. "Corn, peas and walnuts. Whoever it was, they ate corn and peas for supper and maybe some kind of dessert with walnuts in the past twenty-four hours."

"How can you tell?" Chief McAndrews asked. "Are you some kind'a garbage connoisseur?"

Doc Sullivan snorted, "I'm the king of shit. That's what they call me! Ha! Corn and nuts don't get digested in the stomach. They just cruise all the way through and come out the other end. Peas are digested a little better, but…as you can see," he pointed to the round, green orbs, "they, too, come out in the wash."

The police rounded up every known sneak thief. All of them had alibis, however thin, for the time of the robbery. All of them but Jimmy Menenda. Jimmy, who had been vacationing for the past two years at the Minimum Security Prison at Sing Sing, New York, due to, what Jimmy referred to as a mix-up in identity, had just been let out of jail two weeks ago.

Police Chief Emerson McAndrews himself drove to the run-down area of the town known as the Flats. Jimmy and his father, Rags Menenda, resided on the first floor of a three-family tenement owned by Rags. Rags' real name was Giovanno Menenda, but no one, except the police, knew that he'd once been baptized with a different name. He operated a wheelbarrow that went around local neighborhoods collecting old rags and paper. He paid a penny a pound to housewives, who saved and collected the trash. They, in turn, used the few cents they earned each week on small necessities. Rags sold the cloth and paper to The American Felt Company. They, in turn, soaked the garbage in foul smelling reagents, then pressed the resulting soggy mess into industrial grade felt.

The police harbored suspicions that Rags' income might also be bolstered by other illicit transactions, however, as of this date, couldn't prove it.

Jimmy's mother, who may or may not have been married to Rags, had deserted her child early in his formative years by running off to White Plains with a trumpet player. Perhaps, had she stayed, Jimmy might have turned out to be a better member of society. Alas, without a mother's guidance and with the dubious tutorials of a father who pushed a rag-barrow and generally was drunk, Jimmy grew up stealing, brawling and making trouble wherever he went.

"Where were you, James my lad, on the night of May 25th?"

A shrug. "Donno."

"We've got a rather unusual robbery. Has earmarks of your kind of thing," Emerson stared at the young man. "Try to remember. It was two nights ago."

Another shrug. "I musta been home with my father." The senior Menenda chewed on a stump of a cigar and confirmed his offspring's memory.

"You sure?"

"Sure." Jimmy's face split into a grin. They had nothing on him. Nothing at all. "I learned my lesson, didn't I, Pa?"

"Was home all night." Rags waved the cigar. "I swear to it." His face wore a hurt expression. "You guys know me. I'd never lie, would I?"

And with that, the police had to be satisfied.

But the audacity of the robber or robbers stayed with them. Every time any of them saw an ear of corn, a platter of peas and carrots or ate a walnut cookie, the policemen burst into laughter.

None of the stolen merchandise ever surfaced. In month or so, despite a good effort by the Greenwich police, for they had really liked and respected the McCallisters, the file was shifted to a back desk and almost forgotten until the week of July the Fourth, 1929.

***

It was a Friday night. The call came in about ten at night. Steven Laulette and his wife, Kathie, had returned from a night at The Pickwick Theater. They had gone to the early show and waited in line for an hour to get tickets to see the extravaganza of *Broadway Melody*. They'd danced and sang their way home to the modest home six blocks away from Greenwich Avenue.

"You were meant for me...," Kathie crooned.

"I was meant for you...," her husband caroled back.

"Nature made us, and when she was done," they tap-danced up the steps to their front door. *"You were all the sweet things rolled into one!"* Their voices rang out with happy abandon.

"You're like a la-la mel-o-dee…" Kathie stopped suddenly. "Steven!" she gasped. "Look!" She pointed to a rip in the screen door. "What…?"

Steven opened the screen gingerly. He held his arm back, holding Kathie away from any harm, but the front door appeared intact.

"Seems fine." He opened the door and stepped in first. The crunch of glass underfoot stopped him cold. Because of the lace curtains in the window, he hadn't been able to notice that the window in the front door had been smashed. "Oh, Lordy!" he gasped.

Kathie screamed and pulled Steven back out on the porch. "Burglars!" she shouted. The scream brought their next door neighbor running.

The neighbor peeked in, avoiding the glass. He turned to them worriedly and warned them, "You'd better not go in…just in case there's someone still in there!"

"Stay here with Kathie," Steven begged. With his blood running cold, Steven ran to the neighbor across the street who had a telephone, and called the police.

Detectives Third Class Peter Kraut and Charlie Presto answered the call. They arrived to find a knot of neighbors clustered around the Laulette's stoop. No, they were assured, no one had gone into the house since the broken window was discovered. Careful of fingerprints, although they didn't have a great deal of faith in the newish way to capture burglars, Pete and Charlie crept into the house, pulling the light-chain in the hallway. "Anyone here?" Pete bawled into the darkness. "Police! Come on out!" The men listened to the silence and then, rather sure that the perpetrator had fled, truncheons in hand, went into the parlor.

"Pee-yew!" Pete jumped back as Charlie switched on a lamp. "What the hell is that smell?"

"Oh, *no!*" Charlie gasped, "It's that shitting burglar again!"

Again, the swag taken wasn't valuable. "We don't have much that a thief would want," explained Steven. "Gosh! We just got married. They took Kathie's silver cross and chain, but," he looked abashed, "it wasn't very expensive."

"Never you mind, Steven", his pretty little dark-haired wife patted his arm. "The cross and chain was worth every bit of a million dollars to me." She fingered the front of her neck and looked as if she might cry. "Who is so mean as to do this to us?"

Charlie shrugged and ran his hand distractedly through the rich forest of curly dark hair on his head. "This is the second time that this has happened, not that it will make you two feel any better. Some people are just nuts." He shrugged and herded the couple into their kitchen. Peter went out to the cluster of neighbors and interviewed them. No one, except one elderly lady, had seen or heard anything until Kathie screamed.

The elderly lady, a Mrs. Terese Menard, told Peter that she'd heard a car in the street about an hour ago. "There aren't too many cars along this street, especially at night, so I peeked out of the curtains and saw a dark automobile parked a few houses down."

"What kind of automobile?"

Mrs. Menard shook her head. "I don't know anything about them. I don't know one from another," she shrugged with reluctance. "But I could see from the light of the street-lamp, it was a dark or darkish automobile." Peter thanked her and told her to try to sleep and perhaps something more might come to her. She nodded and turned away, her shoulders slumped. "What's this neighborhood coming to, I ask you?" She muttered. "Some fool kids. I'll skin 'em alive if I find anyone prowling around my place!"

Inside, Charlie questioned Kathie and Steven. He asked if they had any enemies. Anyone who might have been jealous that they had wed? Anyone that they'd argued with at work?

"Only that sad apple Alvin Catchpole," Steven made a face. "He was after Kathie all through high school…annoyed her a lot…and wouldn't take no for an answer." He looked pugnacious, or as pugnacious as his young face could manage.

"Oh, Steven, don't be silly!" Kathie blushed and poked his arm. "Alvin would never…he'd never…he'd be too embarrassed to…oh, *no*! Not Alvin!"

***

Naturally, they spoke with Alvin Catchpole the next day. He was a thin, weedy young man with an acne-covered face and a wispy moustache. His mother answered the door and was scandalized that the police were here on her doorstep to speak with her Alvin. "You can't come in here!" She tried to shut the door. From inside the house, a dog began to bark. "Get away or I'll set Lucky on you both!"

"Mrs. Catchpole." Charlie tried to rely on his reputed charm. "Please let us in for a few minutes. We just want to talk to your son."

"He's not here. Now, go away." At her steadily rising voice, the dog began to bark anew.

"Where is he?" Charlie decided if he couldn't be charming, he'd be reasonable.

Mrs. Catchpole started to shut the door. "Mrs. Catchpole!" Charlie decided to be firmer. "Where is your son?"

She shook her head, refusing to tell them where Alvin was, but Charlie's persistence did seem to make her more talkative. Waspishly, she declared, "He'd never…She was a hussy, that Kathie McGregor. Always leading my Alvin on," Mrs. Catchpole sniffed. "She was not worth his notice!"

"So, you know that the Laulette's were robbed, don't you?" Charlie smiled, feeling that he was now making headway. "Glad you keep up with the neighborhood news. I sure hope he comes home soon." Charlie's relentless smile unnerved her. "No matter how long he's out, we'll need to speak with him nonetheless," Charlie Presto was stubbornly firm under Mrs. Catchpole's sour eye. "We'll just wait here, out on the porch, with all of your neighbors watching, until he comes home." Charlie arranged himself, draping one long leg over the railing of the Catchpole porch.

"Ssssst!" Mrs Catchpole's face turned a puce color as she noticed a twitching curtain next door. She pushed the two men into the house. It was a hot July afternoon. The house had all its windows shut and smelled like cabbage. Charlie ran his finger around his wilting collar and gave Mrs. Catchpole his sternest glare.

She capitulated. "He's upstairs in his room or out back in his garage. He's always there or upstairs in his room. He never goes out to bars or … He's a good son. He's always here. He was certainly right upstairs in his own room when…when…"

"When? When was he upstairs in his room?" Pete turned to her. "When was he out in his garage? Just what do you know about our inquiries?"

She nearly collapsed and even Pete felt sort of sorry for her. "I…I…" She turned and called up the stairs; "Alvin. Come down here now." The dog began another round of barking. "Alvin?" She called again. "Must be out in his work shop." She motioned them through the hallway. The faint smell of cabbage and antiseptic followed them. *Too clean in here for the likes of me!* Pete ran his finger around his collar. They went through a spotless kitchen and out the back door. She pointed to a small garage out in the back and watched them, her arms folded across her chest, as they walked to the shed and knocked.

Alvin answered the door, looking like a rabbit trapped in a cage. He was very nervous and reluctant to open the door and let them in. Pete insisted and they pushed their way past him and into the garage.

Charlie and Pete looked about in wonder. *What the hell!* They were in an old building that had formerly been used as a storage shed or a garage. The room was sided with shelving, and filled with household debris, neatly stacked and piled. Lumber, old bicycles, canning jars and garden implements jostled with bushel baskets filled with horsehair and stuffing materials, tin cans and bottles half filled with odd looking liquids. And everywhere, on every surface…there were stuffed animals…everywhere. Owls on perches, bird hung from the rafters, a fox glared from a shelf, and on the table, amid glistening knives and piles of fur and feathers, was the half-stuffed carcass of a squirrel. *Holy cow! What the hell was this?*

"What's all this?" Charlie gaped. The entire shed smelled funny…like wet earth and moldy leaves.

Alvin answered with stiff politeness. "I am a taxidermist. This is my workshop."

"I guess you are." Pete walked around, touching the dry fur of the fox, ducking under a rope that encircled a bird of some sort "Well..." He touched a box filled with glass eyeballs and a basket brimming with feathers of all colors... "Well..." He turned and, with raised eyebrows, conveyed to Charlie that he should start the questioning.

"We're here to talk about the break in at the Laulette residence," Charlie began. Alvin's face took on a greenish hue and he backed himself up against the table that held the squirrel's skeleton. Charlie asked him where he had been the night of the break-in. Alvin had no real alibi, "My mother will tell you that I am home all the time."

"Let's go back into the house and see what she says," All Charlie wanted to do was get out of this creepy dead animal zoo and back into the fresh air.

Mrs. Catchpole confirmed that Alvin had been at home. "He's a good boy, is my Alvin." Her beady eyes, looking somewhat like those on the fox, glared at them, daring them to contradict her.

Alvin stammered his corroboration, "I, um...like to do my pets...and then I, um, like to put my stamp collection into books."

"And do you ever see or speak with the Laulettes?"

Alvin seemed to shrink. He shook his head. "I never see them. I never talk with them." Mrs. Catchpole seemed about to make a remark. She opened her mouth, thought better of it, and snapped it closed. From another room in the house, the dog yowled.

Alvin twitched a bit under Charlie's stare. "I, um, always thought she was really pretty...um, in school and all. Um, that's all."

"And were you angry when she had no interest in you?"

There was a flare of some anger behind Alvin's eyeglasses. He sniffed and shook his head. "She was always nice to me...but she never...well...she...she never..."

Pete and Charlie left the Catchpole home after issuing a stern warning that Alvin was not to leave Greenwich nor to leave the country. As they clattered down the stairs of the Catchpole stoop, Charlie turned suddenly to see Alvin staring out of the window, watching their departure. "Gives me the willies. Waddaya think? He able to do that?"

"Nah. He's a nancy-boy. Tied to Momma's apron strings. He'd be afraid to say boo."

"Yeah," Charlie agreed. "I just can't picture him pulling down his pants in somebody else's house."

"Brrr. He does his little pets, does he?" Charlie shivered. "Creepy."

"Creepy? That's mild! He's beyond creepy. The man is like a dead slug!" Pete wiped his mouth, as if to be rid of the stench of the dead animals. "Creep or no creep, he has no alibi, except for his mother's vociferous promise that he was always at home, every night...whatever night it was...he was home."

Charlie thought Alvin was a pathetic little member of society. Could he be the one who shat on a rug? Not likely that he'd have the courage. He might do some sneaky thing, but pulling his pants down in someone else's house...and don't forget...there were two piles of crap on the floor. Nah, Catchpole wouldn't do anything like that with a buddy watching. Matter of fact, Catchpole probably didn't *have* any buddies...only his mom. Charlie laughed and shrugged, forgetting about Alvin and his stuffed animals.

Chapter Three

"All the world's a stage, And all the men and women merely players"...Shakespeare...As You Like it...

<u>SYNOPSIS</u> – La Bohème - Christmas Eve, Paris 1830 –

Four young bohemian students share a garret on the left bank of Paris. It is Christmas Eve, bitterly cold. Although they are penniless, they have hope and humor to keep them warm. Avoiding the persistence of their landlord who tries to collect their overdue rent, three of the young men exit to the Café Momus, leaving the poet, Rodolfo to continue his work. The enchanting Mimi, clearly suffering from tuberculosis, makes a timid entrance into the garret asking for a light for her candle. It is love at first sight and the couple sing rapturously of their passion before joining their friends at the café. They are joined by Musetta, the coquettish lover of Marcello, one of the other students. Musetta and Marcello's tumultuous romance is re-established after a vociferous argument. The two couples continue stormy relationships – Musetta and Marcello through constant jealous bickering – and Rodolfo through his worry that Mimi's health will continue to deteriorate – perhaps she may die - if she lives in poverty in his garret. They hope their love will survive until the warmth of the spring. Months later, Rodolfo and Marcello end up alone in their garret. Musetta rushes in to tell Rodolfo that Mimi is dying and wishes to talk with him. Everyone tries to keep Mimi alive with medicine and warmth. Rodolfo and Mimi declare their true love for one another moments before she dies in his arms.

*I*t was the worst of dress rehearsals. The programs were lost. No one at the printing office knew to where they'd disappeared. The lights blinked on and off, and Johnston Redmond, the Met's Chief Electrician, hollered at his electricians to "Fix the damn things, at once, do you hear? At *once!*"

Three members of the orchestra were still not in their chairs, six of the Met Chorus were not in their groupings, although the rest of the Chorus strove to hide the gaps.

Massimo Orsini had not yet come into the orchestra pit. Frantically, Garvin McCurdy, First Violinist, craned his neck, seeking the bulky shape of Dean Armandroff, the bassoon player, and two of the viola musicians who were not in their chairs. Garvin offered up a prayer. *Ah, here come a few of the stray lambs. Small blessings…*as a quiet commotion came tiptoeing down the aisle and Lillian Quimby and Kathie Hess, violas clutched behind them to lessen the impact of their late arrival, slid into their seats. *Now where the hell was Dean?*

Garvin's neck swiveled as he searched the chairs. An empty seat gaped between Tom Zeranski, also a bassoon player, and Susan Frangiamore, who played the oboe. Zeranski was keeping his head down, hoping beyond hope that Garvin just might not notice the gap. As Dean weighed about two hundred pounds, had a bush of dark, curly hair and wore garish, unsuitable clothing, it was doubtful that Garvin could miss him. Garvin stared until Zeranski finally looked up. "Where is he?" Garvin mouthed. Zeranski hunched his shoulders. Garvin glared. It was about all he could do.

A moment later, a heavy hand hit Garvin's shoulder and Dean's *basso profundo* voice whispered, "Didja think I overslept?" Garvin made a sour face. Dean was *always* late, *always* madly unrepentant…but, thank goodness, he was here at last. Making a snicking noise with his mouth, Dean lifted his bassoon, untangling it from the paper sack he carried.

"What smells?" Garvin sniffed.

"Pastrami." Dean waved the sack to and fro, puffing garlic and spices into the air. As usual, he was dressed as no other. He favored flowing black garments, meant to shock, and today sported a purple foulard tie at his neck. A self-professed anarchist and political maverick, Dean amused himself by mocking the conventions. Despite his outrageous clothing and snide comments about the government, the stock market and the police, meant to shock all who were in hearing distance, Dean was a good musician with a brilliant, if unconventional mind. Actually, Garvin and Alice Mary thought he was a hoot. But it wouldn't do for Dean to know. Garvin merely chuckled, simply glad that Dean was in his proper seat. He was pleased that all of his chickens had come home to roost on their chairs before Orsini's wrath came down upon them. After one last glance around, Garvin took out his violin and began to tune the strings.

Tom Zeranski leaned over. "Where the hell have you been?" Dean shrugged and began to unwrap the sandwich.

"Smells good," Susan Frangiamore rolled her eyes. "Can I have a bite?" Dean chomped a section away and held the sandwich out to Susan. Tom watched her as she nibbled at the pastrami. She was the most beautiful girl he had ever seen, with her curly hair and her engaging grin. She seemed to like him, too. And they had been dating for three weeks so far. But the pastrami! *Could I kiss her with pastrami on her breath?* He considered the dilemma and grinned, cradling his instrument. *Certainly he could.*

As the performers drifted onto the stage in preparation of Act One, a large wooden scenery partition crashed down, just missing the head of Sergei Andreyi who was singing the role of Rodolfo. The partition knocked over a table, and the vase that was on it fell to the floor, smashing into a million pieces. Andreyi cursed richly in Russian and kicked at the scenery. Urbano Valeria rushed over, and with the help of Timothy Weaver, picked up the partition, checked it over for any damage, and then, with a few blows of a hammer, knocked it back into place.

Francesco, the new man, wearing a large leather apron with capacious pockets holding a myriad of tools, fixed the table, hammering the leg back into place. Then, trying to keep out of the singers' way, Francesco swept up the glass.

Taking advantage of the commotion, with stealth, Morgan McCurdy, Juliana and George Patten and Robyn Benson, the missing members of the chorus, mingled into the group, sighing with relief that no one had noticed their lateness. Robyn, a tall red-haired woman, panted with exertion, her dark eyes darting from side to side. "No one saw us come in late, did they?" She stood still, gazing over the group. "Nope. I think we're safe…this time." The rest of the chorus stood at the side of the stage, waiting until Act Two to move into position.

***

As the orchestra tootled and banged their instruments, Arturo Calle mounted the stage. "Who is missing?" he roared. Sigrid Chalmers, the Assistant Stage Manger, climbed onto the stage and riffled through his paperwork, checking off names.

"Where is Marcello?" Chalmers bawled. Dante Lazzarelli, who was singing Marcello's role, waved vigorously from the wings. Chalmers nodded and made a mark on his list. "I see Rodolfo…um, Colline? Fine, I see you," he made a few more checkmarks. "Shaunard? Fine. And where is Benoit?" Simon Forest put up his hand. "Check…and, who is missing? Our star. Where is Mimi?" He put his hands on his hips and looked from right to left. As he expected, Vivienne du Lac was not on stage. "Is she in the theater? Is she in New York State?"

A chorus of titters greeted his question. "Of course, she is not in the theater!" grumbled Simon Forest. "She's never on time."

Chalmers made a notation on his list. "Where is Mimi's cover?" He peered at the list and ruffled the pages. "Ignatzia Volente? Is *she* here?"

Janet Connelly, the ladies' dresser, rushed over to him and whispered in his ear. He grunted, nodded and made another mark. "Get her out here at once!" He pushed Janet gently toward the wings.

"Trouble. There's gonna be trouble today!" Wringing her hands, Janet rushed out as the performers gathered in a small knot and whispered among themselves.

In a few moments, Ignatzia Volente, who was understudying the role of Mimi, hurried onto the stage. Janet followed her, quickly basting the collar of the green dress that Mimi was to wear in Act One. Ignatzia threw out her hands in dramatic supplication. "I came as quickly as I could. I thought she'd be here already."

Chalmers shrugged. Everyone who sang in an opera was crazy. All of them. Totally crazy. It was beyond his control. And, certainly, the comings and goings of du Lac were beyond his powers...beyond the powers of any mortal. Chalmers made a checkmark at the bottom of the page and, at a commotion in the wings, turned to greet Arturo Calle and Massimo Orsini.

Garvin McCurdy stood up and clapped his hands sharply twice. He then made a graceful motion with both hands, and the entire orchestra, struggled to put down their instruments and stand, giving their conductor their ovation. They clapped for a moment and then Orsini, throwing back his leonine head, graciously stopped the applause and bade them to sit back down.

"Is everyone here?" Arturo Calle's loud voice asked Chalmers.

Chalmers nodded with a half-nod, then, reluctantly informed him that Vivienne du Lac was not yet in the theater. "We have her cover here, however." Ignatzia stepped forward to Calle's glare of annoyance.

"And does anyone know where *our star* is today?" His voice was dangerous. "Is she not aware that the dress rehearsal started at *ten*?" No one met his eye and he muttered and whispered with Massimo Orsini.

Orsini shrugged in anger. 'We will start without her. And we will finish tomorrow night without her, if necessary!" He stepped to his podium and picked up his baton. Garvin and his wife, Alice Mary, their chairs closest to Orsini's podium, heard his oath; "The bitch! I'll kill her if she ruins my last performances!"

Everyone sucked in a breath, aware of Orsini's hatred for Vivienne du Lac. Their enmity went back for years, from the night that she stopped in the middle of her performance as Norma and screamed obscenities at him over the footlights. Orsini had only agreed to this dual appearance at The Metropolitan Opera when he was promised that Florence Easton would be appearing tomorrow night as Mimi in this production of *La Bohème* and then Alma Gluck as Violetta on Monday night's performance of *La Traviata*. Orsini's eightieth birthday was also on Monday night, and the performance of *La Traviata* on Monday, October 18th, 1929, would be his last.

It had been whispered that perhaps, the great Italian tenor, Beniamino Gigli, himself might attend the opening night performance to hear Orsini conduct. Orsini was pleased at the rumor. He had planned to go out in glory. These two performances would be remembered as his final triumphs in a stellar career spanning nearly fifty-five years.

It was only after all the contracts had been signed, all the travel arrangements made, that he learned that neither Easton nor Gluck would be able to sing with him. He was furious on learning that Vivienne du Lac would sing both performances. "I will not do it! I will not conduct for that whore!" Rumor had it that he actually broke one of his favorite batons in his rage.

"Shhh! Maestro. Calm yourself. I have personally spoken with her and she promises...*promises*...that she will behave." Arturo Calle tried to sooth him. "She's had some difficulty herself in her last performances at La Scala and La Fenice. Her voice...well, she is not as young as she once was..."

"Pah! I know that! Everyone knows that! It is ludicrous that she should parade herself on stage as a young and starving girl! Folly! She is a raddled old crow! She has no voice anymore!"

"Ah, Massimo, my good friend." Calle poured them glasses of a fine old brandy he kept for such moments, "The audiences adore her still. They only remember her fire and her brilliance."

"Her fire is out! She has no brilliance! She's a pig! A cow! She cannot hit her high notes!" Orsini's hands trembled in agitation. He turned swiftly to Calle, "And, it is whispered that she is using ether to strengthen her voice!"

"I heard that rumor. No, no, *Maestro*. She is in fine voice," Calle poured yet another brandy, vowing to kill whomever told Orsini about du Lac's ether usage. "She will give you a magnificent performance. I promise!"

And to himself, Calle promised: *"I will wring her neck with my own hands if she makes trouble. I vow that I will!"*

"She has told me, I promise you, that she is thrilled that you will be conducting. She would have no one else." Calle's fingers crossed behind his back. "She admires you like no other conductor, Massimo. She mentions to all that you are supreme."

And with these promises and blandishments, Massimo Orsini had to be satisfied.

***

Worried that Orsini would walk off the podium, Calle motioned and the curtains swung shut. "We will run through the entire first act, come what may. I will make comments at the end. Let us begin!" He climbed down off the stage and went to sit in the third row with Baron David Wessel, Alex Troy, Sir Dennis Staer and three other members of the Metropolitan Opera Company Executive Committee.

Orsini hoped that du Lac would have a heart attack and die. This other soprano, Vivienne's cover, Ignatzia Volante, was adequate. Adequate. Not magnificent as Florence Easton would have been...no, she was merely thought to be adequate. Well, perhaps that was better than adverse fireworks. Perhaps du Lac would stay away. And she...Volante... despite her pedantic performance, was *here* and on *time!* That much was an improvement over the bitch du Lac. He sucked in a deep breath, seeking to calm himself. Damned if he would let that *putana's* actions affect his last two performances. Damned if he would!

He bent to speak with Garvin, then walked off the podium and up the temporary wooden steps that connected the orchestra pit to the stage. The orchestra relaxed. They knew already that the *Maestro* – superstitious as were all of the people who performed at the Met – was going through his own special ritual for good luck. Before every performance, no matter at which opera house, Massimo Orsini, hidden by the curtain, strode the perimeter of the stage surface, touching the curtain from the inside all the way along the front, and making a circle touching as many pieces of scenery as he could. As he made his round, he sang a simple Neapolitan tune. "Mattina, la la.. . la la…"

Satisfied that luck would be with him, the *Maestro* made a sign of the cross and marched back down the steps and back up to the podium. He nodded his head and then glanced at Garvin, his bushy eyebrows raised in question. Garvin nodded that he and the orchestra were ready. Orsini stood for a moment, gathering himself and then, raised his baton. Today, for the rehearsal, he was using the silver baton, given to him by Puccini himself after conducting *Turandot* at La Scala several years ago, just before Puccini's death.

The orchestra moved swiftly, obediently, into the opening notes of Puccini's extremely short, almost non-existent overture. The few bars went smoothly. Calle, with a tiny lamp illuminating the orchestra score he was following, made three notations.

Unexpectedly, the house lights blinked on, off and on again and a curse was heard from backstage suggesting that the marital co-joining of the parents of the electricians might be in question. After a moment, the lights blinked off and the dusty gold curtain rose to show the Act One scene of Christmas Eve in Paris 1830. Calle nodded, happy to note that the scenery looked perfect. That little flit, Forsythe Wicks had done a great job with the props. Perfect. An attic high above Paris, snow covered rooftops glimpsed from the dusty windows. The props revealed a battered apartment, obviously inhabited by a band of bohemians. An easel and dozens of half-finished paintings, piles of books and manuscripts, a lumpy bed, a dilapidated table. The scene conveyed the chill of a garret without sufficient heat, although a battered woodstove stood in the middle of the room. The Act begins as Rodolfo gazes out of the window while Marcello dabs at his painting and blows on his freezing fingertips.

The music swells, then dips as Marcello begins to sing….

***

"It went badly." Calle was angry. "The stage business was clumsy, the singing insipid. You'll all have to do better. Even the lighting, those ruby spotlights…all wrong!" He shook his fist at Johnston Redmond. "Makes Mimi look all washed out. Like a corpse. Change them to rose. And, my God! I thought I'd have a heart attack when the chair broke when Benoit sat down.

Fix it!" He pulled at his hair. "Ah, well, as long as he didn't break his neck." Calle laughed with bitter sarcasm and Benoit, rubbing at his backside, laughed ruefully with him.

"And Schaunard, when you cut the food, raise the knife higher. I want the audience to see that it is a big knife!" Schaunard nodded and waved the knife in question aloft. "Yes, just like that."

"And the music...a few tiny adjustments, *Maestro*..." Calle gestured to Orsini who nodded and bent to speak softly with Garvin. Calle was very careful not to criticize Orsini. The great conductor might walk off the podium! *"Maestro*, you are in charge of the music. I will leave the orchestration...what is yours... to you." Orsini bowed, his face grave, agreeing.

"And now..." Calle consulted the jottings he had made during Act One. "Rodolfo, a bit more *tendrisse* in the *che gelida manina* aria." Rodolfo nodded, knowing that he hadn't put forth his best effort.

"Weaver!" he hollered. "I want the stove to actually work...you know, *work!*" Timothy Weaver shrugged and bent to tinker with the recalcitrant stove. "I want the audience to see the flames. And those in the front rows, I want them to actually *feel* the flames!" He shook his fist at Weaver. "What good is a stove if it won't light?"

He shook himself, trying to tamp his anger, then took a deep breath. *Jesus!* This was the worst rehearsal ever! And would they ever get through it and into the final dress rehearsal? Maybe, by this afternoon. Maybe. Maybe by next week!

He looked down at his pages of notes, flipped a page over and continued his gripes. "And Colline, please do not look as if you have a stomach ache when you are bitching about the cold." Colline nodded curtly. "Gentlemen, a little more action when you are setting the table...and be more animated when the room heats up." He made a sour face. "After all, you are freezing, men...and then you are warm. Act happy about it!"

He stood up and mounted the stage. "Watch me! Happy! Happy to be warm." Calle capered clumsily around the stove, giving the four bohemians his own version of how happy they must appear. To himself he wondered why he'd ever gotten into this crazy business with these astronomically temperamental people. *They were crazy...all of them...stark, raving crazy!* He gathered his wits about him once more. "You were very good, Shaunard, in the bit about the parrot." He gave Claudio Vizzi a graceful nod. "The audience will laugh when you do the puppet. I liked your hand gestures. But remember to wave that carving knife." He turned a page over. "Benoit, you did a fine job...just watch that low note...and watch where you sit! Ha, ha." He then turned to Ignatzia and fussed with her dress.

"My dear, you did well." He turned away from her and made a face, showing the rest of the audience what he really thought of her performance.

"But…who chose this costume? This dress is all wrong on you! You look like an old vinegar-faced virgin in it."

Ignatzia blinked and looked down at herself. Never a particularly intro-spective woman, she thought the green dress was very nice. Calle pulled the bodice lower. "Can we not make this look better? More maidenly, less like a streetwalker but still voluptuous… with a bigger hint of sex. Maybe have your tits show more?" Ignatzia winced, but was experienced enough to keep her mouth shut. Janet came over and Calle showed her what he meant. Janet shrugged, nodded and stepped back saying nothing. When Calle was in this kind of a mood, there was no pleasing him.

Calle continued, "And you did well as Mimi…" Calle patted Ignatzia's rather ample rear end. She was all he had for this moment. He'd try to be kind to her. "I want a little more yearning when you sing about the flowers and the springtime." Ignatzia nodded with dubious understanding. Calle smothered a groan. *She's a cow! Ah, but she's a cow who is here! What else can I do?* "I will work a bit with you after Act Two, in case our *diva* is still absent."

Again, a loud crash was heard backstage and a ripe curse floated through the air. Then some hammering and then a shout, "Where the hell is the toy man's cart?"

Calle whirled and faced the performers, his eyes bugging out, trying to be patient. He sucked in a breath and then let it out, slowly…. "All in all, a pretty good job. Now, let us do Act Two and see what we shall see." He cupped his hands to his mouth and bawled, "Act Two! Everyone on stage!"

***

Sigrid Chalmers again called the performers; "We need Alcindoro here…yes? Fine! And Musetta? Good. Thank you, my dear. I can always de-pend upon you to be ready". Sigrid thanked the heavens for a performer such as Angelique Orloff. She never gave anyone a moment's trouble, always knew her lines, was always on time and ready to sing. A trouper of the first water. He blew Angelique a kiss. And, the blessed woman was beautiful and cooperative and always pleasant. An angel in a sea of self-important vipers! She was well named – Angelique! Our own angel.

He turned and bawled, "Where is Parpignol? Good. And my bohemians? And the children? Excellent." He motioned to a large group in the wings. "The townspeople, the vendors…stand there for a moment. The mammas and the children…over there." He motioned to the stagehands to set up the tables. In the background, Urbano directed the placement of various pieces of stage properties. Forsythe Wicks danced around the stage, placing dishes and toys and properties in their proper places as Chalmers tapped his foot with impa-tience.

"Get moving, lads. You will have the audience going home for breakfast if you don't move faster! Let's go, *Andiamo*!"

Calle climbed back on stage. "Is there any chance that our star might have gotten here yet?" He rubbed his chin in exasperation. "No one has heard from her?" He peered out into the audience. "Can someone get into a cab and see if she has died in her hotel?" He smiled, baring his teeth and conveying that he'd be delighted to hear of her demise. There were a few titters of laugher in the wings.

Calle peered into the darkness. "Yes? Thank you." He tugged at his hair, angry that du Lac was holding up the entire ensemble. "May God strike her dead! How can anyone deal with this?" He turned to inspect Mimi's dress changes. "Yes, that's a little better." Janet retreated, relieved. Ignatzia Volante licked her lips in nervous agitation.

Always ready, as much a professional in her own small way as Angelique Orloff was, Antonina joined the rest of the crowd, standing in front of the small cart that held prettily wrapped boxes of sweets. She adjusted the neck of her costume and touched the string of pearls that she wore – always – when she sang. The pearls were strung on a fine gold chain. There were nine of them, perfectly shaped. Nine luminous blush-colored orbs. They were a gift from her father. The father that she had never known, and she valued them more than she could explain. *"In bocca lupo,"* she intoned, sliding her finger-tips over the satin of the pearls, just as she always prayed at the beginning of her performance, no matter how tiny her part.

She watched Angelique also reach into her bodice and pull out a tiny, sil-ver-framed photo Angelique murmured some quiet mantra, then made the sign of the cross. Antonina nodded. Every performer had his or her own spe-cial ritual to stave off the dreaded Bad Luck of a poor performance. Antonina, herself, always told herself, *"In bocca lupo"*…in the mouth of the wolf… It was the same incantation that her teacher, Alfonso Fazzolini used. It was a good incantation and she had appropriated it from him with his blessing.

Satisfied that she had done everything to ward off problems with bad luck, she inspected her cart. The top of the cart was strung with bright round objects, dangling from strings. Antonina presumed that they were supposed to look like candied chestnuts to the audience. Antonina was dressed in her cos-tume, even though this she really hadn't needed to put it on until noon or one o'clock, when the final dress rehearsal, full costumes, full make-up and wigs, would be performed. Antonina, in the matters of her job, was always more than prepared. She loved the opera, anything to do with the opera, and she was thrilled that her life was filled with opera. She stood, calm and relaxed, ready to sing her five short phrases, shouting out to buy her wares. All thoughts of Peter and their clumsy lovemaking of last night had fled. *La Bo-hème*! She knew it by heart. She could sing every word, every syllable of every aria. She lived and breathed every nuance…every piece of stage busi-ness. *Opera!* This was why she had been born!

She grinned as she watched the children gathering in a rowdy bunch. That little one, Jason. He was prancing around, disrupting the group. She chuckled...he was such a little character! His sisters, Amanda and Alyssa, two little girls with beautiful, clear, young voices, were chasing him and pulling him into his appointed spot. She remembered her own first performance of La Bohème, when *she* was one of the children. The little girl in the red coat. Had it only been two years ago? She'd been such an ignoramus! She'd been so anxious to sing, but Signor Fazzolini, her operatic coach and mentor, would only allow her to perform in a silent role. "Time enough for you to sing, Antonina. There will be years and years when you will be performing."

Naturally, she had obeyed him, even though she'd been dying to sing. After all, if it hadn't been for Signor Fazzolini, she would never even been chosen to be a member of the Met children's' performance group. She looked out into the audience and saw him, sitting in the fifth row and he waved at her. She checked to be sure that no one was paying attention to her, and then, she waved back, *happy* to have even this small part in this wonderful world of opera.

Alfonzo Fazzolini, opera coach to only the best, watched Antonina. She was a sweetheart, a child...well, not such a child anymore. Her curves had grown and her beautiful and natural voice had matured and flowered. He remembered the first time he had heard her sing, perfect pitch, perfect voice, even when she was only a little girl. Under his wise and patient tutelage, Antonina's powers had grown and been perfected. She was ready, at least in voice, to perform arias with the best of them. Such a little chicken, he chuckled to himself, so beautiful and innocent. Her voice was ready, but she still was too young for all the rest of the opera life. The fights, the vicious rumors, the scandals and the sex, the tearing of hair and reputations that followed each *diva's* scramble up the ladder of success, many of them gladly crushing the ones they climbed over. The scheming of those who had aged, or those whose voices no longer soared, trying desperately to regain what they had lost. Using drugs, ether, their bodies, money – whatever they could use – to recapture their prestige and reputations. It was a vicious life, this opera, beautiful on the surface with glittering costumes, champagne and the adoration of the crowds. But, under the surface and behind the curtain, it was a cesspool of greed and dangerous passions. Antonina was too innocent, too untried yet. He would nurture her carefully, a small part here, another crowd scene there, and in a few years, she would be ready to face anything. He loved her; she was like the granddaughter he had never had. He waved again at her, and she waved back, impishly making a face at him. He made a note in his pocket notebook to send her some flowers after tomorrow night's performance. She'd be thrilled. He took his pencil back out and added a notation to send corsages to Francesca and Maria, Antonina's mother and grandmother. He would be escorting the two of them, together with a small contingent of friends, relatives and neighbors from Greenwich, Connecticut, who would be coming to hear the opera and watch Antonina play her little part. Happy, he sat back to watch the struggles of the rehearsal with great interest.

***

"Everyone ready?" Calle turned in a circle and his elbow was jogged by Rudolph Schubin, the Met's Orchestral Assistant. "What?" Calle grabbed again at his hair. "Now?" Schubin's hands moved in fluid gestures and Calle groaned and then nodded.

"What the hell *else* can go wrong today?" He beseeched someone in some heavenly position. "Dear God, please help me not to go crazy!"

Schubin moved off the stage and onto the podium. He bent to Garvin. "The *Maestro* is resting. I will be conducting this part of the rehearsal." Garvin nodded...what else could he do? His wife's eyebrows rose, but she didn't make a sound... simply picked up her violin.

Schubin fussed with the pages of the Act Two Score, making sure he understood all of Orsini's notations. Garvin bent toward his wife's chair. "Dear God! Orsini is in his dressing room. He's sulking. He *hates* Vivienne du Lac and her machinations. Let this rehearsal pass! What a mess!"

Alice Mary pulled her dark black hair back and pinned it neatly behind her neck. She whispered back, "It *is* supposed to be good luck if the rehearsal is bad, isn't it?"

"Hmpf! If that old chestnut is true, we'll have the best damn performance anywhere and anytime!" Garvin picked up his violin and signaled Schubin that he was ready. "That goddamn du Lac! She's the jinx of this whole mess. Where the hell is she? She's making Orsini crazy! I'd like to murder her!"

"Shhh, darling. Someone will overhear you! Then that someone will kill her and you'll get blamed." Alice Mary's pretty face broke into a grin. She patted her husband's knee and put her violin under her chin. Her bright blue eyes sparkled. She was ready. Two rows behind them, Susan Frangiamore watched. *Tom and I will be like that,* she thought. *We'll be married and play in the same orchestra forever. The thought delighted her.*

***

Vivienne du Lac, the object of everyone's anger, was still at her apartment fussing with her make-up as the rehearsal for Act Two began. "Bitch!" she screamed as Celestina tried to pin her hair into a pompadour. "You pulled my hair, you clumsy oaf!" She threw the small bottle that contained her eye make-up at Celestina. Used to this, Celestina merely ducked and stepped back for a moment.

"I'll try not to hurt you, my lady." Celestina smirked to herself. *Bitch? No one was as bitchy as you, my fine lady, my old crow. One of these days, I'm going to pull your hair so hard that it will come out of your head and you'll bleed to death through your pores*. The image pleased Celestina so much that she was able to be gentle for the rest of the hairdressing.

"There! You look beautiful, as always."

"Yes," Vivienne turned her head this way and that. Celestina was a cow, but she did have hairdressing skills like no one else. Vivienne's drugs and that second glass of brandy had soothed her temperament, and she felt on top of the world now. She could sing *any*thing! "I do look well." She bent forward and finished her eyes, loading each lash with a heavy covering of black mascara. She blinked once or twice and then picked up the pot of purple lip cream and a lip brush. *Makes her look like an old corpse*, Celestina noted, smiling serenely. A black nose pushed open the door and a yap-yap announced the entrance of Vivienne's beloved dog, *Poupette*. "Yap-Yap!" The dog made directly for Celestina's ankles.

"Get away!" Celestina tried to shoo the dog away. *Stupid dog. Stupid name.*

"Leave my precious alone! Don't hurt her!" Vivienne made loud kissing noises. "Come here, my darling!" *Poupette* ignored her mistress and nipped Celestina viciously.

"Damn!" Celestina yelled.

"*Cheri!*" Vivienne caroled. "Come to *Maman!*" The dog growled and showed pointed, yellowing teeth.

I'll drown the cur yet! Celestina rubbed her ankle. *I'll kick it to death!*

"Oh my *petite chien*, did that nasty Celestina hurt your feelings?" The dog waddled over and leaped onto Vivienne's lap, digging its claws into her thigh. "Ouch!" Vivienne cried. "Be careful, my little one. *Maman* has to appear beautiful today, legs and all." She laughed, trying for a silvery tinkle of amusement. The damn little dog had nearly clawed her leg off!

Celestina hid her smile of delight. *Serves you right, Madam!* "And what will my lady be wearing today?" *And may the animal shit all over whatever you wear, my Lady.*

"The yellow silk," Vivienne painted her lips carefully and blotted them. Nearly finished with her toilette, she splashed a heavy scent on her shoulders and under her armpits. Celestina brought the dress to her and held it carefully. Vivienne stood and looked at the dress.

"I hate that dress. You ought to know better than to bring that to me!" Her voice rose dangerously.

"But, madam, you asked me…"

"*What* did you say?" Vivienne's eyes narrowed. "How *dare* you contradict me, you stupid cow! Bring me the *other* yellow dress…the one with the polka dots, if you can be so clever as to be able to find what I want!" She tapped her foot in anger.

"Certainly, my lady. I apologize for my error." *I hope she's killed by a falling building!*

Vivienne du Lac, soprano, nymphomaniac, world-famous *diva*, alcoholic, adored beauty, drug-taker, star of every opera house in the world, slid into the dress and readied herself to take charge at the dress rehearsal…on her own time. Celestina noted that it had been difficult to button the dress. Her fine lady was getting rather fat around her waist. Celestina allowed herself a little smile.

"What is there to laugh at, Celestina?"

"Laugh, my lady? I am not laughing. I am smiling in admiration. You look beautiful. You will be a sensation tomorrow night."

Supreme in her own self-assurance, Vivienne agreed completely. "Let us get ourselves to the theater, Celestina. Take the red dress. I plan to wear it in Act One." Celestina raised her eyebrows. *Wait until that Calle learned that Her Highness was going to wear an outfit that he had never seen!*

"Move your fat rump, Celestina. You wasted so much time, we might be late." Celestina sniffed, praying for divine intervention in the form of a heart attack on her mistress. *And may her body fall on top of the rat that she calls a dog and kill it at the same time.*

***

Vivienne du Lac was really her name, a fortunate accident of birth. She grew up in a small village near the outskirts of Paris and from childhood, was a selfish, bullying girl. She was very pretty, however, and her strength in making sport of others made her the leader in a pack of other mean-spirited children.

Her family was a middle-class working family, her father a sales clerk in a butcher shop, her mother a homemaker. They fawned over their headstrong and beautiful daughter, wondering from which genes she had spring, denying her nothing and allowing her to rule their lives.

When Vivienne was fourteen, she lost her virginity to an older man, one who was able to buy her pretty trinkets and articles of clothing. Sharp of mind and venal, Vivienne quickly discovered that an infatuated man will give a girl anything…anything if she performed fellatio on his drooping organ. She progressed through a string of lovers, learning to hone her beauty and sexual skills with each man, then discarding him for the next victim. When she was seventeen, she was horrified to learn that she was pregnant. She chose three of her current lovers, sobbing to each of her predicament…and theirs. As all of the men were respectable, older men, each married to respectable wives, wives with no sense of humor. Each of the men gave her a substantial sum of money to take care of her problem. Vivienne then found an older doctor. She seduced him and he performed her abortion for no fee at all, just her favors. The operation left her sterile, and she was actually pleased with this botched result. Who the hell wanted children? Certainly, not Vivienne! However, the surgery also left her with a serious infection which spread to her lungs and throat. She threatened the doctor. "If you don't make me better, I will scream your actions to your wife and daughters." Frightened of discovery, the doctor sent her into a hospital in Milan, Italy, where she recovered only to find that her voice, which had always been pleasant, seemed to improve, allowing her to begin a series of voice lessons with a retired opera singer.

The opera singer, Signorina Giovanna Vissi, was a tall, thin mezzo-soprano who had sung minor roles at La Scala. Signorina Vissi, who was secretly a lesbian, fell completely under Vivienne's spell. Curious and avid for new experiences, Vivienne encouraged the relationship and the two had a clandestine, torrid affair that lasted until 1900.

In 1900, La Scala was putting on a performance of Bellini's *Il Pirata*. Signorina Vissi, who was singing a small part in the chorus, introduced Vivienne to Giami Sevarino, the elderly man who functioned at stage manager. Sevarino was transfixed by Vivienne's beauty and easily slipped under her spell.

"Giami, I want to sing in the opera," she demanded, after they had made love and he was besotted with her charms.

"*Certamenti, si,* my darling. I will put you into the chorus with your friend."

He smiled in worship and was astonished to hear her anger.

"I don't want to be in the chorus. I want to be the star."

"But...but, you have no experience! And Nina Mascoldi is singing *Imogene.*"

"I want to sing *Imogene!*" Vivienne stamped her foot.

"Impossible!"

"Giami...you do not seem to understand. I *will* be singing Imogene." She wound her arms around him and treated him to her own version of arpeggios. He was lost.

"I...I will see what I can do..."

Unsure that Giami had enough influence, that evening, Vivienne went to a tavern on the rough side of Milan. Avoiding the lewd and bawdy comments from the men in the tavern, she made a few enquiries, each accompanied by a handful of golden coins. At the end of her quest, she found a dwarf by the name of Crespi, who said he was willing to help her. Crespi, crippled and deformed, had a fearsome reputation as a man who would do anything for money. He was exactly what Vivienne was seeking. Vivienne gave him more money than he had ever seen. "You will now work for me. You will be my manservant," she told him. "You will work *only* for me." Something in her expression assured him that she really meant this. He nodded and she continued, "I am going to be an opera star – a *diva* - and you will help me to achieve my dream of success." Crespi nodded again, biting his cheek, his shifty eyes glittering at the prospects of working for a woman who, like himself, had no scruples.

"I will be your man," Crespi pledged. "I will protect you."

"You will do whatever I ask?"

"*Certamente, si.* I will do more than you ask." His face, creased and seamed by his deformity, looked almost happy.

***

On opening night, as the curtain was ready to rise, Nina Mascoldi was nowhere to be found. Poor woman…she was of no particular importance except that she was on the stage where Vivienne wanted to be. She was in Vivienne's way. She was found, several days later, awaking in a villa in a small seaside town near Bari with no memory of missing her performance and a ligature loosely tied around her neck. She had been nearly throttled to death and her vocal chords badly bruised. She never sang again. She could not know it, but she was lucky to be alive. Crespi enjoyed killing, but Vivienne had given him strict orders not to murder the hapless soprano. Vivienne was a gentler person then.

Vivienne du Lac exploded onto the stage of La Scala in her debut as *Imogene.* As the curtain descended, and the audience leapt to their feet, screaming and shouting *"Brava! Brava! Bellissima!"* she became a star…a *diva*…a sensation.

Giami accosted her. "What happened to Nina? What did you do?"

"Me? I did nothing, you stupid man. How *dare* you! The only thing I have done is to rescue your third rate opera. No one could have sung as I did!"

Humble, remembering the thunderous applause, he had no choice but to agree. The critics raved and called her "The Lady of the Lake", and Giami and Signorina Vissi often wondered, in the years to follow, had she cared for them or had she used them? Crespi might have enlightened them, but by that time, he and his mistress were at the Paris Opera House with Vivienne singing *Tosca* to swooning crowds of admirers. Vivienne du Lac was to become one of the most adored leading ladies on the operatic stage. Most people who worked with her disliked her intensely, but no one but Crespi saw beneath the glamorous surface to the viper below.

She was ruthless in her climb to the top and her own insatiable need for sexual pleasures of an unusual type. She had one man killed by Crespi when he tried to blackmail her with his own intimate knowledge of her unseemly love for sex with young children. There was such poverty in Italy at that time that youngsters who lurked in doorways, starving and almost like animals of the night, would do nearly anything for a bit of food and a blanket to keep them warm. And Vivienne took advantage of their pitiful existences.

Crespi often roamed the streets of the poorer sections, avoiding the feral cats. He hated cats and was afraid of them, the only chink in his evil armor. He slinked along, passing out candy, seeking these pitiful children, but only those who were comely and appeared disease free. Sometimes, Crespi bathed the children beforehand, but sometimes Vivienne wanted them just as they were, dirty and barefoot…right off the streets.

Vivienne plied the children with sweet wine and honey and then did unspeakable things to their undeveloped bodies. Such was her avid self-absorption in seeking pleasure that one night, she killed two of the children she abused, a boy of nine and his ten year old sister. She had been drunk with wine and some assorted drugs. In her throes of passion, she had strangled the girl and hit the boy when he tried to save his sister. He bit her and she then shoved him down and repeatedly kicked his head. Crespi had quietly disposed of both of the tiny bodies. He thought it was amusing.

In Paris, one year, when the weather was outstandingly cold and young orphans were freezing overnight, Crespi would go out and find one or two partners for Vivienne on nights before her performances. Usually, if all went well, the children who amused and satisfied her, would go back out into the cold with a handful of *sous*. However, if problems cropped up, some of these children would be put back out, drenched in water by Crespi before he released them, to freeze quickly in the frigid night.

One of her chief rivals in Europe was a soprano named Katarina Schufft. Katarina had been chosen to sing *Tosca* at the Dresden Opera. Vivienne was purple with rage. She felt that the role should have come to her. Two weeks before the opening of *Tosca*, Katarina was walking in one of the gardens surrounding her home when she was attacked by a rapist. The man, described as very short, almost grotesquely so, choked her as he raped her, leaving her bleeding and injured, her throat irreparably damaged along with her spirit. She never was able to sing again. Not surprisingly, the coveted role of *Tosca* was sung by Vivienne to rave reviews. Humbly, she asked the audience to join with her in praying that Katarina Schufft would recover completely from her horrible ordeal.

The newspapers that covered the operatic world were unanimous in condemning the attack on Schufft. They called for the police to put out all efforts to catch and punish the rapist, but, alas, although the police spent months on the fleeting clues, no suspect was ever caught. The newspapers also praised Vivienne for her generous support of Katharine's woes, and lauded her for publically asking her audience to pray for the woman who would have sung *Tosca*. One of the newspapers went so far as to call Vivienne "a saint."

Crespi left Dresden quietly on a train.

Chapter Four

"The day is for honest men...the night for thieves"...Euripides, The Bacchae

The third robbery took place on a Saturday night in July. It was a sultry night and Helen Xander and her good friend, Louisa Mae Sokol walked the six blocks to the Pickwick Theater to see *Blue Angel* starring the German sensation, Marlene Dietrich. Helen and Louisa Mae had become, in the last few years, movie fans. They tried to see every film that the Pickwick featured, enjoying one more than the last.

"She's so beautiful, that Marlene." Helen gushed. "I think she's more beautiful than Greta Garbo."

Louisa Mae disagreed. "I prefer Garbo. She has more mystique." She offered what was left over from her bag of popcorn and the two munched, talking over every scene of the movie as they crossed the Boston Post Road, walking towards their modest homes on Church Street. Although it was only nine o'clock, the night was moonless, hot, dark and sticky around them. Their footsteps echoed and they walked slowly, from one pool of streetlamp light into the next.

Two blocks behind, Helen's daughter, Mary, walked with her great chum, Wanda Lopinsky. Although both sets of women, the older and the younger, had attended the same movie, Mary and Wanda would die if ever one of their friends saw them walking with Mary's mother. It just wasn't the sort of thing seventeen year old girls would do in this modern day and age.

"Isn't Emil Jennings swoony?" Wanda gushed. "He's the handsomest man."

"He hasn't a patch on Gary Cooper," Mary cried. "Remember? In *The Virginian* when Gary said, 'You wanna call me that, smile.' Oh, I thought I'd die!" She shook her blonde curls, "No, Gary Cooper is the one for me."

Ahead, Louisa Mae and Helen had reached the porch of Helen's home. The women dawdled for a moment, finishing their discussion of the movie, Louisa Mae's birthday party on the morrow, and speaking of Mary's new swain, a young man named Gary Felton. Gary's father was a Vice President at one of the local banks and Helen had great hopes for the future. They saw Mary and Wanda cross the street. "I'd better go, dear," Louisa Mae yawned and closed the top of her popcorn bag.

"I'll see you tomorrow," Helen patted Louisa Mae's arm and turned to mount the steps to her porch. Louisa Mae trotted down the street to where the small house she shared with her Aunt Betty sat. As she approached the corner, two bright headlamps bisected the night. And a heavy, dark car lurched around the corner, clearly out of control. There was a growl of a motor and a screech of brakes.

With her foot on the top step, Helen paused, looking down the street. Louisa Mae turned to see what the noise was. From her steps, Helen heard a dull thud, then a racketing sound of metal and wheels. In the dark, the headlamps briefly lit up a shapeless mass as it wheeled through the air. There was a muffled curse and the roar of an engine. The automobile stopped for a millisecond, a door opened and slammed, then its engine roared louder and it disappeared into the darkness, the street now silent.

Helen paused for a moment. What had she seen? Where was Louisa Mae? "Louisa *Mae?*" she called out. "Louisa *Mae?*"

She heard running feet and a shout behind her. "*Mom!* What *hap*pened?"

Helen clutched at the banister and bunched her shirtwaist collar with a clammy hand. On the street, Mary and Wanda's steps clattered as they ran towards the dim pool of light and the small, still bundle that lay on the grass verge.

***

Young Charlie Presto and Cliff Gustafson were catching calls that night. They ran to the patrol car and headed up Greenwich Avenue to the address that had been screamed into the telephone. A cluster of neighbors ringed the body of Louisa Mae Sokol. They pulled the car up to the scene and the headlamps lit up the night. "Geez," Charlie said. His stomach lurched and he fought to quiet the nausea. This was his first dead body.

Detective First Class Cliff Gustafson was an old hand, having seen more death than anyone on the police department except for Chief Emerson McAndrews and Detective First Class Mike Murphy. He took a bit of pity on Charlie. "You take the old lady and the two girls inside and interview them." Charlie nodded, swallowing thickly. "I'll check out the body and wait for Doc Sullivan."

Cliff approached the crowd, asked a few questions and took names and addresses. "Go home now, all of you. Those of you who live on this street, someone will be by in an hour or so to speak briefly with you. Those of you who live further away, we'll come to take your statements in the morning." Cliff noticed that many lights had sprung on in the nearby houses. As soon as Doc pronounced the lady dead and her body was taken to the morgue, he'd begin to knock on doors, one by one. He looked sadly at the body. She'd been a nice-lookin' old lady. Cliff walked around her. Seemed to him that the car had caught her at the top of her legs, the way the legs were bent. Then, Cliff figured that she'd been lifted up and most likely landed on her head. He stepped closer, put his hand under her chin, and saw that the entire side of her head was smashed. "I hope she died quickly," Cliff muttered. "Poor woman."

***

Two cars, one an old black Model T Ford, and one a patrol car, arrived in tandem at the scene. Out of the Ford, Doc Sullivan wearily swung his long-limbed body. "What do we have here, Cliff my man?"

"Hit and run, Doc. Somebody hit this lady and took off."

"Anybody see anything important?"

Cliff shrugged, feeling sad. His mother was about the same age as the lady who had died. "Not much. Two people said it was a dark sedan. One said a dark jalopy." Doc made a sound, then dropped to his knees beside the crumpled heap.

"Know who she is?" His hands were gentle.

"Louisa Mae...um...Sokol. Lives right there." His chin pointed to the house next door. Doc grunted and continued his examination.

The second car stopped behind Doc's. Pete Kraut's red hair gleamed in the streetlamp light as he got out of the car. "What's going on?"

"Hi Pete. Hit and run, looks like." Cliff walked over to Pete's car. "Whatcha doin' out here?"

'We got a call a few minnits ago." Pete looked puzzled. "Far as we know, the shitting bandit struck again right around the corner, two blocks from here." He scratched his chin. "Think the two incidents are connected? Yeah? Me, too."

***

The robbery victims were Robert and Tracy Corcoran. Young parents, they told Pete and his partner for the night, the Greenwich Police's newest patrolman, Phil Moore, that they'd been out with friends. "They drove us home. I mean, they drove us three houses away from our house to Tracy's mother's house. She was watching our children...we have a little boy and a little girl. They were asleep and we picked them up..." He described carrying a child..."I had Timmy and Tracy had Molly. We carried them home...it was only three houses away...and we went from Tracy's mom's house to our house. We live on the first floor. We didn't turn on any lights. Didn't want to wake up the kids." His round, worried face creased. "I dumped Timmy into his bed and Tracy put Molly in her crib. We then closed their door gently and tiptoed into the kitchen. Tracy put on the kettle for a cup a' tea. We sat at the kitchen table for a few moments and then...well, I smelled something bad." He managed to laugh. "Tracy thought for a minute that Molly had, um, you know, made a mess in her bed. Tracy went to check, but Molly was dry and sound asleep. I got up and sort of wandered into the parlor and that's when we realized that..." His face showed his disgust. "There were two big piles on the carpet, and someone...the thieves...had taken our radio and the silver that Tracy's grandmother gave us when we got married."

There was a soft knock at the back door. Phil got up and opened it. It was Bob's next door neighbor, curious and worried. "I heard a car with an engine sort of racing and there was a screech." The neighbor scratched his head. "I did peek out, but only saw a dark sedan going past. Maybe a Ford. Maybe a Chevie or a DeSoto. Sorry, but I really couldn't see. It was so damn dark. Was it the same car that hit poor Louisa Mae?"

***

The Greenwich Police Station, a handsome yellow brick building on Mason Street, saw few murders. Violent crimes were a rarity. Greenwich was a wealthy, generally law-abiding place. The police oversaw what problems there were…petty thievery, drunks, a few prostitutes plying their trade, some fights over money, love, and jealousy, rousting patrons out of speakeasies, battling a bit of booze smuggling…simple things. Oh, certainly there were a few murders, after all…even in bucolic Greenwich, there was greed and hate and killing, but, for the most part, the police had an easy and simple job keeping the peace.

The Greenwich Police Department was headed up by Chief Emerson McAndrews, a tough, no-nonsense copper with a strong feeling for justice and a nose for ferreting out secrets. Chief McAndrews was a tall, strong man, with thinning hair, sharp eyes and a ready wit. He was liked and respected by all of the men who worked for him and managed to keep good relationships with the Selectmen and the Town Council. He belonged to the Rotary Club, the Redmen Society, and the Knights of Columbus. He was happily married and had four children, two boys and two girls.

Underneath him, the police boasted two veteran detectives; Mike Murphy and Cliff Gustafson. Both had joined the force a year or so after McAndrews, and the three of them had worked successfully together for many years. Mike, a large, ham-fisted affable Irishman, was renowned for his street knowledge. He knew every drunk, every speakeasy owner, every thief, every prostitute. He had snitches everywhere. If you needed information, Mike was your man. He was married to the former Nora O'Donnell, and, except for the thunderbolt of Cancer that entered their lives several months ago, the only cloud in their marriage was that no children had been born to them.

Nora had always known monthly difficulties, ever since she had been old enough to begin her menses. Every four weeks, the pain and the cramps and clotted blood were a reminder of what her mother had meant when she whispered about the curse to Nora. Old Doctor Clapps had examined her inside and out and mourned with her when he told her that she'd never be able to bear a child. But she had Mike, and no better husband could a woman have married.

A few months ago, her monthly difficulties had escalated. She finally went, at Doctor Clapps' urging, to a specialist in New York City. Sadly, he confirmed Doctor Clapps' worst fears. "With care, Nora, you'll live out a hundred years." He patted her on her narrow shoulder. "They're coming up with new stuff every day. And who knows, maybe something miraculous will be discovered." The hopes of a miracle, coupled with the prayers of Monsignor Darius, was all that could sustain Nora and Mike.

"We'll beat this together, darlin'," Mike told her every night. She nodded, buoyed by his love and her own simple faith.

"She's bad, Cliff. She's bad." Mike confided in his best friend. "She's not gonna make it."

Cliff Gustafson was a big, burly blond giant, born in Sweden and brought to the United States as a child of three when his parents emigrated from Oslo. He was pale and freckled with bright blue eyes and the fair, nearly white-blonde hair of so many Swedes. He married an English girl, Evelyn Carter, who brought her laughing, sarcastic form of British humor to the marriage. They were blessed with two children, Peter, now eight years old, and Karen, now seven. Cliff's knowledge was in the details. He was a human encyclopedia of facts and figures, names and places. If Cliff had every heard or read something, he never forgot it.

The force was bolstered by several senior policemen. Detective Second Grade Peter Kraut had been on the team for ten years. He was a short, dynamic man with flaming red hair and an unquenchable ability to seek out answers. He was unmarried, although it was rumored that he was seriously seeing a woman from Port Chester, New York. He was partnered with Detective Third Grade Charlie Presto, a younger man with only three year's experience. Charlie was tall and sported a healthy growth of curly black hair, which he kept pomaded and combed in an elaborate crown. Charlie, too, was unmarried. He loved women and was always cheerfully entangled in a romance or two.

Old Herbie Floyd, Desk Sargeant, manned the administrative duties at the station, and a young man with limited mental capabilities named Andy Zygmont took care of the custodial duties.

There were seventeen more patrolmen who filled out the ranks of the department. The patrolmen generally had traffic duty, or walked the beats and the streets of Greenwich. Occasionally, they would patrol with one of the police cars. Each of the patrolmen yearned to be upgraded to the detective branch. A detective had better pay, a more exciting job, and, the best of reasons to be one was that detectives didn't have to wear the heavy, blue serge uniform.

Phil Moore was the last to be hired. He was a young man, fresh out of college. His father had hoped that Phil would go into advertising and join the family firm in New York City. However, Phil had other ideas. He was now a raw and untested patrolman, directing traffic and walking the beat of Greenwich Avenue, but, come next spring, he would be attending law school, hoping to become an attorney who specialized in prosecution.

Phil was fascinated by these thieves who left their special calling cards behind, and couldn't wait to work on the case of The Shitting Bandits, as the case, unfortunately, came to be called.

***

Charlie Presto sat, collar undone, comfortable, at Helen Xander's kitchen table. A cup of freshly made coffee had been placed in front of him in a yellow mug, and a matching yellow plate held two scones baked by Mary Xander that morning. Mary and her friend, Wanda sat across the table as Charlie questioned them. Already, Charlie had fallen in love. Helen Xander had already told Charlie what she'd seen, and, breathless with grief and shock, had gone upstairs to lie down with a cold compress on her forehead.

"Tell me about the evening. Start from when you left the house," Charlie wolfed a bite of scone and picked up his pencil.

Mary blushed, and the pink rose from her modest collar to her cheeks. *My, he was handsome!* "Wanda came over at six-thirty and we walked to the Pickwick Theater. Mom and Louisa Mae..." Mary's eyes filled with tears and she sniffed and dashed them away with a clean, starched hankie. "Louisa Mae!" Her top teeth bit softly at her lower lip. Charlie watched her, his pencil still. "I still can't believe it!" She mopped her face again. "They walked ahead of us. We got to the Pickwick and we all bought tickets and went in." Wanda nodded and sipped at her tea. She could tell that Mary was taken with this handsome young policeman, and he seemed to be rather smitten with Mary. Wanda shifted on her chair and sat back, letting Mary take the lead. They'd been bosom friends since third grade, and besides, Wanda already had a boyfriend.

"After the movie...it was good, by the way. After, we just walked home like we always do. Crossing the Post Road and then coming down Sherman Avenue to Church Street."

"Could you see anything?"

"Well, it was very dark," Mary shivered and Charlie swallowed thickly.

Poor little mite. He'd protect her, he would. "We could see Mom and Louisa Mae. They were maybe a block ahead of us and we could her them talking and hear their footsteps. It was very quiet, wasn't it?" She turned to Wanda for confirmation and Wanda nodded.

"It was hot and sticky. Mary and I were discussing Gary Cooper and Emil Jennings." Wanda ducked her head.

Perhaps this wasn't quite what the policeman wanted to hear, but he seemed interested in everything they had said so far, writing busily in his notebook and saying, "Uh, Hmmm" and "Go ahead".

"Then, Mom got to our house and she and Louisa Mae sort of hugged, probably saying goodbye." Mary sniffed again and Charlie put down his pencil and patted her hand. Wanda hid a grin by coughing.

"We were just coming to our house and then we heard a car. It came around the corner and it had a noisy engine." Mary's face was screwed up with the effort of trying to remember it all exactly as it happened. "I turned to look, but it was very dark. The car was also very dark, a black color, I think. It was ordinary, maybe a little bit bashed up, like a jalopy, but this was almost two blocks away and I really don't know much about cars."

"It was a dark color, all right," Wanda confirmed, "and it was sort of going in a peculiar fashion."

"Driving erratically." Mary added. "As if the driver was drunk or sick or couldn't steer right. And then, the car swerved and went up on the sidewalk where Louisa Mae was walking. I heard...we heard...there was a funny sound. A smacking noise!" Mary's voice pitched upwards. "A horrible sound! The car hit Louisa Mae and we saw her sort of go up in the air, then hit the car's hood, bounce off and fall to the ground." She sat still for a moment, her thoughts inward, reliving the horror.

"And then?" Charlie's question was gentle. "Take your time, Miss Xander." In his mind, he was singing, *"Xander, Xander, I'd like to land 'er!"*

"Oh, please, call me Mary," she offered, and he was amazed at the mushy feeling he had in his midsection. "After all..." her voice drifted off. "We, um, this is, um....well." She shrugged and he touched her hand again. Mary was captivated. Any and all thoughts of poor Gary Felton disappeared.

"Then what happened?"

"Then we heard the car sort of stop for a moment, as if he...the driver, I think it must have been a him." Her eyes questioned Wanda, who hunched her shoulders and nodded in agreement. "And then, he opened the car door and then slammed it shut and then started up the car and the tires squealed and it drove away, around the corner."

"We ran then, yelling to Mrs. Xander. She was stopped at her steps. I think she was in shock or something like that." Mary nodded and looked up at the ceiling.

"Are you worried about your mother?" Charlie asked in a solicitous voice. "Do you want to go up and check on her?"

Mary nodded, nervous. 'Well, go ahead. We'll wait for you." Mary got up and poured a glass of water and took it with her as she mounted the steps.

Wanda continued, "Then, we ran over to where Louisa Mae was and she...well, we could see that she..." her voice dropped to a whisper..."she was, um, you know..."

"There was nothing you could do for her." Charlie wrote another few words. "She'd died." Wanda nodded, not knowing how to say those words.

Charlie finished his scone. He tipped his head and attempted to make the next question a casual one. "Um, how long have you and Mary known each other?" Wanda grinned and began to tell Charlie about Mary…what a great chum she was, how nice she was, how well she cooked…

In a few moments, Mary returned. "I gave her an aspirin. She's just tired and feels awful. It would have been Louisa Mae's birthday tomorrow." Charlie made another moue of sympathy.

"Let her rest. I can come back tomorrow," Charlie said with some satisfaction, "and see if she remembers anything more."

***

Once again, Doc Sullivan viewed the two heaps of feces. "No corn this time," he muttered, poking at the piles. "Nope. No corn. This time we've got *pop*corn!"

"*Pop*corn?" McAndrews held his nose and peered closely. "Yeah, I see the little kernels. "This fella eats a lot of peculiar stuff."

"By jingo, he does. And his friend is eating nuts again. This pile has walnuts and, um, lessee…I think these are pecans." Doc stepped back and wrapped up the debris. "They've got a new microscope up in Bridgeport. I'm gonna have Georgie Zamfino bring them up to see what they can find up there."

"Bridgeport is gonna love you, Doc," McAndrews chuckled as his fertile imagination viewed the scene of some hapless technician opening up the odoriferous packages.

"Ah, they've seen worse up there," Doc washed his hands. "Much worse."

***

The police again went through their lists of usual suspects. Again, they rode down to the Menenda household and tried to implicate Jimmy Menenda in the robbery.

"You guys are tryin' to catch me doin' somethin' wrong," Jimmy complained. "But I saw the light in jail. I ain't gonna steal no more. I'm workin' with my Pa now. Going straight from now on."

And, although the only alibi to vouch for Jimmy's whereabouts was again his father, the generally lying and cheating Rags, there was nothing that the police could do.

"I could get him in the back alley and make him choke a bit," Charlie suggested. "I'm positive I could get a confession outta him."

"That sort of thing was fine back in the good old days," Cliff Gustafson sighed with nostalgia. "They frown upon that nowadays."

"Too bad. He would have sung with gusto when I got through with him." A policeman's lot is not a happy one all of the time.

***

On a Sunday night in September, the police were called to the rural home of Mr. and Mrs. Scott Laulette.

"Laulette?" Cliff scratched his head, as he and Mike Murphy drove up out of central Greenwich. "Didn't we already have a Laulette as a victim of our shitters?"

"Yup. Second time, I think. That was...who?" Mike turned to Cliff to click into Cliff's encyclopedic memory.

"Sure! Steven and Kathie...two victims named Laulette and two Laulette wives named Kathie? Sounds screwy to me. Too much of a coincidence." He paused to check directions. It was very dark and there were few street lamps up on the country roads. "Those first Laulettes lived closer to town." He made a left hand turn. "I think she...Mrs. Kathie Laulette...was the one who lost the silver chain with the silver cross on it." The car approached a side road and a man, standing at the end of a driveway, waved the light vigorously. Cliff turned in and wound down the window.

"Laulette? You the ones got robbed?"

"That's us." The man spat into the bushes. "First my brother a few months ago, and now me. Just call us the Lucky Laulettes!" He laughed, a raw sound, and motioned to Cliff to follow him.

"So what's the story?" Cliff heaved himself out of the car. These particular Laulettes lived in a long, low barn-like house, set into the trees. Pretty place, Cliff thought. Must be nice in the day time. "Anybody hate your whole family?"

"I can't think of anyone."

"Scotty?" The front door opened. A young woman, dressed in a dark skirt and a darker sweater, peered out. "Oh, good. Come on in." She held the door open and Cliff and Mike went into the house.

Mike whistled as he gaped at the huge, open room with barely any walls or partitions breaking it up. At the far side, was a stone fireplace, closer was a dining area, and to the left, a kitchen, separated from the rest of the room by a wooden topped counter. "Great place!" Mike's eyes were gleaming. Wait until he told Nora about this.

"Thanks," Mrs. Laulette beamed. "We love it." She reached for her husband's hand. "A lot of people think we are crazy, but Scotty is an architect and this was how we envisioned living." She gestured towards the fireplace. "Except that we were greeted by that mess when we came home tonight." Cliff and Mike approached the stone edifice. There, in two still-faintly-steaming piles, were the now familiar trademarks of the robbers.

"Sorry, Ma'am." Mike spread his hands out in helpless futility. "Nasty little surprise, huh?"

"This is so weird," Scotty told them, "My brother, Steven, was robbed a few months ago. The robbers must have been the same people. They left the same calling cards." Mrs. Laulette's face registered anger and disgust.

"Well, let's sit down for a moment and we'll get all the particulars." Cliff's kind face was reassuring. "Sooner or later, we'll get to the bottom of all of this."

51

The first thing the police learned was that although the wives of the brothers were both named Kathy, Mrs. Steven Laulette's name was spelled K-A-T-H-I-E and Mrs. Scott Laulette's name was spelled K-A-T-H-Y. "How do you keep them apart?" Cliff asked. "Gotta be confusing."

"Since I'm older, I'm called Kathy One, and my sister–in–law is called Kathie Two." Her smile dimpled. "Simple, really."

Again, Cliff asked, "And why, do ya' think, would the thieves pick on two brothers three months apart?"

"I have no idea!" Scott turned to Kathy One. "Any thoughts, darling?"

She shook her head. "Beats me?"

"We can see what they left behind, but what might they have taken?"

"We've poked around and I made a list," Kathy One showed it to him. "They took my silverware, some cash that Scotty kept in his drawer up-stairs…"

"How much? Do ya' know?"

"A hundred dollars, exactly. And then they took my jewelry box. There was some money in there, too. Maybe fifty dollars." Kathy One's face was mournful. "It took us ages to save up!"

"And any jewels?" She nodded.

Her husband's anger came through. "Son of a bitches took her two rings, one was her mother's engagement ring and one was a pearl ring I gave her last year." His breathing was heavy. "She also lost two bracelets, a necklace and two broaches." He banged his hand on the table. "*Bas*tards!"

"But, thank God we weren't here!" Kathy One, soothed. "The jewelry was insured. It can be replaced. Let's not worry about it now."

"Your mother's ring…you can never replace that!" Scott muttered with vehemence.

Kathy One shrugged. "No one got hurt. That's all that matters." And Cliff and Mike, thinking of Louisa Mae Sokol, had to agree.

Chapter Five

There are people who have money and people who are rich...Coco Chanel

In the mid to late 1800's, social life in New York was rigidly run by a small contingent of enormously wealthy people, people with wealth that had been inherited for centuries. These people looked down upon the newly wealthy, those who made their money in trade, in railroads, harvesters, armaments, or preserved meats. These outlanders were called derogatory names: climbers, *parvenus*, upstarts and vulgarians. No matter how much money they had, the bastions of New York society would continue to ignore them.

In the 1880's, the Academy of Music, New York's only opera house, routinely rejected the newcomers' offers for one of the red and gold boxes at the opera. At that time, a yearly subscription to the Academy cost $2,500, a princely sum. Walter R. Vandersmythe, the wealthiest newcomer of them all, offered the financially ailing Academy the heart-stopping sum of $30,000 to purchase a box. Haughtily, with great relish, he was turned down. After all, who did he think he was?

Mr. Vandersmythe's wife cried at the snub. She had more money than she could spend, and dozens and dozens of beautiful dresses, many of them styled in Paris by Worth, but, if they couldn't join the Academy, where could she show off those dresses, nevermind the magnificent jewels she had accumulated?

Angered at the insult, seeking to make it all up to his wife, Walter R. Vandersmythe had a brilliant idea. He'd start his own damn opera company! Thus, Vandersmythe and seventy like-minded enormously wealthy newcomers who had also been rejected in one way or another by the old guard elite, decided to take revenge. Each put up the staggering sum of fifteen thousand dollars to purchase a box at the new, yet-to-be-built opera house. They purchased an entire block of New York City real estate...the block between Seventh Avenue and Broadway and between 39th and 40th Streets... and the Metropolitan Opera House was built.

Originally, the cost of the theater was estimated to be $430,000, but, as anyone who has built any kind of residence or building will know with rue, the final cost was nearly five times that amount. The cost of just one of the private boxes rose to $17,500 and the most elegant of the boxes, known as the parterre boxes, cost more than $30,000.

The edifice, designed by Josiah Cleaveland Cady, was the biggest opera house in the world. It had a capacity of 3,045 seats, 732 of which were boxes, expensive areas with chairs that were not fastened to the floor, areas with sofas, tables and comfortable seats. All of these boxes had low railings so that patrons in the other boxes could admire – or deride with a snobbish sniff - what was being worn in an adjoining box. These boxes were the vehicles where the wealthy could parade their jewels and costumes. Where they could see and be seen. The stage was large, slightly smaller than that of the Paris Opera and the Imperial Opera in St. Petersburg. The façade of mustard-colored brick was in the Italian Renaissance style. It was going to be showy and dazzling. It was going to outshine the Academy of Music in every way.

The speed of construction was amazing. In less than three years, the opera house readied itself for the grand opening on October 22, 1883. As a matter of the utmost importance, the opening night of the Met coincided exactly with the opening night of the then-failing Academy of Music. Vandersmythe rubbed his hands together in glee. Revenge was about to be his.

The opera house was splendid, all crystal chandeliers, rosewood with ivory and gold plush, with a magnificent golden curtain that swept open on the first night to present Gounod's *Faust,* with Sweden's Christine Nilsson as Marguerite. The costumes were made in Venice, and the performance boasted four intermissions, giving the box holders plenty of time to show off their gowns and diamonds to one another. In 1885, the Academy of Music limped out of business, pleasing Mr. Vandersmythe enormously and giving him great satisfaction, as the box holders from the old Academy scrambled and begged to get boxes at the Met.

The new opera house flourished, but it was not universally acclaimed by all who attended performances there. The auditorium was much too large for good acoustical quality, the view of the stage from many of the seats was partially blocked and the wooden walls made the building a firetrap. Indeed, in 1892, a careless spark from a stagehand's cigarette reduced the building to rubble.

The Metropolitan Opera House was quickly re-built. Fortunately, times in New York were still economically on the upswing and the investors and box holders were still rolling in money. Had the fire destroyed the Met a few months later, it might not have survived the Wall Street Panic of 1893.

The newly reconstructed building was better than before, partially due to the installation of electric lighting. The "U" shape of the tiers of boxes, lit with rows of lights, gave the auditorium an enduring name – The Diamond Horseshoe, although many snickered that the dazzling lights from the wealthy matrons' jewels was the *real* reason that the oval sweep of private boxes was known as The Diamond Horseshoe.

Although magnificent and dazzlingly beautiful, the construction of the back of the stage area left much to be desired. There were no rehearsal rooms for the orchestra, choruses or the *corps de ballet*. They all had to trudge to a nearby building and back again, even in the rain and snow. The basement held little space for the carpenters, and no storage at all for scenery, which had to be trucked from storage warehouses to the alley at the back of the building, stacked – often in teeming rain or driving snow – and held until Scene One had been dismantled and trundled out. Only then could Scene Two be assembled and trundled onto the stage. It drove stage managers, carpenters, and back stage employees insane. And the acoustics were still poor.

Although there were dressing rooms, even the ones for the stars were cramped, with no running water and little space for costumes or changing.

It was a difficult place to play, but, if any opera singer was asked which opera house was the *ne plus ultra*, most would choose the Met.

***

Barbara had studied the history of this unique building. She'd lived with David and his fund raising efforts for many years. She'd listened to his tales of woe – heard about the difficulties of keeping a cultural edifice in the black. She had trod the stage, handled the molting velvet of the great gold curtain, seen what time and the grime of a city had done to the once-glittering chandeliers. She had noted the worn spots on the walls, the floors and the seats, even in the glamour and luxury of the parterre boxes. The poor darling Met needed her and her group of ladies. She made a notation on her list, ticking off first the name of Lady Maltravers-Goffe.

There were seventeen women in the boardroom, including Barbara. She had expected fifteen, but Helene von Vogel had brought her two young daughters. *Good*, thought Barbara, *the more the merrier*. Barbara swiftly ran her eyes over the assemblage and checked off each name on her notepad. Mentally rubbing her hands together, she assessed the worth of their families' fortunes in the hundreds of millions. At the top of her financial list was the Maltravers-Goffe family. Sir Eustace Maltravers-Goffe himself, was worth perhaps seventy million, Barbara had heard. Not that you could tell by his wife's toilette, she mused. Lady Maltravers-Goffe wore a plain silk dress, puce colored. The only concession to the fortune her husband controlled (much of it from his financially advantageous marriage with Lady Maltravers-Goffe), was a long string of large pink pearls that dangled from her scrawny neck. Barbara thought they *looked* like something that came from the Woolworth counter, but Barbara *knew* that they were worth many, many thousands of dollars. Barbara felt sure that Lady Maltravers-Goffe would, when she saw what the others contributed; contribute more than anyone else so as to keep her head high and her status on the top of the highest social and beneficial pinnacle.

Before she became Lady Maltravers-Goffe, she was Cora Lorillard, the eldest daughter of Artemus and Augustina Lorillard, one of the "400" families of New York City. The "400" was a term coined when Mrs. Arthur Seeley, acknowledged queen of New York's aristocratic society, declared publically that in all of New York, there were really only 400 families worth associating with socially. All others were nobodies. Bumptious nobodies.

Comfortable within the arms of the "400", Artemus was the son of the Earl of Fallow and Augustina's maiden name was Netherland, of the New York and Newport Netherlands. Big money. Old, green and enormous.

Seated next to Lady Maltravers-Goffe was another elderly lady whose antecedents went back to the days of old New York society. Corintha Marvel was at least as old as Lady M-G, perhaps eighty. There, all resemblance stopped, for as dowdy and ugly as Lady M-G was, Corintha Marvel was just the opposite. As a young girl, beautiful red-headed headstrong Corintha Lowe slipped the hide-bound severity of her life as a New York debutant and travelled to England where she became the toast of the British Isles. She danced with the Prince of Wales, she drove a team of white horses on Rotten Row, and she returned to New York in triumph as the wife of Lord Henry Marvel.

Lord Henry, an avid archeologist, died in Egypt of a scorpion bite, leaving Corintha a very wealthy young widow. Corintha, who had always adored the opera, gave herself singing lessons and became a minor sensation herself, singing small roles at the Met in her younger years. Older now, but just as beautiful in a mature fashion, she spent her days enjoying her grand-daughter Carey's company and doing good deeds with her fortune. Barbara was sure she would also be a huge contributor, perhaps even fund the new curtain all by herself.

In direct contrast to Lady Maltravers-Goffe's drab dress, Corintha was dressed in gauzy green, with one of the new cloche hats hiding her still-reddish hair. Seated next to her was her grand-daughter, Carey Marvel-Mabley, resplendent in a form-fitting pink linen dress with a hem that reached only to her knees. *Wonder where she bought that? Carey must be the spitting image of how her grandmother looked fifty years ago*, Barbara mused. *Beautiful, spirited and free.* Barbara gave Carey a huge smile and vowed to invite her to luncheon. *I want to know her better, even if she isn't as rich as her grandmother*, Barbara thought. *I want to get to know her even if she didn't have a dime. She looks like a fun person.* Her father, Ambassador Charley Mabley, sat on the Met's Board with David. *Which country does he...what's the word? Represent? Ambass?* Barbara stifled a chuckle and tried to pay attention to Lady Dorothea Staer.

Lady Staer, formerly a southern belle from Mississippi, brown of hair and freckled of face, married to Sir Dennis, who also served on the Board, was agreeing that a group of women... "perhaps we can call ourselves the Women's Guild..." could certainly be able to raise money. "After all, I do most things as well as Dennis," she confided. "And many things I do *better* than Dennis." The ladies laughed with her. "We can replace the curtain - that should be easy. We can certainly either have the chandeliers cleaned and any prisms replaced, or, if they are in very poor shape, have the chandeliers replaced." Her pleasant voice with its honeyed southern tones continued, "I, myself, to get this ball rolling, will undertake to donate the money for the chandelier." Barbara gasped at this unexpected display of generosity and began to clap. Carey and her grandmother joined her and in a moment, the entire room rocked with the clapping of hands. Lady Staer beamed and held up her hands to acknowledge the applause.

"That's going to be the easy part, when we ask for a definite amount for a definite project." She waved her hands gracefully. "But what I think we women would like to accomplish," she turned to Barbara, "If I may steal some of your probably prepared speech, is to continually fund projects for the theater. This ongoing giving will be much harder to sustain." She sat down to cheers and agreement.

"Magnificent, and thank you, Lady Staer, both from this group, if I may speak for all of you, and from the Met." Barbara hadn't thought of ongoing fund raising, but she was quick enough to realize that she should have. Beaming at her committee, Barbara spoke, "I was going to talk about ongoing fund raising, but I thought we could get the group started with a few concrete examples. You took two of my long-winded paragraphs and reduced them in a better way than I could have." Lady Staer nodded gracefully to Barbara's compliment.

"Hmmm, hmpf," Lady Maltravers-Goffe raised her hand. Barbara nodded toward her and acknowledged her. *Ha-ha! She's got to trump old Staer!*

"I must also offer my donation." She stood up and began to fiddle with her priceless pearls. "The new curtain...I think that will be my little way of participating." Her face creased into a smile, with her lips pursed. The ladies began to clap once more. Lady Maltravers-Goffe nodded with self-satisfaction and sat down.

"My! We are going to knock their socks off!" Barbara wrote furiously on her notepad. "David is going to be green with envy!"

Her rapturous remark was greeted by cries of "You bet....We'll show those fellas....Hooray for us women!"

Helena von Vogel languidly waved her hand. "Oh, my, ladies. Am I the only one...? Is all of this, um, masculine raising of funds, ah, a bit ...pushy? Should we, as ladies, um, be doing this sort of thing?" She placed one pink-tipped fingernail on her chin and ducked her head, peering at Barbara from beneath her bright blue hat. Her two daughters, Chloe and Clair, sat forward and nodded in tandem, looking, Barbara thought, like two imbecilic sheep. "I think we should leave all of this *business..." She makes the word sound like typhoid,* Barbara fumed.... as Helena's honeyed voice continued, "to our husbands. After all, we are ladies, not trades people."

Nudged by her mother, Chloe von Vogel timidly raised her hand. She kept herself seated. "I think we should do what my mother thinks." She was clearly uncomfortable, but, encouraged by her mother's second prod, she plowed on. "We shouldn't be doing things that men should do. We are ladies, after all."

Helena nodded, triumphant that she'd been seconded by her daughter. "Chloe sees it in the right light, ladies." Emboldened, Helena stood up again. "We do not chop wood like men, we do not sweat when we exercise, we do not make mannish decisions." Barbara noticed Carey Marvel Mabley's eyebrows raise, incredulous at Helena's mewling. Helena continued: "We are the tender side of men and women. We must behave accordingly and not shame ourselves. Perhaps we can have a tea-party and try to raise a few dollars that way. It would be best."

The younger von Vogel daughter, getting an elbow from her sister, timidly agreed. "Mama is right. Mama is always right when it comes to situations of etiquette." Helena's pretty, non-expressive face creased itself into a self-congratulatory smile.

I'll kill her, the bitch, Barbara fumed. *Why doesn't she flutter and faint right now, the poor little delicate creep? And her two little sheep. Don't they have an independent thought in their empty little heads? Ladies, indeed!*

Before Barbara could reply, Dale Troy rose, adjusted the collar of her shirtwaist dress and spoke. "I'm rather new here. My husband, Alex, is the newest of your board members. I think Alex was asked to join the board because Alex knows how to make money." There was a collective gasp at this bald statement. Dale winked at Barbara and plowed on, "Everyone knows that the Metropolitan Opera is the finest in the world. And everyone knows how much it costs to run. This isn't the Victorian age where women sit in hothouses and wear long dresses and never speak until they are spoken to." Dale seemed to grow taller. "No." she shook her head firmly. "This is 1929. Women are no longer chattel to their husbands. We vote. We can control our own money and our own destinies. I was very pleased to be invited to join this committee," she looked towards Barbara and grinned. "And my husband was very proud that I was asked. He told me that he *knew* that we, as a group of women, would set the tone for women everywhere. My daughters, Ariel Sarah, Abby and Rachel, are too young to be here today." She raised her eyebrows and stuck her chin in the air, "But, I would want them to know that I, as their mother, am just as intelligent and just as capable as their father. I want them to grow up independent and free to do as they wish. I want them to be proud of me. At the dinner table every night, the girls and I join with my husband in discussing politics, finance and the events of the world." She turned to Helena von Vogel and her daughters. "I believe we can keep our femininity, our charm and still be useful, independent woman who can make a difference to the call of culture." Blushing, to loud applause, she sat down. Helena von Vogel's face showed storm clouds.

Ooops, Barbara thought. *What's next?* She saw the open-mouthed look on the face of her best-friend-since-they-were-at-college-together, Judi Miller and heard Brooks Allgood gasp. Three other women averted their eyes, not knowing exactly where to look. Barbara proverbially pulled up her socks and stood up, after all, this was *her* meeting.

"Ladies, ladies," she raised her head and summoned every ounce of her breeding and the determined look that had gained her the presidency of Syracuse University's Gamma Phi Beta's sorority. "There is room here, as in every committee, for everyone's point of view. This committee was convened for the purpose of raising money, as vulgar as it sounds." Judi winked at her and made a sound of encouragement. "With all deference, Mrs. von Vogel, that's what this is all about. We are the wives, daughters, granddaughters and families of the men who keep this opera house as a going concern. They are busy running the business end of this place. I think they will be happy to look to us to help them in ways that remain lady-like," and here Barbara gave Helena von Vogel a warm smile, even though she wanted to kick her right in her lady-like empty head, "but ways that, nonetheless, are practical. We can replace the curtain," her eyes locked triumphantly into Lady Maltravers-Goffe's, "We can fix the chandeliers," she nodded to Lady Staer. "We can see that the sconces shine like diamonds." She saw that most of the women were nodding in tandem with her. *Good! That should shut von Vogel up.* "We, as women, *must* assume the leadership in preserving the cultural heritage that lives here in the Met. We cannot have a dirty, dingy or decrepit edifice!" Barbara's voice became slightly louder. "We have a responsi*bility!*"

Applause from everyone but the three von Vogels rang out. Grudgingly, knowing that she was beaten, Helena gave a shrug, making her rather beautiful face look sulky.

"We'll raise more money than they can imagine!" Mrs. Vandersmythe crowed.

"We women can do anything!"

"We'll show them how it's done!"

"This committee will be a beacon and an example to every other civic enterprise!"

"And, I," rang out Corintha Marvel, "will replace the disgusting fabric on the seats."

"Too deee-vine Grandma." Carey grinned. "You are the cat's whiskers!"

A knock on the door interrupted the burst of laughter. Clemons, pushing a large trolley, maneuvered himself into the boardroom.

"I reckon you ladies must be thirsty after all your work," His smile stretched his face. "Here's some coffee and refreshments for you all."

"Shall we have a bit of a break, ladies" Barbara waved her hands.

"Before we do," Carey stood up, "I'd like to propose that this committee also expand a little more than just fundraising, not," she grinned at Barbara, "that fundraising isn't vitally important. But even more, I feel that we, as women, should look into providing the public with information about what goes on here at the Met." The ladies glanced at one another and nodded, considering the idea. "I just thought of this, so give me a few days to sound out my own idea. I will come back to the next meeting with a proposal for this group, whatever we are going to call ourselves, to also include public relations and some sort of informative action to educating the public about the opera house and the operas....maybe even go into the school systems and try to get younger children to come to a matinee. Get them interested in opera. Most likely, unless their parents are aficionados, few children even know what an opera *is!* I will report further at our next meeting." She sat down, grinning and her grandmother nodded her approval.

"Great idea, Carey!" Barbara was too impressed to pretend that she had already thought of this.

"Carey, I want to help you," Marcia Walls, a young and beautiful fashion photographer, with a cloud of dark hair that settled around her face like a nimbus, spoke out. "I can do photos of rehearsals. Beautiful costumes and the sets. We can work up a program to show the children how much fun it is to put on an opera." She turned around, flinging out her arms, "They'll not stay children, you know. They'll grow up to be avid opera patrons!"

These are my kind of women, Barbara exulted. "Any suggestions of what we might call ourselves?"

"The Metropolitan Opera Ladies Guild," Lady Staer opined.

"A good name," Barbara agreed. "Ladies? What say you?"

"I agree." Lady Maltravers-Goffe stood up and straightened out her hat.

"And I second the motion". Susanne Nielsen Kelly, the heiress to the Nielsen sugar fortune, waved her hand. Up until now, Susanne, a beautiful carefully-touched-up blonde, blue-eyed woman of indeterminate, but mature, age, had been silent. Barbara threw her a grateful look. Susanne winked back, waggling her eyebrows. "I plan on making a donation myself. Perhaps three thousand dollars. It can be used as you see fit," She turned to Barbara and made a half-bow.

"Marvelous! Thank you! That's settled then." Susanne strode over to Barbara and shook her hand. "A fine meeting, Baroness. A fine meeting."

If anyone disagreed, they kept it to themselves. The ladies began to stir and go to the coffee and tea cart. Social chatter filled the air. Helena von Vogel and her daughters left early.

Barbara rubbed her hands together in nervous delight as Judi came over and elbowed her.

"Nice going, Babs. You knocked 'em dead."

***

The United States, in the decade that began in 1920, saw enormous changes. Less than three weeks into the new year of 1920, Prohibition began. Seven months after Prohibition, the state of Tennessee ratified the 19th amendment giving women the right to vote. In 1921, the Sheppard-Towner Maternity and Infancy Protection Act established a federal program to assist women and their newborn babies. Improved education showed the benefits of better diets, pasteurized milk and inoculations against some diseases. The United States was entering a time of hugely increasing prosperity.

World War I had ended, and America stood poised to produce more than ever before. The people of the United States felt confident that their lives would nevermore be interrupted by the prospect of war.

With this confident feeling of prosperity, many new inventions changed the daily lives of Americans. The radio with entertainment and news entered nearly every home; people left the farmlands and moved to urban centers, as convenient transportation and communication proliferated. The automobile exploded into the lives of Americans. In 1920, one household in three had a car; by 1929, almost 27 million cars filled the roads, and credit purchasing of automobiles forever changed the way the United States bought items.

The necklace of electricity that wound throughout the land in the 1920's also changed the way life was. Women were freed from household drudgery as washing machines, vacuum cleaners and refrigerators became household words. The glow of artificial light at night changed the tempo of life. No longer were people bound to get up, work and go to bed with the sun. Toasters, popcorn machines, sewing machines, electric mixers and electric irons were staples in every home.

In the late 1920's, Americans had money to spend. No longer was the world of finance and investing restricted to bankers, wealthy businessmen and those of great inherited wealth like the Maltravers-Goffes and the Staers. As Americans got used to buying cars on credit, it was an easy jump to buying stock on credit. Known as buying "on margin", the buyer paid only a small portion of the purchase price and borrowed the remainder from a broker, pledging the stock as collateral for the loan. This allowed the waitress at the local restaurant, the shoeshine boy, the housewife, the factory worker and the schoolteacher to invest in the stock market. And they did.

It was fun, and they believed that they would get rich just like the flamboyant stock speculators who were America's financial heroes, with spectacular stories of easy and quick riches.

During the latter years of the decade, stock prices rose astronomically. Some stocks rose more than 400 per cent in a year. Everyone was taking a flutter at the game. Taxi-drivers, housewives, the butcher and the baker, the man who sold newspapers, and the lady who took in washing. The market peaked in September 1929. Investors, large and small, were caught up in the race to make a killing. They mortgaged their homes to get ready money, invested their hard-earned life savings, and cashed in secured, but sluggish, unglamorous investments such as treasury bonds to get margin money to buy yet more stock. Billions and billions of dollars in 1929-era money was invested in September as nearly everyone began to speculate on the rising and rising stock prices.

Unfortunately, most of the new investors, and too many of the more experienced investors, didn't have the money to back up their speculative purchases. But who was worried? Almost no one. After all, as the stock went up and up – and, even if it bounced around a bit - it always went back up and was worth even more the following week. If you didn't join in the frenzy, most people thought you were a sad apple indeed.

In some small circles, caution began to raise its head. Not everyone was convinced that the moon would continue to rise. Some knew that – one of these days – the moon would come down with a crash.

Many believed that prosperity would continue indefinitely, others anticipated a disaster. On September 6, 1929, The New York Times warned that wise investors should pay up their loans and avoid trading on margins. On October 2, 1929, the president of the banking association warned that banks were overwhelmed by speculative credit. Some never invested in the roller coaster, some sold their stock at incredible profits, took the money and put it under a pillow, some heeded the cautionary warnings and pulled back. Some realized that financial ups and downs run on cycles....years go by when things are rosy, and then years go by when there is poverty and crisis in the land. Some were wise and heeded the warnings. But many did not.

And the days of October in the year 1929 rolled on.

Chapter Six

Four weeks, you rehearse and rehearse, Three weeks and it couldn't be worse, One week, will it ever be right? Then out o' the hat, it's that big first night! The overture is about to start, You cross your fingers and hold your heart, It's curtain time and away we go! Another op'nin', Just another op'nin' of another show.....Kiss Me Kate, lyrics by Cole Porter

*L*unch was over. It was time for the final dress rehearsal. All of the performers were in costume, from little Jason in his French schoolboy blouse, with his hoop and stick by his side, to Musetta, wearing an elegant gown of pink satin, her abundant dark wig crowned with a pink cartwheel hat adorned with a pouf of pink feathers.

At the end of Barbara's meeting, the group of women decided to go down to watch the dress rehearsal. "We'll sit very quietly in the parterre box behind ours. We'll creep through the curtain from the back. We won't make a sound!"

"Shhhh! They'll throw us out if they notice. Be as quiet as a mouse!"

As Brooks Allgood crept down the stairs, the heel of her shoe caught on a tread. Her ankle! *Ouch!* She muffled a cry of distress and limped down the last few steps. She stood, like a stork, one foot on the marble floor and the other in the air as she tried to put her foot back into her shoe. She didn't see the whirlwind of Dean Armandroff's bulk and he didn't see her. Umpf! They collided.

***

Garvin swallowed nervously. That damn Armandroff! Where the hell was he again? He'd skin him alive!

The subject of his worry was running toward the opera house. He knew he was late. Jingo! Instead of going all around to the stage entrance, he skidded to a stop and then opened the big front door. If he was seen, he'd be castrated. If no one noticed, he'd save seven minutes. The lobby was nearly deserted. Clemons was mournfully mopping the acres and acres of marble, sweeping futilely with a large tufted mop. He saw Dean slide in, touched his forehead, and motioned Dean forward. Not everyone always noticed Clemons and the work that he did...endlessly and over and over again. But Dean, always democratic to all, took the time to greet Clemons ever time he saw him and even brought the old man a slice of cake or a cigar now and then. On Clemons end, the young, brash musician made him smile. *Shoot! What outlandish clothes the young whipper-snapper wore!* Clemons grinned and bent back to his endless task.

Dean softly said hello to Clemons. Grabbing the paper bag firmly, he rushed towards the big swinging door. In his hurry, he collided with a small figure that was bent over on the side of the lobby, standing on one foot. Umpf!

The small figure fell onto the floor with a loud, "Ouch! Watch where you are going, you oaf!"

"Oh my dear Aunt Fanny! I...I'm so sorry!" Dean's composure left him. He reached down to help her up and his heart stopped beating. Her eyes...she was...she was...His mouth opened and closed and he fell in love.

"You *ough*t to be sorry! You ran right into me!"

"Please....I didn't see..." He dusted her dress. "Are you all right?" His soft dark eyes were distressed. Brooks' lungs fought for breath, too. After all, these soft, puppy-like eyes were the eyes that he inherited from his grandmother. Eyes which had seduced a desert sheik. Brooks couldn't seem to look away. Who *was* this man?

"I'm...fine. My ankle....No, It's ..." She put her weight onto him and he helped her to put her shoe back onto her foot. "Thank you." Her foot...her ankle...Dean nearly bit her neck with delicious thoughts. Brooks, herself in a turmoil, bit her own lip and looked up at him through her lashes. "Who are you?"

"I'm Dean Armandroff. I'm in the orchestra. I play...the bassoon."

"Pssst! *Dean*!" There was a sharp whisper from the door. "Get your duff in here right away! Orsini's coming!"

Dean swayed. Part of him knew he had to go, but how could he leave her? Who *was* she? He turned, but the girl pushed him toward the door. "I'll...I'll be back after Act One," His whisper was frenzied. "Will you be....are you...?"

"Yes," Brooks grinned. "I'll be here."

***

In the absence of Vivienne du Lac, Ignatzia Volente was wigged by Victor Calligari, made up by Henry Wu, and sewn into the green dress, with its bodice reshaped, by Janet Connelly. Ignatzia was extremely nervous. It was one thing to be du Lac's cover, to be ready to step into the role of Mimi should the star be ill or injured. But this! What was this? Using her to cover for a temper tantrum? A late night of debauchery? Why wasn't the vixen *here?*

Arturo Calle was nearly berserk. Where *was* she? The house was sold out for both performances, the opening gala of *La Bohème* on Saturday night, followed by the Monday night performance, and the following Saturday's and Monday's presentations of *La Traviata*. Never again would the opera-loving world get to watch Vivienne du Lac sing both leads, and never again would Massimo Orsini conduct these two operas. These incredible opportunities might also be crowned with the possible sensational attendance on Saturday night, October 12, 1929, of Beniamino Gigli.

Once, several years ago, another performance of *La Bohème* delighted an astonished audience when the great Caruso showed up unknown to anyone. Before sitting down, Caruso slipped backstage and tip-toed, as surreptitiously as his bulk would allow, into the wardrobe room. He surprised everyone by appearing on stage in Act Two as the Old Waiter in the Café scene. Naturally, now Caruso was dead, but might Gigli also make a surprise appearance? It just could be! The ticket holders were in a near hysteria of anticipation. And where the *hell* was du Lac?

The orchestra was ready with even the elusive Dean Armandroff in his seat, his bassoon at the ready. Orsini strode to the podium. The few spectators rose to their feet and spontaneously applauded him. He bowed to the third row as Garvin stood up and motioned for the rest of the orchestra to rise. As one, they held their instruments aloft and stood. Orsini bowed gravely to them, and they sat themselves to a smattering of applause from the seats occupied.

A performance by Massimo Orsini was one that few could forget. He was a tall, lean man with a crown of wiry pepper and salt hair. Hair that seemed to have a life of its own as the music intensified. He was extremely dignified, almost without expression off the podium, his face wooden, his eyes, an unexceptional brown, his head nearly too large for his body. It was rumored that his large head hid a brain of unsurpassed magnificence, housing a prodigal memory. Supposedly, Orsini knew, by heart, every note of every score…every musical operatic passage written. Although he did bring a large, much scribbled-upon score to the podium, he never referred to it after the opera began. And as the music soared, Orsini's body came into its own, swooping and leaning to and fro; then bouncing and swaying; then almost dancing, jumping and bouncing, urging his musicians into fantastic, never-forgotten performances. There were people who didn't understand what a conductor did. Some thought he merely waved a baton around, but those who understood music and orchestration and opera knew that the conductor knitted the music and the singing and the action together. A good conductor would produce a wonderful garment…a Maestro like Orsini would produce a *magnificent* garment, one that was fit for royalty. Garvin and Alice Mary, who had played with him several times, couldn't wait for Saturday night!

Calle nodded again to the Maestro. Orsini's head dipped back. "Let's go. Straight through Act One, come what may." Without another word, Calle sat down.

The seats in the auditorium were partially filled with those lucky enough to be invited to the dress rehearsal, which, in many instances, could be more exciting than the performance itself. Many of the backstage and administrative employees filled the box seats, watching what they could not afford to watch on opening night. Sammie Littman, who organized the ushers, sat in the third row next to Hiram Goldblatt. The ladies who had trooped downstairs from the boardroom filled the two boxes behind the parterre box generally occupied by Barbara and David and their guests and Commodore and Mrs. Janice Carson and their guests. Most of the men who were on the Board of Directors sat in the second row. Arturo Calle and Sigrid Chalmers sat together in row five, center, hoping for a miracle.

Orsini lifted his baton, and the music began. In a moment, the curtain opened to the chilly attic of the four bohemians.

All went relatively well until Marcello, Colline and Schaunard made their exits. Rodolfo bent over the table, working hard on his poem. The stage lights dimed slightly and Mimi knocked timidly at the bohemians' door.

"*Chi è là?*" sang Rodolfo (Who is it?)

"*Scusi.*" answered Mimi.

"*Una donna!*" Rodolfo sang of his surprise that it was a woman.

"*Dio grazie. Mi si è speno il lume…*" Mimi explained. (Oh, please pardon me…my candle has gone out…)

There was a crash and a scream. The action on the stage stopped dead. A high voice called out in anger: "What is she *doing? Why* is she singing my part?" The Lady of the Lake had arrived. "Get the silly bitch away!"

"Yap-Yap-Yap!" The little dog, slung under Vivienne's arm began to bark.

The music screeched to a halt. Orsini threw up his hands. "*Madonna mia!* What in the name of heaven is happening?"

Blowing out a huge breath, Arturo Calle got up. He groaned and pulled at what was left of his hair. Wearily, sensing disaster, he walked to the stage. Passing Orsini, he whispered a few words. Angrily, the Maestro broke his baton and shouted back in Italian. "*Va fan culo!*"

"*Some*one had to sing the role!" Ignatzia Volente screamed at Vivienne. "Where the hell were you?"

"Sing the role? I heard your caterwauling," Vivienne spat at her. "If you call *that* singing…ha! My dog could do better!" She swept up the stairs and pushed Ignatzia. "And what is this *rag* you are wearing?" She plucked at the neck of the green dress. In the wings, Janet groaned.

"It's the costume you might have worn had you been here!" Ignatzia was not going down without a fight.

"Pah!" Vivienne's disdain was evident, even to the ladies in the boxes. "You call this a *cos*tume?" She pulled at the dress. "I hate green! I never wear green!" She grabbed the neck of the dress and ripped at it. All of Janet's careful stitching began to rip…..*rrrrip!* The neck of the dress tore away, leaving the audience and the cast with the vision of the strong, grimy brassiere that propped up Ignatzia's pendulous breasts.

"*Aiiii!*" Ignatzia screamed. "You witch! You *putana!*" She grabbed at Vivienne who pulled away. The little dog was torn out of Vivienne's arms and dropped to the ground.

"Yip-yip-yip!" *Poupette* yowled, holding up her paw in feigned pain.

"You whore's mother! You struck my dog!" Vivienne grabbed again at Ignatzia, trying to scratch out her eyes. Instead, she grabbed the already-torn bodice of the dress. She pulled at it until it ripped in two. Ignatzia, standing now in long pantaloons, screamed and ran off stage.

"*STOP! NOW!!!!*" There was no mistaking Calle's rage. He advanced on Vivienne, who had the sense to shrug and say that it was a pity that some people were so touchy.

"Vivienne, I warn you. This is the end! There will be people here tomorrow night who have paid a minimum of four dollars and fifty cents to see this performance! A *fortune*, even in the cheap seats! You must act more professionally! You have three minutes to change into the other dress. *NOW!*"

"Of course, Arturo. You know I will cooperate as best as I can." Vivienne twinkled, waved to the third row (it had been rumored that she was having an affair with Tommy Hillister, one of the directors), and exited to her dressing room. Celestina and little *Poupette* followed, the dog barking and snarling, Celestina trying not to laugh. *You had to hand it to du Lac,* Celestina chuckled to herself. *She certainly knew how to make an exit!*

"Five minute break, everyone. We'll take it from Mimi's entrance when du Lac is ready." Sigrid Chalmers had rushed offstage and returned with a glass filled with a foaming liquid.

"*Brioschi*, boss." He handed the glass to Calle, who looked at it for a moment, then drank it all.

"I'll need more than that, Sigrid. I cannot take her and her antics anymore. I know she is the most famous *diva* in the world. I know she still has millions of fans who want to carry her to and from the hotel. I know all that. After next week, I will strangle her."

"And I'll hold her down for you." Sigrid saluted him with the empty glass. "The woman is impossible."

On the podium, Massimo Orsini held his head. "I will kill her," he nearly cried. "I will rip her eyes out."

"Please, *Maestro*, try to relax. This stress will do you no good." Garvin spoke quietly. He had enormous respect for the elderly conductor and was fearful that this ordeal might bring on a stroke. Orsini sighed and slumped against the lectern. He should have known better. His last set of performances. She would ruin them. He truly should maim her, just enough so that she could never sing again. It would be a blessing to the world of opera. He groaned. What could he *do*? She would turn his last performances into *merda!*

Antonina watched, wide-eyed. She'd worked with difficult *divas* before. But this was more than she could imagine. Her eyes met those of Fazzolini sitting in the audience. He shook his head, indicating his disapproval of Vivienne's temper. *I'll never be like that! Never! No matter how famous I may be!* Antonina vowed to herself. *Never will I be like that!*

Ignatzia, fuming as she stripped off what was left of her costume made a vow also. *I will kill her! Kill her!*

Angelique sighed and retreated to a chair. *This is why I stay as I am.* She rubbed her left foot and decided that she would go up to her tiny dressing room and apply a bandage or else she would be sporting a blister. Always considerate, however, she asked permission of Sigrid Chalmers. "I'll be back in under five minutes."

"Oh, my dear," Sigrid's face showed his worry. "She'll be causing a rumpus for ten minutes or more, I fear." He smiled into her dark eyes. "Take your time."

From her spot, tucked against a piece of scenery in the wings, Antonina kept watching and remembered Signor Fazzolini's warnings about the temper tantrums of some of the opera stars. Before this morning's shenanigans, she'd been an admirer of Vivienne du Lac for many years, listening to her recordings and trying to learn from them. Du Lac's voice was deeper and denser than Antonina's clear, young soprano. But then, she was older and more experienced. Signor Fazzolini had promised that Antonina's voice, too, would deepen and mature as she got older. And it had. She'd gone from a young, beautiful, but untried voice to a more disciplined sound. Fazzolini had taught her diaphragm control, breath techniques, how to shape her mouth to get the best sound from every vowel and every word, how to listen to the orchestra and watch the conductor's hands. He had promised her that she would be a star one day, and she believed him implicitly. She also believed in her own talent. One day, it would be her turn to star.

And how many times had he warned her that the world of operatic temperaments was a difficult and often vicious one. That there were jealousies and violent tempers hiding behind the most beautiful and angelic of voices. "People have been injured...yes and even killed because of jealous madness. Women manipulate men, perhaps with sex, perhaps with, um, other things." Fazzolini had blushed when he lectured her about the depravity that could be found behind the golden curtain of fame. "Men manipulate women, perhaps with jewels, perhaps with sex...You must approach this part of your career with caution. I can protect you somewhat, but...in the end, you will be on stage all alone. This is why I want you to go slowly, learn to live in this artificial world, little by little. You are mature as far as your voice is concerned, but, my darling little one, you are still a child in your heart."

The divas that Antonina had met thus far had been brilliant singers and also stars of generally kind temperament. Today, with Vivienne du Lac's temper tantrum, Antonina better understood what Signor Fazzolini was trying to tell her. This woman – du Lac - was everything that she would never allow herself to be. Today's debacle was a good lesson. From her perch on the stage, she again watched Fazzolini in his seat talking with an elderly man. He looked up and saw her, and waved once more. She blew him a kiss. *Thank you, my beloved teacher. Thank you.*

In the dressing room, Vivienne had Janet throw a bundle of Ignatzia's clothing, make up and trinkets out into the hall. "Let the upstart pick up her own garbage!" she ordered. "Get this goddamn dress over my head. Don't ruin my hair!" She slapped at Janet's hand.

Janet rolled her eyes. What a performance! The stupid bitch was going to have a wig jammed over her head and still she was moaning about not ruining her hair!

Vivienne stamped her foot. "Celestina!" she shouted. "Get my wig ready!"

The little dog growled and tried to bite Janet's leg. Under cover of the ruffles of the dress, Janet kicked hard at *Poupette's* miserable head and managed to make contact. The dog yipped and began to bark; the sharp, staccato, annoying sound that only an ill-behaved small dog makes. Janet wondered if she should re-consider her career choice. Perhaps she should have listened to her mother and become a schoolmistress.

The dress settled around Vivienne's body. Janet struggled to hook it up. "What's wrong?" Vivienne complained. "Why have you taken in the dress?"

"I haven't touched this dress since you tried it on last week," Janet snickered to herself. *The old bat was putting on weight. May she get as big as a house and then burst herself into a million pieces. I hate her!*

"Fix it, you stupid cunt!" Vivienne's wrath was terrible to hear. "Fix it now!"

"Yes, Miss du Lac," Janet's eyes met those of Celestina's in the mirror. *How can we murder her?* They asked together. Janet bit her lip. If she lost her temper and screamed at Vivienne, she'd lose her job. She sublimated her anger by stabbing the points of her scissors into the cushion next to her sewing kit.

"One moment, Miss du Lac," Quickly, Janet snipped one of the seams. "The dress must have shrunk when it was last cleaned." Aware that Calle was pacing the stage, she basted the dress onto Vivienne with large, temporary stitches. "There, that should hold. I will fix it permanently after Act One."

"You'd better." Vivienne twirled herself around in front of the mirror. The red dress was perfect, a dull, heavy velvet that moved with her every step. Most likely, a poor seamstress like Mimi would never be able to own a dress like this one, but damned if she'd wear a drab outfit on stage. She wiggled her shoulders and waggled her finger at Janet in warning. "If you can't do your job right, we'll have to find someone who can."

Henry Wu knocked on the door, opened it and came in with a huge make-up kit. "Ready for your make-up?" He was a tiny, Chinese man with delicate fingers. He was renowned for his talent of perfect stage make-up. Bold enough to be seen in the back rows, yet subtle enough so that the front rows wouldn't be overcome with any garishness.

Vivienne narrowed her eyes. "I can do it myself! Get out!"

"But..." Henry's mouth dropped. He was *always* in charge of make-up, especially for the *diva*. Vivienne picked up a pot of skin cream and threw it at Henry.

"Get out, you Chinese poof!" She screamed. He ducked, dodging the pot of cream. It fell on the floor and smashed open, spreading goo and glass onto the carpeting. Henry shrugged and shook his fist at her.

"So you'll look like the pox-faced whore that you are!" He glared at her back and slammed the door.

"Little faggot!" Vivienne carefully applied more eye shadow, and then outlined her mouth with deep carmine lip color. She stepped back and looked at herself in the mirror. "More rouge. Do you think?" Celestine, used to the mercurial moods and not really giving a damn how her mistress looked, nodded and handed her the rouge pot. Vivienne put two spots of color onto each cheekbone, used a bushy brush to blend the colors and proclaimed herself satisfied. She understood as well as Henry Wu how she should look. Her make up had to be strong enough to register to the patron who sat in the last row, yet be subtle enough so that the patron in the best box wouldn't think that her eye shadow was overdone.

"My wig," she commanded. Celestina gathered Vivienne's own dark hair into a topknot and secured it with pins. She picked up a clean skull cap from the box on the dressing table, slid it tightly over the mass of Vivienne's own hair, and stepped back. Good. Not a hair showed. She then lifted the wig – a mass of tumbled brown curls - out of its leather box. Carefully, she placed it onto Vivienne's head, wiggling the wig until it was straight and secure. The wig was full, with two youthful bunches of curls down each side, making Vivienne look, it was to be hoped, like a young and fragile girl. *Actually,* Celestina thought, *she looked like an old camel.*

"Very good, my Lady". Celestina stepped back. Janet began to breathe again.

Vivienne took one last look at herself, smoothed the red dress over her hips and triumphant, blew her reflection a kiss. "I am perfect!" she proclaimed. "Perfect!" With a haughty swoop, she slammed out of the room, scooping up *Poupette* into her arms.

"May a thousand fleas bite you in your crotch!" Janet flung the insult out, but only after du Lac had slammed the door. She and Celestina looked at one another. "God knows what has already been in her underwear!" Giggling at the thought of a thousand fleas in du Lac's underwear, Janet and Celestina went backstage to watch and see what was happening.

"What the hell are you wearing?" Fausta Cleva gasped. "That's not the dress for this act!"

"Who are you to tell me what to wear?" Vivienne snapped. "Leave me alone*! This* is the costume I will wear!"

"But, Vivienne…darling!" Calle tried to hide his anger. "The lights are not set for that color!" What a pig she was! Too bad someone with such a bad temper could sing as well as she could. The dress was wrong for the character of Mimi, a poor, starving seamstress. No little young lady who sewed flowers for a living would own a dress of red velvet. Red velvet! Wrong! *Wrong!*

"What do I care how the lights are set? Change them if you must!" She flapped her hand. "Don't upset me with such trivial matters." She cleared her throat and began to make small sounds…. "Mi…Mi…Mi" Tucked under her arm, *Poupette* moaned in tune with her voice.

Calle motioned to Urbano. "Can we fix the gels?"

Urbano shrugged and nodded, "If the Queen insists." He went back to the Master Board, where Johnston Redmond had already heard the altercation and was changing the lights to compliment Vivienne's dress, muttering under his breath.

"Thanks, Redmond." Urbano put a placating hand on Redmond's shoulder. 'We'll kill her *afte*r the show is over." Redmond laughed and nodded, making a gesture with his hand across his throat.

"Can you put the dog down, my dear?" Calle asked. "It is a distraction."

"I will. I will," Vivienne crooned to the dog. "She's my little good-luck charm, aren't you, my little darling?" The dog licked at her face. Sensing everyone's displeasure, Vivienne smiled graciously. "I apologize about the dress, but, you know, Arturo, how much I hate green. I could never wear a green dress. It is not the color for me. I do not look my best in green."

Ernest Rattner, one of the stagehands, whispered, "You don't look so hot in red either, you fat pig. You don't look so good in any color!"

Vivienne heard his whisper. "What did you say?"

Rattner hung his head and mumbled. "I said nothing, Miss du Lac."

"You'd better say nothing, you imbecile," Vivienne shook her fist at him. "One more word out of your stupid mouth and you'll find yourself eating garbage!"

"Yes, Miss du Lac," Rattner cringed.

One of the Negro stagehands, Richard Davis, speaking in a whisper; murmured to Janet. "She's all wrong for this opera. That Mimi is supposed to be a young and tremulous waif…a starving young girl. Ha! Here she is, a big, fat old whore trying to look young! It's a joke! A sin!"

"You're correct, Richard. I feel sorry for Orsini out there. It's his swan song and she's making it into a laughing stock."

Robyn Benson stepped away from the group of chorus singers. "I hear she's using ether to keep her voice going." Robyn rolled her eyes. Everyone knew that ether use would eventually ruin one's vocal chords. Only the most desperate singers used it, and then, only now and then.

"Du Lac is so wrong for this!" Janet agreed. "She should have retired."

"Hush!" Arturo Calle glared backstage at the noise. "Quiet!" Richard rolled his eyes and melted into the curtains at the side of the stage. Robyn sauntered back to the choral group.

At the back of the crowd of townspeople, Horz whispered to Roque, "And to think, I was in her bed last night!"

"I can't believe you!" Roque made a face of disbelief. "I know you boasted about it before! I just don't believe it!"

Horz nodded, a maniacal smile on his lips. "It's true. I swear on my grandmother! She was drunk, I was drunk. She collared me and dragged me home. I didn't have a chance of escaping."

"You want me to believe that *she* – a star like her - dragged *you* - a simpleton - into her bed? She, who could have any man? Ha! What do you take me for? Someone wet behind the ears?"

"I swear, Roque. She dragged me home with her. She's staying in this big, old hotel over on Fifty-Sixth. She told me that she had to have it. She couldn't sing unless she had sex." He giggled at the pictures in his brain.

"Ha! Think of how badly you must have performed! Listen to her! She can't hit a note! Ha! Ha! Ha!"

"I'm telling you, Roque. She was amazing."

"Amazing?"

"Yes! Terrible! Amazingly terrible! She was…" his face blanched at the memory… "She was …crepuscular!" Roque turned, his mouth open, at the unusual word. "I mean it! She took off her clothing…I mean, it was dark. Only a candle or two burning. It was embarrassing…God forbid that anyone should see her naked in the light! She was fat…old…she aged all over! Fat wrinkles and jelly. Jelly flesh…her tits hanging down to her knobby knees." He laughed again. "And her cunny, Roque. You know me…I'd screw anything…do anything for a few bucks..." Roque grinned and made a lewd gesture.

Horz continued. "I have a few drinks and I'm not fussy. I'd see any girl on the street…hell, I'd see a *boy* on the street! For a few dollars, I'd do almost anything! But this! This was more than even I could stomach!"

"Why didn't you walk out?"

Horz hunched over, clearly embarrassed. "She threatened me. Said if I didn't come with her, she'd get me fired. She pulled at my clothes, grabbed at my cock...she...she was..." His mouth was tight with disgust.

"But she's a *star!* A legend!"

"I tell you what, the legend is dead. Laid out cold. She was about as exciting as copulating with a dead duck! She was ugly...awful without all of her make-up. Her breath smelled. Her...you know, down there...it smelled! She was a wreck and she kept taking all these pills..."

"Pills?"

"Yeah. I suppose so she could keep going. She was sort of frenzied. She moved like a rusty hinge, trying everything." He scratched at his crotch. "She was inside, outside, under, on top, inside out, upside down...I mean...she was..."

On the stage, Vivienne heard the frenzied whispers. She watched Horz with a cold glare. She sensed, and rightly, that they were talking about her. She whirled and pointed to Horz. "You! You have no talent for anything but lies! No talent at all for singing. None for acting. You...you are *nothing* at all!" She turned to Calle. "Arturo! I want this piece of shit off the stage! Out of the opera! He's a disgrace. Get him off the stage! He's trying to direct attention away from me. He has...no talent at all." She stood, holding her dog to her chest, her chin in the air.

Calle motioned to Horz. "Get off!"

"Me? I protest!" Horz was agog.

"Come with me, old man." Sigrid Chalmers took Horz's arm and led him, protesting loudly, calling for his union representation, off to the back of the stage.

"I didn't do anything! The old crow! The bat! I'll protest to the Union! She's afraid that I am going to say something about her!"

"Hush, you idiot!" Sigrid shook Horz. "Don't worry. I realize you have a contract and we understand how unreasonable she can be. Stay off the stage for now, at least for the rehearsal. Keep out of her way. Help us to get her through this and Mr. Calle and I will not forget it. Let's try to keep her as quiet as we can. Too many fireworks already and we don't want any more fireworks. OK?"

Horz muttered his agreement. "She's a disgrace. I hope she chokes and dies. She's awful...terrible...a harpie!" He shook his fist at Vivienne's back. She can't threaten *me!* Hell! I'll threaten *her!*

Roque grabbed Horz's shoulders and pulled him further back into the folds of scenery. "For the love of Mike, calm down. She's got the attention span of a flea. Lay low for the moment and she'll have forgotten all about this...tomorrow night, she won't recall anything. We'll change your make-up, put a different wig on you...she won't even recognize you." He made a lewd gesture. "And as for your lovemaking, you Lothario, you…try to be a bit more discerning about who you bed down with!" He giggled, a high-pitched noise for such a large young man, "She's *not* the girl for you!"

"Let's try to get this scene rehearsed," Sigrid pleaded. "Let's start again at Act One, from where Mimi knocks on the door…no, nevermind the scenery, we'll just do her business and the Rodolfo's business…to the end of the Act. Then, we'll segue right into Act Two." He checked to see that everyone in Act One and Act Two was either on stage or in the wings. "Everyone just stay where you are…no one leave. The duet will only take a few moments." He glanced at the podium where Orsini was slumped against a chair, holding a large damp cloth to his forehead. *"Maestro?* Are you prepared to go on?"

Orsini shrugged and pointed to his baton, "It's broken," he mourned. "I was so angry that I snapped it in two." He shook his leonine head with sadness. "That it should come to this….this."

Rudolph Schubin hurried to the podium, bringing Orsini a black leather box. Orsini received it with great care, opened it, and took out yet another of his priceless batons, this one a rosewood shaft, tipped with chased silver. He held it aloft and then polished it against his tailcoat. "From Her Majesty, the Queen Mother." His voice was soft. "Covent Garden. I conducted the divine Nellie Melba in *Tosca*. A *diva* of the first water." His voice hardened. "Not like this…this…" he sputtered, getting himself angrier and angrier, "This *pig!*"

Schubin turned and went back into the darkness of the audience. *Thank God the old man always carried six or a dozen batons with him. This was the second one that had been broken in as many days.*

du Lac pranced onto the stage, her little dog still under her arm. She preened in front of the prompter pit, making a moue at Peter Pawlowski, who crouched in the prompter box. From his box at Center Parterre, David Wessel appraised her with a connoisseur's eye. Despite all of her shenanigans, despite her age, she still managed to look regal and wonderful. Like her or hate her, she was a *presence* on the stage. She still sang like a *diva* should. She was a star. He nudged Sir Richard. "She still has it, whatever that means."

"She's still a star," Sir Richard, who had seen *divas* come and *divas* go, nodded. She was old, she was a bitch, but she still had that certain *je ne sais quoi*. That star quality that reached over the stage and captured an audience.

Calle bowed to her, happy that she at last, seemed in a positive mood. Vivienne glanced around to see if Horz had disappeared. Roque stood still, leaning negligently against a piece of partition painted to resemble the corner of the Café Momus. Horz crouched down, behind the scenery, hiding. Vivienne glared at Roque, who smiled at her, his eyes guileless. Vivienne sniffed and took her place outside the door to the studio.

"And, begin…" Calle stepped off the stage.

In her role as Mimi, Vivienne began her part and scratched at the door. "Who is there?" sang Rodolfo.

From beyond the doorway, Mimi called out, "Excuse me."

"A woman!"

"I'm sorry...my light has gone out." There was a noise from the back row.

Ignoring it, Rodolfo continued his short song: "Here..." He opened the door.

Mimi entered, much too resplendent in her red gown, a candlestick in her hand, the dog under her other arm. Despite himself, Calle sucked in his breath. *She looked magnificent, but Goddam it.....the fucking dog!*

Mimi sang: "Would you...?" She held out the candlestick. In the back row, one of the ushers stood up.

"Can't hear a word she's singing! She's gotta be louder." The man gestured, cupping his ear.

As if in answer to criticism of her mistress, *Poupette* yapped and wiggled.

"What do you *mean*, interrupting me?" Vivienne screamed, stamping her foot. The dog barked sharply, scratched Vivienne's arm and she dropped it onto the floor with an audible curse. The dog barked again, then began to whine, pawing at the hem of the red dress. Vivienne screamed for Celestina to come and get the cursed animal.

Calle groaned and pulled at his hair. Vivienne strode to the footlights. "Who says you can't hear me?" The hapless usher waved his arms. "How can you not hear me? My voice is the best in the world! I have the clearest diction. You must be deaf, you imbecile!" She shook her fist into the darkness and peered across the end of the stage, spoiling for a fight. She noticed Clemons, standing in the aisle near the fifth row, leaning on his broom.

"What's that darkie doing out there?" Her voice was tight with anger. "I don't want him in here!" She pointed at Clemons. "He's putting a spell on me! Making my voice too soft! I want him fired!"

Clemons scratched his wooly head. He began to back up, almost tripping in his haste to be inoffensive. "Get him out! *Out!*"

Calle shook his head and went to Clemons. "Please, Clemons. Go up to the balcony where she cannot see you. I'm sorry, my dear man. She means no harm."

Clemons' face was stoic. "She means great harm, Mr. Calle. I'm a good, God-fearing man who never wished anyone bad luck. Until now. She...that woman... has the devil in her." He backed away, picked up his broom and turned. "I will study that God will strike her dead."

"And I hope that a thunderbolt will make your wish come true," Calle slapped Clemons gently on the shoulder, winking at him. "Perhaps she'll die in her sleep tonight and we will all be happier tomorrow." He headed back to the stage. *"Now,* can we continue?" The orchestra picked up Mimi's next line and the rehearsal continued for a few moments.

Mimi dropped her candle. She leaned on the table and the table swayed slightly, making Vivienne stagger to stay upright. She stopped and screamed out; "Who the hell built this piece of shit?" She kicked at the table. Forsythe Wicks hurried over and checked the offending table leg, tightening a screw.

"It's fixed, Miss du Lac."

"You ought to get a job driving a bus!" She snorted.

"And you ought to get a job scrubbing floors!" Forsythe muttered.

"What? What did you say?" She turned to Calle. "I cannot take this any more! Get this buffoon out of my sight!"

"My God!" Calle almost screamed. "This show goes on tomorrow night! Can't we get three lines finished without a debacle?" He turned to Orsini, "Play! I don't care if the building falls down! Just play!" Orsini shrugged and the orchestra began again.

Rodolfo sang of his life and of his dreams. Mimi answered with her plaintive, beautiful song. Calle began to relax, the Act was nearly over.

Tender with emotion, Rodolfo picks up his beloved's hand. His aria, one of the loveliest written, begins: *"O soave fanciulla, o dolce viso..."* His face is suffused with adoration and his voice tells of his love.

Vivienne suddenly burst into raucous laughter. Rodolfo stopped his aria and staggered back. "What is *wrong?*" The orchestra's music ground to a halt.

Vivienne whooped, gasping for breath. "It is you, you aging peacock! How can anyone expect me to make love to an old fat man like yourself?" There was a collective gasp from the onlookers.

"You go too far!" Rodolfo grabbed her arm and shook her.

"Enough!" roared Calle. "I will kill, right here and now, the next person who deviates from the script, the lyrics or the music. *I mean it!*"

"Oh, la!" Vivienne flipped her scarf back and forth. "Such a big to-do over nothing!"

Chapter Seven

"There's no business like show business,
like no business I know..." Irving Berlin

"You must come to the opera with us! There will be no argument about it!"

"Be reasonable, Helena. I hate the opera. I'll stay at home and you and the girls can enjoy yourselves. I'll just fall asleep and embarrass you."

She sighed. He was just...impossible! In her most irritating voice, she ingratiated him. "Must I explain it again to you, Anderson? This is an important night. My social standing is at the center of this! I have the use of Hermione's box. Everyone in New York will be there. Clair and Chloe and I cannot go alone. It would be ...ah, so déclassé! You are an important man and you must be there with me." She turned toward him, her blue eyes narrowed. "And you must be dressed properly!"

He opened his mouth to protest, but before he could utter a word, his daughters began to shrill and cry. He stood watching them, his wife and the fruit of his loins. Three harridans screaming for him to do what he did not want to do.

What good was it for a man to have an important job? To be Chief of Detectives of the City of New York? To earn a good living, ensuring that his wife and children had everything they wanted and more?

Sensing that he was weakening, Helena von Vogel, moved in for her kill. "You will be very sorry, Anderson, if you do not oblige me in this one small thing that I ask of you." He saw the anger and bitterness behind her beautiful façade. "I will make your life hell if you don't."

You make my life hell everyday, Helena. He turned up his hands. "If that is your last word, Helena, then I'll be there as you wish. Your lackey will attend you."

His daughters clapped their hands. As always, as soon as they got their own way, they were happy. His wife, somewhat more complex in her constant quest for something more, simply nodded. "I'll have a taxicab here at seven-thirty. Don't bother to try to order flowers. I'll do it so it is done correctly."

One more stab at me...one more lance in my pride. Anderson merely nodded and went out of the room.

Anderson von Vogel had been born forty-five years ago, right here in New York City. The eldest son of Valentine and Annabelle von Vogel, Anderson was brought up in luxury with the cream of New York society. Valentine, the

President of the Erie and Lackawanna Railroad, and a early member of The Metropolitan Opera Board of Directors, hoped that his elder son would join him in business. But Anderson, named for his maternal grandfather with Annabelle's maiden name, attending Yale University, had other ideas. He graduated with honors from Yale Law School and then joined the New York City Police Department. Outwardly furious, but inwardly proud of Anderson's unique abilities, Val von Vogel turned to his second son, Chaz, and introduced him into the intricacies of running a large conglomerate business. The third von Vogel son, Stafford, studied medicine, becoming a surgeon. There were two von Vogel daughters, Margaretta and Melanie. Margaretta married a penniless artist, and Melanie refused to marry anyone. Her passion was flying and she and her long-time chums, Amelia Earhart and Carey Marvel Mabley were some of the first women to make their living flying airplanes.

Anderson met Helena Cooperstyne at a party that Chaz and his wife, Penelope gave. Helena was the most beautiful woman that Anderson had ever met. She had ash-blonde hair and soft blue eyes, a slender, straight figure and a brittle, sophisticated sense of humor. He didn't realize that her brittle, sophisticated sense of humor hid a streak of nastiness and a heart as cold as the steel that her father manufactured.

Her lineage, like his, was impeccable. Her father was Horatio Cooperstyne, of the iron and steel Cooperstynes; a man who was ruthless at getting what he wanted. Helena resembled her father in that respect. She wanted Anderson. He was handsome, - tall, fair of complexion, but dark of eyes and hair. He wore his hair short and brushed to the side. He grew a mustache that dominated his face, making him look even more handsome to women and dangerous to the criminals that he caught. He was wealthy, despite the paltry salary of the police – even that of a Chief of Detectives. Anderson had a vast trust fund left to him by his doting maternal grandparents.

Helena hated his mustache and hated his job. She felt she could woo him away from the police force and into a private law practice with her father's company and convince him to become a clean-shaven man. After all, if he didn't comply with her wishes, she would simply refuse him her bed.

Almost all of Anderson's friends were getting married. Helena seemed a good match and he gladly entered into the marriage, not quite understanding Helena and her inherent bitchiness. She was triumphant. She got nearly everything she wanted. Nearly everything, as Anderson refused to give up his career in the NYC Police, nor his luxuriant moustache, no matter how she insisted.

Anderson got a beautiful wife, a trophy. A woman who was as stiff as a real trophy of metal; a woman who took pleasure in hurting and wounding others less single-minded than herself. A woman as empty of love and compassion as a china statue. A woman of no humor or kindness. But beautiful. Beautiful, but soul-less. She did allow him access to her body, but only when she wanted the coupling, offering herself to him to get something that she desired.

Helena, who didn't want children, found herself caught twice. After Chloe's birth, she visited a doctor in New Jersey, recommended by one of her more brittle friends. The doctor, who catered to the whims of the wealthy, performed a small operation on her, thus insuring that she would no longer have to go through the embarrassing and potentially figure-destroying times of pregnancy.

Their marriage, never good from the beginning, became a discouraging sham...Helena went her own way, encouraging bored husbands of her so-called friends to dally with her. She had their daughters brought up by a succession of servants, encouraging the two girls to think and act as she did. Anderson, to his discredit, spent little time with his daughters. He found them shallow and silly and paid them very little attention. Perhaps, had he spent more time with them, they...and he...might have become very different people. But alas, driven into deep disappointment by the folly of his marriage, Anderson found his life in his work.

He was respected by his fellow police, lauded for his no-nonsense approach to solving crimes, and considered a credit to the Force. All who worked with him respected him, admired him and thought highly of his skills, although he was a man who gave his friendship sparingly. It was no wonder he spent nearly all of his time in police work.

Pedar Pedersen, his second-in-command, was cut from a different piece of cloth. Pedar was a happily married, jolly and affectionate man with six children. Although a dedicated and devoted detective, Pedar's heart was with Milly and the children. The men on the Force respected Pedar, too, but differently from their Chief. Pedar was their boss, but also their friend. Many of them shared with him their personal problems and concerns as well as work-related issues. With Anderson, there was no gate in the wall between work and personal life. With Pedar, the wall was punctuated with open gates all along the way.

The differences in their temperaments and the way they related to the men who worked with them forged an unusual bond. Pedar softened the boss, and the boss strengthened Pedar.

"I won't be available tomorrow night," Anderson told Pedar. "My wife insists that I accompany her to the opera, of all fool things."

"What's playing?" Pedar loved opera, especially Wagner's offerings.

"*La Bohème*." Even if he eschewed the glories of opera, Anderson was intelligent enough to be aware of that which a gentleman should know.

"You'll like it." Pedar hummed a snatch of Musetta's Waltz. "There's nothing much going on here. Should be a quiet night. Gilligan and Jordan will be covering. Have a good time."

Anderson's face showed his annoyance. "I won't like it."

"Ya, boss, if you take that attitude, you'll really hate it!" Pedar laughed and, after a moment, Anderson joined in.

***

A busy day. Death spent most of his time in Yokohama and Tokyo, cleaning up after a devastating series of earthquakes. More than 120,000 people had to be processed.

***

"You! Girl!" Vivienne du Lac pointed at Antonina. "Get that cart away from my table!"

"But…Excuse me, Miss du Lac," Antonia groaned inwardly. *Oh, no! Was she going to be the butt of du Lac's next temper tantrum?* "The cart is right on the tape." Antonina pointed to the pieces of tape that were stuck onto the stage floor, each taped area showing exactly which piece of scenery or prop belonged.

"I don't care where it is supposed to be," Vivienne snapped. "I just don't want you and your little sweetmeats in front of my face." She appealed to Forsythe Wicks. "Can we move it over three feet to the left?"

"I suppose." Forsythe moved the cart slightly. "Is this better for you, Miss du Lac."

"Somewhat." Vivienne moved her chair slightly to the right. "After all, no one is interested in what she's singing," she inclined her head toward Antonina. "I'm what they came to see and hear."

Antonina rolled her eyes, being careful not to let the *diva* see her.

"Does it now meet with your approval?" Forsythe asked. Vivienne shrugged, as if the matter no longer held any interest for her. Forsythe bit his bottom lip, sighed heavily and made a big production of moving the tape lines to the new location.

"You'd think he would know enough to keep the props away from me." Vivienne addressed her annoyance to all. "You'd never see this happen in Europe."

Forsythe dusted off his hands and glared at the back of Vivienne's wig. "Hope your Majesty is satisfied now" he muttered, but low enough so that only Marcello heard him.

"Can we now begin Act Two?" Calle's patience was wearing thin. "Fine. Go ahead." He walked to the front of the stage, his back to the audience. *"Maestro?"*

Orsini raised his hands and the orchestra began Act Two. The stage was crowded with the tables and chairs of the Café Momus to the center right, and the rabble of a street scene to the left. Street vendors, children, mothers and fathers, students, and hawkers crowded onto the stage. Marcello was pushed here and there by the throng. Schaunard haggled with a pipe-seller and Colline was seen dickering with the rag-man, holding up a coat.

Muriel Durgin, a long-time professional who generally played small parts, pushed her flower cart forward. The Flower Seller screamed her pitch, "Flowers for the ladies!"

The Fish Monger called out: "Fresh fish! Come and get my fresh fish!"

Jason, one of the children, cried: "Mother! I want a sweetmeat!"

Antonina sang out: "Hot roasted chestnuts! Come and buy my wonderful cookies and candies!" She was careful to stay well away from the table where Rodolfo and Mimi would sit.

Mimi paused, tuning her face up to Rodolfo: "Are you going to buy me the bonnet?"

Rodolfo held her arm, gazing at her with obvious adoration: "Hold tight! It is crowded here."

The seller of larks and tiny birds sang: "Buy my fine finches and larks!"

"My fish are the freshest!"

"Flowers for the ladies! Buy a bunch. Cheap!"

"Whipped cream pies! Lovely pies!"

"Gentlemen, please your ladies! Buy my sweets! Come now, I have sweetmeats and caramels. Come and buy!" Antonina sang, dangling a string of gaily tied-up candies.

"Wait!" Vivienne stopped in the middle of the stage. Orsini dropped his baton, and the orchestra stopped with a few squawks and tootles.

"What now?" The veins in Calle's neck stood out dangerously. "What *now*, for God's sake?"

Vivienne's face was a study in fury. "She!" She pointed to Antonina. "Her!" She was almost gibbering with rage. "This wench! She's upstaging me and singing too loudly!" Calle grabbed his hair with both hands.

"She's *supposed* to sing out loudly, Miss du Lac! She's a street vendor hawking her wares."

"I don't like it," Vivienne pouted. "Who does she think she is, caterwauling like that? It diminishes my voice." She stamped her foot. "Make her stop!"

"I cannot do that, madam." Calle's temper was stretched.

"I insist!" Vivienne threw her arms out.

"It's the way the opera was written," Calle spit out the words. "If it was good enough for Giacomo Puccini, it should be good enough for you!" There was a collective titter. Antonina shrunk down, trying to make herself as small as possible.

"I don't like this little girl!" Vivienne's eyes glittered. "She's an upstart! Trying to push her cart in front of me! And her voice is terrible! She shouldn't sing at all. Just have her stand to the side and hold up her pitiful pieces of candy"

Calle laughed. It was obvious to all, even with the few notes and lines that Antonina sang, that her voice was rich and delicious

"Antonina is singing the part exactly as she's been instructed," Calle came toward Vivienne, his hands clenched at his side. "Can we puh-leese get on with the opera? I am losing what small amount of patience that I still have."

Vivienne shrugged. "Of course." She tossed her head. "If you want her to ruin my performance, go right ahead." She began to cough. "It's smoky in here. My throat...." She gripped her throat. "I am not able to sing out for this rehearsal." She waved her hands in the air. "I will whisper my lines and that way, this young girl can shout out and interrupt my concentration as much as she wants. I will save my voice for tomorrow night." She sniffed.

***

Angelique, standing just inside the curtain, grabbed Antonina's hand. "Don't let her get to you, my dear. She can see that your voice is good. She hates anyone who can sing better than she can."

"But...I am just a crowd singer. I'm no one! She's the star!" Antonia clung to Angelique's hand in honest bewilderment. "She's the *diva*!"

"Don't take it too personally. She hates me, too. Wait until my aria," Angelique grinned with dark eyes sparking. "She'll do everything she can to disturb me and get the audience to watch her."

"No! She wouldn't...would she?"

"Watch, my dear." Angelique patted Antonia's hand and dropped it. "She's already jealous of you. You are in for an unpleasant time from her." Antonina nodded, feeling somewhat mollified. She looked out into the audience, trying to watch Fazzolini's reaction to all of this. He was standing up, and his face was thunderous. Fazzolini and du Lac had met and sparred many years ago when she wanted him to be her vocal coach. He had refused with great relish. She had screamed and threatened and even hit him. He had refused again bowed and turned away, hiding his grin under his bushy mustache. Since then, she had loudly proclaimed her disdain for him and any of his protégées. Fazzolini could care less. Actually, he considered it a great compliment that she was furious with him and openly cursed him. To him, it was a mark of his own greatness.

But for du Lac to bother Antonina! *That* was intolerable. His eyes narrowed and he watched Vivienne's antics on stage. She'd better leave Antonina alone. Or else, she'd face his own brand of retribution. His breath hissed out. His own brand could be formidable...very, very formidable. *Don't mess with Fazzolini*, he vowed silently. *I will crush you if you try!*

With a glare at Vivienne, Orsini began the music again, and Antonina sang her lines, loud and clear and as well as she could. She *would not* let Miss du Lac ruin her small performance.

Shrugging to show the rest of the cast that little girls like Antonina didn't matter at all to her one way or another, du Lac only mouthed her lines until the principals were all seated around their table outside the Café Momus and Angelique as Musetta entered, towing her rich, elderly and foolish admirer. The scene centered now on Musetta and Marcello, each trying to annoy the other, each wooing one another with insults and veiled innuendoes.

Vivienne began to move, fluffing her hair, waving her bonnet, using her hands, trying to catch the audience's attention with her over-blown movements.

Why, she is *trying to upstage Musetta!* Antonina was openmouthed with chagrin. *How dare she do all that ridiculous business when Musetta is beginning her aria? How unprofessional and jealous could one be?*

Musetta moved toward Vivienne's chair, standing just to Vivienne's side. She began her famous aria…perhaps the most famous aria in opera. *"Quando men' vo soletta per la via, le gente sosta e mira…"* (*As I walk alone in the streets, people stop and stare at my beauty…*).

Vivienne tried to distract Angelique by waving her handkerchief, but Angelique, an old hand at taming a trick like this, merely pulled it out of Vivienne's hand. She waved the handkerchief with cheer at Vivienne, enjoining the entire cast and ensemble to laugh at Vivienne's blatant machinations to upstage her. Without missing a beat of her own beautiful aria, Musetta stood right in front of Vivienne and sang of the glory of being desired by every man who passed her by. Her graciousness, talent and beauty was evident to all…even those in the back rows. Her almost-cheerful actions to foil Vivienne's pettishness invited the audience to laugh with *her* and laugh *at* Vivienne. Vivienne gasped, her lips thinned in extreme annoyance. Angry, she stopped moving, knowing that she had met her match.

The rest of Act Two passed uneventfully and the gold curtain came down as Marcello and Colline carried a triumphant Musetta off the stage on their shoulders. Vivienne made an annoyed moue, using her fingers in an age-old gesture, just before the curtain passed her on its way down. Antonina clenched her teeth together so that she wouldn't laugh out loud.

In his seat, Alfonso Fazzolini clenched his fist. It was beginning with a great rush. He had hoped to shelter Antonina from all of the machinations of some petty and mean *diva*. He'd hoped that she could spend another year growing up, so that she might be better equipped to deal with this underbelly of the opera. But it was not to be, it seemed. Perhaps he'd speak with Vivienne du Lac later today. Perhaps she might listen to his reasoning with regard to Antonina. He sighed, perhaps his well-intentioned meddling might make Vivienne even more determined to plague Antonina.

***

As the curtain closed, Antonia watched Angelique with dog-like worshipful eyes. *This* is what an opera star was like! *This* is what she would strive for! Graciousness and dignity and beauty and talent. Angelique Orloff had all of this and more! *If ever,* Antonina sighed, *I could even performed one-tenth of how well Angelique performed today, I would be happy and satisfied.* Angelique was magnificent.

And indeed she was. Angelique Orloff, a young widow and one of the most sought-after soubrettes in the operatic world, was descended from Russian and French aristocracy. Her mother, Helen, was rumored to be a cousin to the Russian royal family, who had become impoverished and fled from Russia to the United States, settling in Philadelphia. Some even told a story that Helen, her mother, stripped of her fortune, had worked as a maid to a Philadelphia business mogul, trying to earn enough money to bring up her daughters. Some said that Helen, herself, was a princess, a disposed heiress to the throne. It was well-known that her father, once a member of the French royal court, had fled with his fortune when he became hunted down by those who would overthrow the government. Her sister, Bonita, supposedly a superb equestrienne, had married a Hungarian prince named Dimitroff Dridi. The rumors also said that one sister was more beautiful than the other, one more talented, one more spiritual. Bonita and Angelique often laughed, when they were able to see one another across the seas, at the rumors that swirled.

Angelique's family history held bravery and a sense of patriotism on both sides, although no one really knew any details. Angelique kept to herself and that added to her mystique.

Her genes and delicate bones formed her beauty. She was small in stature, but held herself so that those who saw her thought her tall and erect. On stage, she had the kind of presence that made an audience sit forward in anticipation, even if the role she was playing was a minor one. She had a classical face and abundant dark hair. Her eyes were romantically dark. Her nose and features held the beauty that made poets sing. Although it was rumored that her husband had been French and a resistance fighter, killed while defending the king, no one really knew the details of her history. Other rumors told of the Kimberly Diamond Mine in South Africa; a castle in Scotland and of lives lost in the Boer War. Angelique kept her own counsel. She let the rumors swirl around her. It pleased her to be a woman of private mystery.

It was said that her love of music had begun in her cradle. She was dramatic and passionate, and started formal training as an opera singer at a young age, studying with the famed Clara Meyers and Sam Gordon, debuting in European opera houses. Some even said that the French King himself brought to her Paris to perform.

Some of the rumors were founded on facts. The truth was that she had a young daughter, Anna Emmelina, who had been born in Paris. In 1925, Angelique and Anna came to America, leaving the Paris Opera at the request of The Metropolitan Opera. She lived quietly in a private and exquisite apartment in New York City, sent her daughter to a small private school, and minded her own business. She was so famous and beloved that the owner of Delmonico's, New York City's finest restaurant, had already named an ethereal cake after her.[1]

Antonina didn't care if she had been born in squalor. It didn't matter at all. To her young and impressionable eyes, Angelique Orloff was the most wonderful creature in the world.

As if in tune to her thoughts, Angelique came to her and clasped her hands. "Come up to my dressing room with me. We have ten minutes before they start Act Three." Thrilled, Antonina nodded dumbly and followed Angelique.

When the original Metropolitan Opera building burned, the new one was built with considerably better amenities for those who worked and performed there. The dressing rooms were still hot and cramped and inadequate, but better than they had been.

The world of opera is a floating one, with stars and musicians travelling from one opera house to another in a short period of time. Often, the cast of players is supplemented by a group of people called supernumeraries, called "supers", for short. These people do not sing or act, but are available to fill the stage with a background of crowds.

At the Met, Sigrid Chalmers was in charge of these "supers". He kept a notebook, filled with the names and contacts of dozens of people who were pleased to step onto the stage and play a part, no matter how fleeting or small.

Sigrid's notebook listed the characteristics of each "super", height, national origin, bearded or clean shaven, young or old and, as each opera was being casted, Sigrid called those whom he felt would fill his needs. Lawyers, doctors, society matrons, street musicians, housewives and students might mingle together for an evening, and each was paid a small sum, perhaps a dollar in the year 1929, to be on stage.

The groups of supernumeraries changed into costumes in the basement; the men in the north wing and the women in the south. Each "super" had his or her own locker for storing personal clothing and gear during a performance, and the costumes and wigs were placed, prior to each performance, on a long table that bisected the room. If the costumes were difficult or complex, a team of dressers was sent to help the supers get ready.

The stars of the opera, the tenors, the baritones, the sopranos…they all had their own dressing rooms, and the best of the rooms are doled out in order of importance. Thus, Vivienne du Lac had the finest room, and the smaller of the two other private ladies' dressing rooms was assigned to Angelique. The rest of the cast, the singers with smaller parts like Antonina, used the commu-

---

[1] See the secret recipe for Angelique's Kiss, Delmonico's Restaurant's Special Dessert circa 1928, at the end of the book.

nal dressing rooms; the women's in the 40th Street wing, and the men's in the 39th Street side. Sergei Andreyev was assigned the *ne plus ultra* of the men's rooms, with Dante Lazzarelli and Claudio Vizzi sharing the next best room. Josef Mercurio and Simon Forest shared the next best, and the remainder of the men used the spacious, but never luxurious communal room.

In actuality, all of the fun off stage was in the communal dressing rooms. Each singer brought in bowls of food, dishes of special things to share and enjoy. Some played poker, some knitted or did needlework. Sue Shigeoka and Marcia Parmenter held continuous marathon games of Mah Jongg and Phil Perri and Ralph Bocchetta played hand after hand of bridge. Robyn Benson was completing a huge tapestry. The women, especially, as they spent many hours in the room, brought in gay curtains and pillows to decorate the dressing room and make it as homey and comfortable as it could be. Often, even a star or two meandered to the communal dressing room, instinctively knowing that this was the hot spot of social goings-on and the center of opera gossip.

Antonina spent a lot of time in the communal dressing room. She was, except for the children who performed, the youngest singer. She had formed a friendship with Janet Connolly, the women's dresser, and loved to share her mother's recipes and gossip with Karen Heffernan, a young woman in her early twenties, who also sang small parts. Karen was happy to sing the smaller roles. She hadn't the voice, range nor talent to become anything further, but she was satisfied to enjoy her job as it was.

In her past performances at the Met, Antonina had passed by the stars' rooms, peeking at their splendor, but never been inside one of them. She held back for a moment, propelled by Angelique. "Are you sure you want me…?"

"Get inside, you goose!" Angelique spanked her bottom with affection and propelled her through the door. "I want to talk with you and we only have a few moments."

Antonina gazed around in wonder. The room itself was not huge, but large enough to hold a small piano and a spacious dressing shelf. A basin was fixed to the wall, and there was a comfortable couch and a few chairs scattered around. In the corner, a colorful enameled folding screen provided an area of privacy for changing costumes.

"The rooms are bare when we first get here," Angelique explained. "We can each bring as much or as little as we wish while we have possession!" She laughed, a silvery tinkle. "But don't forget, my possession of this room is terminated after the Monday evening show."

"It is?"

"That's when Patrice Fortesque moves in for a few days. She's doing a one-woman show. She'll occupy the room for three days while she does the performance, and then I get it back again next week when we do *La Traviata*. I will be singing *Flora.*"

"All these candlesticks…" Antonina touched a silver one. "Are these yours?"

"All mine. I like to pray before each performance." She chuckled. "I'll need to pray before this one, what with La Vivienne trying to steal the show!"

Antonina picked one up. "Does it help you to pray?" She had heard the rumors that Angelique Orloff was not only a woman of talent, but also a woman of great faith and spirituality. The beautiful icons seemed to confirm the story.

"It certainly cannot hurt. I always ask God to guide me through each performance…to help me to sing my best."

"I pray, too." Antonina touched her pearls and put down the candlestick. "And these photographs? Who is this beautiful little girl?" Antonina prowled Angelique's dressing area.

"That is Anna." Angelique's voice was soft. "She's my daughter and my heart's delight."

Antonina thought back to all she knew about Angelique Orloff. Angelique was practically a legend in opera circles; an artist who didn't aspire to claw her way to the top. She had been a steadfast and reliable member of the Metropolitan Opera for years and before that, had sung in most of the large opera houses in Europe. She was a rare soprano…someone who was content to sing minor roles and not to be a star. Antonina wondered why…

"Why do you sing secondary roles, Miss Orloff? Your voice is as good as anyone's. Better than most. Don't you want to be the *diva*?"

"My dear, I am going to give you the best advice you will ever get. 'No one can have it all.' That's the simple truth. If you want to be a *diva,* then you must live your life as one, always and always. You will be famous – feted by kings and emperors, but your life will never be your own." She powdered her cheeks and washed her hands.

"When I began to sing, I made a choice. My career or my life as a private person. I might have been a star like Vivienne du Lac. A *diva.* Singing all of the major roles. A life in the glare of publicity…fame, yes. Fortune, yes… but…no husband, no children….one or the other. I chose my privacy." She smiled and picked up the silver photograph frame. "Anna is my life. She is my reason for living and singing and being. I am her mother – full time – and a singer for a small part of the rest. I earn our living singing. It is a job, and not a career for me. I cannot be both a mother to her and a star to everyone else, travelling all over the world, never knowing which city I will be in next. This is not the life for me, nor is it a life that would be best for Anna."

"And this is as you wish it? You don't want to sing the leading roles?"

"You are so young, Antonina. I have been watching you from the wings. I know Signor Fazzolini and understand that he only coaches the best. Those who are destined to be stars. You want it all. I see it." She sat at her dressing table and fussed with the neck of her gown. "On stage, I am Musetta. I stay in character throughout the production. I am always on time. I know my lines and my music perfectly. I never make a fuss..." The two women grinned at one another, thinking of Vivienne's temper tantrums. "But when I go home...when I close the door, I am just Anna's mother. That is what my life is, and I am content with this."

"But there are some singers who seem to do both," Antonina named several, a few men and fewer woman. "I *want* to be a *diva*...Singing is my life and my heart and soul. But my personal life..." she hesitated, a doleful note crept into her voice, "I have a...I have..."

"A man in your life?" Angelique's lips curved in a smile. *Ah, the poor lamb, she is going to have to make a choice that may break her heart...*

Antonina was young enough to blush. She bit her lip and nodded. "Yes, there is a special boy..."

"Is he supportive of you? Does he know how dedicated you are to your art?"

"I think he does. I talk enough about it!" She giggled.

"And does he listen?" Angelique turned around and searched Antonina's face. "Really listen?"

Antonina reflected... "Maybe. He says he understands, but then he talks about how I will be his wife when we are married...." She raised her eyes. "My mother...She's a wonderful person. She overcame enormous difficulties...my father was...well, he wasn't really my father,[2] but he was my step-father..." she gulped. "He was a terrible man and he abused my mother and he was horrid to me..." She sniffed back sudden tears. "I...well, I'm proud of my mother and what she has accomplished. She's a baker. A professional businesswoman. She owns an extremely successful business. She's simply marvelous! You'd adore her and she's going to love you." She grinned, suddenly struck by a thought. "Maybe, after the performance tomorrow night, you can meet her."

"I would love to....but, your step-father? Will he be watching the performance?"

Antonina started to laugh. "No, I really don't think so. He's dead, you see!"

"Dead?"

"Oh, it is such a long story". She gave Angelique a wicked look. "I'm quite sure he is burning in Hell. I hope so, anyway! Maybe one day when you have a few moments, I can tell you..." She shook her head. "It would take too long...but, what's important, is that my mother, despite being a wealthy and successful businesswoman, is – well she's a mother first and foremost. Her family, and even her husband, when he was alive, came first. Her business comes after her family."

---

[2] Ah, and now you are wondering about Antonia and her early life...for understanding about all of this, as well as getting to know Francesca and the other people who came to Greenwich from Italy, you will have to read The Tears of San'Antonio...

"Is that how you would see yourself if you married your young man?"

Antonina's large grey eyes were thoughtful. She tipped her head, thinking. After a moment, she shook her head. "No. In my dreams, I am on stage. I am singing and the audience loves me. That's what I dream of." She stood up as the warning bell for the rehearsal rang. "Is that wrong? I think I love Peter. I've known him since we were children." Her face showed her confusion. "I do love him. I truly do!" Her young face was filled with conflicting emotions. "But, I think I love opera even more." She groaned from her soul, "Oh, Angelique! What should I *doooo?*"

Angelique patted Antonina's hand. "We shall have tea when the performance is over. You will come to my apartment, meet my darling Anna, and then you will tell me your story." Antonina nodded, looking forward to unburdening herself. "And then I will tell you my own story and how I made peace with my own life and ambitions." She picked up the reticule that she would be using in Act Three and motioned for Antonina to get ready.

"Just stay out of Vivienne's way during the rest of the rehearsal. She sees you clearly…she's not stupid. Far from it. She's perceptive and cunning. She knows you are special from hearing you sing your few lines. She fears you already as someone who is already better than she is. She views you as a rival…someone who can usurp her role. She knows she is getting old and cannot sing these ingénue roles with veracity any longer. My advice would be to keep your lines minimal for today. Tomorrow night, sing out as you have never sung before. She will not be able to hurt you then."

She hugged the young girl and the two of them descended the stairs to the stage.

***

Act Three went relatively well. Vivienne did not sing, but mouthed her part. This was not such an odd thing, as many opera stars saved their voices for the actually performance. Even the great Caruso often whistled his arias during rehearsals, hoarding his magnificent voice for the audience.

At the end of Act Three, Vivienne's dog came prancing onto the stage again. *Poupette* interrupted the scene, barking and growling. Vivienne watched the dog's antics, smiling fondly, as if she had personally birthed the little cur.

"Get the damn dog out of here, Vivienne. If I see the dog once more, I will barbecue her!" Arturo bared his own teeth.

"Crespi!" Vivienne called out. Like a wraith, the dwarf's distorted body sidled onto the stage. He bent, fished in the pocket of the malodorous jerkin that he wore, and held out a piece of meat toward *Poupette.*

From behind the curtain, the opera's cat, Figaro, poked his head. The dog saw the cat and began to bark, clawing and scratching, trying to attack Figaro. Crespi, who was fearful of any and all cats…especially Figaro…a *black* cat.

Figaro, noting the presence of an enemy, shrank back. Forsythe Wicks, the property man, ran onto the stage. "Get away from Figaro, you stupid dog!" Wicks waved his hands at *Poupette*. It was well-known that Wicks adored cats and kept two of them at his apartment.

Poupette growled at Wicks and tried to bite him. Wicks kicked out, landing a blow. *Poupette* countered with a bite at Wicks' ankle. Wicks howled and screamed that he would kill the dog. Vivienne screamed also, crying out that Wicks should be fired, or killed or even worse. Pandemonium set in once more. In the midst, Figaro strolled off the stage and into the depths of the curtains.

"Get the dog out of here once and for all, Vivienne!" Arturo Calle thundered. "I promise, if I see or hear it again, I, too, will kill it!"

"Come, *chein*. Come to Crespi!" Now that the cat was out of sight, Crespi became brave again. He waved the meat close to the dog. *Poupette* growled and tried to rip the meat out of Crespi's fingers. Crespi lunged and grabbed *Poupette* by the scruff of her neck. Crespi made a grotesque bow to his mistress and carried the dog, snarling and wiggling, off the stage.

***

At the end of Act Four, the climax of the opera, the character of Mimi dies in Rodolfo's arms, a victim of frailty, freezing temperatures, starvation and consumption. From behind the curtain, Horz muttered to Roque that no one could possibly believe that du Lac could be a tender young thing dying of consumption. "She's a fat old frog! Consumption! Ha! She could live for months off the fat of her stomach!"

From the orchestra pit, Dean Armandroff caught Brooks' eye. He winked and made a motion with his shaggy head. Brooks nodded. "What was all that about?" Carey Marvel Mabley nudged her.

"I'm not quite sure," Brooks shrugged. "I think he…likes me."

"Who is he?" Carey peered into the pit, trying to see Dean's face.

"The bassoon player," Brooks giggled. "Simply the bassoon player."

From her box, Barbara waved to David, pointing to Dale Troy, herself, Alex Troy and making a circle. David had been married long enough to know that Barbara wanted the four of them to meet in the lobby. He waved and nodded, then bent to speak with Alex.

The gold curtain closed. Orsini put down his baton and wiped his brow. The musicians began to put away their instruments. Tom Zeranski spoke briefly with Dean, and then searched the pit for Susan.

The dress rehearsal was over.

"All right, everyone. It is what it is!" Calle came out and gathered the ensemble together. "Tomorrow night, we open." There were movements and murmurs. "May each of you break a leg. Go home, relax, and be here tomorrow night at no later than seven o'clock. The curtain goes up at eight, no matter what! Thank you all, ladies and gentlemen."

Chapter Eight

*...and while the great and wise decay, And all their trophies pass
away...William Edward Hartpole Leeky...On an old song.*

*I*t started in mid-morning...a difficult day in the life of the Greenwich Police. The telephone rang and young Phil Moore, passing the empty front
desk (Herbie Floyd had gone down to the Post Office to mail some police re-
cords to Bridgeport), answered.

"Hey, Mikey. Good morning."

"Phil, I won't be in today. Please tell the Chief."

"Sure, Mike. Is, um, anything wrong? You sick?"

"No, not me. It's Nora. She had a very bad night and I'm waiting for Doctor Clapps to get here. I'll try to be in later."

"Sure," Phil nodded into the phone, his face worried. Everyone knew how
bad Nora was. "I'll tell him as soon as he gets in." Phil grabbed a piece of
paper and wrote himself a note. "Take your time, anyway, Mike. It's a slow
morning."

Death, hovering over Greenwich on an unexpected call, smiled sardoni-
cally to himself. *Slow morning? What do* you *know?*

"Give my best to Nora," Phil hung up just as Chief McAndrews came
through the door.

"That was Mike. Nora's bad and he's waiting for the doctor."

"How bad?"

"He said she had a bad night." Phil shrugged. "Poor Mike. Poor Nora.
Mike said he'd be in when he could. I told him that it's been a quiet morning
so far and I'd let you know what he said."

"Ahhh," Emerson McAndrews sighed and shook his head with doom. "I
worry that she's not gonna make it."

The telephone shrilled again. "Greenwich Police. Patrolman Moore
speaking. How can I help you?" He listened, his face changing, his eyes wid-
ening... "Really?...Gee whiz!..." He chuckled and McAndrews relaxed his
stance. "We'll be right over, Father, um, I mean Monsignor Dario. Don't
touch anything. We might be able to get some fingerprints." He turned to
McAndrews. "You're not gonna believe this one!"

***

Phil drove the patrol car and Chief McAndrews sat in the passenger seat.
The trip from the station to Saint Catherine's Church on Greenwich Avenue

only took three minutes. As they pulled up, the black clad figure of Monsignor Dario clattered down the stone steps to meet them.

"Father Dario. Um, I mean Monsignor…shoot, I can't get used to calling you that!" It had been only a few months ago, Father Dario Sabatino's recent promotion from the Bishop in Bridgeport. Now, his title was Monsignor Dario, and his mother, Maria, was as proud as she could be. However, everyone was used to calling him Father Dario and stumbled with the new title. He shrugged. It would take a few months for the new name to stick.

Dario laughed, chasing the worried expression on his face. "You can call me anything you'd like. Ha, ha. But just don't call me late for Mass! Ha, ha."

"A sample of church humor, I presume?" Emerson McAndrews and Monsignor Dario had been good friends for a long time. They had shared many adventures and many secrets.

"A pretty poor sample, I fear. Ah. My dear Chief." He grinned, and the young urchin that he'd once been peeped out. "But today, we have a strange problem." Always on the move, Monsignor Dario whirled yet again and pulled the policemen with the force of his personality. "Oh, my blessed Savior, come and look at this!" He tugged at Phil's arm and led them into the little garden that separated the Church from the Rectory.

The garden was a famous one. It held an assortment of beautiful statues, all brought to Greenwich from the little town of San'Antonio, Italy, the town from where many of Greenwich's Italian immigrants had come. The statues were of children and animals and represented the holy sacrifices of Saint Antonio's famous miracles, recognized as genuine by His Holy Father, The Pope, himself.

The two policemen came to a halt, gazing in amazement at the statues. Like all of the residents of Greenwich, they were very familiar with the statues. There were six of them that represented the six children who had been taken up to Heaven by Saint Antonio. The statues of the children were surrounded by more statues, but these were of two donkeys, three sheep, two goats and two lambs. This morning, each of the statues of the children, were dressed in various brightly colored clothing. One wore a pair of red long johns, one a nightgown of blue calico. One wore a straw bonnet and a dress of green with an apron over it. One was covered with a cape of dark cloth. One sported a yellow rain slicker, festooned with a bright red scarf, and the last little statue, the one of Toto, was dressed in a sailor suit. The animals, too, were decorated. They had nightgowns draped over them with ribbons, hats and babushkas on top of their frozen stone heads.

"Well, I'll be dipped!" Phil whistled. "What the heck?"

"When did this happen?" McAndrews grinned. "What kinda trick is this?"

"I don't know," Dario shrugged, joining in with a grin. "I was going over for Mass this morning, and here they were!"

"Hah, hah. I guess fingerprints might be a bit difficult here." McAndrews scratched his head. "What do you wanna do?"

"I called my mother to come over and undress them." Dario shrugged. "I guess it's some kind of prank. No harm or damage done." He made a futile gesture. "I just wanted you to see…"

"Well, I have now seen." McAndrews laughed again. "Donno quite how to find and arrest the culprits, though. Anyone missing any clothes?"

There was a clatter of shoes and Maria Sabatino, Dario's mother, came into the garden. Her face was a study in astonishment.

"My dear Mary, Jesus and Joseph! What is *this?"*

"Early Halloween, Mama," Dario told her, and they all burst into hysterical laughter.

***

Back at the station, Phil and the Chief regaled the men with the story of the dressed-up statues. As they all, laughed, the telephone rang once more.

"Greenwich Police. Officer Floyd speaking. How may I help you?"

Herbie listened, his face reflecting what he was hearing. "Yes?....Of course we will…No. Don't touch anything! Don't even go in again. Just put down the telephone and go out, touching *nothing!"*

With the experience of years, McAndrews' ears pricked up and he leaned forward as Herbie finished his conversation. "Uh, huh. OK....What's the address?.....52 Locust Street? OK. Don't go back in and don't let anyone touch *anything*. We'll be right there." He hung up and swiveled around to face McAndrews.

"Jeepers! A bowling trophy!"

"A what?"

"A bowling trophy. Somebody conked him over the head with a bowling trophy!"

"Who?"

"Someone named Stanley Curtin. Dead."

"Call Doc Sullivan." Herbie nodded and picked up the telephone.

Over on Locust Street, Death rubbed his hands and finished doing what he did best.

***

Dean searched the lobby. There she was! She turned, and his heart stopped beating. "Um, hello."

She spoke with one of the women she had been sitting with, they hugged and exchanged a few more words and then she walked to where Dean was standing, his bassoon case resting on the floor beside his foot. "Hallo," she smiled. "Let's take a walk."

From the other side of the lobby, Dean's bedazzled eyes saw Tom Zeranski, his hand in Mary's. The two men leveled a glance at one another. *All is just fine.*

***

At a busy police station, every telephone call might be the one with earth-shattering news. Cliff walked in the front door as McAndrews hollered to Herbie to call the doctor and let him know they'd meet him at the homicide. "Herbie, my man!" Cliff's fine-tuned crime antennae twitched. "You look pale. What happened?"

"Lady called. A Mrs. Ray. She and the milkman...the back door was open. He, um," Herbie scrutinized his scribbled notes, "Mr. Curtin...Stanley Curtin. He's the stiff. They found him on the floor in the kitchen, dressed in his pajamas, and his head was split open with a bowling trophy."

Naturally, Cliff gaped, "A *bowling* trophy?"

"That's what she said." Ernie grinned.

Young Phil asked, "Can I go to see what's what?"

Cliff made a noise at the back of his throat. "Ah, well. You've never seen a dead body, have you, live bait?"

"Nooo." Phil tipped his head, his mouth twisted. "But...I think it will be OK."

"Your day of baptism is here." Cliff bowed, wondering if Phil had any idea of what might be ahead of him. "Is that OK with you, Chief?"

McAndrews smiled, a tender, knowing smile. "Sure. 'Bout time you become a man." He patted Phil gently on the shoulder. "See a little gore. You and Cliff can handle it."

Cliff reared up. "Let's go. You drive...where is it?"

"52 Locust Street." Cliff nodded and grabbed the suitcase that contained all of the paraphernalia that was to be taken to a crime scene where a body had been found. "Let's go to see how our Mister Curtain ended his days." He grinned and the years fell away. "Curtains for Curtin, hey?"

***

Francesca Sabatino Rosato stuck her head out of the kitchen window and pulled on the clothesline that stretched from just outside the window to the old oak tree in the middle of the garden in the backyard. She hauled in her good woolen winter coat and the cherry-red dress that she would be wearing tomorrow night when she went to see her daughter sing in *La Bohème* The crisp autumn air had freshened the garments and she folded them neatly, ready for tomorrow night's festivities. In her bedroom, Francesca held the cherry-red dress up against herself and turned this way and that, watching her reflection in the long pier mirror. Her hair...should she have it cut? Did it make her look too matronly when she pinned it up into the usual coronet? She touched her cheek. Did she look like the mother of a young woman? *Ha!* She snorted to herself. *Not only the mother of a young woman, but the mother of five others as well! Not bad for an old broad!*

"Mama!" It was Rafe yelling.

"Coming!" She patted her hair and placed the dress and the coat on her bed. "Where's everyone else?"

"I'm here!" Rafe grabbed her and swung her up into the air. 'Who else do you need?" He put her down, smacked a kiss at her and turned to the stove. *He's so tall now,* Francesca marveled. *How did my little boys become much taller than I am? They tower over me!*

"What's for supper, Mama?"

"*Pasta alla Norma.*"[3]

"Mmmm. Good." Obviously, the macaroni with an eggplant and tomato sauce agreed with Rafe's raging young appetite. She shrugged. These days, *everything* agreed with Rafe's appetite. And that of his twin brother, Mike. The boys could *eat!* The girls, well...they were a bit fussier. Sometimes Lucia didn't want meat. Sometimes she did. Sometimes Gia wanted butter on her linguini. Sometimes she wanted sauce. Who knew what peculiarities each day would bring?

"Mama? I'm hungry!" Johnny, her baby, her little prince, toddled into the kitchen, followed by Lucia. "Is it time yet?"

"Who is missing? Where is Mike? Where is Gia?" Francesca bustled to the stove and turned up the heat under the simmering sauce. "Antonina's train should be in at five..." She checked the clock. "She'll be here in ten minutes. Lucia, can you set the table? Rafe, get Johnny's face cleaned up." She bent to her youngest. "What were you doing, my brave boy? Working in the coal mines today?"

***

The train that rattled into Greenwich at five was three minutes late. Antonina's weary body climbed down from the carriage and she began the ten minute walk home to supper. It had been a long, long day.

In the Club Car, Dale and Alex discussed their day. "I never saw such a display of temperament! Is she like that all the time? Is *that* how *divas* behave?"

"She's a particularly miserable specimen, I'll give you that!" Alex shook his head. "David told me that she always makes a scene. She always makes everyone's life as difficult as she can."

"Why would anyone want to have her in an opera?"

"She's world-famous. She's du Lac, the crazy, brilliant opera singer! She revels in these debacles."

Dale and Alex descended from the train and got into their car. "Well, I wouldn't give her the time of day! She's snakey and revolting! If she got run over by a taxi-cab, I'd be a happy woman!" Dale made a horrible face. "She's...she's...awful!"

---

[3] See the recipes at the end.

***

Cliff talked about everything but dead bodies on the ride to Locust Street – the way the Yankees kept winning, the latest movie at the Pickwick Theater, his daughter Karen's essay at school – anything but dead bodies. Phil, worrying that he'd throw up when he saw the dead man, swallowed thickly and answered Cliff's chatter with grunts and monosyllables. As the patrol car pulled up in front of the house, Phil's stomach began to knot. *"Please, God, keep me from making a spectacle of myself,"* he prayed. *"Let me be a he-man about it all. Don't let me lose my lunch!"* There was a Round Hill Farms milk wagon at the beginning of the driveway. A brown horse, hitched to the wagon, looked at the two policemen with curiosity and neighed. Cliff and Phil got out of the car, slammed the doors and saw the two anxious people standing outside the front door.

"Mercy sakes!" the woman cried. "What took you so long?" She was a middle aged dame, Phil noted, wearing a cotton housedress with a sweater thrown over her shoulders. She clutched the sweater tight around her. Her hair was wound up in snail curlers all over her head.

"By jingo, you took your time," the man with her wore a blue coverall with "Round Hill Farms" stenciled across the back. He was obviously the milkman, a thin, nearly bald man with long, scrawny arms and legs.

"And you are?" Cliff turned first to the man.

"Tom Cassidy. I'm a driver for Round Hill Farms." He motioned to the woman. "She's Bessie Ray." Bessie, tight-lipped, nodded.

"Tell us what happened," Phil spoke. He was surprised that his voice was so steady. *I wonder where the dead man is. Will I be able to look at him without binging all over my shoes? If I throw up, will Cliff give me Hail, Columbia for not being a professional?*

Bessie shoved herself forward. This was *her* story and she meant to get the most out of it. "I saw that the milk bottles from yesterday hadn't been picked up. They were still on the stoop. I was worried."

"So when I came to deliver the milk…" Tom started to explain. Bessie cut him off.

"I grabbed Tom and told him that I knew…just knew…that something was wrong. All morning, I'd had a premonition that something was going to be terrible." She rolled her eyes dramatically. "I was always like that, even as a child. I always could tell ahead of things happening….what do they call it…clairvoyant…Bessie, I told myself, something is not right across the street at the Curtin's house. You mark my words." She nodded, her eyes bugging out.

"So when I came to deliver the milk…." Tom began again.

"So when Tom came to deliver the milk," Bessie's flow of words continued, relentless as the waters of Niagara Falls, "I said to him, 'Tom, something is wrong. I can feel it in my bones'".

"So I drove Brownie to the Curtin's house. I never have to tell her where to go and where to stop. Nearly twenty years Brownie and I have been doing this route. She knows even better than me where to go." He laughed, a grating noise. "God's teeth! She even knows who gets half-cream and who gets butter!" Bessie glared at him and sniffed.

"Land sake's, Tom. These men don't want to know about your blamed horse!" She clutched the sweater tighter around her bony frame. "I went across the street and Tom saw what I had seen. The milk from yesterday was still on the stoop!" She paused, as dramatically as Gloria Swanson. "We banged on the door." She let the moment stretch out and Cliff opened his mouth to speak.

"No one answered!" Bessie smote her brow. "I told Tom that I'd had a premonition!"

"So we went to the back door...." Tom tried again.

"I said, 'Let's go to the back door,' and we did. Marched right around. We could see through the window." Bessie paused. This was going to be her big moment.

"He was dead," Tom crowed. "We could see his foot and the bottom of his pajama. And the blood!" He stopped, blinking, not quite able to believe that *he* was the one to tell them the important part.

"I almost fainted, let me tell you," Bessie elbowed herself in front of Cliff. "'Tom,' I said, 'I think he's dead.' And I tried the door handle." Her eyes were wide with what she had seen. "We went in...me first and then Tom. I tell you, my heart was beating hard and I was feeling giddy with fear. I knew...I'd known as soon as I got up this morning...that there was mischief in the air." She nodded, solemn and full of her own importance. "And then we saw the blood! My land! He was a'lying in it. All over and around. A pool of blood," she smacked her lips in relish. "A big pool."

"Did you touch anything, madam?" Cliff was impassive.

"Not a thing, officer. I read the newspapers," Bessie's chin quivered. "I know my duty!"

"All right. Thank you both. Can you wait here for a few more moments. Patrolman Moore and I are going to go inside...No, no, thank you Mrs. Ray. It won't be necessary for you to go back in."

Phil followed Cliff's lumbering stride. The back door was wide open and as he stepped through, he saw the body. The man...Mr. Curtin...was lying, sprawled on the floor, face half-turned down. He was clad in green and white striped flannel pajamas. The pajamas were ruched up on the right leg, and the right foot was bare. The left foot wore a scuffed leather slipper. The matching slipper was lying near Mr. Curtin's head, its toe inside the blood, its heel outside. The entire top of the body was encircled by a lake of dark crimson.

"Son of a bitch!" Cliff ejaculated.

There was a buzzing sound in Phil's head. He wondered if he might keel over. And then he saw…the buzzing…the buzzing really wasn't in his head. Oh, no. The buzzing was real. All over the back of Mr. Curtin's head were dozens and dozens of flies. Flies with bright green-yellow bodies. Phil swallowed thickly, putting his hand up to his mouth. The flies were feeding on the blood and body, and then they drifted upward, settling on the windowsill. Phil's face blanched pasty white and he swallowed audibly.

"Take it easy, old timer," Cliff's voice was kind. He remembered his own first dead body. A lady, it was. And she'd been hit by a train. He could see it clearly even now, thirty years later. Her head was on one side of the railroad tracks. It had been severed cleanly from her body and had rolled against a bush, where it lay, face up. Her face was clean and unmarked, her eyes open, staring, vacant, a cloudy blue with the white already turning opaque, like fried eggs beginning to coagulate. The rest of her body was on the other side of the tracks, her arms and one leg ripped off and deposited in three different places. Oh, no. He'd never forget. He understood. "You want to go outside for some fresh air?"

Phil puffed out a huge breath and shook his head. "I think I'll be all right." He stepped closer, careful not to step in any of the blood. "But, gee, whiz!"

"See that?" Cliff pointed to a silver-colored object on the floor next to Mr. Curtin's head. It was a bowling trophy. "That's what hit him." Cliff squatted and peered more closely. "See what it says?" He wiped at his mouth; the flies were unnerving. Even to him. "First Place. Pickwick Alleys. September 1928. Senior Men's League".

"Looks like the part with the arms throwing the ball…the end of it…the little sharp fingers of the man… the trophy…hit him on the head." Cliff leaned and peered at what was left of Mr. Curtin's scalp. "See how the wound is gaping and jagged?"

Phil gulped and leaned forward to observe. He quickly turned his eyes away from Mr. Curtin's wide open staring ones. His glance settled on the trophy with its bloodied edge. "There's a little plaque on the bottom. It says…," Again, Phil balanced on the balls of his feet, careful not to step in the blood or disturb anything. "…Stanley Curtin". He stepped back. "He's Stanley Curtin. He won the God-danged trophy."

"Bingo." Cliff concurred. They called out to ask if anyone else was in the house, then, they gingerly searched the rest of the premises. No one else was there. The house was as neat as a shiny new pin, if you didn't count Mr. Curtin and his body fluids. The bed was neatly made, the pillows fluffed and precisely placed. There were three empty suitcases neatly lined up in the hall closet. The bathroom was clean and neat, towels folded and hung, sink wiped dry, faucets shiny.

They trooped back downstairs. If you didn't count Mr. Curtin and his lake of blood, the rest of the kitchen was tidy. No dishes in the sink nor on the table. A dishcloth, dry, was folded over a chair back.

The dining room looked as if no one had ever used it. The table shone with polish. The dishes were lined up in the hutch. The living room looked equally unlived-in. It had recently been vacuumed; the two policemen could see the tracks of the vacuum cleaner furrowing the rug. The walls of the living room were lined with shelves and each shelf was crammed full of bowling trophies.

"Crimminy!" Phil exclaimed. "There must be two hundred trophies here!" He prowled the room. "His name is on every one of them" He peered here and there, not touching anything, but craning his neck to read the little plates that were affixed to each trophy. "Some of them are like the one that zonked him, little men, throwing a bowling ball, some of them have just one big ball on top of a stand, and these three, are sort of plaques." Phil made an expressive noise. "Old Curtin must'a been one hell of a good bowler!"

The kitchen was a bit old-fashioned, with gingham curtains framing the windows and making a gay apron below the sink. In an alcove off the kitchen stood an old-style ice box, not one of the new electric refrigerators. Cliff took the dishcloth and using it, opened the ice box door. The inside was neat, with left-over foods placed in shiny glass containers. The ice holder held a small, slowly melting chunk of ice, and the inside of the box still smelled sweet with no visible sign of food decay. "Dead maybe a day or so?" Cliff ventured. "Well, let's wait until Doc Sullivan gets here before we mess anything up." Phil nodded, happy to get away from Mr. Curtin and the flies.

They went back to speak with Bessie Ray and Tom the milkman. "Is there anyone else who lives here?"

"Certainly. His wife, Florence. Flossie, we call her." Bessie looked around, as if expecting to see Mrs. Curtain step out from behind the asters and the arborvitae that lined the front walk.

"Have you seen her since...? When did you see her last?"

"Donno," Bessie tried to think. "Maybe a few days ago." She scratched at her nose. "She kept to herself."

"Any children?"

"No."

"Family living nearby?"

"No one." Bessie turned to Tom as if for confirmation. Tom shrugged. He only delivered the milk. "I don't think they had anyone nearby. I think she had a sister in Poughkeepsie, but she died a few years back."

"Friends?"

"They kept to themselves, as I said." Bessie thought for a moment. "But he always went bowling. Maybe three times a week over to the Pickwick Alleys. He was a cracker-jack bowler, I heard. My George went with him once or twice, but George wasn't that interested in bowling." Her face told Cliff just what she thought of a man who went bowling three times a week. "He won a lot of trophies...." Her voice trailed off as she thought of what she'd seen. "A lot of trophies."

"Were they happy together?" Cliff watched her face carefully.

She considered... "Well, I couldn't say, really. They seemed happy, if you met them on the way to church...they were always polite to one another. Seemed sort of affectionate." She reached back, trying to be honest, "But he left her alone a lot. He sure did like bowling...he...well, for instance," she reached up to pat her hair, forgetting that her scalp was a mass of bristling curlers. "Um, he bowled and then went out with the bowling team after each night of bowling. The bowling team...they've been together for a long time. My sister-in-law's cousin Theodore is on one of the teams that Mr. Curtin was on...and he's never around when he's needed. Same thing with Mr. Curtin, I think."

Tom broke in, "She sometimes talked to me when I left the milk in the morning. She'd come to the door with a bunch of carrots or some sugar cubes for Brownie." As if he understood his name, the large horse neighed with some impatience. "Geez," Tom exclaimed. "I gotta get going! The milk...the cream...it's gonna spoil if I keep gabbing to you guys."

"Mrs. Ray, Tom...you can both go now." Cliff patted Bessie's back. "But, maybe we can call on you to help us a little later."

"Me?"

"Yeah, you seem to know Mrs. Curtin as well as anyone. Perhaps we can ask you to look around...after we're all done, of course."

"Look around?"

"Yeah. See if there's anything you can spot. We don't know if she's taken a trip or what. There's no indication that she's packed a bag, but we don't have any idea of what her clothing might be like...you know, did she have a winter coat?"

Bessie nodded, delighted to be included in snooping around the Curtin home. "She had a brown cloth coat with a fur collar. I'd recognize it anywhere. She'd never go out in this weather without a coat." Bessie suddenly realized that her only covering was a woolen sweater. She shivered.

"And Tom, where can we reach you if we need any further information?" Tom gave his address and Phil wrote furiously. "OK, I think you can leave now." Phil checked with Cliff, who agreed, grunting affirmation.

"Should I take the milk?"

"The milk?"

"Uh. The two bottles left outside the Curtin house. No use to anyone now," His lugubrious face showed that the milk would be spoiled.

100

"Leave them for now." Cliff made a decision. "There might be finger-prints or something on the bottles."

"I gotta get those bottles back sooner or later," Tom warned. "The company pays good money for them bottles and I gotta account for every one."

"Tell your boss that they'll get them back. I promise. OK, you can go now."

Brownie's head moved up and down vigorously, agreeing with Cliff's directives. She was tired of standing still, more than ready to get along her route. Tom walked to the wagon, backed up the horse, and, before Tom could climb back onto the wagon seat, began to move down the street. Two houses away, Brownie stopped, knowing somehow that this was where the next delivery should be. Tom ambled along the sidewalk, following the horse and wagon. "Smart horse," Cliff admired.

***

Back at the station, a Mrs. Valerie Lewis had called. She was angry. Someone had stolen most of the clothes on her clothesline, and what did the police intend to do about it?

Herbie Floyd told her that he thought that the clothes had traveled a bit. "Monsignor Dario at Saint Catherine's found all of the statues in the garden dressed in someone's clothing. Are you missing some nightgowns and a red union suit?"

"My husband Alex's union suit!" Mrs. Lewis cried. "What in tarnation…!"

"Why don't you call Monsignor. I'm sure the missing clothes belong to your clothesline and you can arrange with him how to get them back to you."

Mrs. Lewis hung up, gratified that the police in town worked so quickly. Herbie made some notations in the daybook, muttering, "The Case of the Dressed-Up Statues. Closed. Another crime solved by the brilliant work of the Greenwich Police!"

***

Dinner at the Troy household that night was lively. There had been fried haddock for supper and Alex and Dale regaled their daughters with a rehash of the dress rehearsal. "She was a horrid creature!" Dale exclaimed. "But she still has…what does one call it? Pizzazz. Stage presence. Wait until you hear her sing tomorrow night!"

The entire Troy family was going to New York City by train to attend Opening Night at the Met. Ariel Sarah, the eldest daughter, couldn't wait. Ariel Sarah, who was seventeen, had already felt the pull of the stage. She yearned to be a professional dancer. She'd been taking dancing lessons ever since she was a tiny child and two years ago, traded her soft ballet slippers for toe shoes. She'd been to several ballets, but never to an opera. Alex was hoping that she'd change her focus, feeling that the world of professional ballet wasn't quite what he had in mind for his eldest. Ariel Sarah was bright…an extremely good and conscientious student...and Alex thought she should go on to college and perhaps become a teacher or a professor. Dale hoped that Ariel Sarah would set her sights on the fashion world, as her second love was drawing and designing beautiful sketches of avant-garde clothing. Ariel Sarah generally smiled with polite patience when her parents tried to guide her. She knew what she wanted.

The two younger Troy children, Abby and Rachel, were identical twins. At eleven, they spent most of their time reading and writing stories, climbing trees and generally getting into mild mischief.

The three girls were exceedingly pretty, popular with their bevy of schoolmates and friends, and loved sports (after all, Alex was an avid sportsman, too, and rowed three times a week for the Knickerbocker Rowing Club and Dale played at least two sets of strenuous tennis every week). The girls were excellent swimmers and tennis players and, obviously, were the apples of their parent's eyes.

Since babyhood, Alex had included the entire family in discussions on politics and his day-to-day business on the stock exchange. All of them were fascinated by the world of trading and commerce, and dinner conversations fluctuated between political shenanigans and the news of the day to the ups and downs of the New York Stock Exchange.

To induce the girls to get used to handling the family's considerable fortune, Dale's father, Abernethie Ollcot (of the Pittsburgh Olcotts), who was an extremely successful railroad industrialist, had given the girls...his only grandchildren...a large lump sum of money with some stringent stipulations as to the money's use. Ariel Sarah, Abby and Rachel had to invest the money in some profit-making enterprise, and every six months, meet with Abernethie to keep him informed of how the investments were going and how much profit was actually being made.

Guided by Alex's expertise, the girls had invested partly in their grandfather's railroad and partly in the ever-increasing stock of the Radio Company of the USA, commonly called RCUSA (and pronounced as R-Cusa). The stock had increased nearly 400 percent since the children's purchase, and Grandpa Ollcot was proud of their achievements. The railroad stock had also done well, but not nearly as spectacularly as RCUSA. Alex, too, had invested heavily in RCUSA's volatile, but always bouncing back better than ever, future.

The Troy's dogs, two tiny mops of Shih-Tzu canine adorability called Sammy and Delilah, padded into the dining room and settled themselves under the table. They were well-mannered dogs, and would never dream of begging at the table. Oh, no. That would come later in the kitchen.

As dessert was being served by the Troy's serving maid, the talk turned from the opera to finance. "I'm getting worried, Dad," Ariel Sarah leaned forward, leaning her elbow on the tablecloth. "I think the market is getting too speculative." Alex raised his eyebrows as Ariel Sarah continued. "Too many shares are being sold on huge margins of credit."

Rachel piped in, "We've talked among ourselves and think we should consider cashing the RCUSA stock in."

"Really?" Alex smiled proudly. It tickled him that the children were so interested in the world of commerce. "Are you sure? RCUSA has been going up by leaps and bounds."

Abby' made a face, pulling her mouth down in a comical frown. "Too much going up by leaps, Dad, and then going down by leaps and see-sawing all over the place. We talked it over and we are quite sure that the time has come to get out of the stock market."

"And what would you do with the railroad stock?"

Ariel Sarah looked to her sisters, who nodded back to her. "We think Grandfather's stock is sound. The railroad is doing well...not spectacularly, but well. He has seven new terminals and spurs being constructed and the railroad will be continuing new lines out to California next year. Our stock is paid for...no speculation or margins for us!"

"We feel that we can keep the railroad stock, but sell the RCUSA." Rachel nodded. "I plan to ask Grandfather to put my profits..." she paused and her eyes rolled upwards as she figured just what her profit might be..."into bonds for the new hospital here in town."

"The Greenwich Hospital?" Alex was intrigued. He'd been worrying a bit about the volatility of the RCUSA stock, but thought he had time – perhaps until the end of the year - to see what happened. "Why the hospital?"

"They are expanding the main building and setting up a school of nursing to supply themselves with qualified nurses." Ariel Sarah's knowledge was impressive. "I've met with the woman who will be running the nursing school. Her name is Matron Grimsley and she's a good friend of our school nurse. I'm impressed with her vision and the bonds will be guaranteed."

"The income won't be so spectacular, but it is a good rate of return," Abby nodded firmly."

"And we are going to recommend that you also follow our lead," Rachel beamed at her father.

"Well, Jeepers!" Dale's mouth dropped. "You girls seem to have thought of everything!" She spooned up the last of her desert. "What do you think, darling?"

"I think that I am proud as punch with *all* of my daughters," Alex grinned. "I think I should do a little more studying about your suggestions and in one week, I will report back to you. Meanwhile, if you really think that you want to sell your RCUSA stock, we'll call your grandfather on Monday and see what he has to say."

"I have homework," Ariel Sarah announced.

"Me, too," the twins called out in unison.

***

In a walk-up tenement in Brooklyn, Francesco and Concetta DeSarro sat down to their supper...a large plate of *ziti con salcisse*, accompanied by a large salad and glasses of homemade red wine. "How was your day?" Concetta asked. Concetta's day at the sewing factory had been long and difficult. She didn't want to talk about it. Francesco's position at the Metropolitan Opera and the stories he brought home were much better for her digestion.

"You could not believe this woman...she's French, I think and a real *putana*!" Francesco was perspicuous enough, even though they had only been in America for a few months, to recognize Vivienne's true character. People were the same all over, rich and poor, in Italy and in America. "She insulted everyone, even the *Maestro.*" His honest face showed bewildered dismay. "She made remarks about my own work, and that of Urbano."

"Ur*bano?*" Concetta was astounded. To her, Urbano Valeria, who had given her husband his wonderful job, was on a pinnacle nearly as high as the one on which the Blessed Virgin Mary stood. "How dare she?"

"She dared," Francesco grunted. "And even more. She insulted and angered everyone. *Everyone.* From the old man who sweeps the floors to the lovely young singer who pushed the sweetmeat cart." He wiped a trace of red sauce from his chin. "I'd like to put the *malocchio* on her." He made the age-old symbol with his fingers; the gesture that had put terror into the heart of many an Italian man or woman.

"What could she do to you, *caro?*" Concetta got up to clear the table, grunting, as her already heavy belly's tiny burden kicked against her skin. "You are no one to her."

He watched her, proud of her pregnancy. It showed the neighborhood what a man he was. He thought upon the events of the day and grunted, "She could give me trouble. Maybe even get me fired."

"No! Urbano will see that your job is safe!"

"She hates Urbano, too. She hates everyone! You ought to see how badly she treated her understudy. Tore a dress off her."

"No?"

"Would I lie? She yelled at this young girl and tried tricks with the lady that sings Musetta." He shook his head in wonder. "I think everyone would love it if she got run over by a streetcar tonight."

"Do you think you should be worrying?" Her face was tender. She dearly loved her Francesco. He was her light and her heart.

"Well, maybe. That's why I am giving her the curse." He bent his hand up and again extended two fingers into the air. "I wish that she suffers...I wish her to burn in hell."

In Ghana, Death paused for a nanosecond as Francesco's wish pulsated through eternity. *Sorry, my friend, but I don't have this lady on my lists for the foreseeable future.*

Concetta served her husband a tiny, white cup of thick dark liquid. "Here. Enjoy your espresso." She sat back down. "I have an upset stomach tonight and will skip the coffee." She drew a circle with her spoon-tip on the white tablecloth. "Perhaps she could be big trouble, this awful lady who sings and annoys everyone." To ward off trouble, I'm going to take some soup over to Signora Boccadoro. She has the power. Maybe she can do something."

Francesco threw back his head and gulped down the espresso. He stood up and kissed the top of Concetta's sweet-smelling hair. How he loved her! He'd never let any French bitch get in the way of his life, his wife and unborn child or his future. *Never!* Even if he had to manually strangle the woman with his strong bare hands!

***

Dale and Troy had joined Barbara and David for a cocktail at Delmonico's right after the rehearsal. The two couples had enjoyed themselves, anticipating more meetings in the future. At home, eating her dinner, Barbara voiced her approval. "I like that nice young couple." Barbara cut her veal cutlet and slipped a piece to Teddy. "She's smart and she's not afraid to speak out. She came to my rescue today when that idiot Helena von Vogel tried to undermine me."

"Helena von Vogel?" David sipped at his wine. "She's the wife of the police chief, isn't she?" He swirled the ruby liquid. "Seems like she has strong opinions. I've heard that theirs is an empty marriage. She can't stand him and he can't bear her. It's rumored that he stays in the office as late as he can."

"She brought her two daughters to the meeting. Beautiful girls, but with sort of blank, vapid faces, you know what I mean."

David patted her hand. "Not like you, my dear. You may be many things, but vapid isn't one of them." He noticed that Barbara's wine glass was empty. "Let me buy you the other half of that drink." He stood up, courtly and lean, and poured wine into Barbara's glass. She picked it up and saluted him.

"To you, my darling man." They clinked glasses. Barbara cut two more pieces of veal and passed another chunk to Teddy.

"You're spoiling him." David waggled his own hand, with a piece of veal in it, under the table.

"He saved my life today," Barbara was solemn. "If he hadn't barked and delayed me, I might have died in that collision on the street."

"He's a clever doggie, aren't you, Teddy?" Teddy wagged the stump of his tail and agreed, especially when veal was in the offing.

Barbara toyed with her glass and watched the two things she loved best; David and Teddy. "I hope there are no surprise fireworks tomorrow night."

"You mean with du Lac?"

Barbara nodded. "She's a doozey, isn't she?"

"A harridan." David's face was somber. "There's a sense of evil that emanates from her." He held up a hand. "I mean it. There's something about her...she's hell bent on hurting and annoying *every*one!"

"A few more days and she'll be gone...back to France."

"If no one kills her first." David laughed and got up from the table. "I'm going to do the crossword puzzle...makes me relax." He kissed the top of Barbara's head and, followed by Teddy, went into the lounge.

Barbara sat for a moment, finishing her wine. He was such a wonderful husband. Tender, generous and funny. She let her thoughts carry her back. They'd met on the *Aquitania,* sailing from New York to England. She...her name was Barbara Missert then... and Judi were celebrating their graduation from Syracuse. Her grandfather, Frank Labin, a successful Philadelphia businessman, had given her the trip as a gift for her educational success. Judi's parents, who owned the largest department store in Philadelphia, were happy to follow suit. She always remembered what Grandpapa Labin drummed in to her head, "Never borrow five thousand dollars, Barbara. Never, unless you have five thousand dollars under the dining room carpet to replace it, should you lose it." Grandpapa was in horror of being in debt. His other maxim to her was; "You can be happy whether you are rich or poor, but you'll be much happier if you are rich."

Grandpapa hadn't always been rich. He came to America nearly penniless, and clawed and worked his way into business. Among other things, Grandpapa Labin had invented a screw rod that made a toy car whizz along, as well as a mechanism that made toy banks regurgitate their coins. He was a jolly, cheerful man with a sense for what was right and wrong. He gave Barbara her sense of spunk and her joy for living.

When Barbara was growing up, he was well known in the area as a very successful man. Once, Barbara was dating a young man...the nephew of her high school science teacher. Mr. Parker, the teacher, was impressed by Frank Labin's wealth, but leery of just how his wealth had been achieved.

"Barbara, you grandfather...his name wasn't really Labin when her came to America, was it?"

"No, Mr. Parker, it wasn't." Barbara wondered where this discussion was leading.

Mr. Parker beamed at her. "Ah *ha!* His name was really Labinsky, wasn't it? He was Polish, wasn't he?"

"No, Mr. Parker," the young girl said with spunk. "He was a Jew. His name was Labinowitz."

When the pretty young co-eds got onto the *Aquitania*, the first thing they did was look for eligible men. Judi latched onto a group of young businessmen and pried the best one, Roger Miller, into her clutches. The young men were delightful, but Barbara yearned for something else. Someone who might impress her Grandpapa.

As she sat with the group of young men, Barbara noticed a slightly older man leaning with his elbow on the rail of the ship. He was tall and thin, with a trim mustache and had an air about him that made the younger men (except for Roger, of course…as he and Judi married very happily) seem almost callow. He was dressed *differently* …with an almost military bearing. He sported a elegant bowler hat on his close-cropped light brown hair; a bright ascot was at his neck. He was watching her, and when he saw that she had noticed him, he bowed in a courtly manner, doffing the bowler. She grinned at him and he strolled over, using a long, thin cane to ambulate.

"Care for a pink gin?" he asked. *Ooooh!* Barbara felt a thumping in the vicinity of her heart. *He was English!*

As they sat in the Captain's Lounge, she was riveted by his piercing blue eyes. They began to tell each other their histories and, from the very start, she found his mind in tune with hers. She finished his sentences and he finished hers. "Great minds…" he said to her and she agreed. He drank only champagne and when she had three glasses and her bladder protested, she rose to excuse herself. He rose too, and asked quizzically, if she needed to spend a penny. *Spend a penny…what a delightfully English phrase…*She was charmed. Absolutely charmed.

He was on his way back to London, where his family resided. His father, Captain Frederick F. Wessel, was from Denmark, a friend and confidant of the Danish King and King Paul of the Hellenes. David's father had become a British citizen and joined the Royal Fusiliers and the Royal Flying Corps. Captain Wessel then married a beautiful English girl, Frances, who brought her beloved wire-haired terrier dog to the marriage. The dog's name was Teddy.

"If we ever marry," David had promised. "We'll have a wire-haired terrier and call him Teddy." Barbara agreed fervently.

"My father and mother lived on his yacht most of the time," David continued to tell his family's tale. It was called the *Frefrada* and was 64 feet long."

"An unusual name," Barbara remarked.

"Ah, you noticed, you little minx. It's an amalgam of our three names…Frederick, Francis, and little me…David."

Oh, he's from such a distinguished family! Barbara worried herself. *I'm from such ordinary people. Will he find me acceptable? Will he be able to love a American girl?*

How could he help it? At the end of the voyage, they were in love…no, they were in love the moment they set eyes upon one another. At the end of the voyage, if the truth be told, they knew that they were destined for one another. They made such plans…she would meet his parents, then they would return to Philadelphia to meet hers and also introduce David to Grandpapa. They would live in London. They would be happy forever.

One of the other Forces that joins Death, Birth and Mother Nature goes by the name of Fate. Fate is one of the most fascinating of the Forces. Why? Because Fate has a devilish sense of humor. Fate's role is to throw monkey wrenches into the lives of the human beings that come to his attention. And Fate had plans to mess up Barbara and David's plans.

***

A telegram greeted David as he waited for Barbara to clear Customs in England. He saw her eager face as she came over to him. He was a grown man, an officer. Still, seeing her face and knowing what he had to tell her, he nearly cried. "It's from my Regiment, my dear. I believe I mentioned that I am a member of the Irish Guards."

"What does it say, David?"

"It instructs me to go immediately to Belfast. My Regiment is gearing up for a small *fracas*." He smiled to her, showing her how trifling a matter this really was. She smiled back, no fool, she, and wondered if she'd ever see him alive again.

"We have three days, my dear. Let's make the best of them"

And they did.

***

Barbara finished her wine, wandered into the lounge and sat with her embroidery silks as David scratched his head over the crossword. He yelped happily when he finally deduced the answer to thirteen down, a bitch of a clue! She smiled at him and thought, for the ump-teenth time, what a treasure he was. And how lucky she was to have found him again…

She'd returned to Philadelphia, accompanied by Judi and Roger, who were also already planning their wedding. David stayed overseas, tied to the regiment that had made such a man of him. Grandpapa told her that time would solve all problems and, as Barbara cried herself to sleep for a few nights, prayed that his advice would help them both. The months marched by and there was no word. More months and then a year.

She tried to find him by every means possible, writing to the British Consulate, writing to the Irish Guards. But to no avail. David seemed to have disappeared.

Judi and Roger got married, and had two children in quick time. Barbara was godmother to the eldest, a little girl called Nancy. She wondered if she would ever be married. Wondered if she'd ever have a child of her own and wondered what had happened to the tall and handsome man she had met.

A year later, she met a presentable young man. One who made a good impression on her parents, Grandpapa, and even Judi. "You can't keep moping around, hoping that he'll appear out of the blue," her friends told her. And finally, in despair, she came to agree. She married the presentable young man. They were fairly happy. Barbara gave birth to three beautiful children, John, Will, and Susan. She buried herself in motherhood and for many years, it filled her life. The children grew up and had lives of their own. The presentable young man grew older, and, although still presentable, their marriage began to flounder.

Grandpapa was very old now, on his deathbed. He called Barbara and told her, "Cut your losses, darling. He wasn't the right one. The right one was lost to you, but that's no reason you have to stay in a sad and lonely marriage. Get a divorce."

"But Grandpapa! A *divorce!* What will people *think?*"

"You must never give a tinker's dam, darling. You deserve better."

He left her a considerable legacy and she instructed the family lawyer to serve divorce papers. She would travel again, perhaps to Scotland, this time.

It might have been a scene from a romance novel. She was visiting Stirling Castle, wandering off from the group to see the jeweled dagger exhibition. She walked into the darkened hall. *David!*

After their babbling, their cries and their incoherent joy, they sat outside in the chill of a Scottish morning, holding one another and trying to stop the flow of explanations.

"I thought you'd forgotten me…"

"I was captured. I was a prisoner for three years…"

"I tried to trust you…"

"I thought of you every moment…"

"I finally…"

"I despaired…"

"I despaired…"

"I gave in…I finally…"

"I thought you'd forgotten…I weakened. I married the suitable girl my mother had planned for me to marry…"

"I married a presentable man."

"I have three children. Karen, Mark and Peter. They are grown now and live in England."

"It wasn't a happy marriage. We are divorced now…now that it is too late. Oh, David, why was I so quick to…?"

"And why is it too late, my darling? I am divorced, too."

"Oh, David!"

"Oh, Barbara!"

Oh, Fate…

***

She got up from her chair. "How is it going?"

"I'm almost done." He rattled the paper. "The clues are miserable ones!"

She smiled down on him. The beautiful brown hair was nearly white now. They'd been wed for a good long time. And it had been worth the torment and the waiting. Well worth it all.

"Come to bed soon, David. We have a very busy day tomorrow."

"I'm going to take Teddy for one last whiz around the block. I'll be there in a few moments, my love."

***

In a smoke-filled jazz club, the three Negro stagehands sat smoking and drinking beer. The music surrounded them and they chatted idly about the day. "She's a bitch," Stephen opined.

"Worse than my mother-in-law," Richard Davis agreed.

"I saw the way she spoke to Clemons. Called him a darkie." Emmet Matthews finished his last sip of beer. "She could make a lotta trouble."

"Already has."

"Someone should strangle her."

"Someone will, one of these days."

"Can't be too soon for me or for my job. I wanna keep this one for a long time."

"Me, too."

"Me, three."

***

"Can you get through the performance, *Maestro?*"

"She will not best me. I haven't achieved my success to give in to *divas* like her. She is dust under my feet."

"Annoying dust." Arturo Calle poured two more ponies of his best brandy. "She can upset the Angel Gabriel."

"I will not let her upset me or this performance. I swear that to you on my sainted mother's grave."

***

"The woman's a curse," Ernest Rattner told the bartender. His third boilermaker was nearly empty. He drained what was left in the glass and shoved it forward. "Fill it up, Sam."

"Doncha think you've had enough, Ernie?" Sam tried. He really tried.

"Nah, I'm as steady as a rock." Ernest held out his hand. Sam watched the hand as it shook slightly. "Steady as a rock."

"Just one more, old timer." Sam filled the small glass with rye whiskey and poured Ernie one last beer. "It's late."

"Bitch!" Ernie muttered as he quaffed the foam from the beer. "She's tryin' to get me fired."

"Who?"

"This Frenchie opera singer."

"Why would she wanna get you fired?" Sam wiped the bar with a damp rag. Shit, Ernie was always bitching about one thing or another. Ah, what the hell, if men didn't gripe and moan about how life had treated them, there would be no bar business.

" 'Cause she's a miserable human being." Ernie sniffed. "She's got it in for me." He smiled as only a drunk can smile, a sly, knowing leer. "She thinks she can pull a fast one on ole Ernie." He shouted a bark of laughter. "*Ha!* But she doan' know ole Ernie and his temper!"

"Whatchgonna do to her, Ern? Drown her?" Sam looked at the clock. Almost closing time. Thank goodness.

Ernie put one finger alongside of his nose. He winked blearily. "I got some ideas. Shhhh! Don't want anyone to know."

Dear lord. If they only knew. All of the drunks. They all sound the same. "Ok, Ern. Time to wrap it up." Sam held up his hands to stave off Ernie's request for another drink. "Nope. It's time for you to go beddy-bye."

Ernie got off his stool and staggered for a moment. He reared back, trying to see if he'd left enough change on the bar. Bartenders like Sam, they were always your friend while you were drinking and if you left them a good tip. There were three dimes on the bar next to the empty glasses. Ernie burped, then carefully, with the exaggerated motions of the inebriated, picked up one of the dimes and put it in his pocket. "So long, Sam, my man."

"So long, Ernie. Get yourself a good night's sleep."

"Huh! I always sleep like a baby." Ernie wheeled himself around. He peered back at Sam. "And just ferget what I said about the Frenchie, you got it?"

"I got it. Never heard anything at all."

"Thass the best way." Ernie lurched out into the night.

***

The flames of the huge furnace burned red and gold, flaring up to show the shadow of fear. Clemons sat in the old basket chair that he had rescued several years ago from one of the productions. At Clemons' feet, which were clad in bumpy-toed boots which had seen better days, was Figaro, the black cat that lived in the Metropolitan Opera building. All opera houses usually had a cat who was black residing within its walls. A black cat was considered very good luck. Figaro had the run of the building, although he usually spent his evenings reclining on a pile of sacks in the furnace room with Clemons

Clemons' arthritic hands held a peculiarly shaped rag doll. The doll was dressed in a red dress. A snippet of dark hair was crudely sewn, with big and sloppy stitches, on its head.

Crooning an old song that his grandmamma had sung to him, Clemons jabbed the rag doll's head with a long hatpin. "She be evil, she be bad...she make trouble, make men sad." His voice quavered. He was afraid. He picked up another hatpin from the pile on the rickety table. "She's the devil, she's his mate, she make men deliver hate." *Jab.* This time in the region of the rag doll's heart. "I will kill her in the heart, I will kill her in the head. I will mutate her and kill her, 'til she lie down and be dead." *Jab.*

***

"He's been dead approximately since yesterday morning…I need an autopsy to tell you more." Doc Sullivan removed the temperature probe from Stanley Curtin's rapidly decomposing body. "I'll get him to the morgue and do it tonight."

"Thanks." Chief McAndrews rubbed his hands together. "So where's the wife?"

"Think she did this?" With a mighty groan, Doc Sullivan rose to his feet. "Kind of a gory thing for a little old lady to do, doncha think?"

"Either he was kneeling, or a six-foot tall person bopped him," Doc scratched his head. "I don't know how tall she was, but it's doubtful that a small woman could have hit him if he was standing up. The angle is all wrong. Although, he could'a been sitting down, and then a short lady might have done it." Doc Sullivan shrugged. "Any clue as to where she's gone to?"

"She's either kidnapped and maybe dead herself, or she killed him and ran away."

"Any clothes or suitcases missing?"

"Not as far as the neighbor-lady thinks. The whole place is gleaming. If she killed him, did she go around cleaning up afterward? Leaving him bleeding to death while she mopped up the dishes? Had she left the house the night before?" McAndrews clutched at his hair. "Where the heck is she?"

Doctor Sullivan watched the two attendants wrap Curtin's body up in a rubber sheet. "Careful there…don't let it drop!" One of the morgue attendants was a new man. A bit bedazzled by the whole procedure…not so steady carrying a dead body.

"We'll be careful." The more experienced man reassured him. "OK. Now let's get him out…easy, man…easy. That's right." He turned awkwardly. "See you at the morgue, Doc."

***

And last, but not least tonight, after supper, Antonina opened the door to Peter's knock. "Hi, sweetheart." His crooked smile was adorable.

"Hi, Peter. Come in."

"Hey, Peter!"

"How's it going, my man?"

"Peter! Come in. Have you eaten dinner yet?" Francesca smiled cheerfully, but carefully watched the interaction between her eldest chick and the young man she might marry.

"Thank you, Signora Rosato. My mother stuffed me already."

He was charming, Francesca thought. *He was her best friend's adopted son. She had loved him since boyhood. He'd always been a charming child, and now, he was a charming young man. Had he charmed Antonina into making love?*

"Do you want to go to the movies, Antonina?"

"What's playing tonight?" Rafe asked, always interested in the movies.

"*Our Dancing Daughters*," Peter answered.

"Sounds mushy," Rafe shook his head.

"I wasn't thinking of taking *you*." Peter cuffed him cheerfully. Rafe twisted and grabbed Peter's arm, holding it behind his back.

"Enough!" Francesca stated. Rafe looked sheepish.

"I was only fooling around, Mama."

"Hmpf." Francesca gave him her special look. "Don't you have homework?" The first set of Rosato twins…the Rosato boy twins…were in their last year of high school.

"I want to get to bed early," Antonina said to Peter. Her expression was odd, and then she blushed, a deep pink that flooded her face and neck. Peter looked as if he had been hit with a brick. "I mean…I have *La Bohème* tomorrow night…I want…I should go ….in early," her explanation limped to a halt.

He has! She has! They have! Francesca busied herself at the sink. *My daughter is a woman now! My God!*

She knows! Even from the back, I can tell that she knows! Antonina bit her lip and tried to catch Peter's eye, but he was teasing Lucia. *She knows!*

"Well, if you want to be home early, let's skip the movies and just go to Libano's and get some ice cream," Peter seemed oblivious to the tension between mother and daughter.

"I'm finished with my revolting homework," Lucia leaped up. "I'm revoltingly bored now. Can you take Gia and me for ice cream, too?" 'Revolting' was her new word. She used it in every other sentence. It might last for another month or two and then she'd be on to another word and 'revolting' would never again cross her lips.

"Oooohh, please!" Gia joined in. "It would be shattering if you took us." Shattering was *Gia's* word of the week. The second set of Rosato twins, the girls, were in their junior year in high school. They adored being included in what they considered Antonina and Peter's love life. "We'll sit in another booth and leave you two to be shatteringly lovey-dovey." Antonina's face blushed again.

Peter appealed to Antonina. "Well, I was hoping that we could go somewhere alone…" She flashed him a look of annoyance.

"It would be nice if the twins came along." Francesca turned and kept her face averted. She was damned if she was going to insert herself into Antonina's love life. It had been difficult enough to tell Antonina that Carlos hadn't been her real father. And, how could she chastise Antonina for falling in love? After all, she herself had succumbed to Carlo long before he had asked her to marry him. She busied herself drying the dishes.

Peter swallowed his feelings of frustration and tried to keep his mood positive. He'd grown up with Francesca's family...his mother, well, his *adopted* mother and Francesca were bosom friends, from far back to their shared childhoods in San'Antonio. It wouldn't do for him to anger Francesca.

"Come on, Peter!" Lucia begged again. "I need an ice cream soda to wash down all that dusty, revolting arithmetic."

"It will be a short evening", Antonina swung around to face Peter. He was a bit puzzled at her obvious desire to not be alone with him. As for himself, he was panting to be alone with Antonina. Alone in a dark car, parked on a dark street in Bruce Park. A car with comfortable and cushiony seats. After all, she had given in to him last night...she had seemed delighted with their first lovemaking...what was different tonight? Women! Who could ever tell what they were thinking?" He decided to give in gracefully. Perhaps, after the ice cream sojourn, he and Antonina might take a short ride by themselves. It was only a mile or two to the lover's lane atmosphere of the park.

"Sure." Peter feigned his delight and shrugging, good-naturedly rumpled Gia's hair. "Let's get a move on, if you're going."

Francesca turned and picked up her purse. "Here," she handed Lucia a dollar. "This is for you."

"Oh, I'll pay, Signora Rosato," Peter flapped his hand in the air. "My treat." The four of them stampeded out of the door.

"It certainly has been your treat," Francesca murmured.

"What did you say, Mama?" Rafe looked up from his history book.

"Nothing, *caro*. Nothing at all."

.....

Chapter Nine

*"An opera is when a guy gets stabbed in the back and,
instead of bleeding, he sings...Ed Gardner on the Radio...*

"Chief?"

"Yeah?"

"It's the shitting bandit again."

"For the love of Mike!" McAndrews almost screamed. "What happened *this* time?"

"A guy called a few minnits ago. Name of Croker. Robert Croker. Him and his wife," Ernie checked his notepad...."Woke up this morning and saw that their house had been broken into."

"In the *morn*ing?" McAndrews' face snapped back. "The bandit usually strikes at night?"

"Yeah, well, it probably was at night. Croker just didn't notice it until this morning."

This time, McAndrews drove to the scene himself, talking Mike with him. The robbery was on Brookside drive, a pleasant, tree-line road, just off the area of Binney Park. A woman with pale brown, well-coiffed hair was waiting for them as they drove up. "Officers? Are you from the police?"

"Mrs. Croker?" She wore a pink dress which did nothing to hide her curvaceous figure. She smiled pleasantly, although McAndrews noted little lines of strain around her eyes.

"Yes. I'm Linda Croker. Please come in so we can show you...and then get the mess cleaned up."

She led them through a small hallway and into a living room. The room was in shambles, furniture knocked over and one lamp smashed. In the front of the mantelpiece were the now-familiar piles of excrement. "Bobby! The police are here." She pointed, "See?" Her big blue eyes began to tear. "Who is low enough to do this to us?"

A burly man with a crest of white hair came into the room from the back entrance. He had bright blue eyes that looked as if he'd seen it all. And perhaps, today, he had. Croker gave the piles a disgusted glance and hurried to his wife. He put his arms around her and hugged her. "Don't worry, honeybun. We'll get all of this straightened out."

McAndrews walked around the debris, touching nothing, but noting the destruction. His eyes questioned those of Mike's. "First time they've wrecked a house up." He squatted in front of the pile. "I can see the popcorn." He rose up. "I think it's the same guys."

"But maybe one of them didn't eat all day?" Mike's sense of humor burst out. "Let's get out of this room and in to your kitchen, maybe." He shepherded Bob and Linda out. *The poor victims! What did they do to have this mess done to them?* McAndrews followed after giving the room one further backwards glance.

Linda shook her head. "I can't understand....We really don't have any enemies, do we, Bobby? Unless, it's that...no. Couldn't be...ah, well. Coffee?" The table was set for breakfast and an odd-looking glass pot steamed gently on the stove, sending out tendrils of fragrance.

"I'd love a cup." Mike pulled out a chair and lowered his bulk down. "Tell us what happened." He flipped out a notebook as the Chief and Bob Croker took two chairs.

"We got up this morning, as we usually do. We were out last night...got home about ten and went straight to bed. Didn't notice anything," he shrugged his massive shoulders. "Linda went into the kitchen to get breakfast going and I went out on the porch to get the paper. When I got back inside, I noticed the smell." His ruddy face creased with distaste. "I couldn't figure what was up." He rubbed his hands as if he were trying to wash something off them. "I looked around and finally looked into the living room."

"He called out to me," Linda interrupted. "He yelled, actually."

"I yelled out, 'Son of a gun', or somethin' like that."

"You yelled out 'Son of a bitch', or something like that!" Linda laughed. "I suppose we ought to see the funny side of this," she shook her head and the pale page-boy hairdo swung forward. "At least we weren't hurt."

"We've had several robberies like this. Usually, there are two piles of sh.... stuff." Mike's expression was sad. "But this is the first time there has been any damage."

"Is anything missing?" McAndrews queried.

"Our new little radio. It was on the living room bookcase." Linda counted off on her fingers, "A china statue of a fancy lady. It was my mother's. A, um, a big glass bowl filled with pinecones..." She looked up as Bob wig-wagged his face.

"The pinecones are all over the floor. Bastards emptied the bowl out before they stole it."

"I'm sorry." McAndrews words were genuine. These, again, were nice people. People who hadn't bothered anyone. What right had some punks to come into their house and destroy things, nevermind the final insult of the pile of crap?

"I had a sugar bowl filled with quarters here in the pantry. They took that and they also went upstairs into our bedroom. We didn't notice last night, I guess...they didn't make any mess up there. We...it was late and we just took off our clothes and went to bed, not noticing that the jewelry box had been taken." She bit her lip.

"Was there anything valuable taken?"

She nodded. "My pearls...a long string of pearls and my little wristwatch. The other stuff was just costume jewelry."

"What else did you notice?"

"They took some money from my sock drawer," Bob looked sheepish. "Fifty bucks. I know I shouldn't leave money like that, but I like to have some for emergencies."

"Don't tell anyone, but I have fifty stashed in my own sock drawer," Mike confided.

"My neighbor, Joe Naylor, came over this morning. Bad news travels fast around the neighborhood." Bob's face showed irritation. "Anyway, Joe is a good guy. He told me that he heard a loud car last night. He went to his window and saw a dark sedan driving away, fast and loud. He didn't get any license plate nor could he give me any further information, but maybe it was this weasel."

"I think there are two of them."

"Oh yeah!" Croker laughed. "Two piles of crap; two crappy robbers."

"Joe Naylor. OK, we'll go over and talk with him when we're finished here."

The police questioned the Crokers for ten minutes more, but their answers weren't helpful. "Can you leave the pantry, the living room and the bedroom upstairs alone until we can do some investigation?" The Crokers nodded. "Good. We'll have a fingerprint man here and a photographer. Can I use your telephone?" As Chief McAndrews called the station, Mike borrowed Mrs. Croker's rubber kitchen gloves and bundled up the evidence.

"We'll send some men to talk with your neighbors. Maybe someone other than," Mike checked his notes, "Mr. Naylor... saw or heard something more last night. And then we'll submit this mess to the Bridgeport Laboratory. They might be able to tell us some more about the men who, um, did it."

"Really? How?" Linda's eyes were huge with curiosity.

"I don't exactly know." Mike was a little uncomfortable. "Some kinda tests they do."

"Glad I don't have that kind of job!" Linda grinned. "Whew!"

Mike re-checked his notes again. "Mrs. Croker? You said something when we first came in...You said that you had no enemies and then you started to say, 'Unless it was...' or something like that. What did you mean?"

She ducked her head. "Oh, nothing, really." Mike's genial face encouraged her to go on. "Well, Bob does a lot of accounting work. He's the most honest man I've ever known...well, anyway, we have...had, actually...a client who was cutting corners and trying to do some dubious transactions. Bobby and he had a big shouting match because Bobby said he wouldn't work for him if he kept up his scurrilous business doings…cheating his customers."

"Who is this person?"

"Oh, Linda." Croker squirmed in his chair, clearly uncomfortable with this turn of conversation. "This isn't….no. " He shook his head violently, throwing up his hands. "Uncle Bill would never…"

"Uncle Bill? This man who does dubious transactions is your *uncle?*"

"Not really an uncle…we have known him for a long time and he…we…call him Uncle Bill." Linda broke in. "His name is Bill Callahan. He runs a big factory in Port Chester. Callahan's Metalwork."

"Tell us more about him."

Croker's face creased with unease. "I hate to even talk about…well…Bill and I had a falling out over what I felt were unsavory things that he was doing. The upshot of our discussions…"

"Heated discussions," Linda averred.

"OK, Heated discussions…we parted company. It was angry and not pleasant. He called me names like 'ungrateful' and a 'traitor to our friendship'."

"And you called him a crook, I believe." Linda patted her husband's arm and then left her hand there, rubbing him with rhythmical affection. "I'm glad you and Bill are no longer doing any business. Sooner or later, his lack of attention to detail and honesty will come home to roost and we do not want to be associated with any of it."

"I'll take his name and address anyway." Mike wrote the information down. "We think this is part of a succession of burglaries and break-ins, but this one…with the damage done…is a little more violent than the past ones."

Mike and McAndrews got back in the car, leaving the Crokers at their front door, hugging one another and wondering why Fate had chosen them to be the recipients of so much venom.

Actually, Fate had nothing at all to do with it at all.

***

Cliff and Charlie Presto had been out all morning, talking with Bessie Ray and the other neighbors on Locust Street. No one had seen anything out of the ordinary, and no one had the slightest idea of where Florence Curtin might be.

Doctor Sullivan completed his autopsy on Mr. Curtin. The official cause of death was several blows to the head with a sharp instrument. The wounds matched up with the shapes of the bowler's hand and fingers at the top of the trophy that had been dropped next to the body. The trophy was covered with fingerprints, many of them matching fingerprints found in the Curtin's house. Many of them belonged to the deceased. The rest, it was assumed for the time being, belonged to Mrs. Florence Curtin, or to some as yet unknown assailant. In which case, it was imperative to find the whereabouts of Florence Curtin. Had she been abducted? Her life could be in imminent danger, if she wasn't dead already.

The Greenwich Police put out an all points bulletin seeking the where-abouts of Florence (Flossie) Curtin. Description: Sixty-three years old. Five feet, three inches tall, grey hair, generally worn in a bun to the back of the head. Brown eyes, light complexion. No known scars or significant markings. Most likely wearing a flowered housedress and a blue apron (Bessie Ray remembered these clothes and they were nowhere to be found in Florence's closet nor in the drawers). The description ended with a few more sentences: May be dangerous. May be in danger. May be hurt and wounded. Please call.....

***

"I'll drive you down to the train." Antonina's eyes flew to her mother. *Oh no!* "I need some exercise and I want to tell you about the new store." Francesca smiled at her daughter. "It's been so hectic the last few days, what with you and the opening of the opera and me moving the bakery...why, we haven't had a chance to talk. I haven't even asked you how things are going."

I don't want *to talk!* What could she say? Antonina gulped and tried to smile. "Sure, Mama. Let me get my little suitcase and we'll go. I want to catch the 2:30 train." She went upstairs to her bedroom, her steps dragging.

"We'll be cheering for you!" Lucia flung her arms around her big sister. "You'll get the loudest applause of anyone!"

"Thanks, sweetheart." Antonina nearly cried aloud. "I'll try to wave to you with the tips of my fingers."

"In bocco lupo!"

Mother and daughter left the house and got into Francesca's new Nash. She'd learned to drive a year ago and, after getting her license, purchased the car. Delighted with herself, she tried to drive everywhere.

Francesca carefully eased the car out of the steep driveway. "I can drive fine when I go forward. Backward...that's different! I can't make it steer the way I want." She giggled. "There!" The car started down the road. "You ought to learn how to drive, Antonina. It's time. Simeon or Leo can look around and find you a nice, used car. Something a little sportier than this." She patted the dashboard.

"That would be fine, Mama."

"Good. When these two operas are over, we'll look into it." She sang a few bars from Musetta's Waltz. Antonina remained silent. The car turned up the hill toward the railroad station.

"Cara. Are you pleased about the new bakery?"

"Very pleased, Mama. I am very proud of you". Antonina leaned back, re-laxing slightly. It was only three more minutes to the station and if she could keep Mama talking about the store…well, so much the better. "As a matter of fact, I was telling my new friend…did I tell you that Angelique Orloff and I had a wonderful talk yesterday? No? Well, she is the most understanding and marvelous woman, Mama. Not only that, but she sings like an angel." The car turned into the train station parking lot.

"She told me…well, Mama, I didn't mention it last night as there was so much going on, but we had a rash of problems yesterday with Vivienne du Lac."

"The soprano that sings Mimi?"

"Oh, you wouldn't believe how horrible she is!" The car came to a stop. Antonina checked her watch. The train was due in four minutes. Antonina opened the car door and began to get out. "I have to go now. I'll see you all tonight after the performance."

"Antonina," Her mother's tone held her.

"Yes?" Antonina hopped about in anxiety.

"The train isn't here yet. I want to talk to you tomorrow about Peter."

"Peter?" Antonina's grey eyes were huge.

"Mmmm. Peter. You remember him?" She smiled.

"Of course I …Oh, Mama!" Her voice caught.

"*In bocca lupo, tessora mia.* Your mother loves you, you know."

"And I love you, Mama*." She knows and it's all right! She understands!*

But on the train, Antonina's euphoria dimmed. Last night, she and Peter had quarreled violently. She knew he was upset when the twins had dragged themselves along. She knew he'd wanted her alone.

They'd all sat together at Libano's Ice Cream Parlor. Lucia and Gia prattled and chatted, calling out to friends and fooling around. They'd made such a ruckus that the unnatural quiet between Antonina and Peter nearly went unnoticed. (Nearly unnoticed…later, unknown to Antonina, the twins had remarked upon it to their mother). "They didn't talk to each other, Mama. They just sort of sat like they were shattered and frozen," Gia confessed.

Peter drove Lucia and Gia home and pleaded with Antonina to stay with him for another half-hour. "Tell your mother," he'd told the twins, "that I will have Antonina at home by ten o'clock. I know she has a show tomorrow."

Rather than have an argument in front the Lucia and Gia, Antonina had acquiesced. Peter drove the car down to Bruce Park. It was a cold and brittle night and the moon shone on the dry leaves still clinging to the trees and glanced on the fenders of other cars parked in the darkness. In the dark cars, young men and women were snuggling and kissing. This park was the spot for that kind of thing.

"You've been very quiet tonight,"

"I'm tired, Peter."

"Come here, darling." He slid his arm over the back of the seat and pulled her close. She slid over, but her body was stiff. "What's wrong? Are you sorry about last night?" His face was inches from hers, his lips close and inviting. She could smell his familiar smell, a piney aftershave and the scent of a healthy young man. Her body tingled. She turned her head and melted into his arms. They kissed, deep and then deeper and his hands moved to caress her.

She pressed against him, feeling the heat and desire and remembering the incredible feelings of want and how her body had gone crazy with love. She lowered herself and caressed his back and biceps. She *loved* him. She *did!*

He unbuttoned her coat and drew her down on the wide seat of the car. She could feel him, already hard against her. He began to touch her more, murmuring soft things. He pushed up her dress. "When do you want to announce our engagement?" His voice was warm and soft.

She sat up, her ardor chilled. "Engagement?" *Why did the thought of being engaged make her feel as if she were strangling? Isn't an engagement to the man a girl loved what she wanted more than anything else?*

He sat up, adjusting himself. "Well, for sure, darling. After last night...aren't we going to get married right away?"

"I...I don't think I'm ready to be married," her voice was soft and hesitant. "Peter, I do love you, you know, but I want to be an opera singer. I *always* said that."

"You can sing wherever we live, sweetheart. There are lots of choral groups everywhere."

"*Peter!* I have studied and trained for years and years, just like you studied to be a doctor. Choral groups are not what I have in mind for myself."

"And just what do you have in mind?" There was a dangerous edge to his question.

"A career. A real career as an opera singer. Hopefully, a successful opera singer. I believe in my talent and in myself. Signor Fazzolini believes in my talent. People who are in the business think that I can succeed." Her voice was steely. "Why should I get married and stop all of this?"

"Because you'd be my *wife*, Antonina!" Peter was becoming exasperated. "There's no way that Mrs. Peter Bovi is going to be all over the world, traipsing on stages and showing her bosoms to the audience!"

Antonina was silent for a moment, thinking hard. This was her future at stake here, the rest of her life. She had always spoken about her talent; always spoken about her desire to be on stage. "Maybe Mrs. Peter Bovi *will* stay at home and cater to you and your children," she began, "but probably, that woman will not be me."

"*What?*" Peter was stung. He sat bolt upright and slammed his fist on the dashboard of the car. "What kind of girl are you, Antonina? You say you love me, you let me ….we made love last night!"

"And?" Her voice was soft…dangerously meek. If it weren't so dark in the car, he might have noticed that her grey eyes had turned nearly black with anger.

"And what kind of girl would do this? Give herself to a man and not have marriage in mind?" He thought for a moment…he'd always been honest with Antonina…well, mostly honest, anyway… "Before last night, I'd never done anything like that with a girl." A huge lie. *Does she believe me?* He made his voice as plausible as possible. "I wouldn't….never…only the girl I intended to marry." He looked sadly at her. "Otherwise, I never would have let you lead me on." It was a great line. He thought she might be really ashamed of herself and capitulate.

"What? Me lead you on?" Her mouth formed an 'O' of astonishment. *"Peter!* How can you say these things?"

"You're not the girl I thought you were, Antonina," His voice was hurt. "I wonder what your mother or my mother would think of what we did, if you didn't intend to get married."

"They'd think I made a bad mistake," she countered. "They'd think that you weren't worthy of my love." She looked out of the window. "They'd both think you are a cad for trying to force me to marry you."

"I can't believe we are having this kind of argument." Peter tried to change his tactics, realizing that he had gone too far. "Let's forget everything we said tonight and try to mend our romance." *Shit! Who would have thought that she didn't want to be his wife? That this stupid opera stuff would mean so much to her?"*

"I want to go home now." She stared straight ahead.

"You'll be sorry." She didn't answer and they drove home in silence. At her house, he stopped and leaned back to talk, hoping to save the evening. Antonina opened her own door, got out and stalked to her door. She opened it and went inside, leaving him staring after her.

***

In France, Death rushed to take the souls of the seventy-five people who perished in a fire, set by a child who was angry at being punished for teasing a donkey belonging to a street vendor. The high number of unexpected casualties forced death to make many adjustments on his lists. Unknown to them, seventy-five people, marked down on Death's list, were hurriedly crossed off. Most of them lived happy and uneventful lives for twenty or thirty years more. Fate enjoyed this story at the evening get-together more than anyone. *One thing about random chance…it is always random!*

***

Antonina arrived at the opera house early, eager to get herself settled. She had an important performance tonight, no matter how small and insignificant her part. She smiled, as she signed her name in the book at the stage door.

Puccini must have thought her small songs important, not unimportant, otherwise he would not have written the opera the way he did. All of the players, small and large, famous and of no particular fame, made up the musical mosaic of *La Bohème*.

Her smile caught the attention of Sergei Andreyi. *Such a lovely little thing, she is.* "*Bon jour, mademoiselle.* May you break your leg tonight!" Andreyi bowed and Antonina grinned back at him.

"*In bocca lupo, Signor,*" she replied, crossing herself.

No one, not a single performer in the opera, stage or circus...no performer anywhere would wish a fellow actor good luck. To do such a thing would, it was fervently believed, bring down bad luck on the entire ensemble. No one was as superstitious as opera singers or circus performers. They wished one another to "break a leg," or called out the French word *Merde*, or the Spanish word *Mierda* to one another. Italian performers utter "*in bocca lupo*" to one another, insisting that to look into the mouth of a wolf will stave off bad luck. To wish someone a blatant good luck, however, might just call down the wrath of the Faeries or Sprites that hover over all such performances. Some think this is simple hogwash, but the small band of Faeries and Sprites that sit at the lower end of the Force's table, and mete out punishment to those show folk who do not abide by these rules, would not agree.

If, by mistake, a player wishes another good luck, that player must leave the theater, turn around three times, spit, utter a curse word aloud, and then knock to be readmitted to the theater.

As well, no one in the theater would say the name of Shakespeare's epic, *Macbeth*. Instead, they would refer to the play as The Scottish Play, again courting luck and bypassing the curses of who-knows what. No one would properly knit onstage or off (although to knit while waiting in a dressing room was safe), no one would whistle anywhere near the stage (although to whistle one's lines in a dress rehearsal was considered all right), no one would bring a peacock feather onstage or even into a dressing room, and all performers would exit from their dressing rooms on the way to the stage with their left foot first. Laugh at these? At one's peril!

The Metropolitan Opera House, as well as every other opera house and theater in the world, always left a "ghost light" burning, day and night...always. The light is to guide the first performer to the last performer in and out of the theater. Should the light die out, the theater would be dark, and thus, welcoming to those Sprites who inhabit the dark. Actually, the Sprites themselves didn't care if the theater was light or dark, but they enjoyed the superstition and, whenever possible, made sure that any dark theater had some sort of mishap.

Flowers must never be delivered *before* a performance. Performers think that is unlucky and a temptation to the Faeries. But flowers *after* a performance are lucky. The Faeries make sure that, if someone gets a bouquet before a performance, they cause some small silly, but important problem. After all, even the tiny Faeries loved to be feared.

Some believe that having a Bible onstage is unlucky, and those performing a play or opera with a Bible as a prop will simply use the outer cover of a Bible covering another, less controversial book. All costumes or scenery that use the color blue, considered very unlucky, alleviate the bad luck by adding the color silver (considered to offset the curse of blue) to the costume, stage property or scenery.

And, of course, there is extraordinary good luck attached to the opera's black cat, Figaro. If a performer was able to stoop and pat Figaro's fur before a performance, or if the cat allowed one to scratch his back, the performer felt relieved. His or her performance, and indeed, the entire opera was bound to go well.

The superstition was so great that Figaro, a fat, well-fed feline of benevolent temperament, every so often, would wander onto the stage when a performance was going on. When that happened, and the audience noticed the cat, spontaneous applause would erupt, interrupting the performance for several moments and assuring the cast that all was well.

And, cementing the thought that all would go well tonight, was the disastrous rehearsal. One of the oldest superstitions was that a terrible rehearsal will assure a good performance. And yesterday's rehearsal had been one of the worst in memory. Thus, every performer, stagehand, orchestral performer, supernumerary, lighting expert, carpenter, or any who had been in the rehearsal audience...*everyone,* was certain the opening night would go like silk. Be brilliant. Yes, tonight's performance would be a doozy!

***

"Good afternoon, my dear," Angelique took off her cloak and kissed Antonina's cheek. "How is my little star-in-the-making today?" Angelique wore a pale blue dress with a close-cropped jacket trimmed with tight fitting silver fur cuffs and collar.

"Angelique," Antonina's face was pale and pinched, "May I speak with you for one moment?"

Why the poor little sweetheart looks distressed. "Of course, poppet. Come up to my dressing room."

"I wanted to...I had a quarrel last night..."

"With the young man in your life?"

"How did you know?" Antonina was stunned.

"Oh, I guessed. Tell me, little one. What happened?"

Antonina sunk to a seat on a small velvet tuffet. She bit her lip and blurted out the gist of last night's argument. Angelique listened, not interrupting the sad little tale, nodding now and then. "And how do you feel today?"

"I'm terribly upset that we quarreled. Peter and I...we have been friends...boyfriend and girlfriend...since we were children. His mother...well, she's really his adopted mother, and my mother were girlhood chums. And remain best friends. We...everyone always thought that we'd get married...I'd be upsetting so many people if I didn't...." Two tears slid down Antonina's woebegone face.

"You mother, your aunt, or whatever she is, your friends, even Peter, mean nothing to the answer of this question. What do *you* want from your life?"

"I want to sing." Antonina's voice rang out. "Sing as a professional on the opera stage. That's what I have always wanted and that's what I still want." Her grey eyes shone.

"Even if it means that you will never marry?"

"Even that."

"Nor probably have any children?" Angelique's head tipped, questioning.

"No. I understand what I am giving up...but...but, Angelique, it doesn't seem to me that I am giving up anything that will ever make me sorry. I just want to be an opera star." She dipped her head. "Hopefully," she grinned, a bit sheepish.

"And I pray that I will be good enough, when the time comes."

"Oh, darling, you will be even better than that. I am positive." Angelique sat at her dressing table and swiveled the tiny chair around to face Antonina.

"But you love him?"

"Yes, but not enough to marry him right now. And there's another thing that makes me mad." Antonina hung her head. "He's trying to blame me for," and her face bloomed bright red, "making...doing....having loved him. He says if I did that without wanting to marry him, I am some sort of a slattern." Her eyes were enormous.

"Interesting. It is usually the woman who wants marriage and the man who makes the excuses as to why it shouldn't happen." She sighed and turned around, removing the jacket of her dress. Antonina saw that the blue dress, itself, was tied with a silver belt. She nodded, one sharp movement. "I'm going to share a secret with you that only one person knows...well, maybe my daughter's governess, Janine, who has been with our family since Anna was born knows...but no one else." Antonina leaned forward.

"I was married at a very young age to my husband, I loved him very much and he loved me. He was killed in the war. When I heard about his death, I was already pregnant with Anna. I was alone, desolate and my voice deserted me." She fiddled with her necklace and continued.

"Janine was a nurse at the hospital where Anna was born. She helped me with Anna and I felt so reassured with her care of Anna that I asked her to come and live with us, not only as a governess, but as a friend. She did. Janine is not…an attractive woman. Inside, she is beautiful, but her outward appearance isn't too pleasing to the average man. She despaired of never marrying…" Angelique crinkled her nose with amusement …. "not the same problem as you, my dear. She loved children, and she jumped at the chance to come with little Anna and me. As I nursed Anna, my voice came back to me, better than ever." She paused, as if gathering her thoughts.

"I never thought I would love again as I loved Philippe, but then, I met someone…and for the past six years or so, we have been lovers. He…his name is David…he is Italian and lives in Italy. He is a very wealthy man…a Count. Count David della Cuore. He is a banker in international circles and comes to New York with some frequency. He is married, but to a woman who is in a hospital…an institution for those who cannot cope with this life. She became…ill…very soon after their wedding. David told me that she had always been…fragile, emotionally… but that he felt he could help her to be able to cope with the world. Alas, she only got worse and worse and then she wasn't able to function at all. Recently, within the past year, she also contracted incurable cancer, poor woman. He loved her and loves the memory of the woman she used to be, but…she is no longer that woman and he is a healthy man. A man with needs. He is a Catholic and I am a Catholic, and we most likely can never marry. But we have already sinned greatly, as we are lovers." She shrugged. "I have made the decision to forgive our transgression of love." Antonina sat, transfixed at the romantic and tragic story. "How God will look upon our love is something that only time will tell."

"Why are you telling me this?"

"Because, if you truly love someone, that is all that matters. I told you that I only work at my singing as a career, not as a life. Anna and David are my life. My dream is to have a little farm somewhere in the country. Live a simple life. I want to cook enormous meals for David, make dresses for Anna, maybe even milk a cow!" She laughed, a merry guffaw. "I would gladly leave the opera if he asked." Her face drooped. "But, as long as his wife lives, that can never be. This is why I told you yesterday that you cannot have it all. You are destined to be a star, and you can either be a star or be someone's loving wife. Your children's mother. Never both. Not successfully."

A knock at the door interrupted them. James, the young boy who was Rudolph Shubin's nephew and worked as a page boy on performance nights, opened the door. He grinned and his shaggy hair flopped over his forehead. "Ladies. The theater is being prepared! Three hours to performance, Madam Orloff."

"Thank you, James," she smiled at him and he glowed. Angelique's charm flowed from her as easily as a river flows.

She stood up and took Antonina's face in her hands. "That is my advice to you. Not much advice, is it? *You* must choose."

"Oh, no! It is the best of advice. I think even my mother, should I get up the courage to talk with her, will agree." Antonina took Angelique's hands in hers. She bent and kissed them. One by one. "Thank you, my good friend." She stood up. "I will think about this tonight and see, when I sing, if the happiness that fills me is enough." She went to the door. "I think it will be. I think I want to sing."

Angelique watched her leave. "Poor *petite*. I hope she is happy with her life, whatever she chooses." She turned back to the mirror. *Callow, though, this boyfriend of hers...trying to make her feel guilty about making love. There's nothing wrong with physical love. I'd be wondering what was wrong with the lad if he didn't want to make love to her. And, equally, why shouldn't she make love to him? I'd like to talk to this Peter one of these days and see for myself if he is worthy of Antonina.*" She carefully wiped her face with cream and began to get ready. Antonina's troubles were forgotten.

***

One of the railroad cars on the train from Greenwich to New York was nearly filled to capacity with Antonina's family and friends. Francesca sat with her beau, Simeon Meade. Maria sat with *her* old-fashioned beau, Signor Fazzolini. Gia and Lucia sat together, playing Cat's Cradle with a loop of string. The boys, Rafael and Michael, had chosen to stay home. "Opera is boring, Mama," was their excuse. Francesca had excused them on the condition that they stay at home with young Johnny.

Francesca's best friends, Giovanna Manero and Mina Fiorile sat together. Their husbands, Paolo and Sal, also found the opera too much to take, and had prudently stayed home with a deck of cards and a gallon of red.

Peter Bovi, Giovanna's adopted son, sat up front, his handsome face mulish. He was still sulking over his argument with Antonina. *I should have stayed home. Let her sing without me hearing her. Show her how little her attitude and her damn opera career means to me.*

A bevy of Antonia's aunts and uncles filled several seats at the back. Monsignor Dario, Antonina's favorite uncle, told stories of the old days, assisted by pithy comments from Enzo Uccello and his wife Sabina. Leo Del Vecchio, Simeon Meade's partner in the law firm of Meade and Del Vecchio, together with his enormously pregnant wife, Claudette, took up a row in the back, Neighbors, Harold Leigh and Karena Munchauer, Giorgio Zamfino, Guido Sottosanti and fat Norma Palladino brought up the rear. Don Mantaldo, Francesca's good friend and mentor, smoking a vile cigar, sat on a seat all by himself.

And on a later subway from Brooklyn, Vittoria Valeria, wife of Urbano and Francesca's great family friend, traveled to New York, also to watch the opera, partly because of her husband and partly because of Antonina. Accompanying Vittoria was Concetta DeSarro, Francesco's wife. She had never seen the place where Urbano and Francesco worked, and she was excited to see an opera. "You are going to love it!" Vittoria rhapsodized. "Wait until you see what Urbano and Francesco have done with the scenery and the production!"

A car driven by James Drawbridge of Westchester County made its way toward to opera house. In it, next to her new husband, sat Gina Salerna Drawbridge, an old friend of Francesca's from back in their home town in Italy. Gina was dying to hear little Antonina sing, even if the part was a tiny one. She told her husband, "When Antonina sings, there will be a huge amount of very noisy applause, even if no one but her friends and family clapped. We'll make so much noise that the entire theater will sit up and take notice!"

***

Even Vivienne du Lac was on time tonight, not daring to upset the time-table of the opening night, even if she wanted to make mischief. She felt marvelous, just marvelous. Better than ever! Her strange employee, Crespi, had procured a very satisfactory set of bed companions, young and inexperienced, just as she ordered. Young, with empty bellies...so hungry that they did anything that she ordered. Even...Vivienne smiled...yes, even that. It had been an excellent night. She felt sleek and young and her voice felt better than ever. She massaged her throat and smiled. She was ready to make operatic history. She breathed deeply and sang an exploratory note. Marvelous! Her voice was going to be superb tonight! This would be the best performance of *La Bohème* ever! She would go down in history!

Little did she know that both of her premonitions would come true, but not exactly as she planned.

***

The night of Saturday, October Twelfth, was a cold, crisp one, with a shiny moon that lit up the skyscrapers of New York City. The moon paled, however, when compared with the glittering façade of the Metropolitan Opera, welcoming everyone with glitter and warmth.

Opera patrons were arriving early, ready to see and be seen, some by foot, some by magnificent carriages drawn by sleek matching steeds, some by automobiles driven by chauffeurs. This was opening night, and every society woman had purchased what she felt was the most sumptuous dress available. Many of the dresses had been designed by Worth and shipped here from Paris. Some of the dresses cost thousands and thousands of dollars. And the jewels! Every woman there had raided their jewel boxes and bank vaults. Necks, slender and some not-so-slender, were draped with diamonds, ears glittered with rubies and emeralds. Arms were weighted down with concentric rings of bracelets and hands were heavy with monstrous rings.

Mrs. Stuyvesant Burns, one of the richest and most influential leaders of New York Society arrived in a shiny dark carriage pulled by four matching chestnut horses. None of these upstart automobiles for Mrs. Burns! The two footmen who rode the back of the carriage jumped down to help her alight. A crowd had formed...the great unwashed to gape at their betters. A gasp went up as Mrs. Burns turned in a circle, graciously allowing the onlookers to see her gold cape and gold dress, twinkling with canary diamonds. Somehow, she had gotten her dressmaker to sew small operative electric lights along the hem of the cape and all up the sides. The crowd made a noise like an ocean wave crashing. She looked like a moving chandelier, bejeweled with stars that shone and twinkled. Her husband followed her like a drab tugboat follows an elegant, glowingly bedecked ocean liner. In his arms, he held their King Charles spaniel who always accompanied them to the opera. The dog rested on a cushion and was always very well behaved. As the Burns' were, like David and Barbara, not only stockholders, but actually collective owners of the Metropolitan Opera Company, they often brought their animals to performances. Who on earth would ever tell them not to?

The Burns' entered their sumptuous box, one of the better parterre ones. The footmen had already prepared the box with comfortable chairs and cushions, chilled champagne, resting in silver buckets, opera crème chocolates, decorated with crystallized violets from Susan's, the expensive chocolatier shop next to The Russian Tea Room, and frosted grapes on large crystal platters.

Around them, other doyennes of New York society were settling themselves similarly, dressed in exquisite clothing and dripping with jewels. Everyone who was anyone was there, and each peered around, opera glasses up to their eyes, seeing who was wearing what and who was with whom. To many, this seeing of who wore what and who was with whom was more of a thrill than the actual opera itself.

Barbara and David entered their box. Teddy, trotting on a leash, also accompanied them. Teddy seemed to love the opera, and, so that he could see and hear better, was placed on a cushion on one of the chairs, right up in front. Teddy was also decked out in true opera style for the celebrations of an opening night. His collar had tiny sapphires studded into it and he had a tiny satin cape of a matching sapphire color. Attuned to the superstitions of the opera, Barbara had sewn silver sequins onto the cape in a pattern that spelled out T-E-D-D-Y.

"He's anxious for the opera to start," Barbara ruffled up Teddy's hair.

"La *Bohème* is one of his favorites." David put his opera glasses up and reviewed the crowd. "He always sits, raptly listening, especially to the third act duet." He waved to an acquaintance. "I wonder if Gigli will turn up."

"He said he'd be here as soon as his boat docks," Barbara patted the extra chair that was in the front row of the box. The chair was reserved especially for Beniamino Gigli, the world's leading tenor, who was on his way to New York from the La Scala Theater. His boat was to have docked at six. "He'll be here. He wouldn't miss it."

"I certainly hope so," David stood up, the better to see and be seen. He was dressed in British sartorial splendor, crisp white and stark black with only the slash of his scarlet sash and his regimental colors to dazzle on his tie. He waved and bowed to Alex and Dale and then smiled, combined with a wave of his hand to their daughters. Struck by a brilliant idea and grinning, David picked up Teddy. He waved Teddy's front paw to the girls.

"Look, Daddy! Look at the doggie!" Rachel cried, elbowing her twin to pay attention.

"That's Teddy, the apple pie of Baron Wessel's eye," Troy told her. "They just dote on the woofer."

"Ohhh, why didn't we bring Sam and Delilah?"

"Two dogs! Just what we would have needed," Dale rolled her eyes. She waved over to Barbara and pointed to Teddy. *Adorable!* she wig-wagged. Sitting back, she whispered to Troy. "Imagine! Bringing a dog to the opera!"

"Look around you," Troy whispered back. "There are quite a few of them here. Little silly lapdogs on big silly laps."

Ariel Sarah caught her father's joke and sniggered, covering her mouth. The twins then hung over the edge of the box, trying to spot as many dogs as they could. Ariel Sarah, too old to be so silly, sat back, trying to seem sophisticated. If she became a ballerina, she'd be on a stage like this. How exciting! Her cheeks were pink as she dreamed.

***

"Dale looks lovely," Barbara noted. Dale was dressed simply in a pale lemon colored sheath held in place by two narrow ribbon straps. Her hair was piled up on an elegant chignon, and a purple iris was pinned onto the clasp that held her hair-do in place. The girls were charmingly dressed in white organza. Rachel and Abbey's dresses were knee length, with bright sashes, Abbey's dark blue and Rachel's in rose. Ariel Sarah, as befitting a girl who was older, wore her white dress longer, with a purple scarf trimming the modest neck. The twins wore patent leather strapped shoes with white ankle socks. Ariel Sarah's legs were covered with her first grown-up silk stockings and her feet were shod in low-heeled kid slippers. All of the girls wore their long, blonde hair tied back with matching ribbons. "And the girls are lovely. So sweet and dressed just right."

"Look at how they are waving at Teddy," David waggled a one paw byebye and put the dog back down on his chair. Teddy's expressive eyebrows rose and he yawned, his pink tongue curling.

"Look at him! The darling! He's anxious for the opera to start!"

***

In the borrowed box, Helena von Vogel stood, opera glasses trained on everyone, especially those in the parterre boxes, hoping that all of New York society would see that she was sitting in a prominent place. "Look at that!"

She nudged Chloe, her elder daughter. "Look at the jewels on that dress!" Chloe bored with opera and bored with looking at the dresses that perfect strangers wore, made a face.

"Who cares, Mother. They're just a bunch of old rich women."

"Old and ugly rich women," The younger daughter, Clair, agreed.

"Pay attention, girls. These women can make you or break you socially. I intend to get Mrs. Burns' attention. I want an invitation to her Winter Ball. She only invites three hundred couples." Helena leaned further over the edge of the box, "Hello! Mrs. Burns! Oh, how lovely you look! And your sweet dog! How lovely."

Mrs. Burns, shortsighted, had no idea of who Helena was, but she was too nice an old woman to ignore a wave. Peering dimly, she waved back.

"See?" Helena crowed. 'She's acknowledged me!' Her daughters looked at one another, eyebrows raised, and sat back in their chairs. How utterly boring. How soon would all this be over? Then they could go and have lemon ices at Delmonico's.

Anderson sat at the back of the box, numb with ennui, cursing himself for ever giving in to this stupid idea of sitting for four hours listening to fat woman and fat men screech about love. Mentally, he went over the voluminous evidence of last night's jewel heist at the Dakota Hotel. Unable to help himself, he, like Teddy, yawned.

***

In the third row, in the two seats next to the main aisle, sat the two opera critics from The New York Herald Tribune and The New York Times. James Blackburn and Jason Harris, working for competing newspapers, always sat together at openings, causing gossip about their infamous feud over which of them was the best and most discerning critic. Unknown to their public, James and Jason were lovers, conducting a quiet and loving 20 year relationship and delighted that, as of yet, no one, except a few discreet friends, knew their secret. It leant spice to the rumors of the two of them always fighting to be the best critic...jostling to each be better...with more snipes...more critical thrusts...than the other. Their newspaper column fights, slighting one another's critical opera opinions, were the stuff that sold thousands of papers. A good review from either Blackburn or Harris could launch a career skyward. A pointed critical comment could sink a performer forever.

"This should be a good one!" Jason said. "This and the one later this week are the last operas that Orsini will be conducting. I always get excited when I see him. He throws himself so passionately into the music!"

"And I," Jason confided, lowering his voice, "heard that La La du Lac is going rapidly downhill. Her voice is supposed to sound like *merde*. Did you hear that rumor?"

"No! Who told you that?"

"Oh, my lips are sealed," Jason made a zipping motion across his mouth, "and I have thrown the key away!" He tossed an imaginary object into the fourth row. "Now, what do you think will happen tonight?"

***

Backstage, the usual pandemonium reigned. Dozens and dozens of people milled in the dressing rooms, on staircases and in the halls. Everyone was in various stage of dress, some already in costume, some getting wigs fitted, some still in street clothing. Backstage smelled of its own particular odor. Grease paint and wax, gauze costumes, sweaty wigs, stress, worry, and above all, the smell of excitement and anticipation.

***

Vivienne put her dog down. *Poupette* was nervous and began to bark. "Keep that dog quiet!" roared someone from the recesses of the stage.

"Who is criticizing my dog?" Vivienne screeched as Muriel Durgin walked innocently into an imbroglio. The dog, restive and agitated, snapped at Muriel's leg. Muriel screamed and the dog ran amok, growling and frothing at the mouth.

"Get the damn dog away!" Muriel hollered. The dog ran to where Roque and Horz were standing, snarled and bit Roque on the ankle.

"I'll kill the dog!" Roque screamed, holding his foot and hopping in agony.

"Put the damn dog in your dressing room!" Arturo Calle roared. "If I see it again tonight, I will personally throw it in the alley!"

"I'm insulted!" Vivienne snapped. "My dog is a member of my family!"

"As a bitch who leads the parade of bitches, I am sure that is true!" Roque, limping and nursing his ankle, whispered, making sure that several people heard him, but that his voice didn't quite reach the area where Vivienne was.

"What did you say?" She whipped her head around, sensing that he was making fun of her.

Roque groaned and waggled his ankle. "I was merely remarking on your dog's sharp teeth." He looked around, "Does anyone have a bandage?"

Vivienne glared at him, sniffed and went up to her dressing room, carrying *Poupette* under her arm. Muriel helped Roque to a chair and bound up his ankle with gauze and plaster. He, in turn, put a bandage on the small scratch that *Poupette* had inflicted on *her* ankle. "Bitch!" Roque called out.

"The owner or the dog?" Muriel quipped, ruefully rubbing her wound.

Calle approached them, worrying that either might have been really injured. "Will you live?" It was easy to see that Calle was edgy. Du Lac was such an unstable performer when she wished to be difficult. And now, all he needed was that two more performers had a reason to also be difficult. Still, the stupid cur had bitten the two of them. *Had it been me, I would have been pissed off too.*

"I'm just dandy," Roque rolled his eyes. "If I had some poison to give to the dog, I'd be even better!"

"Let's just get everything ready. The less fuss and sensation, the better." He pushed back his hair. "God-damn woman makes trouble wherever she goes!" He paced back and forth, agitating himself as he worried about what else might happen to upset his plans of a smooth performance. "I'm going out front to talk with Baron Wessel. He's an old sparring partner of Vivienne's. I'm going to ask him to go backstage and speak with her for a few minutes. Remind her of the public that is salivating for her beauty. *Ha!* Remind her that people will be talking about this performance – this legendary performance with her and Orsini conducting. – *forever!* Maybe he can talk a little bit of sense into her...get her to behave."

Calle slid himself through the tiny, hidden door under the stage behind the orchestra. He paused for a moment, electrified as always to see the audience clustered around and above him. Thousands of patrons, the rich in their parterre boxes, sipping champagne and dipping painted fingernails into the satin boxes of Susan's opera creams. The merely wealthy, sitting in their cushioned seats. The less wealthy up in the tiered wooden seats...and...all the way at the top, the clusters of hundreds who paid a week's wages or more to merely stand, crowded together, shoulders crushed, to see and hear Vivienne du Lac sing and Massimo Orsini conduct Puccini's most beloved opera. He took a full minute to inhale the sights...the jeweled colors of the women's gowns...brilliants reds, rich golds, the startling blaze of a purple paisley scarf. The dazzle of real jewels...a thousand or more fortunes on display...diamond necklaces the size of hawser ropes...emerald clips...the deep mystery of sapphires...they all glittered and gleamed, fighting in brilliant competition to the huge chandelier that hung above the audience.

"Baron." He bowed to David. "My dear Baroness," He kissed Barbara's hand.

"May I prevail upon you, Baron? I need a favor."

"What can I do for you?" David waved a flute of champagne. "Can I offer you a glass of the bubbly?"

"Thank you." Calle took the flute and drank the champagne in one gulp. "That was good! Just what I needed as this god-forsaken opera gets going! David, my good man. I want to borrow you for five minutes. Five only! I need you to do a good-will mission. To go into the lion's den and sooth our star." David recoiled in mock horror. "Yes, please, my dear man. Just go to speak with her for a moment. Tell her that the audience is salivating for her. That they love her to death; that they cannot wait to hear her beautiful voice pour out of her throat."

"Will that sooth the beast?" Barbara laughed.

"It may keep her from biting someone!" Calle joked. *It may not be such a joke! Who knows what that woman is capable of?*

"She's not really crazy about me…but…duty calls and I am at the ready," David made a mock salute. "Anything I can do for the Met, I will do! I'll be back in two shakes of a lambs tail, darling." He went through the door of the box and around the corner, joining Calle on the floor. "Lead me to her den. Let's hope I come out unscathed….without being covered in blood!"

***

The smooth action of well-rehearsed stagehands and scenery movers went into play. At the back of the theater, stagehands had placed the sections of scenery for Act Two. Behind that was the scenery for Act Three, and even further, lying outside, against the brick walls of the alley, was the scenery for Act Four. Happily, for the well-being of the scenery and the well-being of the stage crew, the weather was cold and dry. On many a rainy night, not only did the men hump wet and slippery flats in and out of the puddles that formed in the alley, but they also had to try to cover the flats and scenery that they had just removed from the stage until it could be properly stored back the warehouse. "No one who designed this opera house had ever worked back stage!" Urbano frequently grumbled.

On stage, Urbano checked the entire back-of-the-curtain area which was set for Act One, to be sure that each and every piece of scenery was in the proper place.

Only then, did Forsythe Wicks bring in the property baskets and boxes for Act One.

The job of a property manager was a difficult and complex one. Each opera had dozens, maybe hundred of properties, or props, as they were called by the theater folk, and each had to be brought out of storage for each opera, then counted, checked and re-checked and then replaced after the opera was finished.

Props for *La Bohème* were even more complex than many other operas. Generally, in an opera, food represented on the stage, wasn't real, but simply made of papier mâché, plaster or wood. However, in Act One and Act Two of *La Bohème*, the food had to be real as it was cut and heartily consumed on stage by the men who played Rodolfo, Schaunard, Marcello and Colline. Thus, Forsythe Wicks and his team not only had to place each knife, each fork, each candle or painting or dish in its proper place, but they also had to be sure that fresh and palatable food was available, and in place, for Act One and Act Two of *La Bohème*.

Everything had to be in its proper place. It was vital. God forbid that Schaunard put out his hand to pick up the wickedly long and sharp knife that would cut the roast chicken, and not find it properly placed on the table! Heaven forbid that Marcello's painting entitled "The Crossing of the Red Sea" wasn't on its easel as it should be! That the cigars and the bottles of Bordeaux weren't in the baskets that the servants carried into the little attic room! That the cold roast beef or the pastries…all real and edible…were not where they should be! That Benoit, the landlord, didn't have his rent papers in his hand as he entered the attic room! No, indeed, the role of the props could not be more important!

Thus, after the scenery was in place and checked, the props were put out, each item in its proper place. Wicks was a fussy, old-fashioned man, small and precise. His very preciseness made him ideal for the position of Property Manager. Very little escaped his prying and ever-vigilant eyes. He checked every item just once more. Only then, after Wicks checked and re-checked, against his many-paged and detailed list, could he give a thumbs-up to Calle or Sigrid Chalmers that all was in readiness for the curtain to rise.

And behind the curtain, dressed in an immaculate set of white tails, Massimo Orsini paced around, touching each piece of scenery, touching the inside of the curtain, humming his little nursery rhyme. He made the sign of the cross and in a few moments, he did what he had to do. He then went back to his room. Just before the curtain was to go up, one of the pages would run to his room to inform him that the entire opera was ready to begin. That everything was in readiness for the music to start. He was now as eager as a young stallion.

The musicians began to file into the orchestra pit, sat down and fiddled with their instruments, giving out mournful tootles and sounds. Garvin took out his sheet and began to check everyone's name off. He looked up and gave a start of amazement. It was still twenty-five minutes to curtain time and Dean Armandroff was *already* in place! Garvin's mouth flapped open. He looked down and whispered to his wife, "By jingo! Armandroff is already here!"

"Astounding!" She agreed, craning her neck to check. "I simply can't believe he's on time!"

"Zeranski, Odams, Hess, Bickle…is Bickle here?…Fine." He made check marks against the list of names. "Anderson...yes…Frangiamore…Littman, Wendy, Littman, Art…who is missing?"

"I think everyone is here." Alice Mary confirmed. "We're ready."

In the lighting booth, men clicked and tested bulbs and gel lights. When Johnston Redmond was satisfied that everything was ready, he made a sign to Sigrid Chalmers, who then checked off the "Lighting" notation on *his* master list.

A page came running to Tim Weaver. "She, Vivienne du Lac, she needs someone to fix her mirror. It fell off the wall!" His anxious eyes and breathless voice told Tim that du Lac was probably throwing a fit in her dressing room.

"Francesco!" Tim spoke urgently. "Get up there and fix her problem, on the double!"

"Si," Francesco was so nervous, he slipped into his native tongue. "Yes, certainly, of course. I mean, certainly, I will do it right now." He ran up the stairs, his bulging, heavy leather tool belt banging against his knees.

He knocked on Vivienne's door. At her answer to come in, he entered. "My lady, what can I do for you?" Francesco was very nervous. This woman had been a virago yesterday, almost causing him to lose his job.

She didn't seem to remember him, or the problems of yesterday. *Dio grazie!* "Oh, will you please fix my mirror," Vivienne's voice was honeyed. "I think the nail, came out of the wall and it fell down. The nail rolled here...under my dressing table skirt." Her slight French accent was charming and her laugh tinkled. Silvery...like the bells in the church. *Could this possibly be the same woman who had screamed and yelled yesterday?*

"It was a miracle that the mirror didn't break!" Vivienne's eyes, their expression already emphasized by the stage make-up, met with his. "A broken mirror would have been bad luck! But it *didn't* break. That means good luck and I know tonight will be a triumph for me!" She twisted on her stool, raising her arms to the ceiling.

Hurriedly, before she lost her temper, Francesco nodded and dropped the heavy tool belt onto the floor. He knelt down and searched under the flounce of the pink fabric that covered her dressing table. Ah! Here it was - the nail. He held it up and she...*la diva* herself ...actually smiled. Francesco rose to his feet and pulled the hammer out of his tool pouch so quickly that the entire contents spilled over the floor, clanking and rolling.

"Santa Maria!" Francesco cursed to himself. "Excuse me, my lady." He scrambled on the floor, on all fours, scooping up chisels and screwdrivers and knives and his big hammer. He stood up, shaken, not realizing that his sharpest, longest knife was still on the floor, lost under the skirt of Vivienne's dressing table. He leaned over the dressing table and repositioned the nail, then hammered it into the wall. He bent, picked up the mirror and put it back on the wall. "Is that satisfactory?"

"Very good. *Merci bien"* Vivienne returned to the inspection of her own face in the mirror. She had forgotten Francesco already. Quietly, not wanting to bring any further attention to himself, Francesco backed out of the room, shutting the door behind him.

From the small, but luxurious room where he rested, waiting for his call, Massimo Orsini burped. His stomach, an organ in his body that had recently ceased to function smoothly, started to ache. This was becoming a real problem. *Such stress that I am under! How can I deal with everything?* He'd check with his own doctor once he got back to Italy. Until then... He opened the door and called to one of the pages. "Get me some *Brioschi* , my son. I have an attack of the stomach."

The page, not quite knowing what to do, brought Orsini's request to Sigrid Chalmers. Chalmers was always ready for this and almost any other mishap. He hauled out a box, opened it and pulled out the blue bottle of white crystals that settled the stomach of almost every Italian in the United States and Italy. "Here, bring this to the *Maestro* together with a glass of water and a spoon."

The boy ran and did as instructed. He knocked on Orsini's door, was told to enter and presented the *Maestro* with a tray.

"*Grazie,* my son." Orsini opened the blue bottle, spooned out a heaping measure of the crystals, and mixed them into the glass of water. He stirred vigorously, clanking the spoon against the rim. "Ahhhh!" Orsini drained the glass. "That will fix my stomach!" He gave the empty glass back to the page boy. "Thank you, my son. You have saved my life and saved the happiness of everyone in the building who would like me to be happy and conduct well."

"Happy to be of service, *Maestro.*" The boy saluted him. "Break a leg tonight, sir." The boy left the room and closed the door.

Orsini watched him go with an absent look. *Should he? Should he not? And should he speak with her and beg her to perform well tonight? Play on her sympathy? After all, these performances – this weekend and the next – would be the last time audiences would see her on stage or see him conduct. Was that enough to make her perform well?* He sighed. *Perhaps. Perhaps it would anger her and she might walk off the stage, leaving him waving his baton at nothing! She'd done it before, and she would do it again! Should he? Should he not?*

***

In the furnace room, Clemons and Figaro watched the flames of the furnace roar red and yellow. "Time we went upstairs, Figaro." Clemons spoke to the cat. "Come now, Figaro, we got business to do." Figaro cocked his black head, as if he understood. Clemons clanged the furnace door shut and the cat and Clemons, using great stealth, went upstairs.

The cast in the women's dressing room began to move toward the door. Even though they were not needed until Act Two, everyone wanted to hear, if not be able to see, the performance of Act One from behind the wings. Karen Heffernan adjusted her wig, looking at herself in the long mirror that framed the communal dressing table. "How do I look?"

"You are the bee's knees," Sue Shigeoka applied one more coat of mascara to her already blackened eyelashes. She, too, stared at herself in the mirror, then stood up. "Let's dance, ladies."

Antonina also stood up and almost tripped over the lace of her shoe that had become untied. "Go ahead," she waved to the rest of the women. ""I have another shoelace in my locker. I'll be along in a moment or two." She felt wonderful, excited and ready to perform. *La Bohème, here I come!*

***

Dean twisted in his seat. He scanned the boxes, searching to see Brooks' face. He stood up, peering into the brilliance of the Diamond Horseshoe's glitter. He saw a waving arm. "Brooks!" he almost yelled, risking a scolding from Garvin.

Brooks saw him and grinned. She waved the red scarf that she'd wound around her shoulders. "So, that's the same guy who was waving to you yesterday at the rehearsal." Carey Marvel Mabley nudged Brooks' arm. "He's rather a hot daddy! What's going on?"

"He's a bassoon player." Brooks kept her eyes downcast.

"And I'm a monkey's uncle!" Carey snorted. "You already told me that part! It's the rest that I want to know about! I can see his eyes yearning for you all the way up here."

"He is pretty cute," Brooks popped a violet cream into her mouth. "We went for a long walk yesterday after the rehearsal."

"You did?"

"Um, we went to the zoo and he told me his life story," she looked up and laughed. "He told me how much he hated rich people and all that they stood for."

"The two of you didn't have much in common, then." Carey deliberately looked at Brooks' expensive kid shoes, then let her gaze travel slowly upward, pausing at the hem of Brooks' couturier dress, stopping at the jeweled clasp that held Brooks' page boy hairdo away from her face. "Geez, Brooks. Your family isn't exactly out sweeping the streets."

"Yours either."

"Sure, but I'm not the one going to see the seals with the bassoon player. What gives? Do you like him?"

"I think he's the genuine ant's ankles," Brooks blushed. "I like him a lot. We're going out for supper after the opera."

"Jeepers! How did you get around the fact that your family owns most of lower Manhattan?"

"It wasn't easy. I let him rant and rave about how horrid the wealthy were, and then I took him for a walk, showing him the hospital that my father endows."

"Clever!"

"Then I showed him where my mother volunteers every day. He's never seen a real home for the aged."

"What did he say?"

"He was sort of speechless. Honestly, Carey, I think he thought that people who had money sat on silken tuffets all day and ate bon-bons." She took another violet cream out of the box.

"Did he apologize for his bourgeoisie mistakes?"

"Well, his mouth hung open after I showed him the two orphanages that I take care of." She bit into the chocolate. "To give him his due, he was astonished. I don't think he realized how much good work we do."

"Us pampered little rich girls," Carey murmured.

"I could have told him about you and how hard you and your grandmother work at the children's hospital."

"That's me, Saint Carey!"

"Well, that's the whole point. You and I and my family and yours, and most of the wealthy people who live around here. We never talk about how much good we do, even though we do an awful lot of charitable stuff."

"Don't make me blush," Carey rummaged in the candy box and came up with a maple caramel. "Naturally, we never say anything. That would be crass," she winked, "and us rich girls are never crass!"

"I certainly gave him something to chew on." Brooks wiggled on her seat. "But under all of his bravado, he's a rather sweet man. Loves his family. Has a great sense of humor."

"And what will happen between the daughter of a tycoon and the bassoon player?" Carey seemed tickled at her little joke.

"I see a great future for us." Brooks waved to a friend of her mother's sitting across the parterre row. "Enough about Dean and me. What are you doing lately? Flying across the ocean yet?"

Carey's passion was airplanes. Ever since she was a tiny child and had seen a plane in the sky, she had been determined to fly. Her grandmother, herself an unconventional woman, gave her flying lessons when she was twelve, and soon, Carey had completed her flying lessons, relished the greasy job of taking apart the engine of an airplane, and had become a bosom friend of America's foremost flight heroine, Amelia Earhart.

"Well, if you cross your heart and hope to die if you tell anyone…."

"What?"

"Well…Amelia *is* planning a flight across the Atlantic!" Carey tried hard to keep the excitement from her voice, but her face was shining with pride.

"Really! A woman to do that? I can't believe it! I mean, it was only a year or so ago, that Lindbergh managed to make it. And he's a man!"

"I know. Promise you won't breathe a word, Brooksie. She's been working like a demon to get the authorities to give her permission."

"They'd never let a woman go!"

"She's making plans at the very top."

"The top? The very top? Like who?" Brooks, who wished she had the courage to go up in a plane, was agog.

"The top top. Mr. Hoover himself."

"The *Pres*ident?"

Carey nodded, biting her bottom lip. "Yessir. My father was able to get his attention and introduce them. Charles Curtis, the Vice-President, is urging Hoover to allow her to try. She's hoping to have her plane ready in a year."

"Wow."

"And I'm helping her to prepare." Carey stared straight ahead. Brooks could see the spot of pink that glowed on her friend's cheek.

"My golly, Carey! What an adventure. Imagine!" Brooks twisted her head, pretending that she was at the controls of an airplane, zooming up into the sky. "Maybe you'll go with her?"

"I think the plane can only hold one human being, but perhaps...if she's successful, I can be the second woman to fly across the Atlantic!" She tuned and grabbed Brooks' hands. "It's so exciting!"

"Gol-ly!"

"And even better...and even more secret..." Carey grinned like a twelve year old child, "We're going to do some wing-walking expeditions in the spring."

"Wing-walking!" Brooks gaped. "Like stand on the wing when the plane is flying? Are you nuts?"

"It's really easy and very safe. Amelia will be the pilot when I go out on the wing."

"Holy Joe! I can't even *dream* of doing something like that! You're a re-markable woman, Carey. A remarkable and crazy woman," Brooks shook her head. "I'll be there, maybe towing my bassoon man with me, to stand below with my mouth open and my heart pounding!"

"I'll wave to you as we zoom past." Carey laughed.

"How do you hold on when the plane goes upside....." But Brooks' question was interrupted.

The door of the box opened and Carey's grandmother, Corintha Marvel, stepped inside, followed by her maid. "Good evening, young ladies." Brooks and Carey leapt to their feet. "Did you see the ridiculous gown on Mrs. Schneider? Looks like a gussied up tramp!" With a grin of satisfaction, Corin-tha sat herself down and slid off her furs. "Who is here?" She leaned over the balcony and began to look at the rest of the opera patrons. "Just look at the Winkelman's box! At her age! She should know better!"

"Have a chocolate, Grandmamma." Carey offered, winking at Brooks. "The curtain should be going up in about twenty minutes."

"What are you up to these fine days, Carey dear?" Corintha asked.

"I'm still flying airplanes." Carey grinned. "And I have just begun ball-room dancing lessons. I'm always trying to learn something new."

"Ballroom dancing. Oh, my! I was always light on my feet. You take after me, darling." She patted Carey's knee. "Keep it up. Good for you, my dear. A girl must have something interesting to talk about." She peered at one of the parterre boxes. "Did you see Gilda prancing about with that horrid young man? He's young enough to be her grandson!" She adjusted the opera glasses so that she could see more clearly. "He *is* rather handsome, though."

"Grandmamma!" Carey pretended to be scandalized. "At your age!"

"At my age, Carey dear, looking at a toothsome man and remarking on his attributes is about all I am capable of!"

Chapter Ten

"...And besides, the wench is dead..."
Christopher Marlowe, The Jew of Malta

James sped along the corridors, banging on doors, announcing that the curtain was set to go up in twenty minutes. Knock, knock! "Yes," roared Sergei Andreyi. "Come in!"

"Sir, twenty minutes to curtain!"

"I'm just about ready, thank you, young man." Andreyi had only to put on his wig, then do the three things that he did before every performance: kneel in front of the large wooden triptych that his grandmother had given him in honor of his first performance at the Kirov Opera in Saint Petersburg, say the prayers that he learned in childhood, and then to fart copiously. These three, in that order, never failed him yet.

Knock, knock! "Yes?"

"Madam Orloff. Twenty minutes to curtain time." Young James eyed Angelique with fervent admiration.

"Thank you, my dear." She winked at him and he allowed himself, much later that night, after all of the ruckus had died down, to remember her face just before he fell asleep. Although she didn't have to be ready until Act Two, Angelique always finished her dressing so that she could watch the opera from the start from the wings. She bent forward and finished the complicated make-up that Musetta wore. She allowed herself a final preening...she did look very good, if she said so herself. And then, she performed the rituals that she always performed. *May I break a leg.*

Knock, knock........*knock, knock, knock.....*

James stood outside Vivienne du Lac's closed door, puzzled. Was she asleep? Already out of her room and ready? He waited a few moments.

Knock, *knock!* Louder this time....sharper, his knuckles making two noisy slams. "Mademoiselle du Lac? Hello?"

"She's probably drunk." Horz Bortel, in full make-up and wig, squeezed against the wall and passed James in the corridor. "Knock harder, maybe she's boozed out," he sniggered.

"I've knocked three or four times," James was flummoxed. "What should I do?"

"Open the bitch's door," Horz flapped his hand. "At worst, you catch her with her knickers down!" He went down the corridor toward the stairs.

Should I open her door? Suppose she is really drunk? Or even worse? Suppose she's not quite dressed? James' hand went to his mouth. He knocked again, this time three heavy raps. *Knock! Knock! Knock!* "Miss du Lac! Are you in there?" He rattled the doorknob.

Rushing steps came toward him. It was Celestina. "Thank goodness!" He turned to Vivienne's maid. "I can't get her to answer my knock!"

The boy was panicked. Celestina smiled at him. "She most likely didn't hear you." She patted him on his shoulder. "Sometimes, she's so enamored with her face in the mirror," her voice was a whispered confidence, "that she wouldn't hear the sky fall." She opened the door and heard frantic barking from *Poupette*. Halfway into the room, she called out, "My lady, the page boy is calling you for curtain." She stepped inside.

Her scream reverberated all the way down to the backstage area.

***

After one glance, James ran away, trying not to vomit. He careened into the walls, thirteen people in the halls and seven more on the staircase, gibbering – screaming - that she was dead… "Dead! *She's dead!* All bloody! She's dead!"

In the dressing room, Celestina bent over her mistress's body. "My sweet Jesus!" she cried. Someone had almost cut Vivienne's head off!

"Yap! Yap, Broooowl!" the dog was frantic, pulling at the leash that lassoed him to the pipe of the hand-basin on the wall. *"Yap! Yap-Yap!"*

She heard the pounding of frantic steps and six people burst into the room at once.

"What the …?" Arturo Calle gaped. "Is she *dead?*"

"See for yourself. Her throat is slashed." Celestina shuddered and pointed, trying not to step any closer to the body. Vivienne du Lac lay on the floor, half of her red dress still bunched onto the dressing room stool. Her body was angled against the stool, and her head, with the throat ripped nearly off, leaned against the skirt of the dressing room table. The grisly gap yawned, with blood and the twisted vocal chords of her throat shining yellowish white, obscene in the harsh lighting of the bulbs that outlined her mirror.

"Here, let me," Urbano Valeria, pushed Calle's unresisting body aside and knelt beside the body. *"Christ!"* Urbano almost screamed. The red velvet dress, so lush and full and lovely on Vivienne during the rehearsal, had now soaked up her life's blood and as Urbano's knee came into contact with it, bubbled and frothed, lapping upward. *"Managia!"* Urbano lapsed into his native Italian, his face turned ashen.

Calle shook himself. "It's nearly curtain!" Murder, tempest, plague, hurricane, whatever…It was his job to show the audience an opera! "Where the hell is her cover?" He turned, shaking Sigrid Chalmers. "Go find her…what's her name? Get her in here immediately!" After all, no matter who had been murdered, the opera must go on as scheduled. There were thousands of people out there!

"It couldn't be...an accident?" Johnston Redmond stood in the doorway, keeping well away from du Lac's body. "She...could she have cut herself like that by...by *mistake?*" His eyes rolled. "I mean...otherwise...God's Teeth! Someone murdered her! *Killed* her!"

"Idiot!" Tim Weaver told him kindly. "Of *course* someone killed her! But then," he reflected in near-hysteria, "*everyone* wanted to kill her!"

"Jesus!"

"My God!"

"I can't believe it!"

"What shall we do?"

"Get Ignatzia...ah, here you are, my dear."

Ignatzia Volente peeked into the room, frightened that the rumors she had heard might be true. "My sweet Lord!" She crossed herself, her eyes huge with horror, warding off the evil that was swirling in the room. "It is true, then? She's been butchered?"

"Janet!" Calle roared. "Get Janet!" he turned, pointing at Celestina. "And you, the two of you...get Ignatzia ready in five minutes flat! We have a show to put on!"

"Yap! Yap, Yap!"

"Shut that dog up!" Redmond ordered. Celestina looked around wildly. *Shut the dog up? How? Kill her too?*

Janet's footsteps clattered and she came into the room, skidding up short at she viewed the horror. "Oh! Oh!" She swayed, almost faint with shock. "What shall we do?"

"Get her ready. Right away!" Urbano made a shooing motion. "Don't disturb the body any more than you have to, but get Ignatzia ready right away! Everyone else, get out of here and let the two women dress Ignatzia!"

The men stumbled out. "Stick the wig on her head." He made a motion with his hands. "I'll get Henry Wu up here in two minutes to do her make-up! *Go, now!*"

***

On the stairs, Calle and Urbano paused. "What the hell are we going to do?"

"We can't just ignore her." Calle's face was aghast. "We have to tell...the police or someone else!"

"Ah!" Urbano snapped his fingers. "I saw...up in the parterre boxes...the Chief of Police."

"You recognized him?"

"His name is...uh, von Vogel...Andrew von Vogel...no, *Ander*son! Anderson von Vogel! I met him several times last year. He's here with his wife and daughters. I saw, through the curtain when I counted the house. I'll send someone to get him."

"Wait! Wait!" Calle thought for a moment. "Not yet! Wait until the middle of Act One, *then* call him to come. Otherwise," Calle stroked his chin, "he might not let us put the opera on tonight."

"You are always thinking, my good friend." Urbano, naturally, saw the wisdom of waiting for a half hour. "After all, nothing will bring du Lac back to life. We will wait. Then, I will get him, personally, so that no one else will know what is happening, after Mimi's aria."

"Jesus! What a horror! I am sure that will be for the best. I will make the announcement that du Lac will not be singing." He nodded, satisfied that they had done the best they could. "The audience will not be pleased that we have used Ignatzia, but when they find out why," he shrugged, "they will have to understand."

"You're not going to tell the audience *why* du Lac is not singing, are you?"

"Are you crazy? Of course not." Calle shuddered. "They'll find out tomorrow when the newspapers come out."

Another piercing scream rang out from above. The two men, jolted by the noise, ran back to Vivienne's dressing room. There, they were nearly transfigured by what had transpired.

"It was the dog," Janet babbled. "The *dog!*"

"Yap! *Rrrrrr!*" Nearly maddened by the smell of his mistress' blood, *Poupette* rushed toward Calle and tried to run out of the room. Urbano reacted with admirable haste and kicked the dog in the ribs. She whimpered, whining and ran back under the chaise lounge at the back of the room.

"Shit! Is *she* dead, too?" Urbano cried. "What did we do to deserve this, Lord? Why are you punishing us?" Ignatzia Volente lay on the floor, the red dress half-on and half-off. Her head rested in a pool of blood, her face white, and one of her legs was bent in an unnatural angle. "What the hell happened? Is *she* dead?"

"Oh, my sweet Lady!" Celestina began to shriek. "Oh, my God!" She pointed and swayed, her body shaking. The head of Vivienne du Lac was no longer attached to her body. It had rolled a foot or so away and lay, like some grisly doll's head, face upward, the eyes opened. Her lashes were artfully made up with heavy mascara. The coagulating orbs were bulging and staring blankly, the entire head surrounded with a slowly coagulating lake of blood. All over the room, decorating the floor like a mad designer's handiwork, were bloodied footprints, some from Janet and some from *Poupette.* The room was a mess - an abattoir of horror!

"*Stop* it!" Janet shook Celestina who subsided, crying and wailing. "What a scene from Hell!" Janet's lip was nearly bitten through and her teeth chat-

144

tered as she tried to explain. "We had to get the dress off Vivienne. When we tried to pull it off...over her head...the head just dropped down. It made a thud and Celestina screamed and backed up, backing into *Poupette. Poupette* just went mad! She strained on her leash and it broke and she attacked Ignatzia, who was standing in shock. She fell...Ignatzia...she fell over the footstool and she landed...oh, my sweet Jesus! I don't think she's dead. I think she's just fainted. I think her leg is broken! Oh, dear, sweet Jesus! What shall we *doooooo?*"

Arturo Calle and Urbano Valeria stood stock still, as the realization of the completeness of the difficulty hit them. "The opera...how can we do the opera?"

"We will have to cancel." Arturo's voice was doom. "We cannot...who could sing...?" His face was ashen. Never, never in his life...never in the history of the Metropolitan Opera Company had an opera not gone forward! And *tonight!* Even worse than ever, perhaps Beniamino *Gigli* might attend!

Urbano muttered, "What else can we do? Who can we get in five minutes to sing the role?"

"How much will you love me if I save your bacon?" Peeping in the door was the beautiful face of Angelique Orloff. "Are they both dead?" Wide-eyed, she gazed at the carnage in the room.

"Angelique! My darling! Of *course! You* can sing Mimi!" Calle's heart started to beat again. He had thought, for a moment, that he might die of rage and frustration. Of Vivienne and her death...why, he had already forgotten her. It was only the opera that mattered.

"No, my dear man. Not me. I don't really know the role nor the movements." Angelique shook her head. "No. I will keep my little Musetta's Waltz." She smiled, a beautiful pussy cat's smile of smug delight.

"Then who...? Who..." Calle's puzzlement was palpable. Angelique winked at Urbano.

"Ah!" Urbano cried. *"I know!* My little sweetheart!" He danced a jig. *"Antonina!"*

"Naturally!" Angelique smiled, complaisant. "Antonina can do it."

"Who?" Calle thought he might go mad. *"Who?"*

"She can sing the role. She knows every movement, every stage action. She can sing it with perfection."

"Who?" Calle almost wept with frustration.

"My wife's best friend's daughter." Urbano leaped, as if stung. "Quickly, Janet! Run and get her. We have only a few moments to pull this all off. Thank God she doesn't come on until the end of Act One!"

"Antonina? The little girl who plays the Sweet Seller?" Janet was thunderstruck. *"She* can sing Mimi?"

"Most likely, better than du Lac," Angelique nodded with firmness. "Go and get her now. Oh, and Janet! Tell Zizzane Fond that she can sing the Sweet

Seller part. She can manage that for tonight." Janet ran off, eager to spread the news, get Antonina and save the production.

In the blood spattered room, Urbano nodded. "Good thinking, Angelique. The rest of the crowd can chime in and cover up for Zizzane if she can't quite remember the lines."

"This *child?* She can sing the entire role?" Calle was still in a daze. "I know she had a very good voice, but this is huge role! She has no rehearsal...how can she...?"

"She's been singing this role ever since she was nine years old. She's Fazzolini's star pupil. She will do it and do it beautifully. I have heard her sing." Urbano smacked his thigh. "You will see, Arturo. There will be magic made here tonight. History! You will have a triumph on your hands!"

She went closer to Ignatzia. "Is she...? Has someone murdered her, too?"

In near hysteria, Urbano babbled. "No, she's broken her leg and is in a faint."

Angelique leaned over carefully, trying not to step into the blood. "Has she...? Is anyone taking care of her?"

Calle stepped outside and called. "Hey! Hey! We need some help here! Please! Right away!"

Angelique was still thinking hard. She pushed at Calle. "Get the doctor. I am sure her leg is broken and she may have a concussion, poor thing." Calle nodded and ran out of the room.

Alone with Ignatzia's broken leg and the headless body of Vivienne du Lac, Angelique shuddered and said a prayer for Vivienne's soul.

As she prayed, she felt a shiver along her spine. The room seemed colder. Death had arrived. Dispassionately, Death took possession of the soul of Vivienne du Lac and spirited it directly to the flames of Hell. Judgment had been instantaneous. She would roast forever, maddened and deranged by the endless torture that would consume her unto Eternity. Finished, Death left to keep a previous appointment in Samarra.

***

Oh, Lord, this night is endless... Anderson was stupefied with boredom. Why, oh, why had he ever given in to Helena's blandishments? He shifted in his seat, thereby earning himself a glare from his wife's narrowed eyes.

"Try to pretend that you might be enjoying yourself, Anderson," Helena hissed. "Here we are, in one of the most coveted boxes at the opera, with thousands of eyes jealous of our place in New York Society." She preened, knowing that others were wondering just who she and her pretty daughters were. "We are on display!" Her voice attempted to cut at him. "Try not to disgrace me!" Venom dripped. Why had she ever married such a boring man? Why couldn't he be more like Count Smirnoff? A gentleman of culture! Someone who appreciated a woman like herself. Helena turned back to perusing the audience, catching the monocled eye of a man she had met at one of dear Katrina's parties. She smiled at him, suggesting, in the brief glance, that a further meeting between them just might happen. And who knows? Perhaps it might. Or perhaps Philippe... Count Smirnoff...the dear man... he had been making suggestions. Whispering in her ear whenever he had the opportunity. Promising delights beyond her wildest dreams. Ah, they were all like that in the beginning. She shrugged. It wasn't like she'd been faithful to Anderson. He was too...what was it? Too provincial. Not exciting enough. Too locked into his dismal job. Uninterested in society and those people who mattered most. If it wouldn't have ruined her, she might have found some way to divorce him. She looked around again. A woman like herself needed a man who could excite her. Stimulate her. Buy her little trinkets and gifts.

***

"Of course, I can do it." Antonina sucked in a huge gulp of air. "I was born to sing."

"Are you sure?" Calle still wasn't convinced. "The entire cast...the entire opera...it will all rest on you. Are you sure you can do this, Antonina?"

"Yes, Mr. Calle. I can." She lifted her chin. Of course she could, couldn't she?

"Go away, Sir." Janet needed all the time she could get. "Please." Calle gave one sharp nod and went out of the room. Sweat pooled under his arms. His entire career rested in the hands of this child. *Please...please...please...let her do well....*

Fate, flitting by, laughed and laughed, amused that this situation had surprised even him. Fate was always the first to see the humor in surprises like this.

Sergei Andreyi pushed into the dressing room. "Antonina!" he called, kneeling at Antonina's side as she stood with a dressing gown wrapped around her underclothes. "I come to salute you and tell you that I will help you in any way, as will we all."

"We will perform this well, Mister Andreyi. I can do this."

"Of course you can, my dear. I will be enthralled with your youth and beauty and everyone in the audience will see that we are in love!" He bent and kissed Antonina's brow.

"I have been half in love with you for years," she teased. "Ever since I saw you as sing *Nessun Dorma!* You have been the man I might have been dreaming about when I kiss my pillow." She dimpled and blushed slightly, causing Andreyi, although he adored his own wife, to fall in love with her then and there.

"You have to leave us now, Mister Andreyi. We have to finish here." Janet pushed and pulled at Antonina, assisted by the now revived Celestina. Andreyi bowed once again and left the room. *She would be fine. She would be more than fine, this little girl. God help us all...she had to be fine!*

They stripped her to her underclothes, then slid the heavy, blood-encrusted dress over her head. "I'll have to take it all up," muttered Janet. Antonina was at least three sizes smaller than du Lac, a tiny thing. "You," she ordered Celestina, "Get on the floor and start hemming. Use big stitches, but not so big that she'll trip over them."

Henry Wu and Victor Calligari came into the room. "Hurry, ladies. We need at least five minutes with her. "Henry, you get to work on her face and I'll brush out," Victor held the blood encrusted wig with the tips of his fingers, "this mess." His fastidious face was crinkled with disgust. "Ohhh! Never have I handled such a thing!" He wiped his hands on a towel. "Such a horror!" He shivered with a delicious shudder.

Outside in the hall, Clemons shivered. In his arms, he held onto Figaro. The cat was unusually agitated, lashing his black tail to and fro. "I stuck pins in her image, Figaro," Clemons whispered into the cat's fur. "I killed her, I did!"

***

Arturo Calle pulled on the white tails of his jacket. "I'm going out now to make…shit…*some* kind of announcement! *Christ Almighty.* Our entire *opera,* our *careers*….all resting on the shoulders of this little girl! May God have mercy on us!"

He stumbled out into the wings, sick to his stomach. "She will be wonderful," Urbano reassured him, patting him on the back. "I have known Antonina since she was a child. She has the voice of a goddess."

Calle pulled a piece of paper from his pocket. "Tell me again, what is her name? *Jesus!* She's the *diva* tonight, and I don't even know who she *is!*"

"Calm down, my dear friend. Her name is…are you ready? Antonina Sabatino. You could say, if you want to gild the lily, that she's been studying with Fazzolini…nah," He shrugged his shoulders, "just announce her. She will make her own history here." He smiled broadly. "You are going to be famous, my good friend. This will cap your career as the most brilliant Metropolitan Opera Director ever!"

As Calle turned back to respond, a huge roar went up from the audience. "What's happening?" Calle tried to peek through the curtains, shoving aside Sigrid Chalmers.

"Oh, my God!" Chalmers gaped. "It's Gigli! He's here!"

The two men opened the curtains just enough to peek through. In Baron Wessel's parterre box, a broad man with waving dark hair was theatrically throwing kisses to everyone in the theater. It was Beniamino Gigli! The most famous tenor in the world! The audience was on their feet, as one, they cheered and whistled and clapped. Gigli clasped his hands together, as if he were just declared the winner in a prizefighting contest. He turned left…he turned right…he bowed…he waved and preened. The crowd adored him and responded with a huge ovation, punctuated with cries of *Bravo! Bravo, Gigli!*

"Thank goodness he's arrived," Calle wiped his brown again. "This will slow down the curtain. Gives us more time to get that girl...Antonina...dressed and ready."

"Oh, she's been ready since she was nine years old," Urbano grinned. He stuck his head out also, "I saw Gigli a few years ago at La Scala."

"Was he magnificent?"

"He sings like a god. His stage acting," Urbano shrugged, "Not so great. He did a double bill there, singing both roles of Turriddu and Canio on the same night. The crowd was mad for him. It didn't matter at all if he couldn't act his way across the stage. When he opened his mouth, people swooned."

Standing in David Wessel's box, Gigli was playing up to the crowd. He grabbed Teddy and held him up. The crowd roared again. Teddy was a placid and well-behaved dog. He reached up and licked the side of Gigli's face and the audience cheered. Gigli waved Teddy's paw. The audience laughed and clapped even more. Barbara was delighted. Teddy was the star of the show!

The cheers subsided. The audience was winding down. Their clapping had nearly stopped. Gigli, knowing that his moment had passed, had the sense to sit down. He murmured some sweet words into Teddy's fur and set the dog gently back on his cushion. "I luff liddle dogs," he patted Barbara's knee. "Beautiful vimmin and liddle doggies." Barbara winked at him and he left his hand on her knee for another moment. David rolled his eyes and pretended not to notice. Gigli, Barbara and David sat back in their chairs, sipping at crystal flutes of champagne, their eyes now upon the stage.

"Now?" Urbano's eyebrows asked.

"Now!" Arturo Calle gave the signal to Johnston Redmond who was at the lighting board. Redmond pushed the button that rang the bell in Massimo Orsini's dressing room. The signal told Orsini that he had two minutes to make his entrance.

Behind stage, every single member of the cast and crew who was not working that moment, gathered. The news of what had happened had flown, from mouth to mouth. Vivienne du Lac was dead.

Dead? How? A shrug...

"I heard she took poison!" Horz whispered.

"Silly boy," Roque tossed his head. "Someone shot her with a bow and arrow."

"Really?"

"A jealous lover?"

"No. It was that dwarf she used."

"Crespi? I haven't seen him tonight."

"Trust me, she's been shot. And I heard that her cover, that Ignatzia woman, was also killed."

"No! Who is doing the role of Mimi?"

A shrug. "Someone from another company."

"No! *I heard it was some one from here.*"

"Who? Who could step in at a moment's notice?"

"It's secret!"

"A secret?"

"Shhhh! Here comes Calle!" They scattered, but came back again, unable to stop crowding together, gathering every scrap of information and gossip. What was *hap*pening?

The entire company was agog. No one wanted to miss one moment of what was to happen. Whatever it might be.

The lights in the opera house flickered.

The buzzing of the audience quieted.

The huge chandelier went dark, the house lights dimmed.

Johnston Redstone pushed the lever that controlled the stage spot. He twisted the spotlight to shine on the exact center of the huge, gold curtain.

The curtain quivered as the Executive General Manager of The Metropolitan Opera Company, Arturo Calle, stepped out, resplendent in his white tails.

He gazed over the heads of the audience, his face remote. His brain was churning as he thought back…*yes. Yes. Yes! That* putana *du Lac was gone forever! She'd never, ever, spoil one of his performances again. Yes!*

The audience rose to their feet and began to applaud.

The opening night opera, *La Bohème*, had almost begun.

"Ladies and gentlemen," Calle began. He remarked upon the honor of having Beniamino Gigli here at the theater. The crowd erupted again in a prolonged, sincere frenzy of applause… Gigli stood up once more and, with his hands in supplication, asked the audience to cease their clapping.

Bowing again to Gigli, paying tribute to his fame, Calle spoke again. He thanked his staff, he thanked Giacomo Puccini, he thanked he remarkable talent of Massimo Orsini, and then he thanked the audience for their support. The crowd again applauded, hyped up even before the program started.

He cleared his throat, harrumphing into his closed fist, took another deep breath and then said: "Due to an unforeseen emergency, the role of Mimi…" The audience, as one, drew in its breath…*what? Mimi! The star? What was happening?* Calle continued: "…will be sung tonight, by Antonina Sabatino."

There was a buzzing sound…*who? Who?*

In the fifth row, an astonished shout went up. *"Antonina!"* Francesca stood up, swaying, her arms raised in the air. *Antonina! Antonina was going to sing the role of Mimi! Gesu, Maria e Giuseppe! God be praised !.* Simeon Meade, sitting next to Francesca, pulled her down, back into her seat.

Quickly, Simeon began to clap and cheer, joined immediately by Enzo Uccelli, who whistled and stamped his feet. In a nanosecond, Signor Fazzolini, Maria, Peter, Mina, Sabina, Vittoria, and all of the others who had known Antonina began to clap and cheer.

"Is this the little girl you know?" Concetta asked Vittoria, whispering in Italian.

"Know! It is Francesca's *daugh*ter!" Concetta leaned over and watched as Francesca nearly burst out of her skin. *"Che fortuna,"* Concetta tapped Francesca's shoulder. *"In bocca lupo!"*

As their little claque applauded madly, the rest of the audience, fearful that they were simply ignorant of this singer, and not wishing to appear ignorant, began to applaud also.

Torrents of sweat poured down the sleeves of his white dinner jacket. *It is out of my hands, now.* Arturo Calle bowed and stepped back between the gold curtains. *I did what I thought was best. God help me, I hope I did the right thing.*

Hovering and curious, Fate wondered what was going to happen. This was too good.

The back door crashed open and a spotlight caught the *Maestro*, Massimo Orsini, as he strode down the center aisle, his leonine head thrown back as if he were the conqueror of Rome. The audience applauded harder, many standing in ovation to his honor. He didn't turn his head, nor did he acknowledge the applause on his march to the podium. His thoughts, whatever they might be on the death of Vivienne du Lac, were hidden from view. His thoughts on a young and untried child singing the lead in this performance were also hidden from view. But inside, his always-sensitive stomach was churning. *Should I have...?*

Garvin motioned with his hands, and the entire orchestra stood up and began to clap and strike their instruments to welcome their master. Patricia Odams stood at her harp; Dean Armandroff and Tom Zeranski hoisted their bassoons, Mary Frangiamore, Leon Venedicktou, Joy Anderson and all of the orchestra saluted the man they had venerated for years.

So honored, Orsini mounted the steps and stood, for a long moment, savoring his due. He turned back to the audience, bowed deeply and the applause surged again. He turned, bowed even more deeply to his musicians and held his hands up. The golden baton with the huge diamond at the tip, given to him by Puccini himself, was waved once in the air, for all to goggle at. *Who the hell is Antonina what-ever-her-name is? And what will she do to my production?* Holding the baton aloft, he mentally shrugged. It was too late to wonder. He had done what he had done. It would be what it would be. He and Garvin touched eyes. He brought the baton down and the music began.

Chapter Eleven

...all I have is a voice...W. H. Auden, September 1, 1939...

*U*ntil *La Bohème*, operas were begun with lengthy overtures. But Giacomo Puccini had done a daring and controversial thing. This opera, this performance that had challenged so many conventional operatic ideas, opened with only a short...very short passage...the music swelled and the gold curtain opened to show the chilly attic. Rodolfo was trying to write and Marcello was slapping paint on his canvas. Both men were wrapped in scarves and sweaters. Rodolfo even had a gaily-colored blanket thrown over his shoulders. Even the audience felt the cold.

From behind the curtain, Forsythe Wicks brushed the hair from his forehead. "Who took the damn knife?" he accused. "Lucky, I noticed! I got a knife from Tim Weaver. It isn't the right kind of knife, but Colline would look pretty stupid out there trying to cut the meat with his goddam dingle!"

"Shhh! It's starting." Francesco, the stagehand, checked again to see that all was well. After all, his wife was in the audience watching. He swelled with pride. *If it hadn't been for him and what he'd done....She would be so proud...and he was so proud.*

The audience was in good spirits, chuckling at the antics of the four men, applauding when the fire roared up in the stove, laughing at the tale of the poisoned parrot. But one could tell...the audience was really only waiting to see what the substitute...and who could possibly be a substitute for the genius of Vivienne du Lac?....who was singing the role of Mimi would do.

The timid knock on the door. *"Chi e la?"*

"Scusi," the two syllables were soft, but heard clearly in the last row, where Neil Odams, the cabdriver, was watching in the "Standing Room Only" spaces.

"Una donna?" Rodolfo was surprised. It was a woman outside the door of their bachelor pad.

He went to the door and opened it. *"Ecco."*

She was still outside the audience's vision. *"Di garzia, mi si e espento il lume"*

Rodolfo opened the door. She stepped in. The audience, as one, sucked in a breath. She...whoever she was... was lovely! A young, tremulous girl...Francesca bit on her tongue. *Antonina! My daughter! Oh, sweet, sweet Jesus! Look at her, Anton! Look at her!*

Mimi held up her candlestick. *"Vorrebbe...?"* (Would you...?)

"Come in for a moment."

"There really is no need..." Mimi's voice was at once embarrassed and yearning.

"Please. Come in" He held the door ajar and Mimi stepped onto the stage. She staggered, coughing. The audience sucked in its collective breath.

Rodolfo started in alarm. "You...you are not well?"

"No...it is nothing," Mimi clutched a tattered scarf over her shoulders, pulling it tight against the chill. She was wearing a red dress. It looked too big for her. She was poor, the audience concluded. Perhaps she had bought the dress from a barrow....second or third hand. She was a pitiful figure. They leaned forward, already caught in her spell.

Act One moved on, the two star performers getting to know one another on stage. No one noticed that Sergei Andreyi was nearly fifty years old, old enough to be Antonina's grandfather. No, he was Rodolfo, a young and vigorous man who had just met the love of his life. The audience was bewitched. The attraction between Mimi and Rodolfo was obvious and real to them. To the audience and the performers who watched from behind the curtains, they...the two on the stage... had truly fallen in love at first glance.

From the back of his box, Anderson von Vogel's attention was caught. He'd sat through the drivel of the four men singing back and forth. *Who cared?* But this...this was different! This was....she was....exquisite. With a few words, she had made him feel the passion, the glory, of operatic genius. *Was this why people came to operas?* His jaw dropped and he was not even aware of it.

Rodolfo and Mimi were on the floor of the darkened attic room. Her candle and his candle had extinguished and she had dropped her key. Their fingers touched and Anderson sucked in his breath. His hand went to his mouth, pressing on his lips. He felt a stirring in his innermost soul. Dean's bassoon played the mournful notes, advising the audience that something big was coming up. Something very big.

"How cold your little hand is!" Rodolfo sang... *"Che gelida manina!"* "Let me warm it for you!" He began his tender aria, telling her of his awakening love. Telling her about his life...his dreams and his hopes. And you, my beloved? Tell me about yourself.

The performers paused, on their knees, as the audience roared their approval of Rodolfo's poignant aria. The wave of cheering went on for several moments, and the two knelt in silence, still as statues, gazing at one another in adoration.

And then, kneeling on the stage floor, holding Rodolfo's hand as if she would never let go, Mimi sang of her own life...her loneliness...her love of the beauty of flowers and the springtime...her voice soared and the audience felt the presence of genius.

"*I look at the roofs and the sky...but when spring comes...the sun's first rays are mine.*"

"Glorious!" Barbara mouthed.

"She's superb!" David whispered back. "She..." His breath came out. There were no words...Gigli watched with intense interest, his dark eyes gleaming.

Mimi's voice soared higher and higher...perfection...."*The sun's first rays are mine!*" Anderson couldn't breathe. He was helpless...there, with her in that cold, cold room, yearning to hold her hand, yearning to make her his own.

Her aria over, Mimi sunk into a heap on the floor, obviously overcome by her fragility and illness.

The audience exploded, yelling and cheering, up on their feet, stomping and screaming, *Brava! Brava! Brava!* The waves of approval crashed and crashed and crashed again, nearly unstoppable....they wouldn't cease...they clapped and clapped and clapped...five minutes...seven minutes...ten minutes...and then, finally...anxious for more, the audience sat down, mesmerized.

"*Where are you, Rodolfo?*" The three other Bohemians yelled from down in the street. "*We're waiting for you!*"

"*I'm up here with a lady!*" Rodolfo called down to them. "*Get us a table at the Café Momus. We will be there in a few moments.*"

"*Aha! He has found his poem at last!*" Marcello remarked as they sauntered off.

Anderson nodded deep within his soul. *Yes, he had found his poem at last.*

And then, the last of Act One, as Rodolfo and Mimi blended their voices; "*Oh, lovely, sweet girl with your face bathed in the moonlight! I see you in the dream I dreamed forever!*"

"*How sweet his praises enter my heart...*"

"*Tell me you love me.*"

"*I love you!*" And as they exited the stage, their muted cries of joy and love echoed not only on stage but in the hearts of all who heard them.

"*Amor! Amor! Amor!*"

Chapter Twelve

"...This onrush of desire surrounds me. It delights me, it delights me...." Music by Giacomo Puccini, words by Giuseppi Giacosa and Luigi Illica...Musetta's Waltz from La Bohème...

*M*ama! That was wonderful!" Ariel Sarah breathed. She, too, would one day be on the stage! Not as an opera star, but as a dancer! The audience would go crazy with applause for her!

"I had no idea! Who is she?" Dale's eyes were shining.

Alex shrugged. "It's certainly not the harridan that rehearsed yesterday, that's for sure."

"I want to be a singer!" Rachel cried.

"Me, too!" Abby concurred. "Nevermind tennis!"

The applause, which had been sustained for at least seven minutes or more, finally died down, although Francesca was nearly hysterical in her clapping, crying and sobbing with joy.

In his aerie, alone in the row behind his loveless wife and selfish daughters, Anderson nearly wept, understanding only now the emptiness of his own life. It could have been so much more!

Massimo, who had exited on a tide of exaltation, returned, joyously slamming open the door, nearly prancing down the aisle to the podium. *She had been unbelievable, that little one! Extraordinary! She made du Lac look like the old crow that she now was! But...where the hell had she come from? And why?* He shook his head, his electric hair springing out. *Who cares? She had been real, this child, making all of the audience, and yes, himself, a jaded old man, believe in love, in the romance of flowers and springtime....ah, she would be a star of the highest firmament now. He'd done the right thing! By God!* Alone, he stood on the podium, listening to the applause that bathed him in its appreciation. He muttered, and only Garvin and Alice Mary could hear him, "And me, Massimo Orsini, the greatest conductor that ever lived, I was the one who began her career. I was the one!"

He smiled, a strangely satisfied wolfish grin, and picked up a rosewood baton with the compass in the tip given to him by Nellie Melba. He nodded to Garvin again and the music of Act Two began.

The curtain opened on a busy square in the Latin Quarter of Paris. On one side, was the Café Momus. The stage was filled with busy people, the sellers of candy and larks...the children playing and pulling at their mother's skirts, the toy man, the beggars, the bustling crowds. And interweaving through them all, the four Bohemians and Mimi, holding Rodolfo's hand as if she would never let go.

Behind the stage, Urbano nearly wept on Francisco's shoulders. "Our little Antonina! She will be a star after this. A star!"

"*Una bella ragazza.* She is *meriviglioso!*" Francesco hugged his good friend back. "And sweet, not like that *putana!* Is she truly dead, Urbano?"

"She is very dead, *amico mio.*"

"No one will weep. She was an unlovely woman."

"But even an unlovely woman does not deserve to be murdered." Francesco shrugged. It was obvious that he had no care as to who killed Vivienne.

"Good riddance." Francesco made a sign with his fingers to ward off the Evil Eye.

In the background, awaiting her cue, Angelique grinned. *Bliss! Simply bliss!* She allowed herself a well-deserved pat on her own charming back. She, with her wisdom and foresight, had saved the opera! She alone had changed the course of history!

"Damn! This is the best *La Bohème* I have ever seen!" Carey shook her head with open admiration. "She's...wasn't she the Flower Seller girl?"

Brooks peered into the orchestra pit and picked out Dean's wild hair. "She was the Sweet Seller," she pointed to the program. "The one that du Lac was yelling at yesterday at the rehearsal. Wonder what happened to Vivienne du Lac?"

"Who cares." Carey turned back to the stage, as Rodolfo and Mimi came out of a shop. Mimi was wearing an old-fashioned bonnet made of white lace, trimmed with little rosebuds. The bonnet had obviously been purchased for her by Rodolfo. Mimi touched it again and again, unable to believe that such a lovely thing sat on her head.

"*Is my bonnet becoming?*" Mimi's look of love touched the hearts of the audience. You knew before this, she never had any pretty trinkets.

You also knew, Anderson nodded to himself, *that she was really in love with Rodolfo, and he was besotted by her. That was the power of their acting. They transcended the knowledge that they were performing on stage! No! This was real...a real love story that he was privileged to be watching.* He swallowed the lump in his throat and his eyes never left Mimi's glowing little face.

"*I want an iced cream!*" Young Jason sang.

"*I want a candy!*" His sister, Amanda pushed him

"*Mama will spank us if we don't behave!*" His other sister, Alyssa admonished them. "*Let's go and see the toymaker!*" The children pushed and ran, followed by the tired steps of their mother.

"*Pies for sale! Whipped cream!*"

"*Flowers for the ladies!*" The stage bustled with the excitement of Christmas Eve.

Young Jason danced across the stage. *"I want an ice cream! Mamma, I'll be good!"*

"Here come the soldiers!" Amanda sang out.

"Oh, Christmas joy!" Alyssa caroled.

"Children, behave!"

Rodolfo and Mimi, joined by his three friends, took seats at a table in front of the Café Momus. Marcello began to mock the obvious affection between Rodolfo and Mimi, mourning that he, too, once had thought he'd found true love with Musetta.

"Ha! You think you have found sweet love. Love is as sweet as honey! But it turns to gall!"

"And speaking of Musetta!" Schaunard poked Marcello in the belly. *"Look who is here!"*

The company turned to see a vision in a deep purple dress embellished with lavish ruffle down each side. The dress swished and rustled and was made for men to admire. An obviously expensive dress. Just as obviously bought by a rich and besotted lover. The vision's red hair, pinned up in a voluminous tumble of curls, was crowned with the most outrageous little hat, a fluff of purple velvet, crowned with three purple feathers that stuck up in the air as if to announce,

"Here I come! Here comes Musetta!"

From her spot at the table, Antonina watched Angelique strut and preen, trying to catch Marcello's eye and make him so jealous, he would pay her some attention. *She was simply gorgeous! The most beautiful woman she had ever seen. Look at her! And not only was she beautiful, but she was generous and thoughtful! Look at what had happened! Here I am, little me, singing the role of Mimi!*

Watching Musetta's antics with Alcindoro, the old fool, Marcello nearly exploded off his chair with jealousy. Knowing of his passion, Musetta pranced around onstage, the conspicuous object of everyone's attention. On her arm, tottering, was Alcindoro, the obviously wealthy old man who had eyes only for her beauty and youth and lusted for both.

The audience then began to enjoy the little farce that was performed before their eyes. Musetta, trying to make Marcello, her old lover, jealous, and to keep her new admirer interested enough to keep buying her trinkets and jewels. Marcello, trying to ignore the one woman that he loved. And old, silly, Alcindoro, yearning to be young again and keep Musetta from straying from him. The plot thickened.

Musetta flitted between Alcindoro and Marcello, whipping them both into a frenzy. It was her due, she shrugged her pretty shoulders, after all, she was Musetta! She began her song...tossing her beautiful head and striking lascivious poses. In truth, Angelique was a small woman, but her shoes, her costume, her hat with its feminine feathers and the way she held her head and body made her seem tall and elegant. All eyes were upon her, dazzled, simply dazzled.

"Quando men' vo soletta per la via, il gente sosta e mira, e la belezza mia, tutta richera en me, ricera in me de capo a pie. (As I walk alone along the street, all the people stop to stare and inspect my beauty, examining me, from head to toe.)"

Her voice, more mature and a bit heavier than Mimi's, lit the imagination of all. Here was a coquette. A woman of such extraordinary beauty that not only men, but even women, fell over themselves to watch her. She loved the attention…Craved it! After all, she was Musetta, the flirt!

Act Two came to a standstill as the audience cheered and clapped at Musetta's song. They knew she was not the star of this opera, but she had the best of the songs; Musetta's Waltz! She remained, poised on one foot, her head thrown back, sure of her beauty, as the entire crowd on the street in front of the Café Momus could not help but look at her in awe.

From his chair, Anderson was impatient with Musetta and her strutting around. Who was she to take the spotlight off Mimi? *His* Mimi! He made some sound and his wife turned around to look at him in astonishment. "Don't tell me you are enjoying this little thing?" she hissed. "You?"

He twisted in place. "It's fine. Fine." *Fine?* He wanted to leap over the balcony and grab little Mimi. Crush her frail body against his to give her strength and warmth…Take her to a doctor, feed her honey and delicious things to build up her fragile strength. He wanted to….was he crazy? *She was an opera singer, for God's sake! Not a real woman!*

The curtain came down on Act Two, with the same insane applause, applause that lasted for ten minutes before the audience would stop. The house lights blinked on and the chandelier burst into brilliance. Dorothea Staer looked up at it, made a tsking sound, and told her darling husband from Scotland, that she was going to buy a new one for the opera.

"Buy them two, my own lovely girl in the moonlight," Sir Dennis' roaring burr could be heard three boxes away. Being Sir Dennis, he didn't care a whit. They'd been married nearly forty years and she was still, to him, the beautiful girl he had met at the quadrillion. He'd swept her off her feet with the Caledonia Highlander's Eightsome Reel and his own tremendous bellowing of his bagpipes. They were married three weeks later. He loved her more today than he had loved her that day.

During the intermission, the audience got out of their seats, some to buy refreshments or a second box of Susan's Chocolate and Violet Opera Creams, each box wrapped and tied with a mauve and gold ribbon. Some to mill around, speak with friends, talk about the marvelous new diva…*where had she come from?* Some wandered, admiring jewels and expensive dresses.

Some, like Helena von Vogel, tried to use the intermission time to push themselves further into the maws of New York society.

Peter Bovi, sitting at the end of the group from Greenwich, slumped further down in his seat. Antonina's performance had been incandescent. She'd been perfect. Brilliant. She'd never marry him now. She was a star and she wouldn't want to be bothered by being a doctor's wife. His handsome face saddened. Little Antonina, his childhood sweetheart. She might have been his wife. Ah, well. It was never going to come to that.

There was a thump, and a bundle of fur came flying over his head. He jumped up. The woman sitting behind him gasped. "Oh, my goodness! Excuse me!"

She was older than he. An attractive brunette, dressed well. She seemed to be by herself. "I didn't mean to hit you with my mink!" Red-faced, she hauled her fur back into her lap.

"If one has to be attacked at the opera, a mink isn't a bad thing to be hit with." Peter stood and half-bowed to her.

Her smile was impish. "I still apologize. I might have suffocated you."

"What a way to go." He turned completely, so that he was facing her. "I'm Peter Bovi...um, Doctor Bovi." He laughed easily. She was very attractive. "In case you injured me, I would be completely able to cure myself."

"A doctor! How convenient." She leaned forward, her full lips parted. Peter was tall and handsome and had a devastating smile. She wanted to pursue this encounter further..."Are you enjoying the opera? I'm Babs Ketchell, by the way. Just plain Babs...not a doctor, I'm afraid." Her eyes invited him.

His eyes answered. "The opera is marvelous. I'm a friend of the young lady singing Mimi." He gestured to the group that surrounded him. "And these are her friends and her family."

"Really?" Babs sat closer and looked curiously at his companions. "Why...did she sing? I mean, what happened to Vivienne du Lac?"

"I don't know. We were as surprised as anyone. No one knew that Antonina would be singing the role tonight." He paused, as if struck by a sudden thought. "Um, would you...I mean...would you care to go to the bar for a glass of champagne? I mean...I feel as if the fur coat sort of suffocated me and I need something to keep my throat lubricated."

"Why not?" She stood up, tossed the mink back, and accompanied him up the aisle.

From her seat, Francesca's eyes met those of Giovanna's. "I thought he might be broken-hearted, but he seems to have recovered."

"Rather quickly, don't you think, my dear friend?" The two women burst into laughter. They had been the best of friends since childhood, shared every dream and kiss and romantic sigh with one another. Shared their happy moments and their despair. They had each loved one another's children.

Giovanna adored Antonina, and Francesca would have been delighted if Peter had become Antonina's husband. But, the two of them felt, this would never come to pass now.

***

Barbara and David, with Beniamino Gigli standing prominently in their box, were inundated with opera lovers who wanted nothing more than to gaze at Gigli in awe. One little old lady had no interest whatsoever with Gigli. It was *Barbara* that she sought.

"Are you the one who is gathering women to raise money to refurbish this falling-down old building?" He voice was rusty, with a pronounced accent...maybe from Spain or South America.

"Why, yes."

"I am La Rue Lopez. I was born and raised in the Argentine."

"How do you do?"

"I do just fine, *Gracias*." The little woman bobbed her head. She looks just like a tiny bird, Barbara thought. "I want to give some money to you and to be a part of what you ladies are doing." Her head twisted to the side.

"How lovely!" Barbara clasped her hands together. "Can we meet?"

"I will call on you." The little lady stepped back. "Here is my card." She handed Barbara a small rectangle. "That young girl...Antonina Sabatino. She is magnificent, but what happened to Vivienne du Lac?"

"I don't know," Barbara pulled at David's sleeve. He shrugged, not having any idea either.

"Whatever it is, I'm glad that she's not singing tonight," The little woman nodded with vehemence. "She ruined a good friend's career and life some time back and I hope she's suffering with some dreadful ailment." She sniffed and turned away, her small personage swallowed up in the milling crowd.

"What did happen to du Lac?" Barbara asked David.

"I'm going to go backstage and find out." David bowed to Gigli, "Do you want to come backstage with me?"

"I will wait until the performance is over. I am astounded at the voice of this new *diva.*" He made an expressive gesture. "What do you know about her?"

"Very little," David responded, "but, rest assured, Signor Gigli, I will be knowing a lot more very soon."

***

The small conclave from Greenwich, including Vittoria and Concetta from Brooklyn, and Gina and James Drawbridge, sat in their seats while Enzo and Simeon went to get the women glasses of wine. As they left, Francesca nudged Simeon. "See if you can spy and tell me what Peter and that lady are up to." He winked and nodded.

"Mama, how did Antonina do that?" Lucia asked. "Get to sing, I mean. She was wonderful, but...what happened?"

"How revolting. I thought that there were always understudies."

"They're called covers," Gia tried to impress her twin. "Everyone knows that shattering term."

"Who cares what they're called...where was she, the cover, I mean?"

Urbano slipped through the small wooden door under the stage and entered the auditorium. "Vittoria!" He called. "Psst!"

"Urbano! Antonina! Such joy!" She hugged her husband. "But how...? What happened?"

Signor Fazzolini, almost weeping with pride, was also asking. "What happened? Was du Lac ill?"

Urbano gathered them in a close circle. "You must keep this a secret for a time. No one knows yet." He lowered his voice, "She was murdered in her dressing room." There was shock and horror on each face. "I have to go and get the police now." He disentangled his wife's fingers from his arms. "Sit still here after the performance is over. I will come to collect you all and we'll go somewhere quiet so that we can talk."

"Psst! Urbano!" Francesco De Sarro's head stuck out. *"Veni qua piano, piano!* Come quickly! The damn dog is missing."

"The *dog!*" Urbano slapped his forehead, forgetting about the police. "I must go, my sweetheart." He turned and wormed his way back through the little door.

The lights blinked once again, signaling that intermission was nearly over. Everyone began to go back to their seats, their boxes, or to the spot that they had staked out in the Standing Room Only areas. Everyone except Peter Bovi and his new friend. They stayed at the bar, sipping champagne and exchanging their life stories. Some of their revelations were true, and some rather embellished. Neither one seemed to care.

And thus, because of *Poupette*, Anderson von Vogel still sat in blissful ignorance through the next two acts, still not informed that a horrendous murder had taken place behind the golden curtains.

Chapter Thirteen

.....Death will come when thou art dead,
Soon, too soon...Percy Bysshe Shelley...To Night.

As Act Three came to a close, Anderson von Vogel, for the first time in his life, was in love. In love with a slip of a girl he had never seen before to-night, whom he had never met. A girl to whom he had never spoken. It was incredible. He couldn't even remember what her name was, but it mattered not. She was tied with golden chains to the beating of his heart.

He had tears in his eyes, she was going to die. She was so ill, so frail, and her consumptive coughing wracked her slender body. No matter that it was all an act, no matter that she was playing a part. His soul was shattered in sorrow. This slender child was ill, and nothing could save her from the clawed hands of death.

Surreptitiously, turning his face so that Helena would never know, he blotted his tears. He coughed, harrumphing to hide his emotions; he tried to swallow the lump of despair that lodged in his throat.

***

"Where are the police?" Calle asked Urbano.

Urbano smacked his brow. "Good, God!" He made a sound of frustration. "I forgot to go and tell him!"

"What does it really matter," With a Gaelic shrug, Calle scratched his chin. "She's not going anywhere."

Urbano sniggered. "She's lost her head over it all!" The two men fell upon one another, trying not to laugh. "Forgive me, Arturo. She is dead and it is really no laughing matter. The police are going to want to know everything that happened." He rolled his eyes. "They are not going to be overjoyed that we waited to tell them about this."

"I will take the blame." Calle shrugged. *I'm glad that I did what I did.*

"No, it was my fault. I just got caught up in the drama and…" Urbano shook his head. "I simply forgot." His eyes widened with astonishment. "Can you believe I am so callous?"

"Not only you, my dear Urbano, but all of us." Calle's face was grim. "They are going to be very angry with us…maybe even wonder if you or I might have cut her throat."

"We are all suspects, I would imagine. After all, it was probably someone backstage. Who else could it be?"

"A tramp?"

"Ha! How convenient. A tramp!"

"Maybe that little man she employed...that dwarf. He always gave me the creeps and I had heard rumors...none substantiated, however, that he was some sort of an assassin in Europe. That he had killed before."

"Crespi. She called him Crespi. Have you seen him here tonight?"

"I hadn't noticed." Urbano shrugged. "I think he was skulking round here yesterday. Crespi. Ha! If only it was going to be that easy."

"I agree. If only."

***

"Who wants to go to the movies?" Cliff Gustafson asked.

"Me!" His young daughter, Karen shrieked. "What is playing tonight?"

"The Marx Brothers in *The Cocoanuts.*" Cliff rumpled her long, pale hair.

"Oooh, I want to go, too!" Peter, his son, chimed in. "Me, too!"

"And me, three!" His wife, Evelyn, laughingly raised her hand. "Come on, let's get ready."

The light-bulb lit marquee of the Pickwick Theater beckoned. Already, there was a line to see the latest in the ever-growing movies shown. Ever since last year and the advent of Al Jolson's debut, the "talkies" reigned supreme on a week-end night. The Gustafson family stood, waiting to get their tickets. Just inside the lobby, they could smell the dizzying scent of popcorn, drizzled with butter. "Is this a funny one, Daddy?" Karen held Cliff's ham-like hand.

"The Marx Brothers are always funny, sweetheart." The line shuffled forward, step by step.

His Scandinavian ancestors had been tall men and Cliff was as tall as any. He towered over the three couples in front of them. With idle interest, he watched the girl in the ticket booth. She had a vapid expression on her face and her bee-stung lips vied with those of Clara Bow. She asked a question of the couple in the front. The couple nodded and the girl pushed a sheet of paper out. The woman wrote laboriously on the sheet and the man dug his hand into his pocket and brought out twenty cents to pay for the two tickets. The couple moved through the two swinging doors into the lobby and the line moved forward. Again, the girl....she was pretty in a dark, gypsy-like way...asked a question of the next couple and pushed a piece of paper out. The woman paid this time, and the man scribbled something on the paper.

There sure were a lot of people going to tonight's movie, Cliff looked back at the growing line behind him and noticed one man who slouched along, his head held at an odd angle. *Wasn't that Alvin Catchpole? The weird guy who Charlie and Pete interviewed about the robberies? What if it was? Even weird guys like the Marx Brothers. And speaking of weird guys, there*

163

were Rags and Jimmy Menendez slouching along, waiting to buy their tickets. His musings on the variety of Marx Brothers' aficionados were interrupted...

Someone was calling out. "Sir? *Sir?* "

It was Cliff's turn. "Four tickets please." The ticket seller was dressed up...*pretty fancy for a little town like Greenwich on a Saturday night,* Cliff thought. *Look at her jingle jangle jewelry and satin dress.*

"Forty cents, please." She was chewing gum and looked bored. Cliff dug the money out of his pocket.

"Daddy, can I have popcorn, please?" Karen pulled at his arm.

"Sure, honey." He fished some coins out and handed them to Karen. "Get some popcorn for yourself and get something for Peter, too." The children squealed and went into the lobby, heading for the glass counter that featured candy and snacks.

"Do you wanna be on our list?" The gum-chewing girl asked him.

"List?"

"Yeah. We gotta list of customers and we let you know what movie is coming and sometimes send you a free ticket or maybe a prize." The girl scratched herself. Her voice was mechanical and she shoved a yellow pad with a pencil attached to it by a piece of string out in front of Cliff. He shrugged and wrote his name on the list.

"What kind of prize," he asked.

"I donno. China or a soup plate." She didn't even look up. "Maybe an ash tray." She yawned and picked at a scab on her elbow. "Put down yer address, so we can send you stuff." The girl's gums chewed, moving like those of a cow. Cliff complied. The girl pulled back the list and snapped off four paper tickets from a slot on the counter. She gave them to Cliff. "Next!" The line moved and Cliff and Evelyn went into the lobby. Karen and Peter had their noses pressed to the candy counter's glass front.

Behind the counter, in back of the fat, spotty girl who was serving customers, lounged two young men. One wore baggy plus-fours with wrinkled stockings drooping over his calves. The other sported a sleeveless argyle sweater and shapeless pants, pegged close at the hems. They were both smoking, cigarettes dangling from their lips. *Louts,* thought Cliff.

"I want pecan fudge, Daddy," Peter cajoled. Cliff, ready to spend...after all...this was a night out at the movies with his whole family... asked Evelyn if she wanted anything to munch on.

She looked at the selection. "What's good?" She asked the fat girl behind the counter.

"Popcorn or fudge," the girl appeared indifferent. "An' we got licorice whips and jawbreakers."

"What kind of fudge?"

"We got peenoosh an' choc'late."

"Peenoosh? What's that?"

The girl rolled her eyes. "Peenoosh! You know, with maple an' walnuts." Her jaws, just like the girl selling tickets, were grinding with chewing gum.

"Ah! Penuche!"

"Yeah! Peenoosh." The girl flicked her eyes to the next customers. "Whaddaya want?"

"We'll have a bag of popcorn, one pecan fudge, one penuche and some licorice whips." Cliff held out a handful of money. "How much is that?"

"Twenny cents," the girl took his quarter and tossed it into a drawer, bringing out a nickel in change. Cliff handed Karen the bag of popcorn, fudge to Evelyn and Peter and put a licorice whip into his own mouth. He gave Karen a nudge, and, reluctantly, she gave him back his quarter. He winked at her and tweaked her hair. She grinned and they went into the darkened theater.

A tinny piano was pumping out music. The Pickwick was crowded, Cliff noted. Everyone liked a good laugh and The Marx Brothers, playing in *The Cocoanuts,* was sure to be a crowd-pleaser. He looked up and around, noting that Rags and Jimmy were seated in the front row of the balcony. He looked higher. The concave ceiling was painted a bright blue…just like a sky…and, as the lights blinked and then dimmed, tiny pinpricks began to glow, just like the real night sky lit up with stars. Karen, leaning back in her scratchy plush seat, gazed up, openmouthed.

"How do they get the stars to shine like that, Mommy?"

"They are very clever," Evelyn patted Karen's arm. "Now sit back…the News of The Week is on and then the cartoon."

They sat back, their feet up on the rim of the seat in front of them. The rest of the audience settled down and the screen exploded into a scene of a golf course. The announcer's plumy voice informed them that Bobby Jones had won the U.S. Golf Association's Amateur championship. The picture shifted to South America where a train, chugging along on the screen, smoke trailing in the air, broke the world's record from Buenos Aires to Chipoletti. The train raced along, covering 775 miles in 20 hours and 37 minutes. Karen opened the bag of popcorn, offered some to each of her family, and shoved a huge handful into her own mouth. The News of the World was of no interest to her.

A chirpy tune announced the cartoon. "Oh, boy! The cat and the mouse!" Peter loved the cartoons. A large, leering animated cat chased a hapless rodent, round and round some lady's bedroom. The mouse, with a huge grin on its little mouse face, turned around and hit the cat on the head with the lady's shoe. The mouse ran onto the dressing table and bonked the cat with the lady's pearl necklace. The children laughed uproariously. Even Cliff chuckled.

The cartoon, with the mouse winning every contest, ground to a halt. Next, a travelogue on the mountains of Spain appeared on the screen. Karen fidgeted.

"Come on, Marx Brothers," Peter begged.

"Did you see the kitty cat necklace that the girl had?" Karen poked her father.

He grunted, half-listening. "The kitty cat in the cartoon had a necklace, too."

"Hmmmm," Cliff nodded.

"That girl's necklace had a kitty cat with big green eyes." Cliff nodded again, but made no comment.

"I'd like a necklace like hers...Oh! Goody. It's starting!" Karen wiggled and turned her eyes up to the screen. A group of gypsies cavorted hugely above, and each of the Marx Brothers popped up, one by one. A small portion of Cliff's subconscious mind gnawed at something. Kitty cat necklace. Green eyes. Walnuts and pecans and popcorn. The *neck*lace! Aunt-by God-Millie's *neck*lace!

Cliff bolted upright. "Evie," he whispered. "I've gotta go to the station....No. You stay here and enjoy the show. I'll walk down. Be careful driving home and I'll see you a little later." He slid out of the row, bumping knees with several annoyed patrons.

With a sigh, wondering what that husband of hers was up to now, Evelyn turned her attention to Harpo Marx, who, in a duet with his brother Chico, was playing a Rachmaninoff tune. She began to laugh out loud at Harpo's facial expressions. With his mop of improbable hair and his endearing, yet peculiar face, he was her favorite Marx Brother. "I like Harpo the best," she whispered.

Karen poked her and said that her favorite was Chico and his gun-finger style of piano playing. "He's the silliest."

The actor...whoever was playing the romantic lead...began to sing a funny song about "Telling me and you, how to do, the monkey-doodle-doo." Evelyn ate a piece of fudge and wondered where her husband was and what crisis he suddenly remembered.

Cliff walked through the lobby. The lights had dimmed over the candy counter and the ticket booth was closed. The yellow pad with all of the names and addresses was gone as well as the two young men and the ticket seller. Only the heavy-set girl who doled out popcorn, candy and fudge remained. She was busy, cleaning up and refurbishing the shelves and candy display. She never looked up as Cliff exited.

***

Act Four began, with the audience transported back to the chilly attic in Paris. Rodolfo and Marcello sang gloomily of how fickle love was. And then, like a ray of brilliant light, Musetta returned. With tears in her eyes, she told them that Mimi was dying. Her last wish was to be back with her friends, in the little garret where she had once been so happy.

Anderson's hands were knotted with tension as he awaited Mimi's entrance. He sat up, shocked, as she stumbled onto the stage, supported by Musetta's strong arms. Henry Wu's skill was evident. She looked dreadful...deathly ill, with a grayed face and sunken eyes. She wore a dull gray dress, and it hung on her skeletal frame like a shroud. Even with the stamp of Death upon her, Mimi's beauty glowed, like a candle in a stormy night. She coughed and clutched at her consumptive chest. Anderson's heart lurched.

Rodolfo lowered her, tenderly, onto a chaise lounge that had been pushed into a position just off center stage. Mimi collapsed, barely able to breathe. Anderson almost leaped out of the box. How could he help his beloved? His Mimi?

The actors on stage, sick with concern and worry, all tried to keep Mimi warm and alive. Musetta stripped off her earrings and sent Marcello to buy medicine. Mimi's little hands were freezing, and Musetta herself left the attic to buy a muff to keep Mimi's hands warm. Mimi clutched at his arm and told Rodolfo that Musetta was a wonderful and generous friend.

Colline sang a eulogy to his faithful old coat, and then, decided to pawn it to buy some nourishing food for Mimi. Schaunard, who had nothing tangible to give, departed with Colline. *"If I can give them the gift of being alone together, then I will do so."*

Rodolfo knelt at Mimi's side and sang to her of his love. He dug into his pocket and pulled out the little bonnet that he had given her when their love was new. "You kept this bonnet, all this time?" Mimi's heart was full. He *did* love her! He always had loved her! He'd kept her bonnet all this time!

They sang of their love, of the past, reliving their joy. There was not one dry eye in the audience. No one, not even the most jaded and callous spectator, wasn't heavy of heart with tears spilling down. Blackburn and Harris, the two critics, wept openly. Their columns in the morning papers would herald the birth of a new star, brilliant in her firmament. For once, they would most likely be fervently in agreement. This young girl was the best Mimi they had ever seen.

On stage, Musetta brought a warm muff and enfolded Mimi's frozen little hands into its warmth. Mimi sighed with the bliss of warmth, at last. She closed her eyes to rest.

Rodolfo sang of their love, and how he would nurse her into the warmth of the springtime. How she would blossom under his tender care. Behind him, on the chaise lounge, the audience saw Mimi's tiny little hand fall out of the muff; they knew, even before Rodolfo, that she was dead.

From one of the boxes, a sharp intake...a gasp...*oh, no! No!*

And on stage, Rodolfo realized that his beloved has gone from him. He dropped to the floor in stunned realization. *"Mimi! Oh, Mimi!"*

***

The audience kept their cheering going for more than fifteen minutes. The principal players bowed and bowed, and Rodolfo had the sense to step back and let Musetta and then Mimi into the center of the stage. The audience stood and screamed, stamped and cried. They would not let the performers off the stage.

Rodolfo bowed to the *Maestro,* beckoning him to the stage. With measured tread, Massimo Orsini strode to the stage. The audience again went into a new frenzy. Massimo bowed deeply, honored and touched. The audience refused to let him descend. He turned and held Antonina's hand, bowed again over it and kissed it. The level of clapping, which had been at a deafening roar, increased…every man, woman and child was screaming, cheering, yelling, clapping and crying. It was delighted pandemonium unseen since Caruso had played *I Pagliacci* in his debut at the Met.

Page boys began to run to the footlights, each bearing an armful of flowers for the performers. The floor of the stage was littered with bouquets, one more beautiful than the next. Antonina stood, transfixed, astonished at the outpouring of approval and delight.

From the center parterre box, Beniamino Gigli leaped over the golden railing. Johnston Redmond saw him and immediately put on the large spotlight, illuminating Gigli's promenade to the footlights. He was helped up on the stage by two of the stronger musicians, Tommy and Dean, who hoisted him with their shoulders pushing his rear end up. Gigli seized Antonina's hand and bowed over it, kissing her hand and then holding her palm to his own heart. He scooped her up into his arms and turned her this way and that, allowing her to be adored and adulated. The audience went mad.

Antonina's eyes sought out those of her mother and then those of her beloved teacher. She blew them kisses and the audience bent forward, trying to see who she favored.

The houselights began to blink and then finally went on. The house was bathed in light from the huge chandelier. The performers finally slipped backstage, accompanied by Beniamino Gigli. There, they were engulfed by a tide of fellow performers, crying, back-slapping, kissing and laughing. They had pulled it off! This performance of *La Bohème* would go down in operatic history!

Chapter Fourteen

"Taffy was a Welshman, Taffy was a thief
Taffy came to my house to steal a piece of beef..." Anon.

This was a decided success. Mrs. Vanderhoof and Mrs. Burns both spoke with me. I know I will be invited to the Winter Ball." Helena's voice was plumy with satisfaction. "You might have been more forthcoming to them, Anderson." She chided. "You never put yourself forward in social situations."

She picked up her fur wrap. "Nonetheless, despite your boorishness, I was able to manage the situation." She sniffed. "I wonder why I even forced you to come tonight!"

Anderson was silent, remembering every moment of the opera. *Thank God she insisted. I might have never known my beloved.*

A rustle at the back curtain of their borrowed box. "Chief von Vogel? I'm not too sure if you remember me." Urbano bowed slightly. "I am Urbano Valeria, the Stage Manager here. We met at the…"

"Of course, I remember you, Signor Valeria. Sam Lamonica introduced us." The two men shook hands. "Your production was memorable. The young lady who sang Mimi…"

"Ah, yes, she is the daughter of one of my wife's best friends. Antonina." Urbano smiled. "Magnificent, would you not say?"

"Magnificent," Anderson agreed.

Look at the fool, Helena watched her husband. *He knows nothing or less about opera. Stupid man.*

"May I introduce you to my wife? Helena, this is Urbano Valeria, who makes all of this magic happen with apparent effortlessness. And these are my daughters, Clair and Chloe." Urbano bowed over Helena's hand and nodded to the two girls, who nodded back woodenly in tandem to him.

"If I may, Chief von Vogel, can we speak privately outside?" Urbano's voice held a tremor.

"Of course. Excuse me, Helena.*"*

The two men stepped outside of the box. Sighing, Helena sat back down, watching the departing audience. "He's never here when I need him," she griped to Chloe and Clair, patting her coiffure. "What kind of a husband leaves his wife like that?" No one answered and so she prattled on: "Look at that old cow," she pointed out a large patroness to the girls. "She's too fat to wear a dress like that!"

"Chief...sir...I am sorry that I have waited so long....but...the original soprano, Vivienne du Lac...."

"She is ill?"

"She is dead."

"Dead?"

"Yes. Someone killed her and left her body, nearly decapitated, in her dressing room."

***

I'm really out of shape, Cliff groaned to himself, as he huffed and puffed the nearly two miles down Greenwich Avenue. Luckily, near the middle of the avenue, he was passed by a ramshackle truck belonging to Mac Ardle's Nursery.

"Hey! Hey! Johnny Tomato!" Cliff hollered, jogging after the truck. The truck screeched to a stop and stood, trembling with its rickety motor misfiring.

"Who is that?"

"Me! Cliff Gustafson!"

"Hey, Cliffy! What the Sam Hill are you doin' runnin' around in the middle of then night?"

Cliff hauled his wheezing body up into the truck. "I'm trying to catch a couple of crooks."

"They run faster than you?"

Cliff laughed. "Nah, they're God knows where, but I know who they are. I'm trying to get to the station." He puffed and sucked a gulp of air. "Jeez! I'm too old to run down the street anymore."

"Wanna tell me more?"

"Not now, Johnny. But you saved my life, picking me up...What are you doing out here so late?"

"Big load of manure, up at the Harriman estate. Took me four hours to shovel it all out."

"Thank God."

"Here you are," the truck shuddered to a stop in front of the police station. "Remember this if you catch me speeding."

"I'll give you a medal," Cliff clapped Johnny on his shoulder as he climbed down. "Thanks again. You saved me from a heart attack."

The station was dim, lit only with a night light at the front desk. "Hey! Anyone around?" Cliff yelled.

From the bowels of the building, he heard Herbie Floyd's voice calling. "Who's there?"

"Me, Cliff. I'm gonna use the telephone." Cliff went to the desk and called Chief McAndrews. "Chief? Can you get down to the station?... Yeah...I think I've solved the shitting bandits case."

There was a long pause at the other end. McAndrews spoke into his telephone: "No shit?" And then a snort of laughter.

"No shit!" Cliff chortled. "Wait until you get here. It's gonna be good...I think."

"I hope so. We got a great canasta game going here."

"Just keep the cards on the table. No peeking. Get your duff over!" Herbie lumbered in to the office. "What's up?"

"Where were you? The goddamn door was wide open!"

"Gee, Cliffy. I was takin' a whiz downstairs. I was only gone a minnit!"

Cliff laughed and went to his locker. He donned his police uniform and hat. As he went back into the lobby, Chief McAndrews' car drove up. Cliff hurried out, strapping on his holster and gun.

"Drive back to the Pickwick Theater. We're gonna first talk to the manager. What's his name? Steinway?"

"Stein*metz*...Harry Steinmetz. What's going on?"

"It was the kitty cat necklace." Cliff explained his hunch. The car stopped at the Pickwick Theater. The show was still running, the lobby dim and deserted.

Cliff knocked at the door behind the candy counter.

A short, stout man with a toothbrush mustache opened the door a crack. "What is it?"

"Mr. Steinmetz? I'm Police Chief Emerson McAndrews." Emerson pushed open the door. Cliff entered behind him looking like some huge avenging angel. Steinmetz stepped back, fearful. *Had they found out about the counterfeit tickets?*

"What's wrong?"

"Your ticket girl. What's her name and her address?"

"What do you want to know for?" Steinmetz queried, trying to bluff. "We don't give out that kind of information."

"Certainly you do." With a ferocious, yet amicable grin, Cliff came closer. "And we want the names of the young ruffians who keep her company behind the candy counter. And the name of the girl who sells the candy, and when we finish talking to them, we'll want to have a long, comfortable session with you."

"Me?" squeaked Steinmetz. "For what?"

"Oh, you'll be told all about it soon enough. Now, where is the information?"

Steinmetz scratched his chin. Nevermind the ticket scam...Was it possible that these coppers also knew that he was skimming the take? He opened the bottom drawer of his desk and pulled out a folder. "The ticket girl is Selena Roxbury. She lives at 207 Harold Avenue." His eyes were wary.

"How old is she and how long has she worked here."

"She's seventeen. Worked here for maybe eighteen months." Cliff nodded, writing in his notebook. He licked the stub of his pencil and flipped a page over.

"And the Rover Boys?"

"The one who is Selena's boyfriend is Ernie Soames. His buddy is Lorne Roxbury, Selena's older brother."

"Are they always hanging around the lobby? Doncha have any scruples about who smells up the place?"

Steinmetz shrugged. "They don't do anything wrong. They sometimes do a few errands for me...take out the garbage...sometimes they even do some ushering here..."

"And the candy counter girl?"

"She just started here two weeks ago. Her name is Arleen Hanulka. She lives in Byram....um, 56 Chapel Street. What's going on?"

"Never you mind, Harry. What time will you be closing up here?"

"The movie's over at nine-thirty. I count the take and bag it up, then check the theater out, then I lock up. And go home."

"Where's home?"

"Are you going to show up at my house tonight?" Steinmetz bit at his lip. His wife would have kittens if the cops came to their house.

"Maybe. Maybe tomorrow." Cliff slapped his notebook shut. "Don't think of taking any vacations to the Riviera."

The two policemen got back into the car and drove off. Cliff twisted in his seat to look back. Steinmetz was watching them leave.

"You think he's involved?"

"For his sake, I hope not. He's scared of something, though."

"Maybe he was bonking the ticket girl and his wife is a jealous woman."

"Maybe. Where the heck is Harold Avenue? Oh, yeah. Off Saint Roch's, right?"

"Right." He rubbed his chin. "Maybe the fat girl at the candy counter isn't involved. She's too new to the Pickwick."

"Again, maybe.....Here's the house." The car glided silently to a stop in front of a two story stucco house. There were lights in several of the rooms. The men got out and walked up a short flight of steps to the porch. Cliff rang the bell.

The curtain the hung in the window of the front door was pulled aside. A woman with her hair in curlers peeked out with worried eyes. She gasped as she saw Cliff's uniform. The chain lock rattled and she peered out. "What's the matter?"

"Mrs. Roxbury?" She nodded, fearful. She opened the door. She was wearing a pink and green chenille bathrobe and on her feet were too-large men's slippers. "I'm Detective Clifford Gustafson. This is my Chief, Chief McAndrews. Is you daughter Selena or your son Lorne at home?"

Mrs Roxbury's eyes grew rounder. She stepped further back, clutching the collar of her robe. "Why? Why do you want to know?"

"Ma'am, please...are they here?"

She gave him a hunted look, turned around and called up the stairs, "Selena! Selena!"

"Whaddaywant?" A screech came from above.

"Come down."

"Wa-hat?"

A yell. "Get down here!"

They saw her come down the stairs. She was barefooted and had a Japanese-type silk kimono wrapped around her. Her hair was piled high on her head and she was still wearing a great deal of make-up. Her neck was bare of any necklace. Cliff noted that her sulky, petulant expression had followed her home.

When she saw the two men, she stiffened. Her eyes widened and she blinked and stepped back up one step. *She's guilty as sin,* Cliff smiled in satisfaction to himself.

"Miss Roxbury? Selena?" Warily, she nodded.

"Is there somewhere we can speak in private?" Mrs. Roxbury gasped again.

"Selena? What's going on here?"

"Please, Mrs. Roxbury. We'd like to talk with your daughter alone." Selena's countenance collapsed and she looked terrified.

"Selena? Do you want me...?"

"Don't worry, Ma. Leave us alone." Selena's voice held a wobbly bravado. Mrs. Roxbury looked ill, but she shuffled away, motioning them to use the living room. Cliff flapped his hand and Selena slowly led them into a neat and clean living room, obviously rarely used. They sat down, Selena on a brown couch covered with a brown, crocheted afghan. Cliff sat on an arm chair, and Chief McAndrews perched stiffly on a hard side chair. They all looked at each other.

"What would you like to tell me about your pretty necklace that you were wearing tonight?" Selena pushed herself further back into the cushions and tried to look as if she didn't know what he was talking about.

"You do remember me from tonight, don't you?" Cliff smiled gently at her.

"I bought four tickets from you and saw your little cat necklace."

She recoiled, clutching at her naked neck, not quite remembering if she was still wearing the necklace or not. Not. Cliff saw a gleam of relief in her eyes. She shook her head, still hopeful that she might be able to fool him. "I don't remember each person. There are a lot of customers."

"And you get each customer's name and address, don't you....?"

She knew that he knew. Suddenly, she began to cry and the torrent of tears dripped through the heavy make-up. She snuffled and knuckled at her eyes. (Cliff and Emerson looked wearily at one another...*the women...they always cried. Did they think that we'll just roll over and feel sorry for them?*). "Selena?"

She wiped her eyes and her nose on the sleeve of the silk kimono. Her face was streaked with the black soot of her eye make-up. "You know already," Her voice was a mumble.

"We want to hear it all from you. Is your brother here, by the way?"

Oh, God! They do *know! They know it all!* "He's...he's out..." Her eyes slid away, desperate now.

"Out robbing some poor schnook who is enjoying an evening out at the movies, isn't he? Him and his good little henchman, Ernie Soames?"

She sniffed again, knowing that the party was over. She nodded.

"Which house are they at?"

She shrugged. "They copied the list and took it. I don't know which house they'll try to...try to....go to."

"Tell us how this all started, Selena. We're going to be speaking with all of you, so you may as well just tell us the truth. It will go better for you."

Like a trapped animal who couldn't escape, she capitulated. "The manager, Mr. Steinmetz, thought it would be a hotsy-totsy idea to get all of the names and addresses of the movie customers. He thought he could send them a little coupon for the next show, maybe give them a half-price ticket...something like that...and get more people to come to the shows. Ernie saw the list and said that all these people were here in the movie theater...for maybe two hours...and their homes were empty. Wouldn't it be a great time to go and see what treasures they might have? And so they started, maybe six months ago, to go and....and...."

"Rob houses?" Emerson prodded. She sighed, and nodded yes.

"So it was Ernie's idea?"

"Yeah...I think he thought of it first. They went to some house and no one was there and they brought back a pile of stuff from there...the cat necklace...I wanted that. I thought it was so nice. They...much of the stuff, they sold. They split the money and gave some to me." She sighed again, wondering if she was going to jail.

"Did the other girl..." Cliff flipped his notebook pages back, "Arleen Hanulka...is she involved in any of this?"

"No. She's a big, fat, stupid lunk. We never much even speak to her. We'd never include her..." Her voice drifted off. *What's going to happen to me? Do they whip people in prison?*

"Did Mr. Steinmetz have anything to do with this?"

Selena shook her head. "No. It was just us."

"Let's go up to your room, Selena." Cliff stood up and motioned to her. She led the way up the stairs, her mother watching from the kitchen doorway with sick and worried eyes, clutching the neck of her chenille robe, as if to ward off pestilence and starvation.

Selena's bedroom was a jungle of scattered clothing, slung over chairs and on the floor. Her bed looked as if it hadn't been made in days. There were cigarette stubs in overflowing ash trays and her dressing table top was a mess of spilled powder and carelessly-thrown-down jewelry. The room smelled like cheap perfume and unwashed laundry. Cliff's pencil picked up a cheap gilt bracelet, a gimcrack ring, and then…the heft of Aunt Millie's gold, emerald and diamond necklace. "This the one that they stole from the first robbery?" Selena nodded, her mouth turned down. "And what else came from their little journeys?"

She sifted through a tangle of chains and bangles. She pulled out a small silver cross on a silver chain, a wristwatch, and a strand of pearls.

"What else," Cliff loomed over her. Making a hopeless face, she went to the closet and pulled out a large wooden cigar box. She threw it on the bed. It disgorged an undigested meal of gold chains, rings, bracelets and necklaces. Cliff poked into the pile and hooked a delicate engagement ring. "I think this is the Laulette's…"

"Tell us about the little gifts that your brother and your boyfriend left?"

Selena's eyes flew to his face and her own face blushed a painful, patchy red. "You mean…?"

"The shit. Yes, my dear. That's exactly what we mean. What prompted them to do such a stupid thing?'

"It seemed really funny." She snorted. "It *is* funny! Think of them people, coming home…and finding…" She giggled and then saw their faces and stopped.

"Very amusing. Whose idea was it?" She shrugged.

"Donno. I guess Ernie had to…needed…and he…and then Lorne did it too…and then they thought it was so hysterical….they started to do it every time." She rubbed her face. "They'd come and bring…whatever….what they found…and then we'd all have a drink and laugh and laugh and laugh."

"Good thing you got to laugh, because you're not going to be doing too much in the way of laughter for the foreseeable future." Cliff stood up. "Get a few things together. We're taking you to the jail." From outside Selena's door, a wail went up. Selena nodded hopelessly, picked some clothes off the floor, and went into the upstairs bathroom to dress. Cliff stayed upstairs with her. McAndrews gathered up what evidence he could see and brought it to the police car, then he went back upstairs and into Lorne's bedroom.

"What a shithole!" McAndrews swore. He thought the room smelled like old socks and cigarette smoke. He opened the top drawer of the nightstand.

There were rolls of bills stashed there, as well as six or seven wristwatches. A newish radio sat on top of the nightstand. Maybe the one that belonged to the Crokers. McAndrews then rummaged in the rest of the drawers, finding three boxes of jewelry under Lorne's underwear and socks. *Why do people think that no one will ever look under the socks? That's the first place we look, right after looking in the top drawer.*

He gathered up as much as he could carry and dropped it into an empty cardboard box that was in Lorne's closet. *And now, let's take a looky-see at the shelf in the closet...that's another spot where things try to get hidden. Aha!* McAndrew pulled down a box filled with silver objects, candlesticks, trinket boxes...some assorted pitchers and forks and spoons.

*And the next most popular spot...*McAndrews went into the bathroom and shoved his hands behind Mrs. Roxbury's neat stacks of towels. *Aha!* A bundle of glass and china objects...*they can never really hide stuff from us...all these petty, foolish, miserable little crooks...they all always put it in the same places!*

As McAndrews filled the car with Lorne's contraband, Mrs. Roxbury stood by the doorway. "What shall I do?" Mrs. Roxbury's hands twisted and untwisted. "Her father...when he gets some...he's gonna kill her."

"Do you have a lawyer?"

"A lawyer!" Even more frightened, she shook her head...no.

"Where is your husband?"

"He's on the nightshift at American Felt...ohhhh, he's gonna be angry."

"I'd get in touch with him, if you can. Maybe try to find a lawyer. You're going to need one for her and your son." Cliff watched her, feeling sorry for her. Both of her children were going to jail. "And, Mrs. Roxbury...we have locked both bedrooms. Your daughter's and your son's. No one is to go into them." She nodded, hopeless and frightened.

McAndrews used her telephone and called Charlie Presto and Pete Kraut. "Get dressed and come over here...Bring your fingerprint kits and be ready for a nice search to see what else you can find."

Cliff drove off with Selena. McAndrews waited at the Roxbury house. Cliff deposited Selena in a cell. "Make her some tea or coffee and make her a few peanut butter sandwiches." He instructed Herbie. "We'll be back in about an hour with a couple of more guests for you." Herbie whinnied with delight. He was happiest when the jails were filled with a few guests and he could cook and clean. *He should'a been an innkeeper,* Cliff thought.

Cliff watched Herbie watch Selena. "Oh, and don't feel too sorry for her. She's not worth it. She's a cheap little chippie who was wearing all the finery that was stolen from honest folks. Don't waste any sympathy on her, Herb."

He drove back to the Roxbury house. As he approached it, he saw a car stopping. It was a dark car, a jalopy...and there were two young men in it.

Cliff walked up, and as he approached the car, the driver saw him and tried to start the car back up. Out of the darkness, Chief McAndrews loomed, slamming his fist on the car's roof. "Don't even *think* of trying to drive away!" Cliff opened the passenger side door. "You're both under arrest!"

Cliff opened the trunk. It was filled with silverware, candlesticks, and several other items. He shut the trunk and sauntered back to the driver's side. Ernie Soames had his head in his hands. Lorne Roxbury sat, hunched forward in his seat, crying. "Little bastards," Cliff commented. "Little shitting bastards."

***

Several hours later, Emerson wearily dropped Cliff off at his house. All the lights were blazing. "Evelyn is obviously still up," Cliff sighed. "Wanna come in for a second or two?" McAndrews, longing for his own bed, hesitated, but by that time, Evelyn Gustafson had already come outside.

"Oh, no! You're both not going anywhere! You'll both want to come in, I *know!"* Her voice was a steel command. "Come and see."

"What? *Oh, no!* It wasn't *our* house that they hit, was it?"

"Come on in, my good men." She shepherded them into the hall. Karen and Peter were in their footed pajamas, their eyes shining with excitement and glee. "Daddy! Daddy...See what the shitting bandits..." There was a delighted giggle from Peter. Saying bad words was delicious!... "have left us!"

Emerson and Cliff shuffled into the living room. There, piled on the hearthrug in front of the fireplace, were two smelly lumps. Cliff sighed, "Shit on. I'm a cop and we've been shit on."

"Ooooh, bad words, Daddy!" Karen danced over to him. "Wait until you see what they stole!"

"What did they take?"

"About fifty dollars from my sugar-bowl," Evelyn griped. "They took our radio, Karen's jewelry box, your grandfather's watch, most of our silver dishes, and the typewriter from your office." She smiled, though. "And, they took some time to go into our kitchen. Remember, I baked cookies last night?" Cliff nodded. He'd been looking forward to some of the cookies after they'd gotten home from the movies. "They ate them all...*and*...they helped themselves to a bottle of milk from our refrigerator."

"They ate my *cookies?"*

"Silly man, yes they did. And, I am assuming that the nice, clean bottle of milk has some lovely fingerprints on it. I will make you all a present of it. I'd never..." she shuddered... "use that bottle again!" She turned around and pointed her finger at the two men. "Now get that mess cleaned up! *Right away!"*

Cliff began to clean up the mess. He stopped, looking sheepish. "I'm such a dumb animal, Ev. All our stuff is in the back of the goddamn car! I was just looking at it and I didn't even realize that it was our stuff!"

"Some crack detective I've married!" Evelyn reached up and gave Cliff's cheek a big smacking kiss.

***

With a sense of heady anticipation, Anderson von Vogel instructed his wife and daughters to take themselves home. Helena was angry. She had planned to have Anderson escort them to Romanoff's Restaurant for a post-opera supper.

"You will have to go without me, if you still want supper," Anderson, his mind already involved in the murder, rushed out of the box with Urbano.

"I'll get someone *else* to take me!" Helena shook her fist. "You always put your work first!"

"Good, good…" Anderson's absentminded answer floated back to her as he hurried down the stairs leading to the back stage area.

*"Bas*tard!" Helena hissed again. "Who needs you?" She gathered their wraps. "Come on, girls. We'll go by ourselves. We'll find …we'll find some-one who *will* give us supper."

***

"No one is to leave." Anderson gave orders quickly. "You can let the au-dience go, but every person attending must fill out a card with their names and addresses and where we can contact them tomorrow." Urbano nodded sharply and assigned six of the ushers to be at each of the exits.

"Call Pedar Pedersen at my office," Anderson rattled out the telephone number to Sigrid Chalmers. "Ask him to call John Dempsey, the Coroner. Tell him to bring Buddy Manger, Abe Featherman…the usual guys…and seven or eight more men with him and be prepared to do a scene of crime in-vestigation." Anderson smiled. "And tell him it is a murder and I want him here in six minutes!" He rubbed his hands.

"Now! I will take a look at the crime scene," he gestured to Urbano. "And no one from the cast," and here Anderson looked around, trying to see if that beautiful girl was in sight. "No one is to leave. After I see what's what with the body, I will be interviewing everyone…first the cast, then your staff, then the rest of the people who work here…everyone. Get them something to eat. It's going to be a long night." He motioned to Urbano and Urbano directed him to follow to Vivienne's dressing room.

"Where's her dog?" Urbano asked Henry Wu as they passed in the hall-way.

"The dog got out of the room. It was barking and going crazy. One of the stagehands….I think it was your friend, Francesco….tried to catch her, but she bit him and squirmed away. Ran…who knows where." He gave a delicate shrug, delighted that the dog and du Lac would never bother him again.

They opened the door. The room was a blizzard of clothing, make-up, fur-niture tipped on its side, blood, and, of course, the head and body of Vivienne du Lac. "*Jee*-zus!" Anderson gasped. "What the hell ....what the *hell!*" He gazed around, incredulous. "Who...? Who made all of this *mess?*" His mouth dropped. "She...did you touch the body?" He turned, aghast..."You never should move a body*! Never!*"

Urbano shrugged, helpless. "I may as well tell you all the bad things we've done, or not done." He stepped into the room. "We not only moved the body, but when we did move it...we had to get her costume off...we...she...her head...it was only attached by a small strip of skin. Whoever cut her throat almost cut her entire head off, and we...well...we...the head...it fell." He sighed. "And then, even worse, when her head rolled over there...the dog jumped out and he frightened the understudy and she fell into the body and the blood. We had to get her out and into a room so a doctor could see her...she broke her leg...and then...and then..." Urbano wound down.

"And what else did you cock-up?" Anderson sat down, completely flummoxed. He'd never seen such a balled-up investigation scene. One that had been so thoroughly messed up.

"Well, we had to get Antonina dressed." Anderson's eyes widened at her name. He tore his mind away from the vision of Mimi and forced himself to be a policeman, not a besotted opera aficionado. Urbano continued, "She had to have the dress. We...we didn't know what else to do. We had thousands of people out there. We didn't want you to know right away. We were afraid that you might not let us put the opera on." He hung his head, pretending to be shamefaced, but secretly glad that he had confessed to all of their transgressions...well, almost off them. There were still secrets that he kept... What the hell else could they have done? He blurted it out; "What else could we do?"

Anderson gave him an exasperated look, then bent down and touched the cold, blood-soaked remains of Vivienne's body. He peered at the ragged cut of her throat, careful not to touch the body. He straightened up and laughed, "Why the hell I am being so careful about touching the body, I'll never know! Everyone and their sister backstage has already been in here, pushing and pulling, stepping in the blood! Tell me, why am I even bothering?"

"I will apologize again, Chief von Vogel."

"Please, call me Anderson. I feel as if we already have been though a washing machine wringer together."

"Fine. I will apologize again, Anderson." Urbano's hands were out in supplication. "I am, of course, Urbano. And all of us, well, we were very bad boys!"

"Ah, well. You meant well, even if you have completely destroyed any clues that might have been here. No one is to come in here now," Anderson ordered. "We will treat this as a scene of crime."

"But...tomorrow..." Urbano looked worried. "Tomorrow we have a matinee with Patrice Fortesque singing. This should be her dressing room!"

"This is crazy!"

"This is opera!"

"Well, Patrice...whoever she is... will have to dress somewhere else." Anderson's voice was stern. *"No one is to get into this room from now on unless I give express permission!"*

Urbano made a face, shrugged before Anderson's authority and then left to tell Arturo Calle to make some alternative arrangements for Patrice.

In the dressing room, Anderson knelt on the floor to examine what he could of the already-disturbed blood patterns. The blood puddle went under the dressing table skirt and Anderson lay flat on the floor, holding up the skirt, to see what he could see. The door of the dressing room opened. He lay still, hidden from view by the heap of clothing and the hassock. He heard footsteps and saw a pair of trim ankles ending in black, lace-up demi-boots. The boots and whoever was wearing them clicked toward him.

He heard a voice..."What a mess! Poor Vivienne." He stiffened. He recognized that voice. Someone rummaged through the objects on top of the dressing table. He sat up suddenly and Antonina screamed.

There was an immediate pounding of footsteps and the door burst open. Timothy Weaver stood in the doorway. He saw Antonina at the dressing table, a drape of pearls in her hand, her mouth open in astonishment. He swiveled his head and saw a man on the floor. "Gotcha!" Tim's considerable bulk leaped and grabbed Anderson's arm. "Hey! Hey!" he yelled. "I got the killer!"

Antonina gasped. "The killer? He killed her?" She stepped back, right into the pool of blood. "Oh!" She jumped. "Oh! Oh!" She slid in the sticky substance, teetered for a moment, and then fell to her knees.

Anderson's head moved slowly from side to side. *Please, God! How many other people would be tromping in the evidence?* He tried to stand, but Tim pushed him back, snarling. "Don't you move! I've got you!" Tim raised his strong fist in the air, ready to punch. Antonina grabbed the hassock and pulled herself to her feet. The hem of her dress was stained with crimson.

"You've got it all wrong, pal." Anderson waved a placating hand in the air. "I'm Anderson von Vogel, Chief of Police."

Tim's face creased in confusion. "Police?"

"Police." Anderson's voice was firm. "Just get Urbano here and he'll vouch for me."

"Police? Are you certain?" Tim's fist wavered. "You...you're not trying to fool me?"

Urbano ran into the room. *"Now* what?" He surveyed the occupants. "What's going on here? This room is supposed to be closed off!"

"Closed off?" Anderson began to laugh as he got to his feet. "The lobby at Grand Central Station has less traffic than this room." He dusted off his hands and wiped them on the dressing table skirt. "There's a knife under this table. It is probably the one thing in this room that hasn't yet been touched. Let's be sure that no one...and I mean *no* one..." He glared at Tim and Antonina... "Touches anything...*anything* in this room!"

"Gee, man. I'm sorry. I heard a scream and I....well...I...I thought..." Tim backed away.

Anderson turned to Antonina. "And who are you and why are you taking that necklace?" *Who was she? She was his heart's delight.* Anderson tried to keep his voice from cracking. "No one is supposed to be in here."

She turned toward him, her gray eyes huge. "I'm ...I am Antonina Sabatino. I'm a soprano...I sang tonight. There wasn't anyone else to sing..." She drew herself up, glaring at him. "How was I to know that you were hiding in here, waiting to pounce on me?"

"I wasn't hiding, young lady!" How had she put him into the wrong? "I was trying, although Lord knows it is a stupid thing for me to try to do in this lunatic asylum you all call the opera....but I was *trying,*" his word was sarcastic, "to see if I might, just *might,* be able to solve a murder!" He glared at her, his blood pumping.

She watched him for a moment, her own blood high. *What a handsome man he was! And how angry he was!* She felt the heat rise in her body. *Anderson von Vogel?* She tipped her head. Gracious...a duchess giving a good-day to one of her lieges. "Shall we make peace, Mr. von Vogel?"

She was the most beautiful girl...no...woman...he had ever seen. "I think we can be friends, Miss Sabatino." He bowed toward her. "And may I compliment you on your performance. It was the best I have ever seen," *And the only opera I have ever seen, but she doesn't need to know that.*

"It is *Chief* von Vogel," Urbano said. "He is the Police Chief."

"Ah, the police chief! Did you see the performance?" *Had he thought her beautiful?*

"Yes. Thank goodness I was here. My men should be along in a few minutes and we will be speaking with everyone involved with the opera."

"Tonight? Now?"

"Yes. I am sorry to detain all of you, but it is necessary that we have a short interview with everyone. I will try to make it as quick as possible."

"Oh. My mother and friends and relatives are waiting in their seats. Can I tell them that I will be late?"

"Certainly. And please tell all of the performers and staff that we will be as quick as possible. If they need to use the telephone, I can open Mr. Calle's office and they can take turns calling home. We will, after we are finished, help to take any of your people to wherever they need to be taken." He stopped, as if struck by a thought. "And, Miss Sabatino, as your family is waiting, I will interview you first...right after I finish what I want to do in this room, if you will all leave now." He bowed to Antonina and she nodded to him, biting her lips.

"Chief!" A group of men came into the room. "Here we are." Pedar looked around, wondering what the hell was going on. "Dempsey is on my heels and three more men will be here within twenty more minutes. He looked around. "Is this where...? Oh!" He noticed Vivienne's head. "Oh, my sweet Aunt Mary!"

"It's a unique situation, Pedar," Anderson smiled. "I will put you into the very confusing picture." He made shooing motions and the room cleared.

"What the hell is going on?" Pedar and Buddy came close to the head and body. "What happened?"

"Damned if I know," Anderson gestured. "This is going to be a doozey."

Chapter Fifteen

"Here comes a candle to light you to bed. Here comes a chopper to chop off your head..." An anonymous nursery rhyme

*U*rbano quickly told Anderson his version of what had happened. "Who do you think are the most important witnesses?" Anderson asked.

"The ones who were involved around the time of Vivienne's murder?" Anderson nodded. Urbano thought back...then counted on his fingers: "Her maid, Celestina. The creepy little dwarf who works for her. His name is Crespi. Janet, the women's dresser, Henry Wu, the make-up man. I think those were the ones who saw her just before....well, just before."

"And who found the body?"

"James, the caller. He's a young boy...nephew of Sigrid Chalmers. He's potsy about operas and wants to work backstage as soon as he gets a little older. We've had him here for two years or more. I don't think he had anything to do with...well..." Urbano shrugged. "He found her anyway. He yelled and then I guess I came and Calle came and maybe Redmond and Weaver were there..." he tried to remember... "The corridor was seething with people...and then, of course, Ignatzia came in here to get dressed. Janet and Celestina were with her. She fell when the dog...and then Angelique and then Antonina were in here...who else...?"

"Just half the population of New York City!" Anderson threw up his hands in mock surrender. "Are all operas this crazy?"

Urbano shrugged. Crazy? Not crazy...but perhaps a little different from the usual, routine of ordinary people's existence. "Crazy? I guess so."

"All right, you keep trying to think and write down *anything* you can recall that could be important. I will interview Celestina and Janet, then Angelique and Antonina....and Calle and Massimo Orsini.*" Had I slipped in her name naturally? Will he think I am trying to see her?* "Pedar will interview Redmond, Sigrid and Timothy Weaver, and Henry Wu..."

Urbano wrote the lists. Anderson continued. "Buddy Manger, my young detective, will interview the rest of the cast, and Abe Featherman will speak with the rest of the stage staff. Marvin Michaels, one of my junior men, will talk to the orchestra and the chorus. These will be very brief interviews, and we'll try to get everyone out of here as soon as we can."

"And then?" Urbano was curious about the aftermath of a murder, as he was curious about everything that impacted his beloved Met.

"We put together a timeline, compare notes, and then try to see if any name or names pop out as worthy of more questioning. Naturally, those who saw her last, or saw her right after the murder, will get the most scrutiny, at least for now. But the second round of questions can wait until tomorrow."

"Tomorrow, you must remember, there is another show going on. The principal singers from *La Bohème* will not be back here until Monday afternoon, as we have another performance on Monday night."

"Another show? Another performance?"

"It's easy to see that you don't know a great deal about opera." Urbano laughed. "The show that is performed on Saturday night is usually performed again on Monday night."

"Is the audience the same?"

"Sometimes, but generally, the box holders share their boxes. Mrs. Smith may only go on Mondays, and she might rent the box for Saturday night performances to Mr. Jones."

"So I can see the performance all over again on Saturday night?" *Oh, joy! Oh, rapture!*

"It will be worth it! With all the publicity, Vivienne's murder getting in to the papers and the roaring success of Antonina's performance, we will not have room for an extra mouse on Monday night!" Urbano was delighted. "Not that I would wish anyone being beheaded, but this will make people flock to see our show."

"And then *La Bohème* is finished?" *Shall I ever see her again after this?*

"Yes, but many of the same performers…the same orchestra…the same chorus…will be performing *La Traviata* next Saturday night and next Monday night."

"La…what?"

"We shall have to instruct you in the gentle art of becoming an opera lover…*La Traviata*. A wonderful opera by Verdi with magnificent music." He jumped up. *"Christ!* I hope Antonina can sing Violetta!" He flashed Anderson a hunted look and ran out of the room, crying for Antonina.

He found her sitting in the audience with her family, telling them her version of what was going on. Peter wasn't there. He had left with his new friend. Antonina didn't even notice.

"Bella!" He embraced Antonina. "Can you sing Violetta?"

"Of course she can," Signor Fazzolini scoffed. "She can sing anything."

Antonina laughed. "I can sing Violetta, *Zio* Urbano. I know it well, as my sisters' eye-rolling will tell you. They are all revoltingly sick and tired of me singing Violetta all over the house. It is one of my favorite roles."

"Dio grazie!" Urbano kissed her hands. "That detective wants to talk with you and then you can all go home." He turned to his wife, "Why don't you and Concetta go home. Concetta, are you feeling well?" She rubbed her

belly and nodded. Who would have thought there would be so much excitement? "Francesco and I will be home as soon as we are able. I think the subway runs until two in the morning."

"The rest of you go on home," Francesca told her group. "I will stay here and wait for Antonina. I don't want her on the train by herself so late."

"I will wait with you," Her brother, Dario, offered. "And Simeon? You, too? Good. It will be late when Antonina is finished here. It will be good to have a few men on the train with you." Urbano nodded and went backstage with Antonina.

Backstage, Antonina grabbed Angelique and the two women hugged and danced a little jig. "Thank you, Angelique! You gave me my chance!"

"You little goose, I only opened the door for you. You had to make the entrance by yourself. May I tell you, you were absolutely remarkable." She hugged Antonina again. "I will tell my daughter tonight that I have met the newest and best of the *divas*."

"But, if it hadn't been for you…"

Angelique allowed herself a little smile of self-congratulation. "True. True." She wiggled, pulling at the neck of her gown. "Come, use my dressing room to change. And you, perhaps, will be throwing me out of my dressing room on Monday! After all, you are the star now and I am merely little Musetta!"

"Oh, no! Whatever happens for Monday, we can share the dressing room, can't we?" She looked terrified for a moment. "Oh, Angelique! This fame thing…it is a lot for me! Faster than I ever could dream. I hope I can cope with all of it."

"It will all work itself out, my petite. You'll have people who will now try to become your best friend. People who never bothered to speak to you before. My advice, even though you haven't asked for it, will be to stay with your trusted old friends. They knew you before you were famous and they liked you anyway." She laughed. "Good that we are now going to share this room. I know you don't want to go into Vivienne's dressing room!"

"They won't let me! They won't let anyone in there! There is this huge police man in there. He…he…" she giggled as if she were a child. "He's the handsomest man I've ever seen!"

Angelique's eyes sparkled. "Hmmm. I cannot wait to meet this man!"

***

"Thank you, *Maestro*. You have been very helpful. I will see you again on Monday night." Anderson stood and bowed over Massimo Orsini's hand. *And now! And now!*

She came through the door of the storeroom that Buddy Manger had set up as a temporary investigation office. She had taken off the drab dress that she'd worn in the last act, the dress that Mimi had died in, and was now wearing her own clothing, a navy blue skirt and a blue and white striped blouse. He had only seen her heretofore with a wig on her head. As beautiful as the wigs had seemed, he was taken a-back by the gloriousness of her silky pale brown hair. She wore it simply…tied at the back of her neck and he longed to run his hands through it and then crush it against his face. However, inasmuch as that might have her thinking that he was an imbecile, he merely smiled at her and asked her to sit down.

She sat, her hands folded in her lap, and waited for him to begin. Her mind was whirling. He was so distinguished looking, so handsome in a craggy way. Must this have been the way *Cio-Cio-San* felt when she first saw Pinkerton? She wanted to throw herself at his feet. Inasmuch as that might have him thinking that she was insane, she merely smiled at him.

"Ah, Antonina." He started. *What the hell should he say to her?* She nodded. *You ass. Who else would she be?* He harrumphed and started again. "Please, if you can. Tell me what happened tonight when you first found out that Vivienne had been murdered."

"I was getting dressed. It was about twenty minutes before curtain. Although I wasn't on stage until Act Two, I love to watch the shows, so I wanted to get down early. Everyone in the women's dressing room felt the same way. This was opening night and, despite the fact that she…du Lac…was a difficult performer, she was revered as one of the leading sopranos in the world. We all wanted to see her sing Mimi."

"Yes? Did you all leave the dressing room together?"

"Everyone left, but just as I was getting ready, I noticed that I had broken a shoelace. I waved them on and stayed in the dressing room…maybe for three more minutes. I got a new shoelace out of my case and fixed my shoe. Then I went down. As I got to the corridor, I heard a lot of noise. People were gathered in groups, and everyone was talking. The rumor was that Vivienne was dead and Ignatzia was going to sing."

"What did you think?"

She shrugged, her shoulders graceful arcs. He held his hands together, gripping them, so that he wouldn't reach out and touch her. "I thought maybe she had a heart attack or some kind of fit." She shrugged again. "Then, someone…Perhaps it was Robyn…one of the chorus members…said that she had been killed." Her head came up and her eyes unfocussed. "I was astonished. Everyone was now milling around and the rumors were spreading. She'd been killed by a tramp. She'd been killed by an old enemy. She…not too many people liked her. Even hearing that she had…she was….she'd been murdered, some people, and I really don't remember who…they said that they were glad that she was dead." She shivered. "Please God that no one ever hates me as much as so many hated her."

"Did she deserve their hate?"

"Perhaps. She was …unpleasant with me yesterday at rehearsal. I felt the lash of her sarcasm." Antonina bit her lip…*her lip…God! Her lip!* "I can understand how angry I might have been with her…and what she said to me was most likely mild as what she said…or did… to others."

"What happened to the other woman….Ignatzia Volente?"

"I wasn't really there, but, from what I understood, she was getting into the red dress…the costume. It was still on Vivienne and they tried to get it off over her head." Antonina began to giggle. "Her head fell off!" Antonina's voice went up in near hysteria. "She….she…the *head!"* She began to shake and Anderson went to her and put his hands lightly…oh, so lightly…on her shoulders.

"Easy, my dear." He held onto her shaking body, holding his own shaking body in check. She leaned forward and pushed her forehead into his midsection. She was weeping. Unable to help himself, he held her close, his face bent to the shining sweetness of her hair. "No one deserves what she…she….Oh! Oh!" She cried like a child, and he held her tight. Her tears soaked his shirtfront and he closed his eyes, wondering when this bliss would be over. She burrowed into him, muffling her sobs, and he found his lips softly kissing her. *I'm only consoling her*, he excused himself. *She needs someone to take care of her.*

What a crybaby I am! What must he think of me? She tried to stop her tears, but they ran down her face. *I must look awful and blotchy! His arms are so strong. They feel so right around me!* She sniffed and tried to wipe her face and then realized that he…he was kissing the top of her head! Soft, tender kisses, kisses meant to soothe…kisses like you'd kiss a child.

She raised her face to tell him that she was better. She saw his eyes, inches away from hers. She raised her face even more….and their lips met. *Such sweetness! Such tender softness!* Their thoughts were as one. They drew apart, searching each other's eyes.

"Ohhh," she said with soft wonder. Her mouth was still open, slightly gaping, and she bit her bottom lip.

What could a man do? He bent again, this time capturing her mouth with some rough passion, shaking, he held her and she kissed him back, unable to stop. *What madness was this? His mustache…I've never much kissed anyone in passion, only Peter…the mustache, it was heavenly…I can barely breathe…*

She pulled back, and a spasm shook her body. "Please, pardon me!" he choked out. "I don't know what…I…I apologize. I was inexcusable!" He harrumphed and tried to smooth back his own hair and stop his pounding heart.

"I…I…I was upset. I…shouldn't have…I don't know what came over me." Her own heart was hammering. *What was that? To be sure, she'd kissed boys before. And even…with Peter….*her face flamed and he thought it was because of his behavior. *But this! This was...mad. Passion. This must have been what Mimi felt when she first set eyes on Rodolfo.* In her innocent confusion and lack of real experience, she could only relate the kiss to a kiss played in an opera. She was flummoxed. It was all more than she could grasp. Her eyes implored him. *What shall we do?*

You swine! How could you treat her so? He castigated himself, yet, he was helpless to do more than stare at her, wanting her more than ever.

A knock at the door made them both leap back. "Chief?" It was Pedar Pedersen.

"Come in, Pedar." He wiped his mouth. *Did she wear lipstick? Could Pedar, who had worked closely with him for years and generally knew every thought that was in his mind...could he tell?*

"I'm finished with my interrogations." Pedar smiled gently at Antonina. *Sweet little thing. The boss looks a little rattled. Geez, I sure hope he doesn't know anything that would throw suspicion on her.* "What do you want me to do now?"

"We'll be finished here in a few minutes. See if Buddy needs a hand with his interviewing." Pedar made a circle of his thumb and middle finger and closed the door behind himself.

"Let's...let's try to finish here." Anderson sat straight in his chair, putting three feet of space between himself and Antonina. She gathered her skirt in her hands and crumpled it up. She nodded, afraid to speak.

"Now, tell me what happened to, uh...what's her name?" *Damned if he could remember anything right now!*

Antonina dimpled, some little place in her brain told her how nervous he was. *Why, he desires me! And I desire him! What kind of woman am I?* Pitying him, she was able to gather herself together. "I am telling you this from what Janet told me. As they tried to get the dress off, I suppose...her head...and the wig...it was nearly chopped completely off...when she tugged at it...it just toppled off and it fell down. Janet said it was as if a bowling ball fell, but I imagine she already told you that." Anderson nodded, afraid to speak. "The dog ...Vivienne had this horrible dog...the dog ran and tried to bite Ignatzia. Ignatzia screamed and tried to get away from the dog. She fell over the hammock. I understand she fainted and her leg is broken or fractured." She suddenly stood up. "They were going to cancel the opera. Who could play Mimi? And then Angelique suggested me." She grinned and her face was lit from within. "I never dreamed that I...well, yes, I had *always* dreamed that I might take over from someone, but not this way! I had practiced Mimi's role for years. I knew every aria, every piece of business, every word of her part. I had watched the rehearsals carefully and thought I could hit her marks and do her stage business...and the others...they would help me if I got stuck."

"You sang like an angel," His face flamed. "I'd never been to an opera performance. I sat, bored out of my mind...and then you came on stage, so frail and so sweet...." He wanted to get up, but, he managed to sit still.

Her face glowed. "Thank you. It means so much to me that you thought....that I sang well." She ducked her head. "I am not someone who pretends modesty. I know I sing well. I knew I could carry the role and make the performance a good one." She sat still...very still... "I always knew I could be a *diva*."

"What does that really mean? *Diva?"*

She blushed, hoping that he wouldn't think her stupid and vain. She knew she was good...better than good. It was her gift. "*Diva* means divine. Of the Gods. A Goddess." She swallowed and he could see the lump in her throat. "In the olden days, a *diva* was really treated just like a goddess. She wouldn't be allowed to walk, lest her feet be soiled by the road. A contingent of follow-ers would carry her from the opera house to her hotel, so she wouldn't...she would be *different* from ordinary mortals." She grinned. "However, I walk on the ground just fine."

He gave a shout of laughter and they looked at one another again. He ran his tongue over his parched lips. "What am I going to do, Antonina? I can't even speak to you without....I've been in love with you ever since you peeped though the door on stage. I don't mean to be this way. This has never, ever happened to me....I'm a grown man, old enough to be your father. I have an important job. I'm married...a terrible and loveless marriage, but, I suppose, all men might say that to a woman that they adore." His hands opened help-lessly. "I don't know what to do."

"It seems real to me, uh...I, uh...I hardly know what your name is!" She cried in total embarrassment, "but I know that I never felt like this either! I have a beau...I have kissed him before, and even...more." She hung her head, scarlet at talking like this to man who was nearly a total stranger. "I sup-pose...if this is how it all happens...and this feeling...it was as if I'd been kicked in the stomach...and I...I wanted you to kiss me...to hold me...I love you, too...whoever you are!"

He crossed to her and took her into his arms again. "It's Anderson, my love. Anderson von Vogel." He kissed her again, but this time a tiny butterfly kiss. "And my name and my kisses are imprinted in your heart. We will be talking a lot more. We will be seeing one another....more." He held her slightly away and she felt bereft, she wanted him to crush her, enfold her...

"This isn't the time...not tonight."

"No. No, you are right, Anderson." She said his name and his gut twisted. "I must go now, if you are finished with me..."

"I'll never be finished with you, Antonina. Never."

"Boss?" It was Pedar again.

"We're just finishing up. I will be speaking again with you, Antonina. Thank you for all of your help." She stood up, smoothing her skirt. "You live where?"

"Greenwich, Connecticut."

"That far? How will you get home?"

"By train. I do it all the time, ride the train here and then home again. My mother, her friend and attorney, Simeon Meade and my Uncle Dario are waiting for me. They will keep me company all the way home."

"And you'll be back to the theater…when?"

"Monday…we have another performance. I will be here in the early afternoon. I have to be re-fitted…another dress…you know…"

"I look forward to seeing you sing, Miss," Pedar nodded pleasantly to her. "I once heard Nellie Melba sing this role, but, from what your fellow performers are saying out there, you are even better!"

Thank God for Pedar. I can always count on him to say the right thing. "I, too, will look forward to seeing you sing again. After the performance, I'll be wanting to speak with you again. Try to remember if there is anything…anything at all, that you can think of…and we will see you on Monday. Goodbye, Antonina. Have a safe trip back to Greenwich, Connecticut."

***

The train racketed through the night. Antonina had spent the first fifteen minutes telling Simeon, Uncle Dario and her mother all that had transpired. She then closed her eyes and pretended to sleep. *Anderson von Vogel. The train wheels made their own clicking sound. Click-a-click-a, Anderson, click-a-click-a, Anderson. What a beautiful, distinguished name. Such a beautiful, distinguished man. And she would be his!* She smiled to herself, *and rather soon, if I know myself.* Then, exhausted, she actually fell asleep.

Francesca watched her. *My darling girl. Nothing will ever be the same for you now. Nothing. May God watch over you and your blazing talent. May God keep you safe.*

***

"Chief?" Herbie Floyd called Emerson early on Sunday morning.

"What's up, Herb?"

"Bad news. Nora passed away early this morning."

"Oh, no! How did you find out?"

"Cliff called. Mike called in. He's pretty broken up."

"Terrible. The poor man and poor Nora." He thought for a moment. "I'm going over to Mike's. Call the rest of the squad and let them all know. I'll be in a little later this morning." He hung up and told his wife.

He met Cliff Gustafson right outside Mike's door. The two shook hands. They'd worked together for a lifetime. They knew how one another thought, how one another would act in any given situation…they were *friends*. "Let's go in."

Mike answered the door. He looked tired and haggard. McAndrews hugged him and Cliff patted Mike awkwardly on his back. "By God, we are so sorry. How are you doing, old man?"

"It was a bad night. She just couldn't hold on." There were tears in Mike's blue eyes. "She was a good woman."

Death, collecting the pure and shining soul of Nora Murphy, agreed. *Wish I could assure you fellows of how welcoming it will be for her in Heaven. Oh, well, when you guys get there…especially you, Mr. Murphy, you'll see. Meanwhile, some of the angels will show her how to watch down over you. You'll see.*

"There's a draft in here," Mike shivered, feeling the passage of some current of air. "Don't know how I'm gonna cope, Boss."

"Take some time off, Mike. Get yourself together. We'll work it all out."

"Nah." Mike shook his heavy head. "I'll take a day or two and get Nora buried in style. Then, I'll be back. What the hell else would I do? She was my life at home and you guys are my life at work. Just because one is gone, I don't want to be away from the other." He allowed himself a rough laugh. "I'll work on bringing all the stuff from our little shitting bandits back to the nice folk who were robbed. That's a good job for me."

"Whatever you want, Mike. Whatever you want."

***

The twins couldn't stop yammering excitedly about last night's thrilling events. "It was shattering!" Gia told her brothers. "Amazing! Antonina was….she was…amazing!" Francesca wondered if shattering was going and amazing was coming. "Wasn't she, Mama?"

"She was shatteringly amazing," Francesca agreed. "Too bad you two chose to stay at home," she cuffed Rafe's shoulder. "You missed quite an experience!"

"How long is our star going to stay in her revolting bed?" Gia complained. "She's supposed to go up the Avenue with us and help us to find a dress for the Halloween Dance."

"She's had a very long night. Let her sleep." Francesca refilled her coffee cup and sat down. "I have to go uptown this morning," she checked her wristwatch. "Simeon is coming to drive me to the new building. We're going to check some measurements to be sure the ovens can fit into the basement and be properly vented."

"You're going to miss having the business here." For the past ten years, Francesca had operated her highly successful baking business from the basement of their home. Now, the business had grown so furiously, the house could no longer contain their family and all of the equipment necessary to serve her ever-bourgeoning list of customers. *Panis Angelicus*, as her bread-stuffs were known, would be moving shortly to a new, larger building right on Greenwich Avenue. The bakery would be three stores away from her sister-in-law, Elena's enormously successful boutique shop, *Eccola!*

"Yes, I will. It was so handy, just going downstairs to bake. I could be home when you all came home from school, I could nurse any one of you who was sick…it was an easy way to run a business." She sighed. "But, those nice simple days are over. I can't cope with the increase in business from here. I just don't have enough room."

"It's a big step for you, you little girl from the hills of Italy," Mike teased her. "One day, you're helping *Zia* Filomande, cooking at the castle, and the next day, you own a building on Greenwich Avenue!"

"We did well, didn't we?" She sat back, luxuriating in the strong cup of coffee. "All of us who came…practically penniless on that boat…Elena, Giovanna, Mina…look at us all." She counted on her fingers. "Elena owns her own business. Santo is the most famous sculptor in the state. Mina owns her own business and her hand cream is shipped all over the United States, Giovanna and Paolo are homeowners with a son who will soon be a doctor. Sabina and Enzo are buying a farm. Dario is the Monsignor of St. Catherine's, Peter is going to be a doctor, Giorgio is the assistant undertaker. Skipper is going to law school, and you four just may…if you study a little more…manage to graduate from high school…." There were howls from her two sets of twins.

"Revolting, Mama"

"Shattering!"

"And," Francesca rolled on, paying no attention to the interruption, "your sister is going to be an opera star. What more in blessings can we get?"

"Don't forget Don Mantaldo and your cookbook with *Zia* Filomande!" Gia reminded her mother.

"Ah!" Francesca nodded once. *"D'accordo! Zia's* book will be published in the spring and Don Mantaldo now owns most of Greenwich."

"Mama?" Rafe wheedled. "Can you teach Mike and I how to drive?"

"Come on, Mama! We sort of can drive a little, but we need you to help us."

"Why not?" Francesca considered. "It will be a help if you two can pick up Johnny and do errands for me. Sure. I also think we should look for another car…for you two and Antonina to use."

The boys broke into yelps of delight. In the middle of the pandemonium, Simeon Meade came in, not bothering to knock. After all, he was an old friend.

"Is there good news?" I heard you all out in the street!"

"We're going to get a new car!"

"A used car!" Francesca corrected. "An *old* used car. And perhaps, if you are all nice to Simeon, he may help us to get one."

Gia threw her arms around Simeon. 'We are *always* nice to you, Simeon. We all adore you!"

"That makes my morning complete. And now, Francesca, are you ready to go and measure your new basement?"

***

It fell to Phil Moore to go around and collect one dollar from each of the policemen. "That way, we can get a nice bouquet of flowers for Nora's wake." He cornered Herbie. "Come on, Herbie, cough up a buck!"

"Alright! Alright." Herbie held his hands up ion the air. "I gotta get it from my coat."

The telephone rang and Phil answered, "Greenwich Police Station. Good Morning. Patrolman Moore speaking. How can I help you?"

Herbie paused, listening. "You did? Really? Gee…we'll be right there! 66 Greenwich Avenue. OK."

Phil swiveled around, hanging up the telephone. "That was Simeon Meade. He and Francesca Rosato are at her new building….the bakery one….in the basement…Florence Curtin has been found!"

"Is she dead?"

"Practically. They…he…said to call an ambulance." Phil looked up the number and called Doc Sullivan as Herbie went to Chief McAndrews' office to break the news.

"Let's go, Phil. Herbie, you keep everything ticking here." They flew out the door.

"Can we use the siren?" Phil begged. He'd never been in the police car with the siren yowling nor the red lights flashing. "Can we?"

"Why the hell not, kid." McAndrews remembered his own excitement…*how many years ago…Ha!* "Let it rip!"

"Is she beaten up? What's the story?"

"It looks as if she's exhausted and dehydrated. She doesn't seem to have been abducted, but that's all that I know." McAndrews whirred the siren again. "Your curiosity will just have to wait a few more minutes."

The car roared through the quiet Sunday streets. It screeched around the corner and drove up the Avenue, stopping right in front of Number 66. Simeon was standing at the curb, waiting for them.

"What's going on? Where is she?"

"In the basement. She's in a bad way. She's evidentially been there for a few days. She's in shock from the cold and she hasn't eaten or even had any water for that time."

"Was she abducted?"

"No…she's…well, you'll hear it from her." Simeon shook his head. "An amazing story."

"Is she tied up?"

"No," Simeon grinned, although a shadow lay behind his face. "You'll have to hear it from her." They went around the alleyway and entered the basement through a rickety brown-painted door. They were in a cavernous cellar. McAndrews thought that this building had formerly housed Tripodi's Plumbing and Heating. Now, the basement was empty, except for a few pieces of furniture and some discarded pipes piled in one corner. The floor was concrete and when they stepped inside, McAndrews felt the cold and damp. The basement was dim. In the slanting yellow light from the high casement windows, they could see two women at the far end.

"Chief McAndrews," Francesca turned and called his name. "She needs urgent medical care." In a chair, huddled into what was most likely Francesca's coat, sat a shrunken visage of a woman. Her hair, grey and greasy, was clumped and lifeless. Her face was ashen and her hands, clutching the coat for warmth, were claw-like.

"Florence," McAndrews called. "Mrs. Curtin! Are you all right?" There was no answer, no stirring from the figure in the chair.

Francesca bent over. She shook Mrs. Curtin gently and then began to chafe her hands, trying to instill some warmth. She thought back to last night's opera…when Rodolfo was trying to chafe some warmth back into Mimi's cold hands…"Help is here now, Mrs. Curtin. The police are here to assist you." Francesca's own blue eyes were wide with worry. "She's freezing. I'm afraid…if she doesn't get help….She's in shock…in terrible shape."

McAndrews came closer and peered into Mrs. Curtin's eyes. She blinked and pulled away. "Why are you here, Mrs. Curtin? What has happened?" *I wonder if she knows her husband's head was bashed in?*

A whisper…a ghostly whisper. McAndrews leaned close. "I killed him." She shuddered and closed her eyes, using her last remaining strength.

"Killed him?" McAndrews whirled at a sound behind him. The hefty, reassuring bulk of Doc Sullivan stood there, satchel in hand.

He pushed McAndrews out of the way and bent to the tiny figure in the chair. "Here, Mrs. Curtin. Drink this…slowly…just sip at it." He held a small flask up to her mouth. She wet her lips.

"Don't want to….I want to die. I killed him."

"Hush. Don't talk now. Let us get you to the hospital. Come on," Doc Sullivan put his hand to her.

She shrunk back into the chair. "No. I don't want to go."

"Do you want to tell us what happened?" McAndrews' voice was gentle.

"I couldn't stand him anymore. All them trophies. He lived for the trophies and his bowling. I wasn't anything to him anymore."

"And?" McAndrews asked.

"He got another one that night. He couldn't stop bragging about it. I wanted him to help me with the kitchen curtains, but no….no…all he wanted to do was wave that trophy around and then add it to the hundreds and hundreds and hundreds of them in the living room. In the dining room. In the bedroom. All over the house. Bowling trophies. Bowling trophies. I have to dust them every day. Trophies and more trophies. I just got tired of it all."

"And?" McAndrews urged again.

"And so I hit him with the trophy." She looked up. "From behind." She rocked back and forth. "He was sitting down, holding the trophy…he could only see the trophy. He didn't ever see me any more. I hit him a couple'a times. He fell over and was dead." She looked up at the policeman. "Then he shut up."

"And then what did you do?"

"Just sat there for a few minutes. I drank my coffee and watched out the window. It was so peaceful. There was no one to talk and talk and talk about bowling. He never – *ever* - shut his mouth. He always bragged and bragged about his bowling and I was so tired of it. I just didn't want him to talk any more."

"I'm sorry," McAndrews spread out his hands. He didn't know what else to say.

"I'm not. I was tired of him and his nattering on." She revived slightly, flushed with the animation of talking. She blew her nose and continued, ready, at last, to spew out all of the details. "Finally, after all of those years of never shutting up, he stopped talking and talking about bowling." She sighed, "Then I cleaned up the house. Did the dishes, polished the counter top." She smiled, a grotesque smile. "It was lovely. So quiet without him yammerin' about his trophies. I was happy then."

"And how did you get here?"

"After I cleaned up, I just went out." She began to shudder and then huge tears began to form in her eyes. She dashed them away with an impatient hand. "I forgot to put on my coat. I walked and walked and I found myself on the Avenue. I was tired, but there was no place to rest. I wanted to lay down and never get up again. Then, I saw the garbage men coming out from behind this store. I waited until they were gone and came down here. The door wasn't quite closed. I came in and found a chair here. I sat down. I was very tired." She slumped down, a small bundle of exhaustion. "I was finished. All finished. I want to die now." She shut her eyes. Her face was pale and waxy.

"Let's get her out of here," Doc motioned to the two ambulance attendants who had entered the basement, pushing a gurney. "Get her to the hospital and I'll be there in two shakes of a lamb's tail." He turned and shrugged as the gurney with its pathetic load was wheeled out. "I'll see you at the hospital."

"Will she live?" McAndrews wasn't sure if he was hoping she would or she wouldn't.

"Donno. Certainly she doesn't want to." Doc wheeled. He stopped, turned back and asked the Chief. "Hey, Emerson? Do you go bowling?"

"Not after today, Sully. Never again."

Chapter Sixteen

"Betwixt her lips and mine...upon my soul...the kisses and the wine..."
Ernest Dowson, nun sum qulis eram bonae

I don't feel much like measuring now," Francesca said to Simeon, her eyes deep and sad.

"Let's just measure the basement, and then I'll take you to lunch." He shivered. "Weird, huh?"

"Frightening." She agreed. He walked the basement, calling out his steps, and she wrote down the figures.

"We'll have the ovens here," she pointed. "And the sinks here, and the storage over there." She wandered into the middle of the cavernous space. "And over here...the work tables. The racks and the proofing cabinets."

"Perhaps a bathroom in that corner. A sink and a toilet." Simeon suggested. "That way, the employees who are making the bread can use the toilet without having to go all the way upstairs."

"You think of everything, my dear."

"I try, Francesca." He turned closer to her. "I want to help you in every way I can."

She turned and up-tilted her face and he obligingly kissed her. The kiss deepened and Simeon wished they were anywhere but in a dirty basement. He pulled back, "Francesca, Francesca, let's get married."

"Simeon! You know what we agreed!"

"I can't wait that long for you, my darling. Johnny is still a child. I can't wait until he's grown. I'll pine away with sadness." *He was joking, but yet, he wasn't. She knew he would be pressing her, she just didn't expect it today. Perhaps, because of that sad and desolate woman...perhaps he had seen the raw and aching loneliness in her eyes....*

"Oh, Simeon. Let's not argue."

"I'm not arguing. I'm stating."

"Is that a legal phrase?" she tried to tease him.

"It's a phrase from a man who is at the end of his rope. There's no good reason to wait. I want to marry you now."

She sighed, a deep, deep sigh. "Let's go to lunch."

He nodded, solemn and serious and guided her out of the basement. He tried to shut the brown door firmly, so that no further murderers might creep in, but the door was warped and wouldn't close properly. "Let's hope that it stays shut. I'll have someone come tomorrow and see that a lock is put on."

They drove to the China Beauty Restaurant and sat in a booth at the back. They both ordered a bowl of egg-drop soup and sat, dipping the crunchy fried noodles into a sweet, sticky sauce. "Well?" Simeon pressed.

"I need more time."

"Do you love me, Francesca? You say you do. When we kiss...when we make love....I believe you love me as I love you."

She toyed with her noodles. He was a good man, an honorable man. He made her laugh, he took care of her and her children. He was prosperous, honest, had an infectious sense of humor, and she trusted him implicitly. He was handsome and distinguished, a respected man in his profession. His love-making made her shudder and writhe with desire. Unlike her first husband, Carlo, Simeon would never hurt her, never cause her or her family pain and heartache. But, ah! Could she love him as she had loved Carlo?

"Francesca?"

She dropped her head and studied the tabletop. *He didn't realize,* she thought, *how much she had adored Carlo. How, despite everything, her passion for him had never slaked. Except at the end, her honest consciousness reminded her. At the end, you hated him! You feared him and you feared for your childrens' lives! And what kind of a woman am I, she asked her innermost self? I once slept with another man, bore his child, and fooled Carlo into thinking that Antonina was his. I did love Anton. I did, but not like I loved Carlo. And Simeon was just like Anton. He looked somewhat like him and acted somewhat like him. A gentle man. A good man. What would he say when she told him about Anton? It had been her own secret, only known by Zia Filomande, who kept her own counsel. And then, of course, she had told Antonina, when the child turned sixteen. After all, Antonina had always hated and feared Carlo and she deserved to know that he wasn't her father. What would Simeon say if she told him all of this? Would he still love her? Feel the same about her?* She looked up. "I want to apologize to you, Simeon."

"Apologize?"

"Yes. Before we make any further plans, I want to tell you that I have deceived you somewhat." She swallowed hard.

"How have you deceived me, darling? What is the trouble?" His face only looked at her with love. "What could be so bad that you can't tell me?"

"Well...." She toyed with her spoon, drawing circles on the starched, white tablecloth...Simeon made her laugh, made her smile. She adored him. Her heart beat fast when he kissed her. She dreamed of him. He would make a wonderful father and husband...She loved him. She gulped in a deep breath...*here goes...win or loose...here goes...*

"I was besotted with Carlo, as I have told you. I was crazy with love and I forgave him almost everything he did to me..." She peered up under her lashes. Simeon sat still, watching...."He really abused me, Simeon. I don't say this to make you feel sorry for me. That was how our love was. Sometimes, I even relished the thought of a fight or even...sometimes, when he was cruel..." She looked straight at him. "Then, when he came back and we ...we...made love...it was even more exciting. I wasn't a very nice person, Simeon. I was too young, and too much in love, and I had no sense of shame."

He nodded, "Francesca, you have told me all of this. I understand. I knew you while the end was coming and I could see, myself, how he controlled you and the children. I loved you the moment I set eyes on you. I knew you were in a terrible marriage to a terrible man. I knew about your struggles, inside and out. I love you in spite of it, or perhaps because of it. I don't know which...all I know is that I cannot face the rest of my life without you."

"But you don't know everything. I have one more secret. A deep secret. Only *Zia* Filomande knew it, and she has never much...except once...spoken of it to me. And only one other person knows....and now, because I love you and want to be sure that you know it all....good and bad...you will know."

"Tell me, Francesca. What is it that disturbs your sleep at night? How can I help you?"

He is such a good man. Will he understand this last thing? Or will I lose him if I tell him the whole truth? Oh, Lord, help me! I love this good man. Will he understand me? "I have told you a little bit about Anton del Guidice, haven't I?"

"The poor, sad, loveless Count. Yes, you have told me about him."

"He was not so loveless."

His eyes narrowed, "What do you mean?"

"I met Anton...the Count...when I first went to the castle looking for a job in the kitchens with *Zia* Filomande. That day...the first day I was there...I met Anton on the staircase. He was dressed for riding and he was tall and handsome and almost like a God to me. After all, he held the lives of my family and all of the other families in the village in his hand. He owned us. I was very impressed with him, and, I know, that he thought I was pretty."

"You are not pretty, Francesca. You are beautiful," Simeon smiled slightly. "You're adorable, captivating...Any man in his right mind would think you were beautiful, even this Count."

"There was an...attraction between him and me. *Zia* saw it right away and she was angry. She didn't want him to like me too much, and she didn't want me to fall in love with Anton. He was a Count, for God's sake, and I was less than a servant. His wife wore silver shoes with diamonds on them and I wore wooden clogs. He was so far above me....in America, life is not like that. People are equal, more or less. But not in Italy. Not then. He was on the top of

198

the mountain and I was a pebble on the sand below. You must understand this!"

"Tell me more, Francesca."

"Wherever I was on the castle grounds, he would be. He always smiled and waved and was never improper towards me. But he was always there. And when I saw him, my heart beat faster. I always looked for him."

"And then I met Carlo and he mesmerized my life. I would have nothing but to marry him. I would have ...and sometimes I did...anything. Anything at all that he ordered me to do. Anton hated Carlo and saw what my life would be like married to him. Anton's own marriage was such a pitiful sham. He wanted mine to be a better one. He knew how bad Carlo was. He tried to warn me, he even tried to beg me to stay away from Carlo, but I was a headstrong girl, used to being denied *nothing...ever!* I was spoiled. I stamped my little foot to get what I wanted. I wanted Carlo and I would have him, come Hell or the end of the world."

"And so we were wed, Carlo and me. And on our wedding night, I saw what a monster lay beneath his handsome, seductive skin. And, yet, Simeon, to my shame, I still wanted him and wanted everything that he was doing to me. He hurt me...I can't even talk about it...and I still wanted him."

She sighed, from deep within her soul. "But one night, I was beaten so badly, so ill-used, that I was sick. Sick with shame and sick from my bruises."

"You don't have to tell me any of this, Francesca. I just don't care what you did in the past. Our love is in the future. Hush, my dear. Hush."

"No. No." Francesca said in a tiny voice. "I can never marry you until you know...It was a dark night and Carlo and everyone else had gone to a *festa*...a fair...in another village. I was all alone. We lived, Carlo and I, in rooms over the stable. I bathed my wounds and took a cachet of medicine that Mina's mother had made up for me. It was to make me sleep. I fell asleep and was awakened by a noise down in the stable. I went down to see what was happening. Anton was down there, stroking the velvet nose of his favorite stallion. He saw me and he saw that I had been unhappy. He saw my bruises and swore that he would kill Carlo. I made him promise to leave Carlo alone. I was crying and upset and Anton soothed me. He was so kind and gentle and sweet....he comforted me and I comforted him...and...and..." She stopped speaking for a moment.

"And?" Simeon's voice was kind.

She tipped her head. "And...well, we made love to one another. Sweet love. Tender love. I don't think either of us had ever had that kind of love before."

She was silent, remembering that night, so many years ago, so many miles away. "And then, I found that I was pregnant. I knew, counting back, that it was Anton's baby, but, if Carlo ever knew, he would kill me. Literally kill me. And then, of course, the baby would die, too. I was in fear and then I was cunning. I just let Carlo think it was his baby. And then, Antonina was born. Carlo never much cared for her. And she had the deep gray eyes of her real father." Francesca's words tumbled over one another as she tried to explain... "One day, I had her in a basket and I was picking tomatoes. *Zia* called to me that Anton was ill. 'Take the baby and go up to see him, my dear,' she told me. 'He is dying and he needs to talk with you.' She knew, you see. She knew that Antonina was Anton's baby."

Simeon reached across the table and took Francesca's hand in his. He held it loosely, his eyes never leaving her face.

"Anton was in bed. He was dying. He wanted to see Antonina one more time. He held her tiny little fist in his hand and tears dripped from his eyes. She was his child and there was very little that he could do about it. He wanted to protect her, though, as best he could. He gave me some jewels that were his mother's. He told me to hide them and use them at some future date to be sure that Antonina would never be without resources. He told me his regret that he and I could never have been together. 'Such a wonderful thing it would have been, Francesca,' he said to me. And then he said that our miserable lives...his and mine...were such a waste of love."

"I put the jewels away...hid them from Carlo and then, when we came to America, hid them from the Customs men." She giggled suddenly. "That's a whole other story." Simeon smiled with a fresh burst of love. *What a woman she was!*

"When Carlo...died...after trying to murder most of my family...*no!* Even before that, I knew I had no more love for him. You knew me then and you knew much of the story, but not this part. What killed my love, finally, was when I realized that Carlo might harm my children, especially Antonina. Then, my love turned to hate and sadness. And then he died. However he died."

"Antonina was so relived when he was gone. All her fear and worry went away. My poor little girl, she was so confused. She had truly hated Carlo. When she was sixteen, I told her that he wasn't her father, wondering what she might think of me...a hussy and an adulterer."

"And how did she feel about you?"

"She loved me as before. But, I could never...now...chide her for loving an unsuitable man. Chide her for having relations. Chide her for being as I had been."

"Is that the end?"

"Yes, I think I have told you almost everything. There are some details...how my jewels saved Don Mantaldo...how we found what Carlo had stolen from the castle...small things. But that is why I hesitated when you wanted to get married. Perhaps you may not want to marry someone who has broken a commandment so easily. Someone who was an adulteress. Someone you might never be able to fully trust." She bowed her head.

He opened a packet of fortune cookies and crushed the contents in his fist. "Maybe you should hear about me, Francesca. Do you think you are the only one who has secrets?"

"You? *You?* What secrets do you have?" Her eyes bored into his head. "Simeon! You are the most decent, honorable person I know!"

"I've never married, you know that. But once, many years ago, I was engaged to be married." Francesca sat back, astonished.

"Her name was Helen. Helen Carstairs. She was rich and beautiful and I adored her. We fell in love and planned to get married. Then, one day, she told me she was having my baby. I was overjoyed. 'Let's get married right away!' I told her."

A week later, she had gone away. I found her...no need to into how right now, but she was living near Boston. I tried to reason with her to come home...to get married right away and no one would know or care that the baby came a little early. She laughed at me and taunted me and told me that the baby wasn't mine and that she didn't love me." Francesca's eyes were huge....a story very similar to her own...only with some slightly different twists and turns. "She told me that she had an appointment to have the baby....eliminated...the next day."

"I have always prided myself on my even temper, but that day, I became unhinged. I screamed and railed and raved at her. She screamed and yelled and raved back at me. I was angry. She was even more angry. She pushed me and I let her. She shoved at me again and I tried to step out of the way. She overbalanced and fell and the baby...the baby...was lost."

"Oh, Simeon. I am so sorry," Francesca touched his cold hand.

"She never forgave me, even though it was an accident and she had already planned to abort the child. She told me that she would tell everyone that I killed the baby...and, in truth, I had, even though it was an accident. I sent her money and she demanded more and more. I paid her for seven years. She died then...I got a letter from her mother so informing me. She died of a miserable disease." He sat for a moment, reflecting.

"We have terrible secrets, you and I. We have both hurt others and been hurt ourselves."

"I never told anyone, not my father, nor my mother, nor anyone...."

"I love you, Simeon." Her smile was sad. "I love you with a grown-up love. A love that has open eyes and a tender heart. I cannot live without you."

"And I love you, Francesca." His smile pierced her heart. "Can we get married now?"

"Yes, Simeon, dear. I think we should get married now. Maybe even tomorrow."

"I will love and honor you for the rest of Eternity."

"I will love you longer than that."

"Egg roll?" The waiter served them. He never understood why they began to laugh and laughed until they had tears in their eyes. He was happy, however, when they were finished and departed from the restaurant. Simeon had left him a ten dollar tip for a lunch that cost a dollar-and-a-half.

Chapter Seventeen

"One sang high, and one sang lo..and the other sang bonny bonny Biscay-O…"
The Wraggle-Taggle Gypsy-O…an anonymous ballad

*M*onsignor Dario opened his prayer book. "To the family and friends of Nora Murphy, may I offer you my sincere condolences and ask you to put your faith in the Lord." He stopped. "Please stand and join me in The Lord's Prayer…Our Father, Who art in Heaven…."

Mike prayed, mouthing the familiar words, but he felt empty. How could he pray when Nora was gone? How could the sun shine? With his head bowed, he couldn't see the hundreds of neighbors, friends, relatives and co-workers who crowded Munchauer's Funeral Parlor. Oh, Nora!

As the familiar words droned over him, the hurt began to recede. He felt the love and sympathy flow around him. These were his friends. And his Nora? Nora had been adored by all who knew her. "May the Perpetual Light shine upon her…" Mike could almost feel Nora's hand on his shoulder. He had to strain to hear her voice telling him to get on with his life. He looked up. Monsignor Dario's eyes locked into his. "She is now with the angels."

A long contingent of cars wound up North Street carrying the rosewood coffin of Nora O'Donnell Murphy to the place where her earthly remains would rest until the day they rejoined her spirit. Emerson McAndrews drove the black car in which Mike sat as a passenger. "She was the best, Mike. A good woman."

"Don't quite know how I'm gonna deal with it all. I'll miss her every moment."

"Of course. Again, Mike, take some time off. Go somewhere. Take care of yourself for a week or two."

"No." Mike's head drooped. "I'd go crazy with boredom. Can you imagine me going to some fancy resort or whatever?" He snorted. "Nah. I'll be back on the job on Tuesday. Tomorrow, I'll clean up the house a little." The snaking line of cars turned into St. Catherine's Cemetery.

"Whatever you want, Mike."

"She was really suffering, Boss."

"She was tired."

"You gotta believe…if you believe anything…that she's at peace. All her suffering is over."

"I'll miss her. I'll miss her."

The gathering was held at the St. Catherine's Rectory an hour after the interment. In the dusk of the evening, stories were told of Mike and Nora...how they met....how she hit him over the head with a bottle of beer when he got drunk at her sister's wedding...how he surprised her with an expensive Easter bonnet in their first year of marriage...The Catholic Daughters Guild supplied hard rolls, platters of ham and turkey and cheeses, bowls of potato and macaroni salad, gallons of coffee and, individually, the women had each brought a special dessert. The men of the parish supplied tin tubs filled with ice, cradling dark brown bottles of beer. In Monsignor Dario's office, a bottle of Jamison's warmed a select few. After an hour, even Mike was laughing, recalling Nora's famous temper.

"Remember that Thanksgiving when I played poker at the Cos Cob firehouse?"

"You won two live turkeys!"

"Yeah, I was dumb Irish drunk and brought them home to Nora, tied by their feet, gobbling and twisting and shitting all over the kitchen. She made me tie them in the basement." Mike roared. "The next morning, they'd gotten loose somehow and they ruined the entire basement. There were broken flowerpots, feathers, dirt, laundry...and mostly turkey shit! Those turkeys had wrecked the entire basement! Took me three days to clean it up."

"I thought Nora was never going to speak to you!"

"Ha! I was worried. And then, on Thanksgiving Day, we had the best damn two turkeys you'd ever want to eat. One with cornbread stuffing and one stuffed with apricots and soda bread."

"She was one hell of a woman, Mike"

"She was, that she was."

Young Charlie Presto brought his new girlfriend, Mary Xander, with him. Mike motioned to them. "She's the one who saw the car accident, right?"

Charlie raised his eyebrows up and down.

"Seems like a nice girl." Charlie just grinned.

"He seems smitten," One of Cliff Gustafson's hands held a bottle of beer, the other a cupcake. "I like it when we get something good out of a crime."

"What a strange set of circumstances." Mike bit into a ham sandwich. "I was so busy with Nora...I never got to ask you, how did you figure it all out?"

"I never connected the situation to the Pickwick Theater. Some of the victims did say they'd been to the movies, but...*everyone* goes to the movies on Saturday night! Some just said they'd been out, and I was stupid and never asked them where they'd been.

"And then, the family wanted to go to the movies. And once I was there, the entire thing was all set out in front of me. I signed the name and address list myself, then saw the fudge and the popcorn. I saw those two punks loitering around, just waiting...waiting...My subconscious must'a been working, 'cause when Karen started to talk about the kitty cat necklace, the whole thing lit up in my head."

"One of those glorious *'Aha!'* moments," Mike swallowed another piece of ham. "They're what it's all about!"

"You feel so damn good when it all falls into place."

"I'd never be anything but a cop, you know."

"What else is there, you Irish Mick, you?"

Mike turned around at a tap to his shoulder. "Hey, Phil! Where's your drink? Come on over here!" He waved at a neighbor. "Nice to see you, Mr. Sargeant!"

"You're gonna be fine, my buddy." Cliff smacked into Mike's shoulder.

"Oh, I'll be fine…a little lonely, but fine. What I really need now is a damn good murder. It will take my mind off of things!"

"Be careful what you wish for!"

***

He and Pedar had gone over all of the original statements. "There are a lot of questions for tomorrow."

"We'll get there right after lunch and start re-interviewing." Pedar stood up and stretched. "I'm getting old, Chief."

"How're you doing, Bud?" Anderson also stood and went to the back wall where Buddy Manger was making a detailed time chart.

"Not bad. I even have some squares filled in." He checked a statement and then made a notation on the chart in the 7:05 to 7:10 square, indicating that three people had seen and confirmed that Claudio Vizzi and Sandor Cali-Curri were playing poker during that time and that Robyn Benson and Karen Heffernan had both been standing together at the side curtain. It was a painstaking job. Across the top of the huge chart were time slots…one square for every five minutes from 7:00 PM, when Vivienne du Lac was certainly alive to 11:00 PM, when her body parts were grotesquely separated and cold with death. Listed down the side of the chart were the names of everyone who had worked or performed in the orchestra, the theater, and backstage.

"Why don't you take a break and come back tomorrow morning and fill in the rest."

Buddy grinned, showing his dazzling smile. "I'm gonna work another hour. I want to finish this pile of reports. Tomorrow morning, I'll do the rest, and then we can see, when we re-interview, where we need more information."

"You're a good lad, Bud." Pedar reached for his coat. "I'm going home. Mollie's made corned beef and cabbage and I can almost taste it already." He turned to his boss. "You want to join us, Chief?"

"I'd love to, but I have a few more things to finish up." He put on his overcoat, and rummaged on his desk for three files, "I'll see you both at the theater at noon."

Buddy looked up. "That Janet...the girl that does the costumes...she's very pretty, doncha think?"

"Very. Are you interested?"

"Well...before I let myself get interested, I'd better find out if she was the murderer!" Buddy chuckled . "Remember Harry Henckles?"

"Who?"

"He's the cop from Brooklyn...about a year ago. Was investigating this murder where someone burned a man alive? No? Remember?"

Anderson snapped his fingers. "I do remember! She...the girl who was also burned...she...? She was a real looker...What was the story?"

"She was a crafty one. She used her charms on Harry. She just pretended to be burned. She set fire to her old accomplice in the...I think it was a jewel robbery... and watched him roast...He was tied up and she watched him...She sat around for ten or fifteen minutes watching him as he grilled on the spit." Buddy rolled his eyes. "Then, she managed to loosely tie herself up and sort of burned a little of herself. The cops came in to rescue her before she got really roasted. Harry was the lieutenant in charge of the case." Buddy chortled, thinking of how easy it was for a pretty girl to manipulate a dumb policeman. "Anyway, Harry thought she was the elephant's trunk and fell in love with her. He had everyone in Brooklyn feeling sorry for her....what the heck was her name?"

"So, what happened? I seem to remember something, but...."

"So he was dating her...shoot, I think he was romancing her, and then it all came out that she was the murderer!"

"Gotta watch your suspects with a jaundiced eye." Anderson chuckled, and then paused as he thought of Antonina....*Could she have killed Vivienne? She had motive, certainly...Opportunity? Certainly...Nah! No, never! Antonina was young and sweet and innocent. She'd never...never...never.* His mind was whirling now, and his stomach began to ache.

It was obvious that Buddy's mind was traveling along parallel paths. *Not Janet! She'd never even harm a little mosquito.* Buddy's disdain turned to discomfort. Discomfort prompted him to raise his voice in protest. "Not *Janet!*"

But hadn't little Janet kicked that obnoxious little dog? Gave the dog a good heave-ho? She could have some violent tendencies. She obviously had a temper, didn't she? Buddy bit at his thumbnail. *Nah!*

Anderson's imagination was whirling along, too. He thought back...*Hadn't Antonina said that she could have throttled Vivienne? Nah!*

The two of them, immersed in justice and love, stood up. Anderson messed up Buddy's full crop of dark hair and left the office.

***

In an hour, he was almost at the Connecticut border. It had been a pleasant ride...hardly any traffic on the Post Road. Now, where was that map?

Twenty minutes of driving on back Greenwich roads…passing homes that were grand, grander and even more grand…here it was…the residence of Alex and Dale Troy. Anderson drove his car through a stone gate and up an imposing driveway.

"Chief von Vogel?" Alex was astonished.

"I'm in Greenwich to interview a few witnesses…you, some of the audience, and the Sabatino girl…"

"I don't really know how we can help you, but come in…come in. We're just finishing dinner."

"I'll wait. I don't want to disturb you."

"Are you kidding? Dale and the girls would kill me if they missed out on being interrogated! They can't wait to tell all their friends about the murder…" He laughed. "Little ghouls."

While the girls listened, spellbound, Alex and Dale told Anderson about their visit to the rehearsal on Friday afternoon. "There must have been twenty people that she insulted and degraded in the few hours that I was there," Dale told him. "She was awful. She yelled and threw tantrums…she was…awful!"

"Who did she insult?"

Alex jumped in; "She ripped the dress off the woman who was her…cover...I think you call it. I don't remember her name…Ignatza, or something like that…and she told her, loudly, so that everyone heard, that the woman couldn't sing a note."

"She didn't say it that politely," Dale laughed. "I think she said that she sang like a dying goat, or some such. Then, she screamed at the old colored man…said he was putting a curse on her."

"She yelled at Antonina. Said that she was trying to upstage her and made her move her little cart." Alex didn't notice that Anderson's face blanched slightly and his jaw tightened. "She screamed at Angelique and tried to distract her when she was singing Musetta's Waltz, she yelled at most of the stagehands, annoyed Massimo Orsini and insulted…more than insulted…one of the chorus men. I don't know his name, a young, blond-headed guy…she insisted that he be fired."

"There were very few people that she didn't chew up. I think you'll find that almost everyone in the theater wanted to wring her neck." Dale was thoughtful. "If you are seeking motive, you will have at least fifty people on your list."

The girls were wide-eyed. Although their bringing up was ecumenical, they had never been privy to inside information on a murder. The three leaned forward…this was fascinating!

Anderson wrote down everything they said, then sighed and laid his pad and pen down. "Thank you both for your kind assistance. I thought I had one or two suspects, but now I have fifty!" He leaned forward to get up. "Thank you for allowing me to interrupt your family's private time."

"That's OK, Chief von Vogel," Alex assured him. "The girls were only giving Dale and me their advice on how we might avoid getting caught in the upcoming stock market correction." He beamed at his daughters.

"You children are interested in the *stock* market?" Anderson was incredulous. Chloe and Clair had no such thoughts or interests beyond wheedling a new hat, more money or an expensive doo-dad from him. Their stilted little minds stopped at fashion and gossip.

"Not only are they interested," Alex bragged, "but they have their own portfolios, which they manage better than I could." He laughed. "I wasn't really paying attention to the upcoming crisis. Now, as the girls have instructed me, I'm selling most of my stocks and re-thinking where I should put my money."

"What's wrong with the stock market?" Anderson asked. "I have been making money hand over fist. My radio stock, for instance, has more than tripled in the past few months."

"It's over-leveraged," Rachel told him, her girlish face solemn. "There's too much speculation and the banks are holding too much stock without enough collateral. If RCUSA falls, there's nothing to prop it up, and you'll see lots of people lose everything."

"Really?" Anderson was astonished. "I don't pay much attention to this sort of thing...I leave it to my broker."

"Our advice," Abby nodded and chewed on one of her pigtails, "is to get out. Cash in now before it becomes a real problem."

Anderson stood up, his eyebrows climbing his forehead. "I am astonished, ladies, to hear how ignorant I have been." He bowed to each of the girls. "I am going to have a long discussion with Mr. Richards, my erstwhile financial manger, and perhaps get out of the market." He turned to go and then whirled back. "And where do you young ladies think my money should be?"

"Perhaps in real estate, Chief von Vogel," Ariel Sarah instructed him with great kindness. "We're going to invest in our local hospital and some of the Greenwich Avenue properties."

"Perhaps we will see you on Monday night at the performance? We were going to give our box to some friends, but we want to see Antonina sing again. She's going to be a sensation, and to think, we were there on the night of her first unusual triumph!"

"Naturally, I'll be there, together with all of the men from our station. I have a feeling that this is going to be a most complex case! I never knew much about opera before, but find myself...well...fascinated with all of it. I think the people of the operatic world are the most fascinating, colorful, crazy group that I have ever come across!"

"I'm going to be on stage when I grow up!" Ariel Sarah informed him. "But I'm going to be a professional ballet dancer."

"I look forward to seeing you dance and clapping my heart out for you. I know you will be a sensation at anything you set your heart out to do." Anderson bid them goodbye and especially thanked the girls once more for their advice.

Anderson started up his car and drove to his second target in Greenwich, marveling at the intelligence and knowledge of the Troy children. He felt diminished and sad. Obviously, Alex and Dale were much better parents than he and Helena had ever been, or could ever be. *I must remember to send the girls some chocolates, he thought to himself. Could be they might save me a heap of money and trouble!*

***

Francesca and Simeon returned to her home. As instructed, in her absence, Lucia had cooked dinner. "What did you cook?" Simeon asked.

"An antipasti, then veal piccata[4] with egg noodles and broccoli raab." Lucia's face was proud.

"And for dessert?"

She winked at him. "A surprise!"

"Sure hope we don't get poisoned," Rafe muttered. His sister hit him with her wooden spoon. "Go...call Johnny and Antonina. I'm almost ready." She fussed with the dishes and reminded her twin that, because she had made the meal, it would be Gia's sole responsibility to clean up the kitchen.

"Depends on if the food is shatteringly good or not." Gia teased.

"Personally, I am hungry enough to eat a horse!" Simeon opened a bottle of wine.

"Hope it tastes better than a horse!" Rafe joked, sliding into his chair.

"Here we come!" Antonina galloped to the table. Johnny, pounding on her head, was straddled across her shoulders, yelling giddy-up.

"I'm glad to see that your triumph hasn't swelled your head too much that you wouldn't be Johnny's horsie!" Rafe joked.

"I promise you all that...no matter what...whether I get famous or last night was the last night of my singing, I will never be snooty or stuck-up. I *swear!*" Antonina tossed Johnny into his chair and plumped herself into hers. "I made a vow after seeing that...that woman...that no matter what, I'd *never* be like her!" She held up her wineglass to be filled by Simeon. "Naturally, I'm sorry that she is dead...such an awful murder...but she...well, she was a very...*confrontational* woman."

"Was she really that bad?" Michael asked.

"The rehearsal...she made everyone feel stupid. She yelled at everyone...she threatened people with their jobs and ridiculed them and made fun of their talents. I don't know what to call her...? A harridan, perhaps. She

---

[4] Delizioso...see the recipe at the back.

was terrible and I think everyone she came into contact with wanted to murder her."

"Even you?" Rafe teased.

"Especially me!"

"Enough about this woman. Let's settle down to our own business," Francesca looked around the table where her family sat, each child shining bright. "Does everyone have some wine...no? Johnny? Some water and wine for you, my little darling. Simeon and I have some news for all of you." She held up her glass, giving Simeon a loving look. "Some wonderful news."

***

At the Greenwich Police station, the phone shrilled. Charlie was passing and picked it up. He listened carefully, wrote down an address and hung up. "We've got a little girl missing. Phil, get yer hat. Let's go."

"She was at the playground with her friend, Danielle Gillespie. They always walk home together; they've been best friends since they were two years old. Danielle lives across the street." The distraught mother twisted her hands together. "I saw Danielle and asked where Louise was. Danielle said she didn't know. She said they were playing and then Louise just wasn't there any more."

"Mrs. Lutten, do you have a photograph of Louise?" Charlie spoke with great kindness. "Kids, you know how they are...she's probably at another friend's house and didn't realize how late it was."

"She's never done that before," Mr. Lutten sat on the couch, a hurt look on his stunned face. "She's a good little girl...always."

Charlie took the photograph. It showed a lovely child, in a starched yellow dress, her hair in tight pigtails, a huge grin on her face. Charlie felt tears pricking at his eyes. *Oh, Lord! Keep this little girl safe from harm!* "Is this a recent photo?"

"Yes," Mrs. Lutten whispered. "Her school picture."

"How old is Louise?" Phil asked.

"She's nine. She'll be ten the week after next. " Mrs. Lutten began to cry. "She's just nine. Oh, please, please...find our daughter!"

"Tell us what you can, Danielle," Phil bent down and patted Danielle's head. "Tell us everything that happened, starting from when you and Louise got to the playground."

The curly-haired child screwed up her eyes and tried to think. "Louise and I went to the playground..." They'd reached the playground at about three in the afternoon. The playground was filled with children, most of whom they knew. There were a few mothers there, and one older sister. "I think Mrs. Higgins and Mrs. Bold were there, and Sally's big sister, Susan." Danielle tried hard to remember. "We played on the swings for a while and then a few of the boys came and we all started to play dodge-ball. I think...I don't remember…Louise wasn't…." Her eyes were big with fear. "It was getting late and all the kids began to go home. I looked for Louise, but she wasn't anywhere…so I came home." Danielle shrugged. "I didn't know she was going to run away, Mommy!" Her mother clasped her close.

"Why would she run away, Danielle?

A shrug. "I don't know…"

"Was she unhappy?" Danielle shook her head and shrugged again.

"Did she do something…bad? Something that might make her parents mad?"

Again, Danielle shook her head and shrugged. This sort of conjecture was above her. "Do you think she'd go…where? Back to school? To someone else's home?"

"I don't know." Danielle stuck her thumb in her mouth. She was an adorable child, with a sprinkling of freckles dancing across her nose. She probably had pink cheeks most of the time, but today, her face was pale with worry and the fear of she-didn't-know-what.

Giving Danielle's parents a knowing glance, Charlie got down on his knee in front of Danielle… "Were there any strangers around the playground?" Any…fellows that you don't know? Grown up men?"

Danielle shrugged. "Maybe"

"Can you try to remember?" Danielle's mother came closer and hugged Danielle to her chest.

"Was anyone's Daddy there?" Danielle's mother asked. "Or a neighbor man?"

"I don't remember!" Danielle began to cry. "I don't know!"

Charlie and Phil wrote down the names of the playmates that Danielle could remember. Danielle's mother supplied them with as many addresses as she could.

"Thank you, Danielle," Phil rumpled her hair. "You've been a big help". Over Danielle's head, her mother and Phil looked at one another in worried concern. *Where the heck was Louise?*

***

So this was where she lived. Anderson slowed the car and pulled up in front of a huge hedge. The front walk was highlighted with a white arbor. Anderson imagined it in summer, cascaded with roses. He got out of the car and stepped up to a wide, friendly porch strewn with saggy, comfortable chairs, all well-used. He saw that lights were on and he could sense movement within. He rang the bell.

"Mama! It's a man!" Johnny brought Anderson through to a huge, open room, redolent with delicious smells. A large, round table dominated the room, and the table was crammed with people. It was obvious that he had interrupted a family meal.

He saw her immediately, sitting between two younger girls...she jumped up, as if stung. "Oh! It's *you!*" She fell back in her seat.

"You may not remember me, Mrs. Sabatino," he addressed Francesca. "But I am Police Chief Anderson von Vogel of the New York Metropolitan Police."

"I remember you, Chief," Francesca dimpled at him, wondering why her daughter sat still, like a stunned kitten. "You and your men asked some questions after the opera." She motioned to him, "Please sit down....Lucia!" A young girl with a mop of dark curls and bright blue eyes quickly got up and pushed her chair towards him. Awkward, he sat. He was next to Antonina, and, as the table was crowded, their thighs touched and quickly separated. Had she felt the zing of electricity?

"Have you eaten, Chief von Vogel? No? Lucia, bring the Chief a plate...no...no, I insist. We can talk better if you are filled up." She flashed him a charming smile and he could easily see from where Antonina's beauty sprung.

"And it is Mrs. Rosato, Chief...not Sabatino". He looked confused. "Antonina has taken my maiden name for her own stage name."

"Ah?" He tried to focus. *Rosato...Sabatino...Rosato...*A large plate was placed in front of him. On it was a heap of noodles, covered with two slices of a breaded meat, some lemons and a sauce. On the side was a portion of a green vegetable which he had never seen before. It smelled like heaven.

"Eat." Francesca ordered, and, outmaneuvered and hungry, he fell to. "We can talk afterward." She gave several orders. "Gia, make some coffee...do you like espresso, Chief von Vogel?" He managed to mutter, between chewing and swallowing the ambrosia on his plate, that he didn't know what espresso was.

"Like strong coffee, but better. You can try it, no?" Her voice lilted, with a trace of Italian. "You know Antonina, but this is the rest of my family...My mother, Maria Sabatino" ...an older version of Francesca, faintly recalled from the crowd at the opera, nodded and smiled at him... "My fiancée, Simeon Meade." A good-looking, distinguished man with nearly white-blonde hair gave him a sympathetic and friendly bow..."My sons...the terrible twins Michael and Rafael. My twin daughters, Lucia and Gia, and my little sweetheart, Johnny, who met you at the door." Johnny grinned and waved his fingers.

Unasked, the twin girls got up and cleared the table, then went to the stove and began to fill a strange-looking coffee pot. One of them...*they looked exactly alike...how the heck did one know which was Gia and which was Lucia?*...came back to the table with a tray holding tiny cups and saucers, and a fistful of spoons, forks and a pile of dessert plates. "Let the poor man eat in peace," Francesca admonished as Rafael...*or I think he's Rafael*...began to ask him questions.

212

What a great family! Anderson envied. *See how they all help their mother and each other. Fat chance I'd see Chloe or Clair jump up and serve a guest.*

Anderson made a face as he chewed at the green vegetable. Johnny laughed. "He doesn't like the *broccoli raab*, Mama!"

"It's not that I don't like it," Anderson sputtered at the slightly bitter taste. "I just never had this before...never even heard of it," He laughed, putting them all at ease. "Is this a typical Italian meal? I don't think I've ever had Italian food before...but, please, Mrs. Um, Rosato...this is the best food I have ever tasted!"

"You can thank Lucia," Francesca laughed with him. "She cooked the entire meal." The twin that was, apparently, Lucia, ducked her head, a slow blush making her perfect, heart-shaped face even prettier.

"How do you tell the twins...all of them...apart?" Anderson mopped up the last of the lemony sauce with a piece of fragrant, hot bread. "Good grief! That was marvelous food!"

"Lucia has the face of a camel and Gia the face of a goat," The young man named Michael told him.

"And you can tell revolting Rafe from revolting Mike because Mike has revolting horns growing out of his revolting head and revolting Rafe has two heads!"

"Now that you are no longer a stranger," Simeon laughed easily. "Let's have espresso, and shock you again and then how about that surprise dessert?" He leaned both elbows on the table. "When I first met Francesca, I was astonished at how dumb I was about all things Italian." He waggled his nearly white eyebrows at Francesca. "And then I was astonished at how much I *loved* everything Italian!" Out of the corner of his eye, he watched Antonina. She kept her head down and didn't look at von Vogel. *What did that mean?* Always attuned to his beloved, he could feel the curiosity steaming from Francesca's head. *What was all this?*

"Ta-Da!" Lucia produced a tray with pastries heaped on it. They were tubes of a longish shape, filled with some sort of cream, sprinkled with what looked like chopped chocolate. Anderson had never seen anything like them. "Ga-nol!" Lucia announced, then whispered loudly, "The word is spelled c-a-n-n-o-l-i, but if you say 'can-no-lee', everyone will know you are not Italian."

"Ga-Nol," Anderson parroted. "Whatever you call them, they look fantastic! Thank you, Lucia." The girl beamed.

"What do you think, Mama? Shattering, aren't they?"

"As Chief von Vogel said, they look fantastic." Francesca lifted one off the tray. She winked a Simeon, held the pastry up and then crammed almost half of it into her mouth. Anderson gaped. He had never seen a grown woman stuff her mouth like that! The rest of the table, except for Antonina, began to laugh.

With cream dripping, Francesca nodded. "Mmmm!" She rolled her eyes. *"Meraviglioso, figlia mia. Meraviglioso!"*

"Grazie, Mama mia." Lucia dimpled and passed the tray around.

Anderson watched for a moment, shrugged, his eyes wide and mischievous, then stuck the pastry halfway down his own throat. His senses inhaled a delicious mouthful of scented thick cream and crackly crust "This is marvelous!" he choked out, spitting pieces of crust onto the table. "This is incredible!" He turned to Lucia, licking the residue off his mouth. "Where did you learn to bake like this?"

He looked around, astonished, as everyone, even Antonina, fell about in hilarity. "What? *What?* What did I say?"

Antonina leaned forward, letting her leg come into fleeting contact with his. "How could you know, Chief von Vogel? My mother is the most famous pastry cook and baker in the State of Connecticut...maybe in the entire Forty-Eight States of the United States of America! Naturally, all of us...even the boys...can cook and bake. We all learned it from birth."

"Really? Oh, my!" He bit into the rest of the cannoli[5] and then muttered, "I can see...and now I understand..."

***

Gia poured each of them a tiny cup of dark, steaming liquid. Rafe got up and handed Simeon a crystal bottle of some clear liquid and Gia then placed a small dish, containing what looked like coffee beans, on the table. Simeon passed around a selection of miniature goblets.

"This is espresso," Antonina had decided to speak, Francesca noted. "And, if you'd like, you can either pour some of this *sambucca*...sort of an anise liquor...into your espresso...or you can have a little glass of it..." Here, she poured a tiny cordial glass full of the *sambucca* and handed it to him. She held up her hand and then dropped three of the coffee beans into the glass. They floated on the surface. "These are called either 'The Father , The Son and The Holy Ghost' or 'three mice', however you like." She laughed again at his confusion.

"As you get to know them, it all sort of makes sense." Simeon told him with pity. "Until then, just nod your head like a puppet."

Anderson sipped at the bitter, strong brew. It seemed just right to offset the richness of the cannoli. He picked up the tiny glass, swirled it to get the coffee beans moving, and then sipped. He coughed as a tiny rivulet of hot fire raced from his mouth to his gut. "Wow!" Again, he made everyone laugh.

"Basta! We have made this poor man – a stranger - the target of our laughter!" Francesca's smile was warm. "And he has been a good sport about

---

[5] Again, kindly go to the end if you want to astonish police chiefs who might just stop in for dinner...

it all." The entire table broke into applause, admiring Anderson. He glowed. He *wanted* them to like him. He liked them too, for themselves…not only because they were her family…"And now, you children, clear up and go and do your homework. Rafe, please put Johnny to bed and read him a nice story. I think this lovely police chief has things of a serious nature to talk about to Antonina, Simeon and me."

***

It was nearly nine o'clock. "Let's put out a bulletin to the radio station and get a notice into tomorrow's Greenwich Time," Chief McAndrews, hoping for an early night, stretched, resigned now to going home…again…later then he had expected. "Say: MISSING…LOUISE LUTTEN, 9 years old, colored, 3 feet 6 inches tall, approximately 65 pounds, black hair in pigtails, dark brown eyes….Last seen at the Julian Curtis Playground yesterday at approximately 3 PM…last seen wearing a navy blue sweater over a white blouse, navy blue skirt, navy stockings and black shoes. Anyone who has seen anything suspicious or unusual, PLEASE IMMEDIATELY contact the GREENWICH POLICE." He sighed. "God help her."

***

"Simeon and I were at the performance. We were absolutely shocked, and thrilled…now, remember, we had no idea of why du Lac was not singing, nor of why her understudy wasn't able to sing…when we heard Antonina's name. I was shaking with excitement." She reached over and took Antonina's hand. "My daughter has wanted to be an opera singer ever since she was a tiny child. She's worked and studied…and I, for one, think she has the best voice in the world."

"We'd waited, Francesca and I, when the performance was over and Urbano…Francesca has known Urbano and his wife as a courtesy aunt and uncle for many years…" Simeon broke in.

"His wife, Vittoria, and I…and Antonina, when she was a tiny girl…all of my children, except Johnny…we came to America on the same boat. Lucia was very sick…she might have died had it not been for Vittoria…we have been fast and faithful friends ever since…" Anderson knew there were many stories behind Francesca's rush of words. He smiled gently at her.

"At any rate, to go on with what might interest you instead of stories about our family, we know absolutely nothing about Vivienne du Lac." Simeon shrugged. "Only the story that Antonina told us about the rehearsal."

"Perhaps we can talk a bit?" Anderson turned to Antonina.

Francesca nudged Simeon and made a motion with her chin. *Let's you and I go and leave these two alone.* "We'll leave you to talk. If you need us, we'll be upstairs," Simeon shook Anderson's hand. "I look forward to seeing you again. We'll both be at the performance tomorrow night."

"Oh!" Anderson shot up. "Antonina's performance! I almost forgot in all of your gracious hospitality and food!" He fished in his briefcase. "Here are

the two New York newspapers with the reviews of the opera!" He spread the Herald Tribune out. On the front page, in large headlines, was: OPERA STAR MURDERED.

"du Lac's death is on the front page, but here…" He paged to the Entertainment Section. Blazoned across the top of the front page was: "THE QUEEN IS DEAD…LONG LIVE THE QUEEN!" And below that, in large type: "NEW STAR GLOWS ON THE MET STAGE! ANTONINA SABATINO SHINES BRIGHTER THAN THE SUN – SINGS BETTER THAN ANYONE HAS EVER SUNG MIMI! – MASSIMO ORSINI BRILLIANT AS HE CONDUCTS MET ORCHESTRA – THE *MAESTRO* IS STILL THE MASTER!

"Oh, Mama!" Antonina gasped. "I didn't even think of the reviews! Oh…*Oh!*"

"I've read them three times myself," Anderson grinned. "You are going to find yourself praised in a thousand different ways. The whole world now knows what I saw last night." He picked up her hand. It was ice-cold. "You were…indescribable…the most moving performance…perfect…" He was almost choking, Francesca noted. *I wonder if he is married….Antonina is avoiding looking at me….I wonder what is going on here….*

"The New York Times," Anderson handed them the second paper. "Jason Harris did a four column review. He called you 'the most remarkable thing that has been on the stage of the Met in decades.'" He turned to the Theater Page and read a snippet: 'Her voice has a pure, incandescent quality. Mimi lives…remarkable in one so young… her career should rise like a meteor.'" He scanned the rest of the review. "Hard to say which critic was more fulsome with praise."

Simeon touched Antonina's shoulder. "You are now famous, Antonina." Anderson watched her as she blushed scarlet. And then, on a very sober note, he said, "I hope it doesn't change you too much."

"Why don't you take the papers up with you, Simeon," Antonina folded the papers and handed them to Simeon. "I'll read them later." Simeon and Francesca shared a telling glance, took the papers and left Antonina and Anderson together.

"Alone at last," Anderson grinned. "Or is that too trite a thing to say?" He turned toward her and picked up her hand. "I should be an objective, impersonal policeman, but I can't wait to tell you that I thought of you all day."

Her eyelashes were like delicate fans against her pink cheeks. Shyly, she looked up at him. "I found myself waiting to see you again."

"Did you?" He gnawed at his lip. "I told you when we first, uh, met, Antonina…I'm married. You're an unspoiled child and I'm a man who has many piles of dirty laundry. I'll tell you once more…I had an unhappy, loveless marriage, but, that's probably what all married men might say to a young girl like yourself. I can't help it. It's true. I've seen you and spoken with you for a total of fifteen minutes. I'm…I'm…well…I can't get you out of my mind. Is there such a thing as love at first sight? I can't think or sleep or eat…I just want you."

"This is such a…I'm…I don't know what to say or do!" Her aguish was palpable. "Almost all of my life, I thought of two things; that I'd sing on the opera stage, and that I might be Peter Bovi's wife. He's…he was my boy-friend…we have been neighbors since we were children…everyone expected that we'd…and then…Vivienne was murdered, and I got to sing. And then…you." She looked at him with longing and confusion. "When I first saw you…I don't quite….I don't…"

He stood up, reached down and kissed her gently on her cheek. "It's late, my bruised little bird with the sweet voice. I've stumbled here and made you upset."

She shook her head. "I'm not upset. I'm gloriously happy." She grinned and his heart turned over and over. "But…it *is* late and I need to get ready for tomorrow night's performance."

"There's all the time in the world for this…whatever it will be," Anderson took his coat and hat from the stand. "You and I are linked through some wonderful, celestial chemistry." His smile was charming. "You get a good night's sleep and we'll talk before the show tomorrow."

"You *will* be there?" Her face was lit.

"Naturally. I will be wherever you are." His face was still. "That's what my life will be like from now on."

"We will be happy, won't we, Anderson?" His name was like honey.

"We will be." He bent again and kissed her. She turned her head and met his lips, sweetly, gently. And then, he went out into the night.

***

His last stop in Connecticut was at the Greenwich Police Station. The lights were still shining and he could see several patrolmen milling around. He knocked at the locked door.

"I'm Police Chief Anderson von Vogel, from the New York Metropolitan Police." He introduced himself.

"Emerson McAndrews. Chief here in Greenwich." Emerson pumped his hand. "Nice to meet you." Emerson's eyes asked.

"As I am investigating a murder that touches on a few of your good citizens, I wanted to let you know that I will be poaching…a bit…into your territory."

"Sit down and tell me what's going on…" Emerson invited, offering Anderson a cigar. "It's always something, isn't it? We just got ourselves the worst problem a few hours ago."

"What happened?"

"Little girl gone missing. Sweet kid by the name of Louise."

"How long has she been gone?" Anderson leaned forward, his mind delving. A policeman never stopped being a policeman.

"Seven hours or so...she's nine...nearly ten years old."

"Shit."

Emerson shrugged. "I sure hope she got mad at her mother and is hiding somewhere."

Both men felt a draft...a swift passing of some cold air...somewhere near, and both men's hearts dropped. They had been cops too long to think that Louise was simply hiding.

Emerson lit his cigar. "So, tell me what brings you to our fair town?"

"Murder. Have you heard that a famous opera singer who was to sing at the Metropolitan Opera had her throat cut last night?"

"I did hear something about it...didn't our little Antonina Sabatino get a chance to sing the role?"

"Do you *know* her?" Anderson's chilled heart began to warm.

Emerson's laugh boomed. *"Know* her? Ha! I know the whole family!"

"I met them tonight. Francesca, the mother... and her fiancée Simeon..."

"Fiancée? Good ole Simeon! Finally got her to say yes!" He slapped his thigh. "There's a long tale associated with the family. The father...what a terrible man he was!"

"The father?"

"Carlo Rosato," Emerson spat the name out. "He was a swine...a rat, and even worse." In his mind, Emerson re-played the scenes of madness that Carlo had caused. "But he's gone...dead, and no one grieves for him at all." He shrugged. "Everyone was...what's that fancy word? *Shadenfreud?* You know, delighted that he was dead." The smoke came out of his mouth in a puff. "So, anyway, tell me about the opera singer's murder."

"*Shadenfreud* is right in my murder investigation, too. There wasn't a person in the opera house, even little Antonina, who liked Vivienne du Lac. There are dozens of possible suspects and really no clues at all."

It was after midnight when the two men shut off the lights of the police station and went home...Emerson, six blocks away to a warm kitchen and a dinner kept hot for him, no matter how late he came in, and Anderson, sixty miles away to a dark and chilly house.

Chapter Eighteen

"Men have been swindled by other men on many occasions. The autumn of 1929 was, perhaps, the first occasion when men succeeded on a large scale in swindling themselves..." John Kenneth Galbraith...The Great Crash

*O*ne of the most pleasurable things about the morning was sitting with David, usually in a sunny spot in front of the window overlooking Central Park, sipping fragrant coffee and reading the New York Times (David) and the New York Herald Tribune (Barbara). David really preferred The Times of London, but, even with the newspaper being shipped over on one of the new and quick-crossing ocean liners, it was always delivered at least month late.

"Damn and blast!" David read a particularly galling editorial favoring the Labour point of view. "Suffering idiots!" David never held back on his opinions.

Teddy, wise in the ways of a typical morning, moved closer to Barbara and nudged her leg. He was rewarded by a piece of buttered toast with rough-cut marmalade. Teddy adored buttered toast with rough-cut marmalade.

"What a wonderful review!" Barbara delved further into James Blackburn's opera column. "Blackburn says that you are a genius to have found Antonina." She giggled. "If only they knew the truth!"

David gave her a glare of pretended hurt. "If I were able to choose an alternate to Vivienne, I certainly would have chosen Antonina."

Barbara choked. "You had no idea of who Antonina was! Even when she came through the door, coughing and looking so ravishing, you didn't know what to expect!"

David crashed the paper onto the floor. "You've cut me through...like a sword! Of *course* I knew who Antonina was!" He scrabbled in the hidden recesses of his brain. "I had always known about her abilities," he bluffed with grand abandon. "Signor Fazzolini and I had discussed her future often. We were waiting for an opportunity...and then, when du Lac was murdered...well, my dear Barbara, it was...it was....well, as you know, my idea took root then and there." He waved his hands, as if conducting the orchestra. "I always was able to improvise, darling. I always believe in looking ahead."

Barbara's scathing answer was drowned out by the buzz of the intercom connecting to the main lobby. Delighted at the interruption, David roared, "Who goes there?"

"Anderson von Vogel, Baron. May I interrupt your breakfast?"

"With great pleasure, my lad. Please ascend!"

Anderson settled at the table, accepted his third cup of coffee for the morning, and then got down to business after a few preliminary remarks about Teddy's beauty and intelligence.

"Before I even begin to talk about the murder investigation..." he turned toward David. "I consider you one of the most intelligent and insightful men I know..." David's lean face beamed. "I've just had a most interesting conversation about the volatility of the stock market. I've been advised..." (and here, Anderson grinned to himself – what would David think if he told them that his three sources were three schoolgirls?)... "by three independent sources, to liquidate my holdings, especially those in radio, banks, and steel. What is your opinion, if I may be so bold?"

David harrumphed, while his agile mind jumped to assimilate the stock market situation. He had been noticing that the market seemed over-priced...no stocks could keep climbing so astronomically, could they? "Yes, yes. I agree. I have been speaking with my advisors also." Barbara shot him a quick look...*in a pig's eye you have!*

David shot *her* a quick look. *Just because I haven't discussed it with you, doesn't mean that I haven't been right on top of it all!*

Anderson, a master of decoding that which was never said, rubbed his hands together. "Then you advise me to liquefy...to sell some of the stocks?"

David had recovered completely. His lightning-fast intelligence, once aware of what the situation was, had already gathered all the loose ends that had floated his way during the past few weeks. "Yes, my liege. I, too, am going to sell my precariously placed shares." He held his coffee cup out to be refilled. Barbara complied. "I am selling RCUSA, my American Steel, much of my bank stock and also...the stock I have in Aurelian."

"Aurelian? I thought their cars were selling at a great clip."

"Put your money in British cars, Anderson. The American built cars...well...especially Aurelian...pieces of junk, that's all. Pieces of junk." He bit off a large piece of toast. "What are you driving these days?"

"A have a Pierce-Arrow." Anderson's brow was creased. "Should I worry about Pierce-Arrow?"

David shrugged and put years of wealth into the movement. "I always drive Rollers myself."

Barbara rolled her eyes mischievously, "And his sweet baby Rolls is baby blue, like a robin's egg."

Anderson laughed. "I can't afford a Rolls Royce, never mind a baby-blue one!"

"Piffle! A great car is a great investment!"

Barbara began to rise. "Anderson, while you two argue about cars, I have a meeting to attend at the Met."

"I'll only be a few moments more...I must take off my unofficial hat and put my police hat back on. I really didn't mean to veer off onto financial matters. I need your recollections about the rehearsal and the night of the opera." He reached into his briefcase and brought out his notes. "Now, tell me, Barbara, what you noticed at the rehearsal..."

***

The doorman waved a cab over for Barbara. The cabbie stopped and leaped out. "Good morning, Mrs. Wessel!"

"Oh! It's you!" Barbara recognized her voluble driver from a few mornings ago. "Neil? Was it Neil? You have the wife who plays the harp?"

"That's me...Neil Odams...you re*mem*ber me?"

"Of course!" Barbara settled herself in the seat. "As a matter of fact, I'm going to the Met this morning, too."

"I saw you and your mister there on Saturday. I was up in the attics." Neil laughed. "Wasn't she *mar*velous! I never thought I'd have a story that I could tell my children...not that I have any children yet...about how I saw opera history being made!" He steered the car around a recalcitrant brewery wagon.

"You should have come down and met Gigli."

"Pshaw! *Me?* A cab driver! He wouldn't want to be bothered by someone like me."

"He's a very nice man...He wasn't always a famous opera singer. I think his father was a green-grocer and Gigli delivered tomatoes and peppers for him....He will enjoy meeting you – a devoted and knowledgeable fan."

"Next time I see you and Mr. Gigli, I'll run right up to you!" Neil joked.

"Well, I'll be there tonight...same box, same time. I'm not too sure if Gigli will be joining us, but if he is, I'll expect you to stop!"

"Well, I'll see.....I can't wait for Sabatino to sing again. She's such a little mite! But her voice! The power of her lungs! Who could believe that she could carry the whole opera? Patty tells me that she had no rehearsals...no preparation. Just came up from nowhere and sang like an angel."

"I can't wait for tonight's performance," Barbara agreed fervently. "She's going to be a huge star." The cab slowed down as traffic stalled in front of The New York and International Bank building stood. "Neil?" Barbara started slowly...

"Yessum?"

"Do you and your Patricia own any stock?"

"Sure we do. Like every other red-blooded American, we've put our savings into RCUSA...made a bundle of money, too."

"Really?" She didn't know whether to say anything or just to keep quiet. Was it good advice or silly?

"Yup. We don't want to stay here in New York City. Patty and me, we want to go north...go to Maine."

"Maine?"

"Yup. I have my eye on a little fishing boat. I always wanted to be a fishing boat captain...to work on the water."

"Really?" Barbara couldn't imagine living away from a big city. She loved the hustle and bustle...the noise and the energy. "Maine? Do they have bears in Maine?"

"I sure hope so!" Neil laughed. "I've got a cousin up in a place called Kittery Point. Lots of fishing up there. We plan to save a little more, sell our stuff down here and buy a little cottage up there." As the traffic ground to a dead stop, Neil leaned back over to talk. "We've even got a name for our boat," he laughed, a bit red-faced.

"What will you call it?" Barbara really *liked* this young man.

"We'll call it *The Captain and Patty.*" He squirmed on the seat. "Do you think that's a silly name?"

"I think it's a wonderful name." Up ahead, traffic started to move again and all around them horns beeped and men cursed.

"Here we go..."

"Neil....this is really none of my business...I mean how you handle your savings and all...but..."

"Yeah?"

"Maybe...my husband says...maybe you'd want to think about taking your profits from your stock now...." She launched into a short explanation.

"You think we should sell?" Neil skillfully swooped his cab right to the front entrance to the Met. Again, he leaped out of his cab and opened Barbara's door with a bow and a flourish. "I mean...things are going so well with the stock...it's doubling and then doubling again....do you really think...?"

Barbara paid him and again, gave him a generous tip. She enjoyed talking with him, but maybe she should have just kept quiet about the stock.... "I'm not telling you what to do, Neil," She stepped back as he heaved himself back into the driver's seat. "I just...I..."

"I'll talk it over with Patty. She's the smart one...Thanks again, Mrs. Wessel." He tooted the horn with a flourish. "See you and old Beniamino tonight!"

***

Charlie and Cliff did the house-to-house investigation, while Phil and Pete conducted a circle search of the playground at Julian Curtis School. Phil drew a sketch of the playground, then divided the area into eight slices. Each slice was marked with stakes and yellow ribbon, and was the responsibility of one patrolman. The eight patrolmen started in a tight circle together, their heels touching. While Phil supervised, the men crawled outward on their hands and knees, parting grass blades, and combing through asphalt and gravel to find anything...*anything*...that might help them to know where a little girl might have disappeared ...or help them find anyone who may have removed her, either forcibly or by enticement, from her happy playmates. As their slice of area widened, the men worked harder and harder. The flatness of the playground area changed to brambles and bushes and then a gully on one side. The other side dipped into a street.

Anything found...a cigarette butt, a piece of paper, a torn match book cover, whatever...was marked with a stick. The patrolman then yelled and Pete came over, tied a pink tie to the top of the stick, retrieved the piece of potential evidence and put it into a clean brown paper bag.

The men went over a half-mile of ground this way, thereby covering a circular mile. Vectors 1, 2 and 3 went into the woods and yielded more secrets. Vectors 4, 5 and 6 stretched into the road. And what did they discover? The list read:

Three cigarette butts. Two from Vector 1 – section 5, and one from Vector 5 – section 3...The two butts were from Chesterfields cigarettes, the single butt from a Lucky Strike.

One metal can opener found in Vector 2 – section 4

A navy blue button, badly scratched and weather-worn, found in Vector 1 - section 5

Two empty beer bottles, Schlitz beer, Vector 3 – section 5

A red-pattered bandanna, torn – Vector 2 – section 4

Two balls – both showing weather wear – Vector 2 – section 5

One dog collar – red – with a scratched brass plate reading "Lucky". Vector 3 – section 5.

One woman's slipper – for right foot – made of green chenille – new. Size 7 ½ - Vector 3 – section 5

One skate key on torn lanyard – found in street – Vector 5 – section 6

Eleven pieces of assorted paper – Three were torn from cigarette packages. One was half of a Pickwick Theater stub

One crumpled and ripped piece of notebook paper. Listed on it were the words: LET, ½ TUR, P.O., POT

One receipt from Wee Care Cleaners, dated March 8, 1929 for repair of a brown pair of pants

Two matchbook covers, one from The Bruce Park Grille, and one offering to make a weak man into a man with Sampson-like strength in just three weeks.

One envelope, torn, with half the address showing: It read:...34 East Elm Street .....wich, Conn.

Two candy wrappers – one from Black Jack's Taffy, one from Necco's wafers

Two metal screws – Vector 4 – section 5

A torn piece of navy blue ribbon, new

Seven burnt matches, found in various places.

One half-eaten donut, relatively fresh, Vector 2 – section 2

Two rusty tin cans, one found in Vector 3 – section 4, and one found in Vector 6, section 3

***

"Make anything of this stuff?" Phil shrugged, touching the paper bag that held the donut piece.

"Might be her hair ribbon," Pete offered. "She was dressed in navy blue."

"We'll check with her mother." Phil sighed. "Gee." The two of them had miserable thoughts of a little girl, maybe abducted, maybe even worse…

"Check and see who lives on 334 East Elm, 134 East Elm, 234 East Elm or whatever." Phil scribbled on his notepad.

"And see if anyone has reported a lost dog named Lucky." Phil made another notation.

"How 'bout this list?"

"I think the list is groceries."

"How so?"

"LET is for lettuce. POT is for potatoes…1/2 TUR…half pound of turkey?"

"And the P.O.?" Phil wasn't convinced. "Is that for Peas Only?"

"Smart ass kid!" Pete laughed. "Lessee…prunes? Prunes and onions ? Potatoes and…and…who the heck knows?"

"Only Fu Manchu. And he knows everything!"

"OK, smart boy. While you have nothin' else to do, search out every woman you see who is dressed in a bathrobe." Pete snickered. "See if she only has one slipper on!"

"Like Cinderella?"

"Just like Cinderella."

***

"Antonina, can you come up to my office?" Arturo Calle intercepted her as she came into the stage door.

He shut the door. Antonia looked around with curiosity. She'd never been in this part of the building. The office was cramped and slightly shabby, the walls festooned with pictures of various opera sets, stacks of papers and files, and photos of some opera stars autographed to "Darling Arturo…" and so forth.

"I want to again congratulate you on your beautiful performance. I am presuming that tonight, you will be repeating your triumph."

Antonina blushed and ducked her head. "Thank you," she whispered. "I never imagined that I would get to sing Mimi in such…unusual circumstances. I wish that Mademoiselle du Lac….I'm sorry that she…." She threw up her hands, hoping that he understood her confusion.

"What's done is done." He smiled in what he hoped was an avuncular way. "We are taking up a collection for Ignatzia. Janet is bringing her a fruit basket. She's resting at the hospital, but will be able to hobble home in three days. We are hoping that she can soon be back at work here."

Antonina delved into her purse and brought out a dollar bill. "For Ignatzia," she offered. He opened a drawer of his desk and added the dollar to a bulge of money.

"Thank you, my dear. I'll add your name to the get-well card. Now," he dusted his hands as if to be rid of the specter of Vivienne du Lac and Ignatzia. "We must talk about your new contract and what we are to pay you."

"Oh!" She was clearly astonished.

"Well, my dear, you sang the lead. We can scarcely expect you to sing Mimi for the same money…what do we pay you anyway?"

"The same as any minor walk-on, Mr. Calle. Six dollars a day for rehearsal days, Ten dollars for a performance."

"Is that what we pay you?" He seemed surprised.

"Was it too little or too much?" He had underestimated her.

"Harrumph. Whatever…now that you are singing Mimi…Saturday night and tonight…and we can presume, can we not, that you will be singing Violetta next week on Saturday night and on Monday…?"

"Certainly," she dimpled.

"We thought you would, ah, that your salary would be, um, ah, greatly be increased, ah…" he handed her a sheaf of papers.

"What is this?"

"Your new contract," He fiddled with his pen.

She glanced at it. "Ah," she said.

"What do you think? A fortune for such a little girl!" His face beamed with good humor.

She riffled through the pages. "I think I should get a bonus for Saturday night's performance," she began. He blinked. "It should be for… um…I think…four hundred dollars." *A colossal sum! Will he balk at paying me so much?* "And then, I will take the contracts to Signor Fazzolini and my step-father-to-be."

"Who…?" Calle felt as if he'd been punched. *She should have jumped at the offer. Jumped like a happy gazelle!*

"Simeon Meade. He and my mother are to be wed rather soon. He's an attorney."

"An attorney? Well, yes…I see…" *An attorney! Sweet Saint Anthony! An attorney! And I thought she would be putty in my hands!*

"I'll recommend that you and Simeon meet to finalize the contract." She grinned. "This is so exiting to me, Mr. Calle! But, as I plan to move to New

York City, so as to be closer to work, I will immediately need the bonus amount so that I can find and rent a decent apartment for myself."

"Er…yes, certainly." He rubbed his chin. *Sweet Saint Anthony!*

***

The house to house inquiry hadn't turned up much. Ten men had gone up and down the street where the Lutten family had resided for sixteen years. The men then fanned out and went door-to-door on all of the nearby streets, then on the street that the children would use when going to and from the playground to the Lutten house.

One woman said she had seen a man who looked foreign…a big, burly man with dark hair and a moustache. "I think he had a truck."

"What kind of truck?"

"An old one," It was the best she could recall.

"Could have been the vegetable man," Charlie opined. He made a note to check with Gennaro Bastinglia, the fat man who delivered fresh vegetables in his old truck every Tuesday and Friday to the housewives of the area.

An elderly man told them that a dark-colored sedan had been cruising up and down the street. "The car went slowly up the street, then turned around and went down the street. Then, about six minutes later, went back up, turned around and went back down." The man spiced up his narrative with hand motions, zooming back and forth.

"Was there only one person in the car?"

"Donno."

"Was it a man?"

A shrug.

A teen-aged boy who lived across the street from Louise Lutten told Charlie that he'd seen "a lady with a little girl that sort of looked like Louise…she was a colored lady and the girl was colored. The lady had a big hat on and the girl had a kerchief tied over her head."

"What was the lady wearing? A dress?"

"Yeah, a dress."

"The color of the dress? Did you notice?"

Another shrug. "Maybe yellow and green. "I think the hat was yellow."

"Can you remember what the little girl was wearing, other than a kerchief?"

"Maybe a white top…" The lad screwed up his eyes. "I…I…I don't remember. I'm sorry." He scratched his chin. "Maybe we kids can help you and look around for Louise. We all really feel sad that she's missing."

"Thanks, son. We're going to ask for volunteers." Charlie took his name and address. "We'll let you know. We can use all the help we can get." Charlie's shoulders slumped as he walked away.

***

As Anderson had indicated he'd be at the Metropolitan Opera House as of one o'clock on Monday afternoon, Dr. John Dempsey, the Coroner for the

City of New York, thought it might be fun for him to bring the autopsy reports directly to Anderson.

An opera lover himself, Dempsey hadn't been able to get tickets to Saturday night's performance, nor had he been able to find anyone to sell him tickets for tonight. *Everyone and his Aunt Nellie wants to see this little lady sing. Fat chance that I can sneak in.* Armed with his official paperwork, Dempsey sailed through the stage door. *I'll just hang around. They're doing the dress rehearsal in a little while and I can see that, if nothing else.*

"What's the autopsy say, John?"

Dempsey tossed the packet onto the desk in front of Buddy Manger. "Not much in the way of surprises. Appears that her neck was cut…most likely from a right-handed person standing in back of her. I am proposing that she was seated, perhaps at her dressing table. I am also proposing that the person was standing in back of her, pulled up her head, perhaps by her hair, and slashed her throat in one enormously strong cut."

"Could it have been by this knife?" Buddy held up the cellophane envelope holding the knife that was found under Vivienne's dressing table.

Dempsey gave it a short glance. "I don't think so. The weapon was sharper, narrower…perhaps like a surgeon's scalpel."

"Maybe you were here, Doc," Anderson joked.

"Ha. Ha." Dempsey gave him a nasty look. "Not quite a surgeon's scalpel, but *like* one."

"How was it different?"

"From the tear pattern and the pieces of vocal chord slashed, it was wider than a scalpel, but narrower than a regular knife. It was very sharp…almost like a stiletto…" He shook his head. "Don't know that I have ever seen any weapon exactly like this one."

Buddy dropped the package on the desk. "Hmpf" he said. "Too bad." He checked his notes. "There is a knife still missing. The one that was to have been used in Act One. The character of Schaunard…I think…uses it to cut a chicken on the stage. It was missing before the opera started."

"The cut was clean…severed the jugular and the two arteries. The blood gush would have been horrific…like Niagara Falls in spring flood. Look at the splash pattern," He showed them blood that was splashed as far as the wall by the windows. "Whoever stood behind her would have been drenched in blood." He made a sweeping gesture. "Gutted with blood. Their clothing, or costume, or whatever they were wearing would have been soaked. Their hands, even maybe their face." He scratched his chin. "Unless, maybe, they wore a cover-up or some kind of coat that completely protected them."

"There wasn't anyone…no one has said that there was anyone, who was covered with blood. No one noticed anyone with blood spots on their costume or clothing. Someone would have noticed." Dempsey shrugged. He could only tell them what was what. The deductive process…well, that was Anderson's job.

"And then there was this knife…"Anderson showed Dempsey the knife that had been under Vivienne's dressing room table skirt.

Dr. Dempsey shook his head. "Nope, that's not the weapon, either."

"Too many knives floating around," Anderson mused.

"Yeah, and none of them the right one." Buddy sympathized.

Anderson continued, "We'll make a search for the murder knife and for whatever bloody costume we can find…We're going to go over this mausoleum inch by inch."

"Won't be easy. This is a huge edifice…old and with lots of secret places…easy to hide something which might never, ever come to light."

"We'll have to do it." Anderson shook his head in frustration. *"Nothing* about this murder is easy." He wandered around the room, picking up a perfume bottle from the dressing table, sniffing it and putting it back. Buddy and Dempsey watched him. He kicked at the hassock, held the torn leash up and threw it down. He pushed the chaise lounge out of the way…shoved it hard, and it slid forward, offering a glimpse of a large, black object behind it. "Hey! What's this?"

Anderson reached down and, with the tips of his fingers, pulled up the corner of a large swath of black velvet cloth. Buddy pushed the chaise lounge further away so as to better see.

"It's a …what? Some kind of costume?"

The cloth was large and, when spread out, seemed to be a cloak or robe. It was black, and had some sort of hood.

"Feel it," Anderson ran his fingers over the plush. "It's stiff and…it's got stuff that's dried on it."

Dempsey reached out, fingered the cloth and then put his glasses on. He took a sharp knife from his kit and scraped off some of the dried material into the palm of his hand. He sniffed it, then spit into his hand.

"Is it blood?"

"Yeah." Dempsey's palm, where the spit had mingled with the dried material, was tinged with a rusty-colored emolument. "I wonder if it's hers."

"Maybe someone wore the cloak so they didn't get covered with her blood." Buddy held the cloak up. "I'm almost six feet tall. This is a big cloak. Perhaps a tall man's cloak? This is most likely our murderer's protective shield."

"Or maybe a short man who was a murderer wore it." Anderson sighed. "Just to confuse us a little bit more. John, can you take it and see if you can tell us anything more about it?"

"Sure. I'll do my best. These new tests can tell us whether it is animal blood or human blood…and we can tell what blood group it came from…but…I think we'll find that the blood is Vivienne's. That will confirm that she's really, really, *really* dead, but not tell us one rabbit fart's worth of who killed her."

Anderson sighed. "We'll do the best we can. Gather as much as we can." He looked around, wondering what he might have missed. "And Buddy, ask around and find out who the cloak belonged to. Is anyone missing a costume, maybe from the wardrobe department?" He dusted his hands. "Was the cloak here, or did someone bring it in here with him, knowing that cutting Vivienne's throat would make a god-awful mess."

"This gets weirder and weirder. What else is stuck under the furniture in here?" Buddy peered under the chaise, but was rewarded with nothing but dust and dog hair.

"Glad you volunteered, Bud. As soon as we're through in here, I want you and one of the patrolmen to do a search of everything in here. Maybe we've missed something vital." He swung back to the Coroner. "What else can you tell us from the autopsy?"

"She ate two hours before she died….we are putting the time of death at between 7:20 PM and 7:45 PM, which is when the young boy called her. Not a lot of time".

"And only three hundred people passed by her door in those fifteen minutes," Anderson groaned. "Thanks, Doc."

"If you care, she ate rare steak and fried potatoes, drank wine, and ate some chocolate." He plunked his bulk on the corner of the desk and swung his leg. "Most interesting, though, was that she ingested ether…probably inhaled it…about five minutes before her death."

"Ether?" von Vogel and Manger were both astonished. "What the hell did she do that for?"

"An old operatic trick, or so I am told." Dempsey's expression was smug. *What other Coroner would know such a thing?* "When an opera singer's voice is going to pot, they sometimes suck in ether a half-hour before they sing. It's illegal and dangerous, but I am assured that it is commonly done and probably rather effective."

"Ether? Doesn't it…smell funny?" Anderson thought back to a tooth extraction he had suffered last year. He could still bring back the nauseatingly sick-sweet odor of the gas they had given him. He shuddered. "Whuh! Ether!"

"I understand that no ether, nor any container that would have housed the ether until it was used was found in her dressing room." Dempsey checked a page of notes. "Don't know what could have happened to it. It's rather volatile stuff. Dissipates in the air, although it stays for a while in the throat tissues."

"We think her manservant…a dwarf…wouldn't you know this idiotic case has not only a missing dog, but a *dwarf*…known as Crespi…was here in her room. Maybe he brought the ether to her and then removed all traces."

"Crespi? Have you interrogated him? Could he have killed her in some sort of argument and then taken away the evidence – the ether - of him being with her?

"Can't find the slippery bastard. We've checked her apartment. Someone was in it, by jingo. The place was ransacked – everything turned inside out - and her maid says that money and jewelry are missing."

"Could the maid have taken it herself?"

"Her name is Celestina." Anderson shook his head. "No. She was here, backstage, while du Lac was murdered. She didn't go back to the apartment, although it's possible that she, herself, murdered du Lac before she came backstage. She's certainly on our list of suspects. But, she never went back to the apartment…she was very upset and stayed all night with Janet…what was her last name? The dresser…?"

"Connelly," With a grin, Buddy chimed in. "Janet Connelly."

Anderson grinned. "Buddy is keeping his eye on the toothsome Janet. He's quite interested in all that goes on with her." He waved his hands. "Nonetheless, the maid was either here or with Janet. The apartment was tossed and robbed by someone else. And as far as we can tell, no one has seen Crespi since."

"Whatever happened to the dog?"

Anderson shrugged. "I have no idea. Someone said that the dog ran away...perhaps it's still hiding somewhere in the theater. Maybe it got outside somehow…I don't know." He spread his hands out. 'Everything connected to this case is screwy."

"I hear that anything connected with the opera can be screwy."

"Anything else in the autopsy that we should know about?"

John Dempsey thought back. "The head sustained a few bruises after death."

"Huh?" Pedar tipped his head. "After death?"

"Yup." John grinned, enjoying himself. He always enjoyed the really gruesome details, and got a lot of satisfaction in telling his cohorts about the messy bits, as he called them. "Remember, we were told that her head was hanging by a few strips of skin?" He circled his own throat and faced them with a contorted expression. "We were also told that, when they tried to wrestle the dress over her head, the weight was too much for the little strips of skin…the entire head fell off." Pedar grimaced. He had a soft stomach. "The head probably bounced on the floor and then rolled around a little." Dempsey did some jazzy footwork, pretending to kick a soccer ball around. "The fall and the subsequent knocking about caused a lot of bruising on her face. Posthumous bruising, we'd call it."

"Thanks, John. You've ruined my lunch," Pedar complained.

"Anytime I can be of help," Doctor Dempsey bowed. "Also, naturally, with her head coming off as it did, the skin and tendons in her neck and vocal chord area were posthumously damaged. Got all messed up with dust and whatever was on the floor where it rolled. Dog hair and other stuff. Ha Ha! Goes without saying." He put his glasses into his top pocket. "Now, what would *you* say if I wanted to sit out in the audience and watch the rehearsal? I can't get any blamed tickets for tonight, and I'd love to hear the opera." He put his hands together in supplication. "I swear, I'll be as quiet as a mouse."

"Go on out. Try to find David Wessel. Baron Wessel. Tall, very distinguished man...he's probably sitting in the third row or in one of the parterre boxes. Tell him who you are and that I sent you out to watch. You can pretend that you're part of the investigative team. See if you can spot the killer."

***

"Are you Patricia Odams?" Barbara trotted down the aisle and into the orchestra pit, then over to the harp. A curvy woman with bright blue eyes in a lively, attractive face turned to her. Her pretty mouth opened in astonishment.

"Me?"

"Yes. Are you Patricia? Neil's wife?"

"Oh!" The woman stood up, knocking the music off the stand. "I know! You're the woman that Neil drove here!" She dimpled. "Oh, my! He was so impressed with you!" She blushed. "I...I don't remember your name! I'm horrified!"

"It's Barbara. Mrs. Wessel." Barbara smiled.

"Oh! That's right. I'm Patty. Patricia, but everyone calls me Patty."

"I'm so impressed with your skill. Playing the piano, organ and harp here." Barbara patted the beautifully carved golden harp. "I'm afraid I'm hopeless at any kind of musical skill."

"Yes, but you do work here, don't you? Neil said you raise money for the Met."

Barbara blushed. "I...I volunteer here. Yes, I do raise money, or I hope to raise money. I've just formed a group...we're going to call ourselves the Metropolitan Opera Guild, or something like that. It's all women and ..." She pulled an empty chair over and sat down. "The men...our husbands...some of them are not really happy that we've stuck our noses into their business."

Patty's blue eyes rolled in understanding. Men were like that sometimes.

"Anyway, we're going to raise the money for some new refurbishing." Barbara pointed upwards. "Get a new chandelier...or at least get that thing cleaned up, take down that tatty old curtain and get a beautiful new one. Maybe re-upholster the chairs...that sort of thing."

"Patty! Are you ready for..." Anatole Goodman approached, his hands filled with sheets of music. "Oh! Baroness Wessel! I didn't know you were down here!" His fair face flushed.

"I was just thanking Patty for her husband's kindness to me." *Oh, oh! My secret is out! I'm now the Baroness...no longer plain old Mrs. Wessel!*

"Oh, please. Don't mind me!" Anatole stumbled backwards, clearly embarrassed.

Patty and Barbara watched him and then, both burst into laughter. "I hate it when I have to be the Baroness!" Barbara rued. "Some people, like poor old Anatole, can't handle the title! They get all flustered."

"Well," Patty stated bluntly, "I'm a little flustered myself! You're the first Baroness I have met." She laughed, "But I liked you before and I'll try not to let it get in the way!"

"Thanks, Patty. Sometimes it does get in the way." Barbara stood up. "And I'd better get out of your way. Obviously, you're busy." She turned to go. "Oh! I invited Neil to come to my box at intermission. I want David, my husband – and yes, he's the Baron and the reason I'm the Baroness– to meet him."

"He'll be tickled pick." Patty waved goodbye.

***

"Celestina? Thank you for coming here." Faustia Cleva waved Celestina to a seat in the crowded office of the Wardrobe and Costume Department. "I understand you were with Mademoiselle du Lac as a ladies' maid for seven years?" Celestina nodded, wondering where this meeting was going.

"You made all of her clothing?"

"I made some of it, Madam. Some of it was made by couturiers or designers, but I maintained it all, repaired it and took the dresses in or let them out…" Celestina allowed herself the luxury of a grin… "As Mademoiselle du Lac grew larger and smaller – generally larger!"

Faustia guffawed and clapped her hands together. "A good answer!" She smiled. "I know you are far from your home in France, and I presume you no longer have a job?"

"That's correct," Celestina's naturally good humor drooped. "I don't think…I haven't been paid for…." She threw out her hands. "I don't know what I am going to do!"

"We have a position here in the Costume Department. One of our long-time employees is retiring. Janet suggested that you would be an asset to us. Would you be interested in working here?"

"Oh! Oh! I would be honored." Celestina's eyes filled with tears. "Thank *le bon Dieu!"*

"Good! Please go and see Jessica Dingley in the Office on the third floor. She'll get you all set with information on pay and so forth." Faustia stood up. "I'm happy to have you with us, Celestina. You have been through a harrowing ordeal."

"It was awful! I'm very grateful. I think I can stay with Janet for a few days until I can find a place to live." She stood up and danced a little jig. "Thank you! I am so happy!" She turned to leave and then stepped back.

"And I will no longer get dishes thrown at me in anger. I'll no longer have to watch her toying with little girls and boys in her quest for sexual pleasure. And best of all, I won't have to put up with that miserable little dog! Oh, almost, I would pay you!" She turned again. "Almost!"

***

"Let's see...?" Anderson and Pedar looked at the time chart that Buddy had produced. "Who, just on opportunity alone, might have killed her?"

"On motive," Buddy mourned, "*every*body would have killed her."

"How so?"

"She tried to upstage Angelique Orloff. She insulted Antonina Sabatino and tried to shove her off stage. She insulted that singer, Hort...Horz Bortel – Criminy! Who names these people? – She insulted him and said he wasn't much good and then tried to get *him* fired. She ripped the dress off Ig...Ig.....Ignatzia – see what I mean about these names? – the lady who was her understudy. Also screamed out loud that she...the Ignatzia person...sang like a dying goat. Made allegations about the talent of Massimo Orsini. Yelled at several of the carpenters and the stage people...um, Francesco DeSarro, Stephen Gibson and Ernest Rattner. Also cast aspersions on Tim Weaver, the guy who is head of the carpenters. Made the old man who does the furnace...Clemson? No, Clemons. Clemons. He...she...made him leave the audience. Made fun of the leading man, too. Said he was too old and not sexy and said she couldn't sing with him and pretend that he was young and handsome." Buddy sucked in a breath. "Oh, and she had brouhahas with Mr. Calligari, who does the wigs and Mr. Wu, who does the make-up...is that enough? Geez, she made an enemy of everyone! Everyone!" Buddy knuckled at his mop of dark hair. "Oh, and I heard a rumor...a rumor only, but several people seemed to know about it...supposedly, she...Vivienne...was having some sort of affair with one of the men from the Board of Directors here."

"Who?" *Not Wessel? Don't let it be Wessel!*

Buddy checked his notebook. "A Mr. T. de Witt Hollister." Buddy spelled the name, stumbling over the pronunciation. "I'm not too sure how you say it."

Anderson could do nothing but laugh. "OK, you poor schnook. So half of the people in the theater had reason to kill her, nevermind the other six hundred people who weren't in the theater that she insulted somewhere or somehow."

He stood up, "Do you have a list of those who were physically able to get into her room between 7:20 and 7:45?"

Buddy nodded and handed him three sheets of paper.

"All these?" Anderson croaked.

"Not pretty is it?" Buddy laughed.

"Not at all. I don't think I've had the pleasure yet of speaking with Mr. T. de Witt Hollister. I didn't see his name on the attendees for Saturday night. Maybe he's one of the people who has his box on Monday nights only."

"Huh?" Buddy looked confused.

"Some people share their boxes. I'll explain it later." Anderson tucked the list into the clip board he carried. "Let's go out into the audience. They're doing a quick rehearsal, and I think it will benefit all of us to see it and see the suspects and the production crew....it might help us to see who is who now that we know what we know...which is mighty little."

"Oh, Chief?" Buddy had one last thing.

"Yeah?"

"The black velvet cape. I hate to tell you this, but there are maybe a hundred of them around."

"Oh, no!"

"Yeah. They use them all the time. People wear them on stage, as opera capes or ladies capes over their gowns. People wear them if they're in costume and want to step outside to have a cigarette or go over to the delicatessen around the corner. They use them to cover up if they are having make-up applied. They use them if there is a draft. There's one hanging from every hook in every room and behind every curtain." His handsome face was glum.

"Rats. I thought we had a good clue there."

"Nope, as usual, with this opera crowd, we have nothing...nothing at all."

***

She heard a groan...and then another. Who? Who was groaning? She tried to open her eyes, but they were sticky and hard to open. A groan again...*why it was me! I'm groaning! Where am I? What...? What...?*

Some primeval instinct took over. *I must see if I am hurt.* She moved her arms and her fingers, her legs and her toes. She hurt all over, but she could still move. She rubbed at her eyes and tried to pry the eyelids open. She could see...*I'm in some kind of dark room. I'm on the floor. Under me is a blanket and I am chilly.* She reached out with her right hand and touched cold concrete. *Or I think it is concrete.*

"Mommy! Mommy!*"* Silence. Fear moved into her primal space. *"Mommeeeee!"* She rolled over, groaning aloud. "Help me, Mommy!" Her head hurt. Had she fallen and hit it? She touched the back of her head with a tentative finger. *Ouch!* That hurt! Her mouth felt funny and her spit tasted of some metallic flavor. She was thirsty.

She stood up and nearly fell down again. She was dizzy and the darkness disoriented her. She peered up and could see the dim outline of two windows or openings, boarded over. A tiny amount of light seeped through thin chinks. She took a few tentative steps and then the dizziness ceased. She looked around.

It was a smallish room, perhaps the size of her bedroom at home. There were two windows, both on the same wall. A heap of stones or coal lay on the floor under the window. There was a rickety table and a chair in the left corner and a rickety door to the right.

Hoping against hope that it might lead to her freedom, she opened the door. Alas. Inside was a tiny room with a chamber pot and some torn up papers. She shivered, thinking of her prison. Someone had thought of everything.

She buttoned up her sweater. It was getting colder.

On the floor was the thin blanket on which she'd been lying. A small, lumpy pillow was lying on the floor and another blanket, a little thicker, was folded next to it. She picked it up the thin blanket and shook it, then placed it down again, doubling it up, hoping that it would be a little more comfortable. She placed the pillow on top and then draped the thicker blanket over her shoulders.

On the table was a metal pail and two brown paper bags. The pail held some sort of liquid. She sniffed it. She stuck her finger in, swished it around and then smelled her finger. Then, she licked the liquid off her finger. *Water, probably.* Carefully, she lifted the bucket and took a gulp and swallowed it down. *Would it poison her?* She took a second mouthful, swished it around in her mouth, and swallowed it. *I could have spit it out, but maybe this is all the water I will have.* She was acting on animal instinct now.

Slowly, she opened one of the bags. There was a loaf of wrapped store bread and a small jar of peanut butter inside. *No knife or spreader*, she noted. OK, who needs a spreader? She opened the jar, stuck in her finger, and scooped out some peanut butter. She licked it. It tasted wonderful. She licked the rest.

The other bag held a glass jelly jar, and the jelly, if that was what was in it, was imprisoned by a layer of wax. She poked at the wax with her finger, and it slid sideways, opening a half circle into the jelly. She stuck her finger in and licked it. *Grape.*

She dragged the chair over to the wall where the windows were and climbed on top of it. The windows were much too high for her to see out of. She thought for a moment and put the pail, the bread and the jars of peanut butter and jelly on the floor.

Sucking in her breath, she dragged the table over to the window wall. *I'm making a lot of noise. I hope the bad men don't hear me and come and hit me.*

She stopped what she was doing and stood for a moment. *Why do I think that there is more than one bad man?* She shrugged.

The table was heavy and it took her a long time to push and pull and shove it up against the wall. She then put the chair on top of the table, leaned her backside against the table and pushed herself up onto it. She stood up, holding onto the chair, and then, with great care, stood on top of the chair. Almost! She could almost see outside. She gripped the window sill and stood on tiptoe. She saw, through one of the cracks, a dusty yard enclosure...a high wooden fence and a lot of bramble bushes. From the way the light looked, she guessed that it was afternoon.

She hit at the window with her fist, but she wasn't strong enough to make the window break or even dislodge the large pieces of wood that were nailed up. She did manage to break off a sliver of wood. She wondered if, given enough time, she might be able to chip away at the wood and enlarge the tiny gap she'd managed to make.

With a weary sigh, she got down, being very careful not to fall. She moved the table back, but not as far back as it had been. *I'll leave it closer to the wall, and when I know more, perhaps I can do something. Right now, this is all I can do.*

She replaced the pail on the table and then brought the bags, the peanut butter, the jelly and the bread up. This time, she was more refined. This time, she scooped out the peanut butter and smushed it on one slice of the bread. She then scooped out a finger-full of jelly and plopped in on top of the peanut butter. She covered the slice with another and pressed the two together. *If Mommy could see me now, she'd yell at me for not being neat.* She thought for a moment. *If Daddy could see me now, he'd tell me that I was doing a good job in bad circumstances.* A wobbly grin lit her face and then she began to cry.

***

It was fascinating, Anderson thought, to see the opera rehearsal. Like being inside out. On stage, Calle was reviewing Act One with the four Bohemians. Tim Weaver, a red spotlight glinting on his round glasses, was tinkering with the ever-difficult stove mechanism, and over in a corner, Antonina, dressed in a yellow muslin costume, was being fussed over by Janet Connolly.

He was in the third row. Buddy and Pedar sat with him. Behind him sat Baron Wessel, John Dempsey and a large man with a huge white mustache whom Anderson had never seen before. Anderson twisted to see the rest of the audience.

In the boxes, Barbara Wessel sat with three elderly women. Several young ladies occupied one of the other boxes. Anderson noted that the young ladies were very animated, waving at someone...where? Ah! A burly young fellow in the orchestra wearing a colorful red and purple scarf. The young fellow held up an unwieldy instrument and waved that in the air. He was grinning and bowing and clowning around. At a nudge from a red-haired fellow sitting next to him, and a glare from the violinist who seemed to be in charge, the burly young man, noticing that *Maestro* Massimo Orsini was approaching the podium, gave a start and sat down. Anderson marveled; the goings-on in the orchestra and audience were almost as exciting as the opera itself. Well, not quite...the opera stage held Antonina and nothing could be more exciting than that.

Arturo Calle clapped his hands together, acknowledging Massimo Orsini. "Thank you, *Maestro*. Now that you are here and ready, perhaps we can start..."

Orsini bowed graciously and bent to speak with his First Violinist. At that moment, there was a roiling of the curtains at the back of the stage. Abe Featherman, one of Anderson's detectives, burst through. His eyes wildly scanned the audience and located Anderson. With a loping gait, Featherman nearly ran straight through center stage and trotted down the makeshift staircase.

"Chief!" Featherman whispered urgently, bending down to kneel at von Vogel's side. "We've *solved* it! We got a con*fession!*"

Chapter Nineteen

And his eyes have all the seeming of a demon's
that is dreaming....Edgar Allen Poe, The Raven

They leaped as one and ran up the stairs, their feet clattering and announcing their exultation. On stage and in the wings, the players, the staff and the employees watched, openmouthed.

Who confessed? Did they find Crespi? Was it him?
Thank God we've got the son of a bitch!
Who? Who killed her?
Thank God Antonina is safe!
Who confessed?

Abe Featherman brought them to the small room the police were using as an office. They burst in.

Marvin Michaels, the youngest of the detectives, sat at the desk. In front of him, cowering in a wooden chair, was Clemons, the elderly janitor.

"What's going on?" Anderson stopped short.

"This gentleman came in and told me that he was responsible for killing Vivienne du Lac." Michaels voice was proud. "He's confessed!"

"Mr. Clemons?" Anderson turned. "Did you murder Vivienne du Lac?"

The old man nodded, his face sad.

"Tell me, Mr. Clemons," Anderson pulled a chair up and sat next to Clemons, "How did you do this?"

Clemons, who wore a grey cardigan, fished his hand toward his pocket. Marvin Michaels jumped up, drawing his revolver. "Hold on! Stop or I'll shoot!" Michaels' revolver was pointed right at Clemons' heart. Clemons stopped, his hand midway in the air. Shock blanched his seamed old face.

"Please, Marvin. Put that away." Anderson held his hand up. "I don't think...I don't think we need that just yet." He made a tiny motion and Pedar moved quickly to Marvin's side, deflecting the trajectory of a bullet, should it be fired. Marvin's face showed anger and confusion.

"What were you going to take out of your pocket, Mr. Clemons?"

"Jus' this..." Clemons reached, slowly and carefully, his eyes never leaving Anderson's, into the pocket of the grey cardigan sweater. He pulled out a curious stuffed item, a grotesque doll with long, black yarn sewn onto the knob that was its head. "I made a spell." He offered the doll to Anderson. "I killed her with the spell."

The door to the office squeaked open. The head of a black cat appeared, followed by a sinuous feline body. "Figaro!" Clemons smiled for the first time. "You good cat. You came to help me."

As if in agreement, the cat lashed its tail and jumped, light and lithe, landing on Clemons' lap. He stroked the cat and murmured soft words.

Anderson watched and the hair prickled on his arms. *There are more things in heaven and earth, Horatio, than are dreamt of in your philosophy...* He held the doll in front of him. It was a crude thing, with a painted face, two dots for the eyes and a slash of red for the mouth. The doll was pierced in several places with pins, and one of the clumsy arms appeared to have been burnt. "Is this supposed to be Vivienne du Lac?"

Clemons nodded, stroking the cat.

"And how did you kill her?"

The old man looked around at the phalanx of police surrounding him. He ducked his head.

"Did you try to burn her?" Anderson pointed to the doll's hand.

"I wished her to be dead." The old man whispered. "I stuck her. I made the spell. She was the devil and I killed her." The cat rose up from his lap and jumped to Anderson's lap. With a quick, slashing paw, Figaro swiped at the doll, knocking it out of Anderson's hand.

There was a quick intake of breath. Marvin Michaels reared backwards and crossed himself. Anderson tickled the cat under his chin and the cat arched its back, made a circle with dainty paws, and settled on Anderson's lap. Anderson reached down and picked the doll up. The cat watched the doll, its tail lashing back and forth.

"Mr. Clemons. Did you actually kill Vivienne du Lac, or did you *wish* that she was killed?"

"I wished her dead. I prayed that she would die and that her evil soul would be burning in hell." His face was set and stony. "I made her die."

Death was always attuned to his name. He hovered, pitying the poor old man who wanted the power that he alone had. *No, my dear sir, you did not make her die. Only I, or a mortal who kills, can do that. Not you, you sad old soul. You did not cause her to die...*

"Mr. Clemons, it is a dangerous thing to wish death upon another." Clemons watched his face and nodded, unsure of what Anderson was saying. "But wishing death and killing someone are two very different things. Let me ask you again, did you cut her throat?"

Clemons shook his head. "No, sir."

"Did you go into her room?"

"No, sir."

"Did you touch her?" Clemons shook his head with vigor.

"You only wished that she die?"

"Yes," Clemons voice was a whisper. "And then she did die. I think I killed her because I made a spell for her to die. She did die."

Anderson picked up Figaro, got up and deposited the cat on Clemons' lap. He patted the old man's shoulder. "Sometimes, I wish bad luck on someone I don't like. We are all human here, Mr. Clemons. She was a very difficult woman to like."

"She was evil." Clemons' lip stuck out. "I'm glad that she's dead." The cat's tail lashed back and forth. "I wanted her to be dead. That way, she wouldn't make any more trouble."

"There are many people who will agree with you, sir." Anderson sighed. "But you didn't kill her, Clemons. You can go back to work now." The old man's rheumy eyes began to fill with tears. "And thank you for coming to us. We appreciate your honesty." He shook Clemons' hand. The old man stood up, holding the cat over his shoulder. He stroked it once or twice, and then went out of the door.

Anderson held up the doll. "Well!"

"Well is right," Pedar's breath whooshed out slowly. "Poor old codger."

"He's either a poor old codger, or the smartest man in the world." Buddy mused. "Now, we'll never suspect him."

***

"Signor," Antonina took a moment to creep down into the audience. "How are you?"

"My darling. You were so lovely. Your voice…perfect. I can teach you no more!" Signor Fazzolini kissed Antonina's hand.

"Don't be silly, Signor! I have so much more to learn from you. This is just the beginning." She giggled, her face impish. "But, as my sister would say, 'Isn't this shattering!'."

Fazzolini, who had known all of the Rosato children since they were tiny, laughed. "At least it isn't revolting!"

"On a more prosaic note, my dear teacher, I need some assistance from you."

"What is it, my dear?"

"I think it is time for me to move from home." She made a face of gloom. "I need to be by myself and to grow up. I love my mother and my family, but…." She spread her hands out in supplication, "I think this little bird must get out of the nest."

On stage, there was a slight commotion as the stove refused to light and Tim Weaver came out and kicked it, muttering nasty names at the contraption. The orchestra stopped playing and tempers began to flare again. Antonina giggled. "At least the rehearsal is going badly enough so that the performance will go well."

Fazzolini bowed his head. "There's always something. Ah, child. Your mother will be devastated when you leave, nevermind Maria and the rest of the family." He shrugged, "But, I think I agree with you." His craggy face was fierce with concentration. "Ah! I have a good solution, if you agree." He turned to her with a conspiratorial smile. "I have a dear friend...perhaps you have heard me speak of her? Joanna Joseph? No? Well, perhaps I never told you about her...She is a widow, but they never had any children. Her husband's name was Joseph Joseph...an easy name to remember." He laughed, a dry, papery laugh. "He used to work for the Met as a stagehand...it was a long time ago, before Urbano began to work there. Anyway, Joseph died. A heart attack. And Joanna, who was always a wonderful seamstress, kept herself busy making costumes...not ordinary costumes, but sumptuous things. Like *Turandot's* robes...costumes that glitter with jewels and embroidery. She is mostly retired now, but still occasionally does some special order from the Met. At any rate, she and Joseph owned a brownstone, a few blocks from here. She rents the top floors to a few select tenants. And I think she has a vacancy." He got up from his seat. "I am going to confirm if this is so right now."

"That would be perfect!" Antonina clapped her hands. "But...I'm not sure how much my salary will be...I have the contract that Arturo Calle gave to me. I wanted to talk to you and to Simeon about it....I thought the two of you could advise me on what is a fair compensation."

Fazzolini raised his eyebrows up and down a few times. "Aha! A contract, you say! Yes! Simeon and I will make very sure that you are paid fairly, and perhaps a little bit better than fairly! You saved the performance on Saturday. You are saving it again tonight and you will shine next week in *Traviata*. You have brought immense publicity to the opera house. I think the American word for what you did is called 'saved their bacon.' Ha! A good way to say it! Ah, yes! We will see that the compensation will pay your rent at Madam Joseph's apartment and maybe have a few baubles left over for some bread, wine and cheese." He laughed. "Ah, yes! A little bit left over!" He kissed her cheek and nearly ran up the aisle in his haste and happiness.

***

As rehearsals go, this one was average. Anderson, Pedar and Buddy climbed back down, skirting the action on stage, and sat back into their seats. Anderson was delighted that the debacle with the old man had only lasted ten minutes or so, and, thus, he had not missed Antonina's entrance as Mimi.

"What's the story about?" Buddy whispered. "I missed the beginning." As the four Bohemians cavorted on stage, Anderson quickly explained the beginning plot.

On stage, the old landlord, Benoit, was being plied with drink. He waved his glass in the air and tried to put it on the table. It fell, crashing into a thousand pieces.

"Damnation!" Arturo Calle jumped up. "Can't you be more careful?" Benoit sheepishly pushed the pieces of glass under the table with his feet.

"Nevermind, nevermind!" Calle waved away Francesco who came on stage with a broom. "Clean it up later! My good God! Be careful!"

The Bohemians finished their stage business and Benoit stumbled off the stage. Marcello, Schaunard and Colline exited, gleefully going to the Café Momus.

"And now, Rodolfo is just finishing…" Anderson waved his hand and settled back to watch. "Shhh…she's coming now." Buddy, not quite catching the entire plot, sat back, too.

A knock on the door of the attic…. *"Who is there?"*

A soft voice… *"Excuse me…"*

Rodolfo is surprised… *"A woman!"*

And then…there she was… *"I'm sorry. My light has gone out…"*

Anderson gave a convulsive shiver and leaned forward, his jaw dropping. As Antonina moved about the stage, trying to light her candle, she sneaked a peek at the audience. She turned her head a fraction and winked at Anderson. No one, except Anderson and Barbara Wessel noticed. Anderson gasped. Barbara wondered. Buddy looked over at Anderson. *Geez, the Chief must really like this opera stuff!*

***

"Some of them were awful to me." Antonina was nearly in tears.

"Tell me what happened," Angelique was careful not to laugh. "This is something that was bound to happen. You could never move from being a part of the chorus to being a star and not expect some kind of complications."

"I went to the women's dressing room to get the rest of my things…my make up and my shoes…As I came in, everyone was talking, but then…they all stopped. I felt as if they were all staring at me." Her face was doleful. "A few…my good friends Karen, Robyn and Sue and a few others…they were great! They told me how proud they were of me and hugged me."

"They are good friends," Angelique agreed.

"Yes. Sue and Karen hugged me and Robyn even gave me a little bouquet." She pointed to a glass jar filled with violets. "It was so *nice!"* Antonina's voice squeaked upwards. "But some of them turned their backs on me. *Why?* I didn't do anything to them!"

Angelique shrugged. "Most things that are going to happen to you from now on will be good things, my little poppet, but…and you'd better get used to it and take it in your stride…some people, even your old so-called friends…will be jealous of your success. They forget how hard you have worked. They ignore the fact that you saved the performance." She patted Antonina's shoulder. "There will always be those who do not wish you well, my dear." She picked up the little vase and sniffed the sweet scent of the violets… "Your true friends will remain true. The others…well, just be as nice as you can to them. It will annoy and confuse them!" She laughed. "You will learn these little lessons about your new-found fame. Some of them will be bitter, but most of them will be as sweet as you are."

Janet knocked at the door and peeked in. "How are we doing, my ladies?"

"We are the snake's hips." Angelique caroled. "And how is that handsome young policeman who stares at you all the time?"

"Buddy?" Janet blushed. "He's swoony, don't you think?"

"He's certainly a sweet-patootie, as the modern girls say," Angelique agreed, the up-to-date lingo sounding strange.

Maybe we should say that he's the ant's ankles." She laughed merrily. "And you, my little Mimi, what are you going to do with your police chief?"

Antonina started, gasping. "Can you tell?" Janet grinned, winking.

"I can tell, my sweet. I notice everything. The man is besotted with you…and you are also caught up in some…fever…"

"He's married," Antonina mumbled. "I don't know what to do."

"Follow your heart, but don't forget your head, Antonina. Please remember that you cannot have it all. You must carefully choose."

Janet made one last adjustment to Antonina's dress. "And don't forget that we are your friends. No matter what." She patted Antonina's shoulder.

Angelique sighed. "Ah, young love. So beautiful. Both of you." She fussed with her hat, pinning it more securely to her wig. "I'm ready."

"Moi, aussi!" Antonina got up. "Oh, Janet! This is so much fun!"

"Thank you, Vivienne du Lac!" Angélique made a mock salute.

"Thank you, Vivienne du Lac !" Janet saluted back.

"Aren't we awful?" Antonina gurgled. "However," she turned around, as if expecting to see Vivienne's ghost lurking, "No one thanks you more than I do, Vivienne du Lac!"

***

She must have been exhausted. She lay, cuddled on the cheap blankets, curled into a ball of misery. She awoke…had she heard a click? It was dark, the only chinks of light coming through the boarded up windows. *It's early morning, I think…* She struggled up, brushed off her clothing and went to the little room to use the chamber pot and clean herself as best she could with the torn up newspapers. She wrinkled her nose. It smelled in there, but what else could she do? She was glad that her captor…captors?….had been thoughtful enough to at least give her a place to pee.

Her eyes adjusted to the dim light. On the table, was another brown bag, and the water pail was full again. She sighed. She'd have to trust them that they'd keep her fed. Thus, she tore a corner piece off the thinnest blanket and dipped it into the pail of water. She used this as a wash rag and cleaned her face and teeth, then, she washed herself, hating that she and her clothing smelled from sweat and fear. She wrung out the cloth over the chamber pot and hung it on a bent nail that stuck out from the window coverings.

She was already bored and frustrated. To make her day seem bearable, she...before investigating the contents of the new bag...spent a few moments shaking out her bedding. She moved the bedding over to the wall underneath the windows, where the light was best. She folded it neatly and propped the pillow up against the wall. There! Now, she could recline in as much comfort as was possible.

Now to the bag. First, she noticed that the groceries that had been left yesterday were still there. That was good. She unfurled the new bag, smoothing it. Perhaps it might come in handy. She thought of Robinson Crusoe and how he saved everything, not knowing when it might come in handy on his little island. She, too, would use every scrap...every little thing...to keep herself fed and in good health. She'd use her mind and everything at her disposal to keep from being bored and to plan how to escape.

In the bag was an egg sandwich, still warm, a glass bottle of milk, still cold, and two jelly donuts. Shrugging, she sat down and ate. The food was delicious and she licked every last crumb.

Her careful concern with the empty paper bag caused her to think back. A month ago in school, her teacher, Miss Lillian Kelly, had asked the class to write a short report entitled "Who Is The Most Intelligent Person. Real or Imagined, Alive or Dead?" The students had to name their candidate and then explain their reasons.

It was a very thought-provoking challenge. Who? *My goodness*, Louise had pondered, *there are so many intelligent people that I know...my mother, my father, Grandpa Lutten, Uncle Rory...the President, Mr. Hoover.*

Or someone who was already dead...President Abraham Lincoln? Pastor Alexander? She'd chewed on her yellow pencil...

Or imagined...did that mean a person in a book? Jesus? She'd always thought of Jesus as being wise and loving, but was that the same as intelligent?

Certainly Jesus was intelligent...he was God, wasn't he...sort of? And God was really intelligent, so, Jesus must be intelligent, too.

She looked around at her friends and classmates. Some were writing furiously. Some looked out the window or up into the air, seeking some inspiration or the thread of an idea.

She shook her head, perplexed. Miss Kelly was rising. "Children, you have six more minutes."

Who? Who could she say was the *most* intelligent? She bit her lip and began to write....

***

Fazzolini reappeared as the curtain came down at the end of Act Three. He grabbed Antonina and whispered to her that Madam Joseph had a vacancy on her fourth floor and yes, she would be pleased to rent it to Antonina.

"We'll walk over there after the rehearsal and you can see it for yourself and meet her."

"Thank you, Signor! I can always count on you to help me when I need it most."

***

A handsome and vibrant man came down the gangplank as the S.S. Hamburg arrived on the West Side docks. He was tall, with dark, curly hair and a luxurious mustache. His eyes were dark and, if one looked close, one might notice something sad and weary lurking there. His clothing was expensive and just a bit different from the average American's clothing. He commandeered a taxi and rode to Angelique Orloff's house where the sadness disappeared. He was greeted with rapture and delighted frenzy by both Anna Orloff and her governess, Janine.

"Dear David! Why didn't you tell us you were coming?"

"Shhh! It's a surprise. You mustn't tell your mother." He hugged Anna and made her promise…cross her heart…. "She'll be home for a quick supper in a few hours. You must not let on that I am here."

Anna promised. "I'll keep as quiet as a mouse. Mims will never suspect anything. I swear."

"I have borrowed a box from Sir D'allee. He saw the show on Saturday and agreed to let me use it. You and you and me…" he pointed to Janine, then Anna and then to himself… "We're going to the opera tonight. We'll sit in the box and see if your Mims notices us."

Anna giggled and both Janine and the Count watched her pretty face. *She'll be a beauty…just like her mother….*

"Oh, she's going to *faint* when she sees you!"

"She's going to jump for joy!"

"Remember…not a word!"

***

Act Four started with a small disaster. The entire lighting board refused to work. Johnston Redmond cursed and banged and called down the names of the gods. Finally, he thumped the board with his fist in complete frustration…and, of course, the board responded meekly, working like a charm.

"Let's get this finished," Calle exhorted. "Then you can all go home, rest and be here for the performance." He laughed. "And I can go home, get drunk and pray!"

The Act began and Rodolfo sang of his doomed love. His voice, poignant with longing, remembered Mimi's little hands…he sat at his table, and the chair splintered. Rodolfo, in mid-aria, fell to the floor

"Stop!" Massimo roared, hitting the podium with his baton. *"Stop!"*

Marcello helped his fellow Bohemian to his feet. Francesco ran onstage to pick up the offending chair.

"Tim! Are there no chairs in this entire opera that do not need repair?" Calle nearly screamed. "Can you fix them so that this doesn't happen again?"

Stephen Gibson helped Francesco re-nail the offending chair. Emmet Matthews and Richard Davis brought their tools on stage and checked the other chairs, making sure that all of them could withstand the force of a Bohemian throwing himself down.

From the wings, Emmet Rattner watched. *Why bother even going out there to work. Let the rest of them do it. I'm not gonna break my tail around here much more. Not after I write my little letter about what I seen.*

I'll ask for five thousand dollars for my silence...maybe even ten thousand. There's no problem about the money. Rich is rich...the so-and-so can afford it...I'll be set for life. He turned and drifted back into the area behind the curtains. *Thought no one saw, huh! Well, I saw!*

The remainder of the rehearsal went without further glitch. The small group in the audience stood and clapped, voicing their delight and approval.

"Bravo!" Calle crowed. "It is done!" He opened his arms, encompassing everyone. "You were all wonderful." His breath whooshed out. "I was wonderful!" Everyone laughed, the tension broken. "All right, my friends. I want everyone here tonight at 6 o'clock. Go home, go to a bar, go and rest...whatever. Be here on time and ready to make opera history once more!"

***

"This is my best friend, Carey Marvel Mabley," Brooks introduced Dean.

"You did a great job with the bassoon," Carey laughed, her hand engulfed by Dean's paw.

"I am definitely the ultimate bassoon man," Dean joked. "Although my pal, Tommy, might take issue with that." He chuckled. "Now, are you two ladies free to have a bite of early supper with me before I have to be back here?"

"Oh, I have a prior engagement," Carey was tactful.

"Are you sure? I have a little German restaurant to take you both to. Have you ever had wiener schnitzel?" Both girls shook their heads.

"What's that?"

"Come on, Carey. Stay with us for supper. You'll never forgive yourself if you don't taste wiener schnitzel," Dean's voice was persuasive. Carey looked at him with speculation. He *was* a handsome devil. He *did* have lots of charm. No wonder Brooks was smitten.

"Yes, Carey. You needn't feel that we have to be alone!" Brooks rolled her eyes. "Dean and I can be alone *after* the performance. He's definitely taking me out to Delmonico's afterward, where we can gaze into one another's eyes." Dean guffawed and wiggled his eyebrows in a suggestive manner. *What a woman she was!* "Come with us."

"Fine." Carey gathered her coat. "I'd hate to say that I missed wiener schnitzel...whatever it is!"

***

"Can I have supper with you?" Anderson slid next to Antonina. She smiled at him, but shook her head.

"Oh, Anderson. I never eat before a performance. I'd just throw up everything. And not today, even if I did eat. I'm going with Signor Fazzolini. I'm going to look at an apartment for myself." Anderson's heart began to beat with a thick, erratic thump. *An apartment! She'll be alone and not at her mother's house! An apartment!*

Antonina winked as her own stomach lurched at the thought that, somewhere in the future, they might be alone together. "Perhaps we can have supper after the performance. My family is taking me to Delmonico's and you can join us." Defeated, Anderson nodded.

"All right, Antonia. I'll wait for you no matter how long it takes." He touched her sleeve and she shuddered, thinking of what might be at the end of the waiting. "I'll go over to see my stockbroker. I will be watching you tonight from Baron Wessel's box. You'll feel my adoration floating through the air." He wanted to kiss her, but they were in the midst of several dozen others. He satisfied himself, badly, by patting her on the shoulder.

And so, with not much else to do, Anderson visited Mr. Richard Peabody and instructed him to sell his RCUSA shares. At the same time, David Wessel was visiting *his* stockbroker with a similar request. Neil Odams, double parking his cab, stopped in to see the fellow who helped him with his small amount of investments. The fellow, after Neil's departure, thought for a while and then made some adjustments in his own investments, too. And in Greenwich, Simeon Meade spoke with his bank manager, as did Alex Troy and his three daughters.

Chapter Twenty

*"There is no cure for birth and death save to
enjoy the interval....George Santayana...War Shrines*

THE MOST INTELLIGENT PERSON

By Louise Lutten

The most intelligent person in the world is my mother. Why? Because she can cope with anything. She's a woman with not much schooling. She had to work when she was young to help support her family. And she works now to support our family and be a breadwinner together with my father (who is also very intelligent, too, but I can only have one person in this essay). She didn't have the benefit of learning about literature or mathematics. But that didn't stop her...no, no! She can fix anything. She can stop a bruise from hurting with a kiss and a piece of ice. She can fix the faucet on the sink when it drips with some sticky tape. She can stretch our food money (of which there isn't much) so that we all...me, my mother, my brother, my father and my grandfather...all have delicious meals, even if it is only sweet potatoes and greens. Last Christmas, when my father's job closed down, she managed to give us wonderful presents...things that she or my father made by hand. She takes what is around her and makes it into more.

When my day is gray, she always manages to make me smile. She loves me with both arms open, and she loves the rest of her family the same. She also manages to give money to people who are even poorer than we are and then give some to the church, too. I do not know how she makes such magic, to seem to always have more than she really has. It is remarkable.

I love my mother and would put up a statue in the park to honor her. The statue should be right next to the statue of Abraham Lincoln and George Washington, who are, I am sure, also very intelligent people. But not as intelligent as my mother.

Miss Kelly stood in front of the class, her hands filled with a pile of papers. "Class, I am very proud of your essays," Her bird-like head tipped to one side. "As you all know, there is no one answer to the question of who is the most intelligent person. There are millions of answers, and all of them are correct."

"Let me tell you who my own choice is." She smiled. Each child sat up in anticipation. This had been a difficult exercise. Who would Miss Kelly choose?

"Intelligence is a ephemeral thing...who knows what 'ephemeral' means?...Yes, Danielle?...Correct! Very good. Ephemeral means hard to hold onto. Vaporous. Difficult to pin down. That means what intelligence might mean to you may not be the same as what it means to me. It *could* mean that you are really smart. Louis Pasteur was very smart. He discovered that milk could be heated and then cooled rapidly, therefore killing the bad bacteria. And what do we call this discovery? Yes, Milton? Good. Pasteurization. He also discovered a vaccination against rabies. He had a brilliant mind...but only in the scene of science. Was he the most intelligent man?" The class didn't know whether to answer yes or no. They waited for Miss Kelly to lead them.

"How about William Shakespeare? He wrote brilliant plays and sonnets. His use of the language still is unsurpassed. Was *he* the most intelligent?"

"My own opinion, class..." And the class began to breathe with relief. Miss Kelly was the bee's knees. She was going to tell them what she thought. "...is that a man or woman who used his or her head...who makes the most out of a given situation...is acting with great intelligence. And that intelligence can be used in many different ways, not just science, not just literature or medicine or law."

She went to the blackboard and began a list of names. "All of these people are very intelligent. My choice...and you may or many not agree with me...is that Robinson Crusoe is the most intelligent man."

The class, as one, sucked in its breath. Crusoe? He was in a *book!*

Anticipating them, she spoke, "He was a fictional character. The book was written by Daniel Defoe, and it is based on an exploit that a real person experienced. The man was a sailor by the name of Alexander Selkirk, and some say that Robinson Crusoe was the first English novel published. Many of you have read it, yes?" There was a show of hands, Louise's and Danielle's among them. "Here was a man, set upon a deserted island. To live, Robinson Crusoe had to be very, very intelligent. His very life depended upon it. He had to find or make shelter, figure out what he could eat and how to find or catch it. He made the most of his environment...the little island...and everything within. A nail, a shell...they could be the difference between life and death to him. He did very well, as you may remember. He used his brain...used his intelligence."

She wrote 'environment – using it all' on the blackboard. "And that, children, is *my* idea of intelligence. Using everything to its fullest."

She began to walk down the aisle, doling out the corrected essays. "Each of you gets an 'A' for the content. I have also graded these for neatness (Miss Kelly was big on neatness) and spelling (she was also very big on spelling).

"Some of you chose American heroes – Abraham Lincoln and George Washington - some of you chose leaders from other times and other countries – Napoleon and King Solomon. Some of you went to literature to choose – Jules Verne…a very interesting choice," She bent and patted Ricky Sommer on his head. "Some chose Jesus – always a good choice." She placed Sue Casey's paper down. "Some picked artists and dreamers," She put Danielle's essay down on her desk. "Leonardo da Vinci and Michelangelo. And one student chose a relative who exemplifies practical and admirable intelligence in our day-to-day world." She gently placed Louise's essay down on the desk. "Please show this to your mother, my dear," she smiled and patted Louise with affection, "It will please her very much."

***

The house-to-house search offered a few meager crumbs to the Greenwich police. No one had really seen anything, if you discounted the few hysterical reports of a Chinaman with a long pigtail who was seen dragging a little girl, the three sightings of wild and bearded men, ten feet tall, who, with their pack of rabid dogs, roamed the neighborhoods with a truck, grabbing old women and children. There was nothing at all of any substance.

Two years ago, Chief McAndrews reminded his men, a little girl named Alice Farella, age eight, had disappeared, never to be seen again. Alice had lived in the general vicinity of the Lutton household. Her parents, sad and dispirited, had finally moved away. *Even though they moved, they can never move far enough to forget their daughter*, the Chief mused.

At the time, the police had also conducted a search and a house-to-house with not a single clue. Alice was a well-liked young girl, in no trouble scholastically or with her parents. She was never seen again.

In the nicest of towns, there is always a cadre of suspicious people, and Greenwich, for all of its splendor and wealth, had its share of these such people. The police two years ago, and now, dutifully rounded up these people…and most of them were men, although there was a particularly odious woman named Mae Washburn, of whom, it was rumored, buried the dead bodies of unborn babies….

These people were asked to accompany the police to the station house, either willingly or unwillingly. There, in the stark privacy of one of the interrogation rooms, these rag-tag specimens of humanity were asked many questions as to their whereabouts on the day or days in question.

Augie Gazzarra, Benson Pinchett, Bruce Candlewick (a/k/a The Candle) and Corbin Eckert, all of whom had decided proclivities to paying much too much attention to young girl children were grilled incessantly. None, although each of them was involved in petty crimes such as shoplifting and/or being drunk and disorderly, were involved in either child's disappearance, then or now.

Other local miscreants who were often in trouble, although the trouble wasn't connected to a prurient interest in female children, were also rounded up and leaned upon. No one knew anything, or, at least, no one was saying anything. The police were stumped and nearly frantic.

Mike Murphy spent an evening in the seedy bars of Port Chester, New York and Cliff Gustafson did the same in the booze houses in Stamford, Connecticut, each displaying wads of cash and offering even more to the person who might come to tell them a secret or two about this disappearance. The police promised absolute secrecy and absolute immunity. Even this tactic brought nothing home.

Mr. and Mrs Lutton were living in a nightmare of despair, afraid to hope, afraid not to hope.

***

"Ohhh!" Concetta was hit with a wave of pain the intensity of which she had never felt before. She bent sharply, trying to free her stomach from the line of fire that traveled up and down and back again, making her nearly scream. "Ahhh!"

"What's wrong?" Francesco jumped up. "You're not ready...for...are you?"

"It's not supposed to be for another two weeks!" The pain subsided. Concetta straightened up with slow concern. *"Mamma mia!* That was powerful!"

"I'd better call Vittoria," Francesco started for the door. Concetta called him back.

"Wait. *Aspetti.*" She tipped her head, testing herself...."I think I am fine now." She went to the sink and pumped herself a glass of cool water. "I'm fine." She splashed a few drops of water onto her forehead and sighed. Thank goodness, the contractions had ceased. "Francesco, if this is a baby girl, I want to name her..."

"Vittoria said it was going to be a boy." Francesco had great faith in Vittoria's midwifery skills. "We'll name him Francesco, after me." He nodded, as if there were no other choices for a boy's name. "If Vittoria is mistaken, and I doubt that she will be, we'll name the girl Giovanna, after my sainted mother."

He missed the glare that Concetta gave him. *Nevermind Francesco or Giovanna.* This was going to be her baby and she had some ideas of her own. She'd deal with this problem when the time came. She turned to him, smiling and was hit with another contraction that doubled her up. Francesco ran and knelt by her side, trying to ease the pain from her belly to his own strong shoulders.

It doesn't work that way, my lad. Birth, hovering close by, waited with cheerful anticipation. *This one is a big one and he's coming rather soon. And you, my sympathetic man who loves his wife, are helpless to do much more than mop the sweat from her brow and tell her that you love her.*

"Get Vittoria. *Now!*" She groaned again and tried to stand upright.

Francesco dithered...should he leave Concetta in such pain? Should he run to get Vittoria? What the hell should he *do?*"

From some depth of intrinsic knowledge, bred into every woman since time immemorial, Concetta screamed..."*Now! Now!*"

He ran.

***

Also in Brooklyn, in the Italian immigrant area, in the brownstone house across the street from the one where Birth was hovering, Death approached. Birth and Death had worked it out last night. A 98 year-old-woman, Serafina Insinga, suffering with terminal lung disease, was released with gentle sleep into Death's care. Her soul winged its way to Heaven...she had been a kind soul, except for the hatred that she harbored for her middle son's wife. This hatred had real roots. The daughter-in-law *was* a selfish slut who had cheated on the middle son from the time of the marriage. In His judgment, God was able to understand Serafina's hatred, for, after all, on balance, her life had been exemplary, except for this one thing. The angels awaited her.

After this chore was done, Death looked in to find that Birth was nearly finished. Naturally, as Vittoria had said, a huge baby boy had been delivered of Concetta, and all that remained to do was to watch Vittoria joyfully and calmly deliver the placenta, wash the baby, wrap him up and place him at Concetta's breast.

Birth then traveled to the Bronx, where a forty year old woman easily gave birth to her sixth daughter. Death had more to do. He had to go to Jerusalem as the Arabs were attacking the Jews at the Wailing Wall.

***

"We are calling him Frank."

"Not Francesco? Not after his father?"

Concetta kissed the soft top of the baby's head. "After his father, sort of...but he is an American. Not Francesco...Frank!"

Vittoria nodded. "What would you have called her had I been wrong?"

"Joan."

"Joan? What kind of Italian name is *Joan?"*

"I told you. This is America and my children will have real American names." Vittoria shrugged and agreed. After all, Concetta was in charge.

And with the honor that went with helping with the delivery, Vittoria dipped her hand into the bowl of warm olive oil and made the sign of the cross over the baby. "I baptize you Frank in the name of The Father, The Son and The Holy Ghost."

"Frank," Murmured Concetta. "He might be a priest. Father Frank. How does that sound?"

"He might be a doctor, a lawyer, or a man who delivers vegetables." Vittoria laughed, smoothing Concetta's hair. "This is America and he is a proper American. He can be *anything.* Now, *bella mia.* Close you eyes and get some sleep. Our men are going to the opera house now for tonight's performance." She giggled, struck by a thought. "But no opera performance can rival the performance you just put on!"

"You'll stay near?" Concetta was exhausted, but not so exhausted that she wasn't concerned about her new son."

"Have no fear. I will stay with you and your new American son, Frank, my friend. *Sogne d'oro…*have dreams of gold. You deserve them."

***

"Thank you Madam Joseph. It is perfect for me." Antonina's excitement bubbled over. Unable to help herself, she twirled around, her arms extended. "This is the most beautiful apartment in the whole world!"

Joanna Joseph smiled at the child's exuberance. "Well, my dear, the apartment *is* very nice. We had a schoolteacher who rented it previously." She pointed out a few of the features. "I'm rather fussy about who I rent to, but as Signor Fazzolini recommended you…well, that's all I need to know."

She brought out a lease and Antonina, feeling rather grown-up, signed her name and paid six month's rent in advance. Madam Joseph, pocketing the money, was sure that Antonina would be an excellent tenant. *An opera star…what a cachet for me! I wonder where she sang before? I've never heard her name before that rather unsavory murder last week. Ah, well, if Alfonzo has her as a pupil, she must be magnificent. Perhaps I can get some tickets to go and see her.* "When do you want to move in?"

"Will tomorrow afternoon be all right?"

"Certainly. Here is your key, and…do you have much in the way of furniture to move in? I ask because if you do, I will have the man who helps me here on hand to help you or your movers. He is honest and charges a reasonable amount to help."

Antonina laughed. "Movers! How droll! I have absolutely nothing! I will be bringing my clothes and a few personal belongings." She blushed. "I have always lived at home…with my mother…and now that I am singing some leading roles, I think I am grown up enough to stay in the city." She dimpled. "My mother and my grandmother will be coming very soon to inspect the apartment and to meet you. They are worried that I might be going to live in some kind of an amusement park or flea-bitten establishment…This lovely place will make them so happy. It is lovely and so clean and, one can tell right away, that it is respectable. Oh, yes, Madam, Joseph, they'll be so pleased to get to know you and to be assured that nothing bad can happen to their little girl in such a nice place as this!"

***

She spent the day playing tic-tac-toe with pieces of coal from the pile and slivers of wood that she snapped off the bottoms of the boards that covered the window. She pretended that she was playing with Danielle. Danielle was the 'O' and she was the 'X'. She moved from one side to the other…on the window side she was herself, and on the door side, she was Danielle. Perhaps it was inattention or simply laziness on Danielle's part, but the 'X's' nearly always won.

It wasn't the most fascinating of pastimes, but it did make the day go by quicker.

She'd tried to get some amusement from reading the torn-up squares of newspaper that her captor or captors had placed on the floor next to the chamber pot. They were all in numbers, something about stocks…she hadn't the faintest idea of what they meant and, even using her best imagination, she couldn't manage to do much with the squares except fold them to see if she could make a paper hat.

In between the games, she did exercises. Robinson Crusoe would keep himself fit and ready for anything that might come along. Any tiny opportunity. She did one hundred jumping jacks, crisscrossing her arms above her head and counting out loud. Then she ran in place, one hundred steps…then a relaxing stretch and bend…then one hundred more.

As the afternoon sun slanted through the chinks in the window, she remade her bed for something to do. This time, she put it against the wall, with her head facing the door. Just in case. When she lay down, she noticed that there were some letters scratched on the wall, way down near the bottom. She lay down to see the letters better. Someone had scratched 'AF was here' on the wall. Louise wondered who AF was. Had there been someone else imprisoned here? She wondered if she should scratch her own initials on the wall underneath AF's…perhaps tomorrow…it would give her something to think about.

She prepared her supper. One jelly sandwich, and one peanut butter sandwich…a big drink of water. She wondered who, if anyone, would come in to the room in the dark of night. She shivered.

Chapter Twenty-One

"I feel about airplanes the way I feel about diets.
It seems to be that they are wonderful things for other people to go on..."
Jean Kerr, The Snake Has All The Lines.

" *Y*ou're going to the opera again? I thought you were bored stiff!" Helena
was astonished when Anderson returned to their apartment and changed
into his formal attire. She waylaid him just before he was about to leave.

"You were the one who urged me to go." Anderson spoke stiffly to her.
He felt guilty. "I found I was wrong. I enjoyed the performance greatly."

"Hmpf," Helena sniffed. "You might have told me. The girls and I have been
asked again to go tonight by Hermione. The girls don't wish to attend. They are
staying home tonight. I'm sharing Hermione's box. Naturally, I'll have to sit in
the back, as she is also coming tonight accompanied by her boring husband and
her boring son. She heard what a sensation that Antonina woman was and she
was angry that she had missed it. "Helena fingered her diamond necklace, the one
he had given to her (because she insisted on it) after Chloe's birth. "Perhaps you
should see if we can purchase a subscription for ourselves. We are an important
family, Anderson, and I think we should have our own box."

"Helena, I am going to the opera tonight because the soprano was *murdered*
on Saturday night. This is not a pleasure evening for me. This is part of my investigation.*" Not a pleasure! If only she knew, she'd kill him. Cut him. Strangle him.
Have him killed by as assassin. He mused. I wonder if this might be how the
thought of a murder begins? When a wife suspects her husband of...what? Adultery? Is that what I've done? Adultery in my mind? Adultery in my heart and
soul? Adultery. Hmmm. Helena has been an adulteress for years. I could cause a
scandal and divorce her. Would I do that? Is murder in one's heart when a husband discovers he hates his wife and loves another? Is this how those poor
bastards that I arrest start to think? And could I be one of them?*

He realized that Helena's voice had stopped. What the devil had she been
saying? "I beg your pardon, Helena. I was thinking of something else. What
was it you said?"

"I asked you if you would be sitting with us. There is an extra chair". *Oh,
I pray that you will not sit with me, Anderson. You would cramp my evening's
plans of anticipated delight with Philippe.* "After all, you left us high and dry
on Saturday night. Very annoying, Anderson. The girls and I had expected
you to escort us to supper and you left us so impolitely."

"I repeat, Helena. I was called backstage because of a *murder!*"

"Well, it was very inconvenient for *me!*"

"It was rather inconvenient for Vivienne du Lac, also." Anderson found himself snapping.

Helena drew herself up, highly insulted at his tone. "Well! I don't know what to make of you! It was bad enough that you left us…and now you insult me with a crude jest!"

"I will not be sitting with you tonight. I will be working." He placed his top hat on his head. "I hope you enjoy yourselves."

"We'll be dining afterwards with Count Smirnoff," She threw out the name as a challenge, hoping to reduce Anderson to teeth-grinding jealousy. "He was kind enough to be at my beck and call."

"That's nice." Anderson bent to fix the strap of his spat. "I hope you and the Viscount have a fine dinner."

"He's a count…not a viscount!"

"Whatever you say, Helena." Anderson's voice held nothing but polite boredom. *He used to be jealous. He used to love me, didn't he? He knows. He knows that I've been cheating on him. He doesn't care at all. The bastard.* He continued; "Most likely, you will see me here and there tonight. As I said, there was a murder and finding the perpetrator is my job." He opened the door. "Goodnight, Helena."

She sniffed as he exited. "Weak excuse!" she muttered. "Weak man!" *Why did I ever marry someone like him?* She looked at herself in the long mirror on the hallway wall. *You're still beautiful, Helena,* she told herself. *You look ten years younger than your age,* she exulted, smoothing her dress down. *Anderson's fire has gone out, if he ever had any! I need a man with fire! Philippe is fascinated by me.* She leaned forward and adjusted the flowers on her dress, placing them lower so that they accentuated the swell of her bosoms. *Anderson hadn't even noticed the flowers. Probably just as well. He'd want to know where they came from and he wouldn't be pleased to know that Philippe had sent them to me. Who am I fooling? He doesn't care at all. He'd most likely be relieved that I have found someone else to dance to my tune.* She smiled at her reflection and thought of the upcoming supper for two. *I'll make Philippe dance…and dance…romance…and pay and pay. Not only pay attention to me, but pay for pretty things, necklaces and perfumes…And Anderson, well, perhaps I will divorce him anyway, make a sensation in New York City! Scandalize them all! It might just be the making of me as a woman of mystery …one who dazzles men. And then…well, who knows what may happen?*

***

Whoever was coming to her prison…the man…for Louise was positive it was a man…would most likely be back again tonight. Louise was determined to stay awake, keep watch, and then make a tentative plan to escape.

At this moment, with the limited knowledge she already possessed, her plan had two potential parts.

The first part was to attempt to escape through the narrow windows. She thought she could pick away, piece by piece, enough wood shards to make an opening.

As it was still daylight, she felt that she had some time to experiment. Again, she shoved the table under the windows, climbed on the chair and scrambled onto the table top, pulling the chair up with her. She pushed the chair firmly under the window and stood on it. She pried another piece of wood away, breaking her fingernail in the effort. Sucking at her sore finger, she rested for a moment, then sighed and got back to work. The hole was bigger and she, again standing on her tiptoes and pulling up on the window frame, could see out of the window. There seemed to be a square yard, surrounded by a high wooden fence beyond. The fence measured, by her reckoning, six or seven feet high. She was a good athlete. Good at jumping and climbing, but could she get over that fence? Perhaps.

She tried to measure herself and the space of the window frame. She was thin, and she thought that she might be able to wiggle herself through. But how to get up high enough to get to the window? She could stand on the chair that she put on top of the table. That barely got the top of her head to the sill of the window. She wasn't sure that she could shinny herself up high enough and still have the strength and balance to smash the window and wiggle through. Difficult to overcome.

She looked carefully at the chair. It was a plain, cheaply made wooden chair with a ladder-type of back. She shook it, trying to see if it might come apart. It might. If she could get it apart, she could then use the ladder back to climb up a little bit higher, using the top of the chair as a push-off. That would get her about a foot-and-a-half more height. With the foot-and-a-half, could she then climb out? Perhaps.

And then? Could she not only get herself through the windows, but also shove the chair back through? If so, she could then lean the chair back against the fence and then, it would be easy to climb over. Perhaps.

And what lay beyond the confines of the fence? A higher fence? A dog that might rip her to pieces? She shook her head, disgusted at her own pessimism. If she could get out of this room and over the fence, she could do anything!

And her second plan of escape? That would be to stay awake and somehow be quick enough to run out of the room when her jailer came in at night to refill her water and empty her chamber pot. Could she do that? Perhaps.

Tonight, I'll have to keep myself awake somehow. Pretend to be asleep when he comes in. Watch him and see what he does. Then, I'll have to see what I can manage. She thought of Robinson Crusoe managing to find food, managing to make tools, managing to finally escape the prison of the island. She thought further of her mother managing to find the wherewithal to make a happy Christmas out of the scraps and leftovers of a year of poverty. Robinson was inspirational, but he was only a character in a book. Her mother was real.

She settled down, telling herself that she would sleep lightly for an hour. Hopefully, when her jailer came in, she'd be able to wake up and watch.

***

The Metropolitan Opera was ready again, like a bride at the altar, waiting for the audience to fill its seats and standing areas, waiting for yet another triumph of operatic spectacle. The lights sparkled, the doors beckoned, the ushers, immaculate in their finery, picked up the programs and stood, ready for the gush of customers. Already, the parterre box-holders and those who were to be seated in the grand tier were marching in, grandly arrayed in silks, satins, feathers and furs, the women flashing diamonds and rubies and emeralds at their throats, on their ears and on their fingers. The men, dressed in stolid white and black, showed glimpses of color with scarlet sashes, gold cummerbunds and the gleam of military decorations festooned across satin waistcoats. Who was wearing Worth? Have I seen that dress before? Who had one of the new Chanel gowns? And – oh, look at her! She's wearing a five-year old Poiret kimono! How gauche!

Dowagers paraded up and down the aisles, visiting other boxes, petting dandified lap dogs, cooing over a necklace or a hemline.

"Were you here on Saturday? Did you see the new soprano?"

"My dear, not only was I here, but I actually spoke with Vivienne du Lac just *moments* before her death!"

"No! How was she? Do you think she had any premonition…?"

"She looked haunted. I thought to myself…you know how sensitive I am…I said she looked…haunted!"

"How lovely you look, Maude! Such a beautiful gown!"

"And you, Natalie! I haven't seen that dress before, have I?"

"My dear Ambassador Mabley! How good to see you again! I spent a delightful afternoon with your niece, Carey."

"Lady Staer! She's the bane of her mother," The Ambassador twinkled. "Always up in one of those new-fangled airplanes." He bowed low over Dorothea Staer's hand. "Have you met The Honorable Athol Wolf?" He introduced them and then turned his attention to the bottle of champagne resting on the tiny glass-topped table.

In the aisle, Barbara and David, with Teddy tucked under David's arm, waited to enter their box. Barbara carried a white satin box of Susan's Chocolates and a page-boy, behind them, staggered under the weight of a silver cooler filled with ice and champagne. Barbara wore a silver chemise, beaded with green peridots and tiny bells that chimed faintly as she moved. "I feel as if I'm walking with Big Ben," David rumbled, secretly pleased that his wife was gathering so many envious glances.

"Anderson von Vogel is sitting with us tonight." Barbara turned, smiling and waving at Judith and Roger Miller. "I'm not sure if Gigli is coming, but I'll have them bring an extra chair, just in case."

"Who has the fourth chair?" David eased Teddy's bulk down on the cushion and stood, leaning over the balcony, assessing the crowd.

"Anderson's sister, Melanie. You met her at the reception for Amelia Earhart, do you recall?"

"She's also a flyer, isn't she?" David had great admiration for women who dared to do unconventional things. He'd never give Barbara the satisfaction, but he was secretly very proud of her for wanting to raise money for the opera. He thought of Barbara presiding over her meeting, then thought of a female flying a plane. "And she's a pretty thing, isn't she?"

"Almost as pretty as I am," Barbara winked at him. He bent and kissed her cheek.

"No one is prettier than you, you sweet patootie, you!"

"Boop, boop-a-doop!" Barbara did a slightly risqué, impromptu dance move. "Oh, Melanie! Here you are, you sweet thing!"

"Oh, you kid!" Melanie answered back, waving her arms as if dancing the Charleston.

David clutched at his heart. "Ladies! This old geezer cannot deal with all of this vamping!" Melanie laughed in delight and kissed David's cheek. "Is my brother here yet?"

"I think he's backstage. Sleuthing, you know."

"Then, I'm popping over to say hello to Carey and Brooks." Melanie slipped back out. "I'll be back in two shakes of a lamb's tail, as David always says."

***

Francesca and Simeon, together with their friends and neighbors from Greenwich, found their seats in the Orchestra Section. "I'm here, and you're next to Simeon," Francesca motioned to her brother, Monsignor Dario. "Mina, you're in 306, Giovanna...308 and Sabina and Enzo...you two are right behind me in 404 and 406." She shrugged out of her coat and sat down. "Mama...you and Signor Fazzolini are over there." She waved her mother to a pair of seats. "The program! It's been changed! Oh! Look...here..." She read: " 'Mimi, a poor seamstress....Antonina Sabatino'...Oh! I'm so proud!" She nearly dissolved into tears of joy. "My daughter! An opera star!"

She turned at a hail from behind. "Mrs. Rosato! Good evening!"

"Mr. von Vogel! I didn't know you'd be here." Francesca rose and took Anderson's outstretched hand. *If it is my daughter that you wish to impress, you'd better be here!*

***

"Unfortunately, tonight is business, Mrs. Rosato." Anderson tipped his head to Simeon. "We have a killer to catch."

"Do you have any idea of...oh, perhaps I had better not ask," Francesca dimpled. "I'm sure that you have your methods." She grinned at him and he saw how much Antonina resembled her mother. "May I introduce you to my family and some dear, dear neighbors and friends?" She turned. "This is my brother, Dario Sabatino, also known as Monsignor Dario. And here are Enzo and Sabina Uccello, Giovanna Manero and Mina Fiorile...all neighbors and great friends...all from the same little village in Italy. And you remember my mother? Maria Sabatino." Maria dimpled. "And this is Signor Alfonso Fazzolini, Antonina's singing *professore*." Anderson bowed and shook hands. "And, of course, you already know Simeon."

"Simeon..." Anderson shook hands. He felt lightheaded, meeting all of these people who knew Antonina so well. He saw Francesca watching him...*did she know? Could she know?* "How pleasant to see you again. I'm looking forward to hearing Antonina sing again. I was delighted and charmed on Saturday night to hear her, but tonight...well, it is different....um, now that I know her...um...even better."

A grown man blushing, Francesca noted. *Hmmm.*

To extricate himself from his own asinine comments, Anderson changed the subject. "How have the Greenwich police been doing with regard to the little girl who is missing?"

Simeon rescued him. "I was speaking with Chief McAndrews this afternoon. They have no clue at all to her whereabouts."

"What little girl?" Mina asked. There was nothing that happened that Mina wasn't curious about.

"A nine year old child from Greenwich. She was last seen at the playground two days ago."

"I hadn't heard!" Mina, who had a round little face with two dark, snapping eyes, looked very concerned. She turned to Simeon. "You should have told me!"

"Told you?" Simeon looked confused.

Mina pulled at his sleeve. "Francesca should have let you know." She sat down and closed her eyes, seemingly folding herself up. "I can sometimes see things..."

"Babies...yes," Francesca turned to her friend. "But this sort of thing, Mina? You can see *this?*"

"Perhaps," Mina massaged her temples. "When we get home, Simeon. I want you to go to the police. Get some item...perhaps a beloved toy...perhaps a nightgown...something that the child wears or plays with..."

"You think you can...?" Anderson didn't know quite what to say. Did this little woman consider herself a fortune teller? He almost laughed, but realized that the rest of them were nodding in agreement.

"Oh, Mina! If only you can see..." Francesca grabbed Mina's hand.

Mina shook her head. "I cannot promise. My gift...well, for babies and for women, yes. This...this child...I can but try." She bent her head and looked into her own clenched fist. "Perhaps."

Anderson tried not to look incredulous. Sabina leaned forward, over the seat. She seemed to sense his incredulous doubts at the notion that anyone might be able to see into the future or discern where a child might be abducted. "You will be surprised at her powers." Her voice was low and urgent. "She has a gift from God." Her husband, a funny-looking little man, nodded solemnly.

"If you say so..." Anderson tried to sound neutral. "I hope...I..." He ended in lame confusion.

Francesca patted his hand. "Trust her. We Italians from our little village have some powerful gifts...some are easily seen and some...well...what can it hurt if Mina tries to see..."

I'm certainly not going to begin a silly argument with Antonina's mother, for God's sake! "I bow to your knowledge," Anderson thought he'd said just the right thing. "Was Antonina excited tonight?"

"Excited! I thought she was going to take the early morning milk train! She's so thrilled about all of this. And her new apartment!" Francesca laughed. "I suppose it is normal for one's children to grow up and depart their mother's warm nest."

"Not only warm, but food-filled!" Simeon laughed. "She'll probably starve without your baking and cooking."

"She'll manage just fine," Francesca nodded with stout conviction. "She's a sensible girl. It is a good time for her to learn to live as an adult." Francesca's eyes slid past Anderson's. "She is growing up and it is time for her to become a grown-up, with grown-up freedom."

"Freedom to make her own mistakes!" Mina suddenly laughed. "It is a different world here in America."

"A good world. Different, but fine, all the same." Francesca averred. "She's coming home tonight, but will take herself and her belongings on the train into New York tomorrow. We may not see her for a week."

"A week?" Simeon seemed surprised.

"Certainly. She has *La Traviata* on Saturday night. It's a whole new opera for her, although I am sure she is as ready as she was to take over *Bohème*. She'll be getting her things together and settling into her apartment," She turned back towards Sabina. "Signor Fazzolini swears to me that the landlady will keep an eagle eye on her, haven't you, *Professore?*" *Was she mistaken, or did Anderson suck in his breath?*

"I will guard her as I would guard the jewels at the Vatican," Fazzolini smiled with tenderness.

Sabina poked her husband's midsection, "Fazzolini would never let anything happen to her."

Anderson coughed. "I, um, ah...I will be driving up to Greenwich tomorrow at noon. I am seeing your Chief McAndrews..." *This will be news to McAndrews, but I will make sure he doesn't give me away...*" I, um...I, ah...will be driving back in the mid-afternoon. Um, If I can be of some assistance," he bowed towards Francesca, "Uh, perhaps, uh, Antonina...I could...she...I might drive her back here. Um, with my car and her things, perhaps it will be easier."

"Perhaps it would," Francesca inclined her chin.

Mina broke in. "When you come, please come to my little store," she ordered Anderson. "I will show you what I mean about my powers...perhaps."

"It would be my pleasure," Anderson agreed. *Anything to do with Antonina and her family and her friends would always be my pleasure.*

Behind him, the opera house was filling...He glanced up to see a young woman waving wildly at him. "Melanie!" He called, waving back to his favorite sister. He knew she couldn't hear him, but he waved his arms anyway to indicate that he'd be with her in a few moments. Francesca glanced up at the young woman and then waited for Anderson to speak.

For some reason, he blushed. "That's...that's my young sister." He smiled and his mouth softened with affection...and Francesca understood the powerful attraction a man like this might have for her daughter. "She...her name is Melanie. She's a live wire. An independent young woman who loves anything to do with airplanes."

"*Air*planes?"

"Yes. She an aviatrix. She flies them." He found that he said it proudly. "She's a friend of Amelia Earhart...perhaps you have heard of her?"

"Heard of her!" The woman called Giovanna squealed. "She's a heroine! Imagine, going up in the air in one of those flimsy contraptions! Oh, my!"

"You'll have to meet my sister one of these days. She'd think it was wonderful if you'd like to take a ride up with her."

"Really!" Giovanna's voice was reverent and her eyes sparkled. "Up in a plane! Oh! Paolo would have a kitten!" She grinned. "But maybe I would go."

"You? Up in an airplane?" Francesca scoffed. "Not on your life!"

Giovanna pretended to be insulted. "What do you know? I was always the adventuresome one. You, Francesca, were always the coward." The two old friends laughed. "Up in a plane? Of course I will go!" She pulled at Anderson's sleeve. "Tell her that she has a pupil down here and perhaps we can meet at the intermission and talk." She watched Francesca's astonished face. "Humpf! I'd love to fly! Who knows, perhaps there is a new career for an old lady like myself. I can become a pilot!"

"You're a brave woman, Mrs. Manero," Anderson marveled. "I'd never do that."

"What? Your sister is a pilot and you've never been up in a plane?" Giovanna was surprised. *How could anyone miss an opportunity like that?*

"Not on your Aunt Nelly!" Anderson pretended to cower.

"Why not?"

"I'm a coward. I'm afraid of heights." He laughed, albeit ruefully, waved and went to see his now-famous sister.

***

Backstage, all was proceeding smoothly. Antonina's new dress for Act One and Act Two had been completed. It was a deep blue print with silver lilies sprinkled all over. Instead of being made from a rich fabric as the accursed red velvet dress had been, more suitable for a King's ball instead of adorning a poor seamstress, this dress was fashioned from soft, faded cotton. Antonina stood, rigid and still, with Janet making last minute alterations so that the dress fit perfectly.

"I like this dress better than the last one."

Janet crossed herself superstitiously. "Brrr! The last dress! I'll have nightmares until I die about that dress!"

"Are you nervous?" Angelique, sharing the dressing room with harmony, asked.

"No. On Saturday, I knew I could do it, but was worried about all kinds of peculiar things….who killed Vivienne? Was the murderer still lurking around the opera? Would everyone help me on stage? Now, I think that the killer is no longer here. I think her funny little man killed her."

"Crespi? Why would he kill her?" Angelique buckled her shoes. They were an important part of her costume, as she had to kick one of them off in Act Two.

"Perhaps they quarreled about his salary?" Antonina was too young and too happy to be worried. And besides, Anderson was out there…somewhere in the throng of people…her voice would find him…and she'd be singing to his heart, even though everyone would think she was singing out her love to Rodolfo. She slid her pearls out from under her bodice and said her mantra. *"In bocca lupo".*

At the dressing table, Angelique was also going through her ritual, touching her treasures and murmuring her own prayers. She paused as she finished her ritual. "Funny…tonight, I am thinking of my dear friend in Italy." She winked at Antonina. "Perhaps, at this very moment, he, too, is thinking of me."

"I am sure that he thinks of you twenty-four hours a day!" Antonina bent and kissed Angelique's cheek as the door opened and Henry Wu with his paint-pots and blushes came to do their make-up.

"Ladies!" He announced with a flourish. "I am here!"

***

Twenty minutes to curtain. Dean Armandroff was not in his seat. Tommy Zeranski poked Susan. "Where's our sheik?"

She pointed to one of the parterre boxes. "Up there. Not far from his new sweetie."

Tom stood, trying to catch Dean's eye without anyone noticing. "Come on down, you clown!"

Up in the box, Dean flapped his hand at Tom, signaling that he'd be right down. "I've gotta go. We're almost ready to start."

"I'll listen for your mournful notes," Brooks took his hand. Carey, with a giggle, rolled her eyes. Actually, she thought Dean was a wonderful catch for Brooks, and naturally, Brooks was a superb catch for Dean. The two of them…from such different backgrounds, but both earnest and funny people, learning, because of their attraction to one another, that such things as background and even political leanings can be overcome if love comes calling in the right way.

"Don't forget," Carey admonished him. "We're going up in a plane tomorrow. You and Brooks, me and our other friend and wonderful pilot, Melanie von Vogel."

"I'm a little frightened, Carey," Brooks shivered. "An airplane…wow, it's so high up there…"

And I am terrified. There is no way that I am setting foot onto a little contraption like that! Fly in the air? Do you think I am insane? But, of course, that's not what came out of his mouth. "I can't wait!" He tried for a tone of excited confirmation, but Carey thought his words were said in a tone of shaky bravado.

No way that he can un-say them, she chortled. He was stuck on his own manliness! "Great! We'll meet at the aerodrome tomorrow. At eleven…that will give us time to get in a flight over the city. You are not going to believe how beautiful it is zooming up the Hudson River and seeing all of the tall buildings. You know, they've started construction on The Empire State Building! Wait until you see it from on top!"

"By jingo, I can't wait." *Zooming up the Hudson River! He'd rather walk on hot coals barefooted!* With a heavy heart, Dean got to his feet. "I'll see you ladies at intermission…I'm on my way to the pit." He gave Brooks a chaste kiss on her cheek and lumbered down to take his seat with the orchestra. Garvin watched him approaching and winked at him. Morosely, Dean gave Garvin a wave, sat down and began to tootle on the bassoon…mournful music. *If you only knew, Garvin. Tomorrow, I am probably going to die in an airplane crash. Me and Brooks. Just falling in love...our whole future before us...and the whole thing will be doomed just because we were so stupid as to let Carey talk us into this suicide mission. If you only knew!*

* * *

Behind the stage in the small office that was being used as their interrogation room, Pedar and Buddy finished their lists. "OK, these people are the ones who have no real alibi...they might have had an opportunity to kill her...no way for us to know yet."

"Read them to me."

"Sure, boss. All of the performers...that's nine stars, fourteen secondary performers, all of the kiddies, the people who played the mothers, the Farm Women, the soldiers, the Townspeople and all of the understudies." Buddy rolled his eyes.

"How many is that?"

"At least fifty."

Pedar sighed. "Well, the orchestra has an alibi...all of them, right?"

"Everyone but the Maestro."

"I thought he was in his little room until he got called, no?"

"Unfortunately, no. He has that good luck thing that he does before every performance where he trots around the stage, touching the curtains." Buddy shook his head. "They're all nutsy, these show people. Everybody has to do some idiotic thing or else they'll have bad luck!"

Pedar sighed again. A deep sigh, from his very soul. "And we have your little girlfriend and the other dresser girl, Celestina. Then all of the executive staff and whatever members of the Board of Directors were wandering around. Oh, and all of the chorus members. Well, most of them, anyhow. A few were together with someone else the whole time...but most of them went here and there...to the toilet, to make a telephone call, over to the curtain to take a peek at the house..." He hit the top of his desk. "God's teeth! We may have to interrogate half the city of New York!"

"And don't forget Crespi."

"If I ever meet Crespi, I'll tell him what I think of him."

"I wonder what happened to the dog?" Buddy got to the end of his list. "She can't still be alive, can she? And how about that Board Member who supposedly had an affair with du Lac?"

"He's off the hook. Lucky for him, he's been in South Africa for the past month."

"He's the only one, really, that we are sure didn't murder her. Jeepers! Everyone had the opportunity and everyone would have loved to see her dead!"

Pedar threw up his hands. "Let's get out of here and watch the show. It's ten minutes until curtain."

Buddy laughed. "Listen to you…'until curtain'…you're hanging around here too much! You're even starting to spout the lingo!" He stood up and threw the list on his desk. "Come on, Janet showed me the best place to watch from. We'll see everything."

***

The gong sounded, telling the audience that the opera was about to begin. The buzz of conversation heightened as dowagers, postal workers, millionaires, paupers, musicians, wealthy patrons, librarians, bankers, teachers, construction workers, professors, students and every other category of avid music lovers drifted to their assigned spots. Anderson, on his way to the Wessel's box, stopped for a moment to exchange a few words with his sister and greet Carey and Brooks. As he turned to survey the house, he caught sight of Helena, sitting in Hermione's box with Philippe Smirnoff. The two were engrossed with one another. *Good. Perhaps she'll leave with him and I won't have to bother with her tonight. No, she'll see me sitting with the Wessels and she'll come over during intermission. It wouldn't be like Helena to miss the opportunity to hob-nob with a Baron and Baroness.*

He passed the two seats that were reserved for the opera critics. The two men, looking like two identical penguins in their formal livery, were just settling themselves down, gossiping like old ladies. He nodded to them. "Good evening, Mr. Blackburn. Good evening, Mr. Harris."

"Oh, Chief von Vogel! So exciting! I saw you here at the opening!" Anderson noted that Jason Harris spoke every sentence as if it ended in an exclamation point.

"I was astonished to hear about Mademoiselle du Lac's untimely death," Anderson thought he put it well.

"Oh, that!" James Blackburn's hand flashed upwards, as if to flick Vivienne's death away. "But how about the divine Antonina Sabatino? Divine, do you think? Better than du Lac? The best I've ever heard, do you think?" Harris was the king of exclamation points, Blackburn spoke in question marks.

"I thought she was fabulous." *Fabulous! She was an angel! Perhaps I will always speak in exclamation points, also, when I am speaking of my Antonina!*

"We both wrote gushing reviews! She is such a treasure!"

"Where did she come from? We have an interview with her after tonight's performance, isn't that right, Jason?"

"Better than Nellie Melba!" Jason's hands clasped together in delight. "Better than Adelina Patti! Rapturous! We await her performance! Sublime!"

"We'll see you during the intermission, won't we?" James caroled. "We'll tell you just where we were when the murder occurred, won't we?" He giggled. "We've never been in on a murder before, have we?"

"Perhaps one of us did it! Oh, what excitement!"

The lights flickered, telling the audience that there were five minutes to curtain. Anderson said farewell to the critics and slid into the Wessel's booth.

"There you are, Anderson!" Barbara got up and kissed his cheek. "Would you like to hold Teddy while David pours you a glass of the bubbly?" Anderson liked dogs, and Teddy was a particularly nice hound. Nodding...for after all, what else could he do?...he scooped the obliging Teddy onto his own lap. Teddy licked his face and turned around once, then lay down with the bottom of his snout on the railing.

"Teddy does love *La Bohème!*" Barbara cooed. "He's not very fond of Wagner, much to David's annoyance."

David made a moue, raised his eyebrows as if to ask, what can one say when one's wife spouts inanities? and handed Anderson a flute of champagne. "There are little nibbles on the table, dear boy. Just help yourself. And if Teddums gets too heavy, please let me know."

"Who is that handsome man over there in Sir Richard's box?" Barbara had just noticed someone she had never seen before. "Who is he with?"

"A lady and a young girl," David trained his opera glasses to the left.

Barbara fluffed her hair. "Gorgeous man. I must find out who he is and get an introduction."

"Are you thinking of leaving me for another?" David's voice was sardonic.

"Oh, never, darling. You're the bee's knees." Barbara giggled. "But I am always looking to meet gorgeous men. After all, I have you and Anderson here...why wouldn't I want another gorgeous man?"

David blew her a kiss. "Barbara, you light up my life." Anderson smiled. The two of them obviously adored one another. His smile slipped. *Why wasn't my own marriage any good? Is it me or is it Helena? Or both of us? How much I have missed!*

"Oh, David! Look! There are the Troys!" Barbara waved at Alex, Dale and the girls.

"Good man, that Troy," David lifted his champagne glass in salute. "Barbara, my love, would you like the other half of your drink?" He waved the champagne bottle in the air. *David was always so thoughtful*, Barbara thought. *He makes everyone feel as if they are a cherished guest.*

The Troy daughters waved to Anderson. They spotted the Wessel contingent and giggled at the sight of Teddy. Rachel sighed again. *We should have brought Sammy and Delilah. They would have behaved, wouldn't they have?*

The chandelier blinked and the opera house was dark for a moment. A spotlight shone on the opening of the gold curtain. To enthusiastic applause, Arturo Calle stepped out.

The audience held its breath. What was he going to say?

"Ladies and gentlemen, good evening. As you may know, I am Arturo Calle, the Executive General Manager here at The Metropolitan Opera House." He paused and the breath of every attendee paused too.

"Last Saturday, the opera suffered a great loss with the death of Vivienne du Lac, one of the greatest sopranos ever to sing." The audience burst into applause and Arturo stood still until they stopped. "Through a series of complex situations, we were able to introduce you to our newest star, Antonina Sabatino singing the role of Mimi in our production."

The audience screamed their approval, clapping and cheering and stamping their feet. Arturo smiled at them. "I'm happy to know that you think she is as wonderful as I do." Again, the audience went into hysterics.

"I want to thank you for your patronage and your enthusiasm. You are the most wonderful audience in the world and I love every single one of you." He paused for a heartbeat. And now, *La Bohème!*" With a practiced motion, he stepped back into the folds of the curtain and disappeared.

The chandelier flashed once more and the doors at the back slammed open. *Blam! Blam!* The dignified, yet electric figure of Massimo Orsini paraded down the aisle, bowing left and right to the thunder of applause. He climbed to the podium and opened the ebony box that held his baton-of-the-evening, a thin gold scepter with a large ruby embedded in the top. David murmured that this baton had been presented to Orsini by the Empress of Russia at a performance of *Prince Igor*.

"How many batons does he have?"

David shrugged, "Hundreds. Each more valuable than the other. Some are pens that write. Some are daggers. Some hold an ounce or two of whiskey. Some are electric and light up when he plays. But no matter what they are or do, they are all worth a fortune!"

The *Maestro* greeted his orchestra and shook Garvin's hand. Garvin replaced his violin, tucking it under his chin, ready to perform…

Orsini nodded firmly, took a deep breath and swelled his chest out. He brought the baton up in the air and then… "Ta TUM!" The opening notes of the brief overture sang out. The curtain slowly opened to huge excitement. Would this young and untried girl…would she sing as well as she did on Saturday? Was she as marvelous as everyone said she had been? Could she sustain her voice? As one, the audience sat forward, eyes staring…already enthralled….but no one, not even Antonina's own mother, was as enthralled as Anderson von Vogel.

.….

Chapter Twenty-Two

"They who dream by day are cognizant of many things which escape those who dream at night..." Edgar Allan Poe...Eleonora

It got darker and darker. Her eyes were heavy and she lay down, determined to keep awake by angling her head against the wall so that her neck was bent and cramped. Unfortunately, she kept drifting off, waking with a jolt as her head snapped downwards as she fell asleep. She tried taking off her shoes and her socks, keeping her legs and feet out from under the blankets. It was chilly in the room and she hated to have cold feet. Perhaps the discomfort would keep her awake. Despite the cold, she fell asleep.

Her eyes snapped open. *What was that?* She was instantly awake. Instantly ready. A chink sounded...a chain being unlocked? She strained, moving her head slightly so that her ear was positioned as close to the door as she could, and still make her jailer believe that she was sleeping. Another noise...a grating sound...the door being pushed open...slowly...slowly...She slitted her eyes and saw a dim pool of light. A lantern being held? The door opened, making the grating noise.

She felt him before she actually saw him. A young-ish man, slender, wearing some dark shapeless clothing. He wore glasses and wore his hair in a long-ish cut. He stood over her and she breathed evenly and let herself stir slightly. He shaded the lantern, most likely moving it behind himself. She moaned and snuggled, holding the pillow half-on her face, shielding her eyes from him. This way, she could peep at him and he might not be able to see that she was awake.

He stood over her for a long time. She decided, it was most likely a minute...but it felt like a long time. He reached out his hand, and she clenched her teeth behind her mouth so that she didn't recoil from him. He touched her hair. It was a gentle touch, but she nearly vomited.

At home, before this nightmare had started, it was Louise's job every night to go out to the backyard and feed the chickens that he mother kept. There were ten chickens, and they resided in a small coop tucked inside of a wire and wood fence. Louise had one favorite chicken. She'd named her Ramona. It seemed like a very glamorous name. Ramona was a prodigious layer and there was always a warm, pale brown egg under her feathers.

After Louise had taken Ramona's egg and the other eggs laid by the other chickens, she'd scatter chicken feed and meal on the ground. The chickens were always delighted to see her and ate the meal as fast as they could. Ramona seemed especially glad to see Louise and even let her pet her black-and-white feathers. But when Louise turned to go and closed and locked the chicken coop door, Ramona would stand and stare at her, asking her for something, but Louise didn't know what it was.

Louise now knew. Ramona wanted to be free. She was well-fed, watered and had a comfortable home. She was petted and scratched. But she was a prisoner.

The man stepped back. He put the lantern down and went back outside the door. He returned immediately, carrying a pail of, Louise guessed, fresh water. He put the new pail down, picked up the old pail, and went back outside the door.

He came back in carrying an empty, Louise guessed, chamber pot and a pile of newspapers. He went back into the little room she now called her bathroom. She heard a clink as he placed the clean chamber pot down, then a scrape as he picked up the used chamber pot. She heard him ripping the newspapers into smallish squares. This took about two minutes, Louise guessed. He then carried the used chamber pot out the door, came back in with two paper bags. He placed them on the table and picked up the lantern. He came to her bedside again, stooped down once more and touched her hair. She schooled herself to breathe softly and naturally. She schooled herself to not scream. She schooled herself not to move.

She felt that he'd stood up. She kept her breathing light, but stirred slightly and turned her head into the pillow.

In a moment, she heard his footsteps go out. The door was shut, and she heard the chinking sound, she guessed, of the chain or lock being replaced.

The night was still. She sat up and put her socks back on, tucked her cold feet against her calves, and discovered that tears were running, unchecked, down her face. She got up and went into the little room. She used the chamber pot and then went to her pail to wash her hands and face. Feeling somewhat better, she lay down. She could have looked into the two bags, but she wanted to save that activity for tomorrow.

If he does this every night, I can escape...I think. There are maybe one or two minutes while he goes into my bathroom, rips up the newspapers and changes the chamber pot. If I can leap up and run out, I think I can escape before he can catch me. She shuddered. What would he do if she didn't get out in time? Would he be angry?

What was beyond the door of her prison? Could she escape from there? Would he hurt her if she was unsuccessful?

She shrugged. She sure wasn't going to spend the rest of her life eating peanut butter sandwiches and having her chamber pot emptied out by a stranger. Certainly, she would try to escape. Otherwise, she was no better than a chicken.

***

Two things happened as Mimi crept through the door of the bohemian's chilly attic. Well, three things, actually. The first was that the audience, as one, stood up for Antonina's entrance. She stayed at the doorway, waiting as the applause thundered about her. *This is my life! This is what I was born to do!*

The second thing was that, under cover of the pandemonium of clapping, Antonina peeped her eyes up and connected to the eyes of Anderson von Vogel. It was only a millisecond, but the glance lit each of their hearts.

And the third thing? As the applause died down, she entered the room and began the ever-beautiful meeting of a man and a woman who were destined to fall in love. As Mimi and Rodolfo told one another of their lives, Figaro, the Metropolitan Opera's cat came onto the stage.

The audience was first to notice, as Figaro was behind Mimi and Rodolfo.

A few cried out; "The cat! The cat!"

Mimi turned to see Figaro jump onto the table. She smiled and, without missing a note or planned stage gesture, managed to stroke the cat. Rodolfo, following her lead, also stroked Figaro's back. Figaro, enjoying his moment on stage, arched his back and purred.

"It is good luck!" Francesca whispered to Simeon. "The cat is the best of good fortune!"

The audience chuckled. It was clear that they knew of the superstition. A cat on stage means the performance will be stellar…even more special than before. They whispered to one another and vowed that this was a night's performance of which they would tell their grandchildren. A miracle of an opera!

Mimi sang that her key was lost. She and Rodolfo knelt on the floor, seeking the missing key. Figaro jumped off the table and pushed his nose into Mimi's hand. Delighted, she added an extra line. *"Welcome, dear little cat. We need your help. The cat will help us find what is lost!"*

The consummate professional, Massimo Orsini signaled to his orchestra to follow her lead. The orchestra, watching their *Maestro* with one eye and watching Antonina with the other, adjusted their music. Dean had all he could do to not whoop out his delight. *This was opera! This was what it was all about!*

Some people wondered just what it is that a conductor does. Why, if the orchestra knew its part and the opera singers know their parts, does an orchestra need a leader? To the unknowing and uninitiated, it was a question, but to those who knew music and orchestras and operas, the question was a silly one. Like a chariot driver guiding six or eight spirited horses, the conductor held the reins to the successful mingling of the singers, the orchestra and the entire stage production. He kept the tempo and the action together, easing up on the violins, if the soprano was a beat late. Increasing the sound of the trumpets if the tenor was having a problem reaching his high note. Slowing down the tempo if the action on stage didn't quite match the score. He was the genius, gathering all of the sounds and timing of the opera together to give the audience a performance to be remembered. A good conductor did this and produced a good performance. A great conductor, and there were very few of this breed, transcended the music and the singing and the stage directions to give the audience a show that melded the separate items into one that was greater than the sum of its parts. A great chef did this with humble food ingredients; a great photographer did it with a photo that dazzled the eye. A great *Maestro*, like Orsini, brought brilliance to those who watched and listened to him.

And when he saw the little black cat walk out on the stage, Orsini smiled and performed his special type of magic.

Rodolfo touched the key and hid it in his pocket. The audience chuckled at his little deception. Figaro pawed at the pocket and Rodolfo also added a line: *"Shhh, little cat. Do not tell her that I have hidden the key! She is my love and I must keep her here until she realizes that she loves me."* The audience went wild as Orsini deftly re-gathered the music. In the midst of their frenzied applause, Figaro disappeared from the stage. This performance would be talked about for a hundred years.

***

Act Two opened to the colorful bustle of the Latin Quarter on Christmas Eve. Sue Shigeoka sang the part of the Sweets Vendor and Ruby Stevens was plucked from the chorus of mothers to sing the few lines given to the Female Beggar.

And then…the spectacle of Musetta hit the stage! Again, Angelique was resplendent. She had the audience eating out of her hand. They laughed, they chuckled, they admired her saucy character. She whirled and strutted, and every eye was upon her. She turned to sing her song. She felt…what? Something…something…she whirled around one more time, and Massimo Orsini's genius, sensing that she was not quite ready, adjusted his music to wait for a beat or two.

Antonina, close to her on the stage, was aware that Angelique had seen something in the audience. Something that had made her heart stop. As Musetta whirled around that one extra time, Antonina saw tears of joy in Angelique's eyes. She saw the 'O' of Angelique's mouth open in delight. What was it? Who was there? Under cover of the audience's rapt attention of Musetta's incomparable waltz, she searched the audience, seeking the reason for Angelique's ecstasy. She saw a man, sitting in one of the boxes. He was with a young girl and an older woman sat behind him. The eyes of the man and the young girl reached over their box and centered on stage. Was this Angelique's lover? And her daughter, perhaps? Yes, Antonina reasoned, singing her part, which at this moment was minimal, with half her brain while the other half watched Angelique. Yes! Yes! Yes!

And when Musetta's Waltz was over and Angelique stood, her hand thrown up in triumph, the applause thundering and thundering around her, Antonina could feel the love that shafted from the stage to the box and back to the stage. *Ah, Angelique! My dear, dear friend. How happy I am for you!*

***

As the curtain closed for intermission, Ernest Rattner put his plan into action. *I'll be a rich man by tomorrow. Ha! I'll be set for the rest of my life!*

***

The curtain came down on another night of triumph. There were nearly fifty curtain calls and the audience stood on its feet for more than twenty minutes, refusing to let the orchestra, Massimo Orsini, Angelique, the rest of the cast, and especially Antonina off the stage. The flowers were piled three feet high. The accolade went on, and on, and on, and on....

At last, the house turned the lights up and the performers disappeared behind the curtain. The entire house was buzzing:

"This was the performance of a lifetime!"

"She is the finest *diva* in the world!"

"Imagine what she will do next week in *Traviata!*"

"Angelique Orloff sings Musetta better than anyone! Anyone!"

"She's the most beautiful..."

"Not as beautiful as Antonina Sabatino!"

"I prefer..."

"What a show!"

No one missed Vivienne du Lac at all. No one even mentioned her. Her murder had been eclipsed by Antonina's stunning performances. Only the newspapers headlines and the police seemed to recall that Vivienne had been brutally killed only a few evenings ago.

***

At Delmonico's, the tables were filled with the opera patrons. At the big table under the window, Urbano and Arturo held court with James and Jason and a few members of the Executive Board and their wives.

Francesca and Simeon sat with their Greenwich contingent. Anderson and Antonina sat with them, although both of them had been invited to join several tables. "My family comes first!" Antonina laughingly refused. Instead of being annoyed or angry, her simple statement made her stock soar in the eyes of those she had refused. She didn't realize the truism that exclusivity makes a person even more valuable. Had she known, she still would have sat with her family and old friends and neighbors.

From their seats across the table, Francesca and Giovanna locked eyes and signaled to one another, *"What is going on with Antonina and this Ander-*

son von Vogel?" Giovanna had already told her best friend that Peter hadn't been at home since last Saturday night. He had called, which was good, as Paolo had been a little worried about his son. It seems that his liaison with the wealthy socialite with the mink coat, Babs whateverhernamewas, had borne fruit. He and she had taken a drive to Philadelphia in her automobile. Peter told Giovanna that Babs was an heiress, and that she owned several cars. He sounded like a cat with a huge bowl of cream at his disposal. He said he would be back at the end of the week, in plenty of time to get back to his studies. Ah, well. What can one do with young people? Giovanna adored her son, but he was a man and would do what he wanted. A good mother was one who kept her opinion to herself.

At a small table in an enviable alcove, Angelique sat, her face looking as if she'd swallowed the sun, with her companion, Janine, her darling daughter, Anna Emmelina, and the love of her life. Angelique wore a Worth gown, a deep, bottle-green chemise with a webbed netting that dazzled.

Antonina made sure that she stopped to say hello and congratulate Angelique on the triumph of her Musetta, even though the real reason she wanted to visit Angelique's table was to be introduced to David della Cuore...*Count* David della Cuore. He was extremely handsome, with an open, smiling countenance. It was obvious that he was in love with Angelique and adored little Anna. Antonina winked at her new and dear friend. *I approve! I approve with all my heart! He's so devastatingly handsome...almost as handsome as Anderson!* It was a sign of good, solid friendship when two women could converse with a wink and a nod.

"We are all going to try your dessert tonight," Antonina offered. "I understand they sell more of this cake than any other dessert."

"My mother's dessert is the best!" Anna bragged, rolling her dark eyes. "Last time, I ate two helpings!"

"I'm not sure that I can eat *two!"*

"You must try," Anna was convincing in her girlish charm. "When I told the girls at school that Mims had a dessert at Delmonico's that was named after her, at first, no one believed me." She grinned and the Count ruffled her curly hair. "And then Catherine Vanderbilt came here with her grandmother, and saw it on the menu. She told her grandmother that the cake was named for my mother and they both had a helping." She smiled, a smile of great satisfaction. "So all of the girls knew that I wasn't making anything up."

Antonina returned to her table. "We will all have to have the special dessert named in honor of Angelique. It is called 'Angelique's Kiss', and I insist that we all try it."

Mina joked, "I wonder when they will name a dessert after you, my pet?"

Francesca laughed, "If Gia and Lucia were here, they'd suggest that Mr. Delmonico name Antonina's dessert 'the shatteringly, revolting, best cake ever'.

Simeon excused himself and went to visit with Arturo Calle. "I will be in New York next Wednesday with Antonina's mother, to whom I have the great fortune to be engaged." He paused while the men at the table offered their congratulations. "Yes, Francesca is meeting with her publisher at eleven o'clock. Would that be a good time for me to come to your office to discuss Antonina's new contract?"

"Is...Mrs. Sabatino? No...ah, Rosato? Is she a writer?"

"She and a dear old teacher and comrade, *Zia* Filomande, have written an Italian cookbook. Wattles and Webberstein is publishing it next year."

"Goodness! A cookbook! How fascinating this family is!" Calle paused and checked his pocket memorandum book. "Wednesday...that's the 16th, right? Eleven o'clock would be splendid. Will you come to my office? Good." Simeon bowed and returned to his table.

"I've known Simeon as a friend and as an attorney for many, many years," Urbano whispered to Calle. "You are going to be handsomely fleeced!"

Calle laughed. "She will be worth it, whatever it is! She has the potential to be the greatest soprano ever."

"I agree."

"I have an opening in the schedule for next Sunday. I'm going to have her do a benefit special...let's suppose we earmark all of the profits for the fund for indigent opera singers..."

"And what will the benefit be?"

"If I am going to spend a fortune on Antonina's contract," here he grinned. "I'm going to have her do this concert. I think I'll have her sing ten arias...Maybe *Inneggiamo, Quando, rapito in estaisi, Vissi d'arte, Un bel de vedremo*...and a few others...the best of the best, you understand."

"I have no fear that you'll get your money's worth."

Calle winked and slapped Urbano's back. "She will do magnificently out of this and we will do magnificently out of this, my friend. It will be a marriage made in heaven."

***

As Simeon sat down, there was a stir at the door. Buddy Manger rushed into the restaurant, looked around wildly and spotted Anderson. Anderson rose to meet him. "What's wrong?"

"Two problems, boss." Buddy was wheezing, slightly out of breath.

"Only two?" Anderson smiled. "How bad can this be?"

"Well, one isn't too bad. They found the dog...the little dog that belonged to Vivienne. She's dead...maybe been dead two days. Looks like someone kicked the pup to death." Anderson's eyes widened. No one had any good words for the dog, but still...this was terrible.

"And the second thing?"

"The second thing." Buddy slowed his breathing down. "The second thing is worse. We found one of the stagehands…man named Ernest Rattner…dead. His body was hidden behind some canvas on the side of the stage. He was killed by a blow to his head."

"No!" Anderson gasped. "What more do you know?"

"It was one of them sandbag weights…they hold up scenery, you know? We think someone coshed him over the head with one."

"I'll be right with you." Anderson turned back to the table. "I'm sorry, we have an emergency back at the theater. An accident to one of the stagehands. I have to go back there." He bent and spoke softly into Antonina's ear. "I will see you in Greenwich tomorrow about noon."

If she was disappointed that he was leaving, she didn't say so. She squeezed his hand and her luminous eyes told him that she would dream about him.

Chapter Twenty-Three

"Oh, if I had the wings of an angel...over these prison walls I might fly..."
The Prisoners Song, by Robert Massey

At the Opera House, Death had come and gone, bringing Ernest Rattner to be judged. As a tornado was devastating a small island in the Pacific and several hundred island residents drowned, Death did not wait to see the outcome of Rattner's afterlife. Rattner had been a poor specimen of a human being, full of petty crimes and small transgressions...stealing a few dollars here and drinking rot-gut hooch. He'd smacked around a few women, but in his immature mind, they had firmly deserved it. And then there was this recent business of blackmail...the recent business that hadn't worked out so well for Rattner. God took it all into account. Rattner's horrible upbringing, his lack of any parental love and his inherent weakness of character. God was in a good mood this day and gave Ernest Rattner the benefit of the doubt. It would be Purgatory for a long stretch...after that, God would revisit the matter.

As they entered the opera house, Buddy and Anderson found Dr. John Dempsey bending over the slumped body of one Ernest Rattner, formerly a stagehand with the Metropolitan Opera Company. On a chair, watching the doctor, was Clemens, the old janitor.

"Hey!" Dempsey greeted Anderson, waving his foot as his hands were occupied in probing the body. "You've got a real slaughterhouse out here! If it isn't the soprano, it's the stagehand."

"The Coroner as a humorist," Anderson deadpanned. "Perhaps we should put 'and be able to snap out jokes at a moment's notice' into the job description." He squatted next to the doctor. "What's up?"

"Clemons, here was cleaning up...putting everything away after the opera house closed down. He found, uh, Mr. Rattner under a pile of draperies or canvases or whatever you call these," he kicked at a heap of material on the floor.

"Is that correct, Mr. Clemons?"

"Yessir. I do up all the floors after everybody goes. I check the whole place. First thing, tonight, like usual, I goes up to the fifth floor...check everything, and then go down, floor by floor. I saw a closet open near the accounting office. I went to shut it, but then, donno...curious, I s'pose...I opened the door. That lady's dog was lying on the floor." His eyes rolled over to the far corner where another bundle, smaller, was heaped.

"Did you bring the dog down here?" Clemons nodded.

"By yourself?" Clemons nodded again.

"And then what?" *Enough of the nodding.*

Clemons leaned forward, letting his hands dangle down. "The dog was surely dead. Been dead a while. I got a blanket from Mister Calle's office…he has one on his couch…I wraps up the dog and carrys him downstairs. I came through the back door. I was gonna bring the dog to the garbage, but, when I came through here, I saw a shoe stickin' outta the canvas back here. I put the dog down and looked." He shook his head. "Now, I didn't do any voodoo on this man. Nosir. I didn't stick any pins in. I had nuthin' to do with this here man being killed. Nosir."

"We'll keep the dog's body, Clemons. Is there anything else you think we should know?"

"Nosir."

"Fine. Thank you. It's all right for you to go about your work now, but please, leave this area for us to care for."

"Yessir. Thank you, sir." Clemons lumbered away. The black cat, which had been hidden under Clemon's feet, also got up, stretched, and stalked away, his tail swishing from side to side.

"I heard that cats were supposed to be lucky in the opera." Buddy watched the cat go. "This one wasn't so lucky for Mr. Rattner."

"Tell me, John. What happened?"

"He was hit from behind. Fell forward on his face. His nose was broken, most likely when he smashed into the floor. See the blood? One hard blow. Feel here," he pointed to the back of Rattner's skull to the place that looked caved in and bloody. "Smashed his skull. Most likely into his brain. I'd say death was nearly instantaneous and probably done about three or four hours ago."

Anderson looked at his watch. It was just past midnight. "Before eight?"

"Right about then, give or take a half hour. I'll see more when I open him up tomorrow. Anybody know what he ate for supper or who he ate with?"

Anderson and Buddy shook their heads.

"Could it have been a woman who did this?" Anderson queried.

"Perhaps. If he…this Rattner…was say on his knees, a woman or a short man…could have been the dwarf… could have easily inflicted this kind of a wound. But if Rattner was standing…hmmmm," He straightened the corpse out, Let's see…he seems about five feet, maybe nine or ten inches tall…well, then the assailant would have to be six feet tall or taller. See?" He explained about the angle of the blow. "Then it was most likely a man."

"Do you think it was the same person? Did this killer murder Vivienne du Lac and are the two murders linked?"

A shrug. "It's a rare event at the opera, a murder, and now, we have two in less than a week."

"When do you want to start inquiries?" Buddy was happy that the killer most likely wasn't a woman.

"We'll have to wait until Monday when everyone comes back here to start Saturday's rehearsal." Anderson stood up, groaning. "I'm getting too old for all of this nightly gallivanting. Ohhh!" He rubbed the small of his back. "Can you take a look at this dog, John? I know dogs don't really fall under your lordly jurisdiction, but take a peek anyway, huh?"

Dempsey also stood up, making a sound of agony. "I'll be a dermatologist in my next life. No stooping down." He bent over the lump on the floor and peeled off the blanket. "Dead as a doornail," he muttered, stroking the dry fur. "He's been dead for at least a few days...see here? See the maggots?" Buddy averted his eyes. *Nevermind seeing the maggots.*

"How did he...I mean she...how did she die?"

"Hmmm? Perhaps a kick...seems like there is a soft spot here on her head...see?"

"So the dog was killed with a blow to the head a few days ago and Ernest Rattner was killed by a blow to the head tonight." Anderson shook his head. "Why?"

"Who hated him?" Buddy asked.

"I don't know much about him. He was on the list of people who might possibly have killed Vivienne."

"So were seven hundred others." Buddy was glum. "These people are just gonna get killed...one by one...and we'll never know who did it or why."

"We'll get to the bottom. We always do."

"Maybe."

"Nevermind maybe. We're the God-damned New York Metropolitan Police, aren't we?"

"Yeah, that and a nickel will get us a cup of coffee. I am telling you again: these opera people are nutty! Nutty! Let's get the boys in here to get the bodies out, rope off this area, as they have a God-damn ballet dance program here tomorrow afternoon, and get the hell out of here!"

"Best idea you've had all day."

***

Anderson opened the door of their apartment. It was about two in the morning and he tried to keep his noise at a minimum. The apartment was dark. He felt his way into the kitchen to get a cold drink. As he poured a Vichy water, he heard a sound in the living room. Stealthily, he crept to the door and opened it soundlessly. He stared, shocked.

There, in the living room, was his wife in the arms of Philippe Smirnoff. They were kissing passionately and both of them were completely wrapped up in one another's arms. Helena's dress was pulled away from her body and

Smirnoff's hands were on her breasts. They didn't notice him standing there until they broke apart.

"My God!" Smirnoff leaped away.

"Anderson!" Helena screamed. "What are you doing here?" She tried to get her clothing back on.

"Watching you, my dear." He waved the glass of Vichy water in the air. "But, please, do not let me interrupt you." He bowed to Philippe, strode by them and went upstairs to his dressing room.

He sat down on the day bed and drained the water, then pressed the cooled glass to his forehead and rolled it back and forth. He was dead tired and started to giggle, nearly in hysterics as he reviewed the scene in his mind. His eyes began to tear. Was he laughing or crying? He lay back, chuckling feebly, closed his eyes, and was instantly asleep.

Downstairs, clutched in one another's arms, Helena and Philippe were also in hysterics. *What would Anderson do?*

***

The larger bag held two sandwiches and two cinnamon crullers this time. One was a bacon and egg sandwich, still warm, and one was a liverwurst and cheese sandwich on rye bread. *Goody, goody. Who knew how happy one could be with two sandwiches and two crullers. Was this how prisoners in the war were slowly lured into telling secrets to the enemy? Huh! She'd eat, but she'd never surrender.* She delved further into the bag. At the bottom was a bottle of cold milk, a room-temperature bottle of soda pop and, surprisingly, a small metal bottle-cap opener.

I wonder if I can use the bottle opener as a tool to help me chip at the wood over the windows?

Using her time, she folded the bag and neatly placed it on the table with the other bags. She thought that if she used a piece of rock, she might be able to make marks on the bags...use them to record the dates...*how long had she been in here anyway? Let's see, it was a Thursday that she'd been playing with Danielle...or was it a Friday? I can't remember!* She took a piece of rock and tried to write on the paper, but the rocks were too hard and wouldn't leave any marks. She stuck a finger into the liverwurst and made three dots on the edge of one of the bags. It should be either three or four. *And perhaps I can escape tonight and it won't matter if it is three or four.*

She picked up the second bag. Something jingled inside. She opened it up and tipped it over onto the tabletop. A deck of cards and a small ball and jacks set rolled out. Louise's eyes lit up. *How nice! Well, not so nice that I am here, but nice that my jailor thought to give me something to do. It was getting awfully boring playing tic-tac-toe with no one else.* It felt traitorous to be happy that her jailer had given her playthings that made her happy. But, she was so bored, that she was happy that he'd given her the toys. Being a captive was a funny thing, she decided. It made life seem upside-down.

She ate the sandwich, relishing the warm and runny egg, taking teeny-tiny small bites so as to make it last longer. While she nibbled, she wondered just why her jailer had captured her. She wondered about the jacks. *Did he want a little girl to play with?*

Fortunately, Louise was a young and innocent girl. She had no idea of why a man would kidnap a little girl. No idea at all.

***

Anderson woke up with a start. He'd been dreaming that Helena had killed him and strung his body up in the middle of the stage at the Met. He shuddered and padded to the bathroom.

It should be fascinating to see what she's got to say for herself this morning. He dressed, not hearing any sound at all, and went into the kitchen. Chloe and Clair were at the kitchen table and Marie-Ange, the maid, was serving them breakfast. The girls were arguing, but stopped when he came in.

"Where's mother this morning?" Chloe took her orange juice and gulped at it.

"I have no idea," Anderson asked Marie-Ange to bring him a cup of coffee. "I'll be leaving for work in a few minutes, thank you, Marie-Ange."

"She's not here," Clair buttered a piece of toast and then slathered jelly on top. She took two huge bites. Anderson noticed that Clair's face was showing red spots and, as he looked closely, he also saw that her dress was too tight. *Perhaps she shouldn't eat as much as she does,* he mused.

"What are you girls doing today?" He rarely paid them much attention, but after the surprise of last night, he felt that they just might be getting short-changed, not only from himself, but from Helena.

Both of the girls shrugged, clearly not interested in a dialog with their father.

Feeling unexpectedly sad and hopeless, he sighed, wishing that his life had gone along on alternate paths. *If it had, I might never have met Antonina.*

"Why do you have that dumb smile on your face?" Clair asked.

"No reason. No reason at all."

***

She spent the day playing solitaire and bouncing the ball, trying to scoop up the jacks. It made the hours pass. She spent an hour or so, by her own reckoning of time, doing her exercises, and then tried to fold the paper squares into the shapes of boats. She chose the three that looked the best and floated them in the pail of water. Two sank and she christened the one remaining as the winner.

She took a short nap, so that she'd be wide-awake when her captor came to visit tonight. She also took a piece of the coal and wrote on the wall, just below the other inscription; 'LL was here'. Again, she wondered who AF was and how long ago he or she had been in this room.

***

He drove to Greenwich, again enjoying the ride and the countryside. It was a few minutes past eleven when he got to his destination. He spent ten minutes exploring the vast main street, known as Greenwich Avenue. Here was the building that would be Francesca's bakery. Here was the store that, he had been told, Antonina's Aunt Elena owned. Here was the church where Monsignor Dario ruled. He passed taverns and feed store, a jeweler, a library, a school, and a store that sold women's clothing. And here was the building where Simeon Meade had his law practice. A swinging sign in front announced 'Meade and Del Vecchio. Attorneys at Law'. It was a pleasant and prosperous town.

At eleven-thirty, he parked in front of Antonina's home, climbed out and was tackled at the knees by Johnny Rosato. "Hey! Anderson! Come in for lunch!"

Francesca greeted him. "We'll have some lunch, then I want to have you go to Mina's store. Antonina will bring you there. Then you can come back and we'll stuff your car with all of her suitcases and bundles and you can take her to Madam Joseph's house." Francesca's face was solemn. "I expect you to take very good care of her for me, Anderson. She is my treasure."

"You are a wise woman, Francesca. She is my treasure also. I think you have noticed that."

"I entrust her to you. I know that I need not worry that you will care for her as I would." Anderson bent and kissed Francesca's cheek. She nodded firmly and led him into the house.

The lunch was as sumptuous and yet simple as he had expected. A plate of sliced olives, salami, cheeses and tomatoes was placed in the center of the table, accompanied by a large basket of the most delicious bread he had ever tasted. This time, Gia and Lucia sat at the table and the twin boys, Mike and Rafe, acted as waiters.

"Do you children always help at meals?"

"My children always help at everything!" Francesca laughed. "Although I was married, my husband was never here much." Anderson was astonished at her candor. "And, since I was a woman who worked full time…even *more* than full time, and a mother of six children, my own children have always been expected to pull their share of our load." She smiled and touched Rafe's hand as he took away her empty *antipasto* plate.

"We always worked," Antonina agreed. "Everyone who lives around here works hard…all my friends and all of our family. We worked in Mama's baking business, even if we were only old enough to just fold or stack the boxes. We helped Enzo deliver bread and cakes, we help with special catering jobs, we weed the garden, cook meals, clean the house." She looked around and laughed. "You are all going to miss me and my special cleaning methods!"

Her brother Mike waved a plate filled with some sort of tomato-sauced objects. "I'll have your room now and I will not miss you at all!" He put a white jar down on the table. *"Mangia!"* He exhorted the group as he sat and unfolded his napkin.

"And please...what am I eating today?" Anderson inhaled a delicious aroma.

"These are *ravioli,*" Francesca explained. "They are squares of pasta, stuffed with a mixture of ricotta cheese, eggs, fresh parsley and black pepper."

"You can put some extra parmesan cheese on them," Lucia showed him, "Then some extra sauce." She offered a sauceboat filled with tomato sauce.

Anderson ate for several minutes, rapturous and silent. "You like them?" Maria inquired.

"Oh, yes. Yes, indeed." Anderson had to stop himself from licking the left-over sauce from his empty plate. "And may I have some more?"

After stuffing himself, Anderson and Antonina were shooed out of the house by Francesca. "Go to Mina's. Antonina will show you the way. She is waiting for you."

They drove back to Greenwich Avenue. Three doors away from the building where Francesca was to house her new bakery was a small shop. "She calls it *Sogne D'oro,*" Antonina explained. "That means 'dreams of gold' in Italian. It's an unusual store, or it will seem unusual to you. I grew up with Mina and her ability to understand about babies, so I am used to her powers. She's a midwife. She has an uncanny ability to care for expectant mothers. The babies...she can see what is going on in the womb," Antonina stumbled over the word. Her face was suffused with an embarrassed blush, but she soldiered on. Anderson stifled a grin, wondering if his heart could hold his love for this wonderful girl. "She's always been able to tell if the baby is healthy, if it will be a boy or a girl...honest, I know it sounds, um, funny, but she *does* have this gift." She turned on the seat, her hands making graceful gestures.

"Why would I not believe you, my sweet," he said, relishing the fact that he could call her endearing names. "Everything about you...ever since I met you...has taken on some magical aura. I saw you sing, I was transported into a world I never knew existed. Your family introduced me into their warmth, their foods, and now, why should I suspend my beliefs at a woman who can tell if it going to be a baby boy or a baby girl?"

"You're making fun of me." She grinned. "You'll see."

They got out of the car. The shop looked closed. Anderson saw a red painted door flanked by two large glass display windows. The sign above, painted in dark blue on a red background, read 'Sogne D'oro...Dreams for Sale'. In one window was a display of glass objects. Fragile orbs, glistening with gold and silver, decorated with jewels, were hung from a ceiling of make-believe clouds. As he glazed at the glass balls, some breeze made them move slightly...they turned, casting kaleidoscope patterns of colors. He shuddered and then wrenched his eyes to the other objects in the window.

On the bottom were pedestals made of marble holding crystal jars of mysterious substances. "Those are her creams and ointments," Antonina told him. "She makes face creams and creams for your skin." She pointed to beautiful glass containers, filled with oils. "Those are her perfumes and oils. She makes each one especially for the person who buys it. Some are for finding a lover, some for a happy home. Some are for sweet dreams and the answers to questions only asked in one's heart or soul." She put her hand on the doorknob, but he stopped her and went to the other window. This one held mountains of soaps, piled haphazardly against fabrics of tapestry and fantastical embroidery. Scattered here and there were pictures in ornate frames and small statues of incredible beauty. Heaped on a marble table were tins and containers of tea. Silver teaspoons and other tea-making objects were placed carelessly here and there. He gazed, entranced already.

"I feel light headed," he spoke softly. "This...these things...they make me...yearn for...I don't know." He shook his head again, as if to clear cobwebs away. "I want...I want to want to open the door and go in."

"She has powers," Antonina put her hand on his arm and felt the hardness of the muscle underneath. She shivered, her mind dwelling on what might happen when he took her back to New York. "Come on. Let's go in."

As they opened the door, a tinkle of bells sounded. The shop was dim and all around him, Anderson was aware of shapes and colors that swirled and glittered, making an assault on his senses. He felt slightly disoriented, almost dizzy and found himself reaching for Antonina's hand.

"Ah, Chief von Vogel." She appeared from behind a velvet curtain, a tiny woman with a round, sweet face. Her hair was wild and curly, and framed two button eyes that twinkled. She held out her small hand and he was surprised at the strength and warmth of her grip. "Welcome to my little shop. Come in and sit...here."

At the rear of the shop was a round table, covered in a pale green embroidered cloth. The embroidery traced dragons and exotic plants and was picked out in glowing threads of scarlet and gold. He sat, almost in a trance. He was aware of a faintly spicy odor in the air, like incense in a church that he only visited in his sleep.

He sat and Antonina sat too, but slightly behind him as if she already knew what Mina wanted her to do. Mina rubbed her hands together. *She looks like a little witch*, he thought. *A funny, sweet little witch.*

"What do I do?" His voice seemed to echo.

Mina smiled, bewitching him further. "You will know…"

He tried to answer her, but couldn't seem to speak.

"I will bring you tea first, and then, I will try to help you. One of the police-men brought me a toy from this child, Louise Lutton. I will try to see what I can."

She glided behind the curtain and returned, almost immediately, carrying a tray. On the tray were three unusual glass tea cups, one gold, one scarlet and one a deep green, and a large pot that was made of swirled glass encompass-ing all of their colors. She poured them each a cup, and the smell of the steaming tea was the same smell as the spices that surrounded him. He re-ceived the gold cup and he held it with both hands. The steam from his tea tickled his senses. He sipped, and the hot liquid permeated his eyes and his ears and his fingertips. *A witch indeed.*

"And now," the witch said, her voice a hypnotic sing-song, "I will try to see…"

Anderson wanted to speak to her, but his mouth was dry and he seemed unable to open it. He sipped at the tea, hoping that it would sooth his lips, but it only made his head buzz with confusion.

She brought out a small stuffed rabbit and put it on the table. "This be-longs to Louise," she told him. "She sleeps with it every night." He shivered, thinking of a child who was not in her own little bed.

"And my things…" She reached down and brought up a bundle of cloth. She placed it on the table. In the center of his mind, where he couldn't quite reach it, he felt a sense of movement. He suddenly had a vision of his mother, bending over his bassinet and kissing him. He saw her eyes and the love in them. There was a song…a lullaby…from long ago, that rang in his ears. He raised his eyes from their inward stare and watched her open the bundle.

The covering of the bundle was of some old cloth, plain, white and obvi-ously well-used. As it unfolded, he saw a heap of bones and feathers, some oddly-shaped stones, a shell or two and several jewels that looked like real jewels…he saw a ruby and an emerald and a dark purple stone that he didn't recognize…the jewels winked and reflected. He felt a presence…an actual jolt…as Mina's tiny hands began to lift the objects, pulling them up and then letting them drop back. She picked up the rabbit, held it to her cheek, then placed it in the center of the table. She heaped objects over the stuffed animal, letting them fall in ways that only she could understand. One of the jewels, a ruby, dropped onto the rabbit's floppy foot.

He knew that Antonina was in back of him, but she seemed very far away. There was only him and Mina, and this strange assortment of objects on the old cloth. The objects seemed to give off a glow and a warmth, and he felt as if the rest of the store receded into darkness, leaving only the contents of her bundle and the confusion in his mind.

He looked at Mina. She was pale and concentrated, her eyes at first wide-open, and then closed and shuttered. She was at once with him and yet remote, somewhere in her own universe. She muttered and shivered and then, as if a bubble had burst, she sat back, drained of whatever powers had gripped her, her breath hissing out.

The dimness left the room. Anderson shivered and felt Antonina's hand again on his arm. When he looked at the table, the bundle and the rabbit had disappeared.

"She is alive." Mina's voice came to him from far away. "I feel her and she is well, but troubled and lonely. She is in a cage of some sort, perhaps not a real cage, but trapped somewhere. You must comprehend that I do not understand a lot of what I feel. I can only tell you what it is and perhaps you can make some sense of it. There are animals and yet not animals. There is lust and unnatural passion hovering over her. There is another child calling…I don't know…She *must* be rescued." Her voice hissed out. "We *must* find her." Anderson shivered again and felt a great weight pressing against his heart. He saw his mother again, but she was receding from him. He tried to reach out his arms to capture her, but she was gone.

He didn't remember how they left the store. He didn't remember anything, but there they were, driving away. His mind swam into focus. Antonina sat beside him, her hand on top of his.

"What the hell happened in there?"

"Magic. Some magic. I told you, she has a power."

"Where is the child? Why can't she lead us to her?" There were tears in his eyes. "Why can't she just tell us where she is?" In his frustration, he hit the steering wheel. "Animals and not animals. Another child. What does that *mean?*"

"She can only tell you what comes to her. Please, you have to understand. It isn't like some quiz where the answer pops out." She stroked his arm. "Let's go to see Chief McAndrews. He said he'd be waiting for us at the police station." She guided him around the next corner.

"I've had some dealings with Mina Fiorile and her 'powers'," the Chief confided. "She does have some supernatural gift. It's inexplicable, but if we can figure out what she saw in her mind, we may be able to find Louise." He rubbed his hands together. "Write down just what she said and leave it with me. We'll mull it over and see what we can come up with."

Anderson wrote out, to the best of his recollection, everything that Mina had said and done. He was going to leave out the part about his mother's ghost, or whatever he might call his experience, but thought he had better include it. "This stuff about my mother," he muttered. "I…it was so odd…but, even though it makes me feel like some sort of fool, I guess you need to know it all."

Emerson patted his arm. "Who knows? We all would love to have our mothers back with us, even for a moment. Perhaps that part of the rigmarole was for you and not for finding Louise. Who knows?" He shrugged. "Certainly not me."

"If it helps you to find this child, I'll dance naked in the streets."

Emerson rolled his eyes. "I'll keep that in mind."

***

The car was loaded with Antonina's clothing, personal belongings and a few bits and pieces of furniture. A huge hamper of bread and other delicacies was stuffed into the back seat, and Simeon came out with six bottles of Enzo's home-made wine for them to take. "I won't starve, that's for sure," Antonina was excited and a little nervous, even a bit embarrassed. She wanted to leave and she wanted to stay. Was this what growing up was?

"The food will keep you for a day or so, until you get a chance to do some shopping." Francesca searched her daughter's grey eyes. Whatever she saw there seemed to satisfy her. She kissed Antonina. "Take good care of her, Anderson."

"You'd better," Simeon said, only half-joking. As the car started away, a yell was heard. Mina was running toward them.

"Wait! Wait!" she cried, waving her plump arm. "I have something for you!" She came to the side of the car, panting with exertion. "My good Mother of God! I am too old to trot like that!"

"Mina, you came to say good-bye to me. Thank you." Antonina jumped out of the car and swept Mina in a hug.

"I came to say good-bye, yes. But also to give you a present." She handed Antonina a large silvery bag, tied at the top with a red ribbon. "Open it when you are ready."

"Ready?"

Mina's eyes twinkled. "You are a girl from my own village. You have powers too." She made a pushing gesture, urging Antonina back into the car. "When you are ready, open the bag." She winked and stepped back.

"Good-bye!" Antonina called, waving. "We'll see you all Saturday night at *La Traviata!*"

Chapter Twenty-Four

"Come live with me and be my love…" John Donne, Songs and Sonnets

Janine took Anna to visit the monkeys at the zoo. "We'll meet you for a light supper at Romanoff's," Angelique told them. "You enjoy your outing and Uncle David and I will talk." She and David waved good-bye and watched Anna skipping away, her hand tightly clutched in Janine's.

"I have to leave in the morning. My ship sails back at eleven."

"Oh, David! So soon?"

"I came to see your triumph as Musetta and I came to talk very seriously with you." He kissed her and the seriousness of their conversation wandered and wandered. At last, he set her upright. "Now, we have very little time and I have much to tell you."

"Please."

"Patrizia is very ill." Her eyes flew to his. "She's dying. They called me to come as they do not expect her to last until the end of the week. I won't be able to see you sing in *La Traviata*, but…"

"Oh, my darling! Have no apologies to me…poor Patrizia. She's suffered so." Angelique crossed herself and whispered a prayer for the woman whom she had never met. The woman whose husband she loved beyond life itself. "Tell me about it."

"The cancer…it is the end. She's been sedated, although, God knows, she's been in her own little life for twenty years. She doesn't know anything at all. No pain, no happiness, no fear." He sighed. "I wish things had been different. I wish she had been able to have some sort of a normal life…" He took Angelique's hand in his. "But then, my darling, we would have never been together." He sighed, torn between his wife, whom he had loved as best he could, and the woman that he *had* loved for many years.

"You did what you did. You have been faithful to her in your own way. No man could do more."

"No. It was impossible. She…she never even recognized me or anyone else in twenty years. She has the mind of a three-month old. She cannot feed herself, sit up, think, or smile." His face was grave. "She is in a coma now, and I will be with her at the end." He buried his head in his hands. "It is the least I can do for her."

Angelique touched his forehead and bent to kiss him there. Her kiss was sweet and light. "You must be with her, David. I will pray for her. Poor, tormented soul. I am positive that God will take her into heaven and that her life there will be a happy and peaceful one."

"I will be back when I have wrapped up my affairs in Italy. I have given the bank my resignation."

"You…your resignation?"

"Yes. They have made it impossible for me to continue working there…things that you won't understand, but things that no honest man could put up with…they wanted more than my principles could allow. Devious things. Dishonest machinations. And so I told them that I was leaving. They were rather upset with me. They cursed me and told me that they'd block any opportunity I might have for future employment," he laughed bitterly. "I gave them my life's blood and they spit at me."

"They will miss your acumen greatly." Angelique knew how clever David was. She understood that his cunning and vision had pulled the bank out of many a precarious situation. "What will you do then?" Her heart beat fast. She hoped…but she dared not hope.

"I am coming to you," He smiled at her and her heart turned over. "You always told me that you wanted to live on a farm." He stood and took her hands in his. "I have liquidated all of my stock and my assets. I think the stock market is in a poor position. I've made a fortune, but now…well, I think I am buying a farm and getting myself married to an opera singer…So will you marry me when I am free, Angelique?" She shrieked and jumped into his arms, crying with delight.

After an interval which was prolonged and private, she told him that she would gladly leave the stage to be his wife. "Only if you wish, darling. The farm…if you like it as well as I do…is in Duchess County. Only an hour from New York City. And funny thing…one of the people who was at Antonina's table…an old man…sort of odd looking? Ears that stuck out? You do remember him? His name was Enzo. He told me that he, too, was buying a farm in Duchess County. Isn't that a coincidence? He said that he was a gardener and had worked for Francesca, Antonina's mother, his entire life. He told me that I should grab this farm." David's handsome face was bemused. "He was odd, but somehow, I think he knew what he was talking about…It sounds as if it all was destined by Fate!" He laughed. "Anyway, the farm…It has three cows and a horse or two. We'll add a pony for Anna and maybe a nice steady mare for Janine."

"Oh, David! I am afraid…I am so happy that I am terrified that the Gods will see my bliss and punish me."

"Never, my love. The two of us have suffered sorrow. For the rest of our lives, we will care for each other and make Anna very happy. I don't care if you sing or don't sing. I'm proud of you and delight in your voice, but you can sing for me every night or you can sing for me every night and for an audience every week or so. It is up to you."

"We don't have to decide just yet, do we, David?"

"Whatever you wish, my dearest." He kissed her again and then leaped to his feet. "Hurry! We'll be late for dinner!"

***

He made the acquaintance of her landlady. Madam Joseph watched, unsmiling, as he carried all of Antonina's suitcases and boxes into the house, loaded the tiny elevator, and staggered the load into the new apartment. He opened one of the boxes and pulled out one of the bottles of Enzo's wine. "Madam Joseph, this wine is from Antonina's family friend. He made it himself." She took the bottle, still not smiling. Antonina opened the hamper and brought out a still-warm loaf of bread.

"And this is a loaf of bread that my mother made," She handed the loaf to the landlady. "Mama will be here this Saturday night to hear me sing and then she will spend the night here. I know she will want to meet you, so I have asked for a complimentary ticket for you to see the opera."

The stern countenance broke and Madam Joseph grinned happily. "Thank you, my dear. I will look forward to seeing you sing." She turned to Anderson. "As you know, I have made dozens of costumes for operas." He nodded, delighted that Antonina had found a way to please her. "One of my last costumes was the ball dress for Violetta."

Violetta? Who the hell was Violetta? Some opera star? He nodded, pretending to be impressed. Madam Joseph said her farewell and closed the door, leaving the two of them alone.

"Who the hell is Violetta?" He asked helplessly. "Do I know her?"

Antonina fell into the sofa, laughing until her stomach hurt. "You goose. I am going to have to teach you all about opera. *Violetta* is the lead character in *La Traviata.* I am singing *Violetta* on Saturday!"

He sat next to her, bemused. "I have a lot to learn, don't I?"

She turned toward him, a little timid. "So have I. I'll teach you some things and you can teach me some things."

He crushed her to him.

Later, she opened Mina's package. There were several things in it. One was a golden vial of perfume. She opened it, smelling the scent of carnations, her favorite flower. She dabbed some on, behind each ear and then between her breasts. She smiled as she thought of dear, dear Mina...Mina who knew things...

There were several sacks of bath salts, and Antonina grinned as she thought of the huge, old-fashioned bathtub that rested in the next room. There were three bars of sweet-smelling soap, a wisp of a nightgown made of some gossamer pink material, and several packets of herbs and medicines. She laughed and blushed as she read the instructions on the packets. God bless Mina Fiorile. God bless her.

***

She heard the clank and chink of the door's lock. She rolled into the position she had practiced. He came in with the lantern. He put the lantern down and came to her bedside. She kept her eyes closed, not daring to have him suspect that she might not be asleep. She thought that she'd be terrified, but she only felt a deep calm and certainty. She had to do what she had to do. It was tonight or never.

He went back out of the room. She heard the splash of water as he staggered in with a full pail. He put it on the table. He took the old pail out. She tensed. Soon. He came back in, carrying the clean chamber pot and a pile of newspapers. He stopped then…something different…and she was terrified that she wouldn't be able to escape tonight, that he wouldn't give her the opportunity. Her heart thumped and she was terrified that he would hear it.

He went over to her, put the chamber pot down, lay the newspapers on the floor and squatted next to her. He touched her forehead, stroking it gently. His hand traced the contour of her face, down her cheek and then he touched the side of her neck. His hand felt like the touch of a snake. He murmured some words and then his hand brushed her shoulder. She forced herself to lie still and breathe softly. She thought she would die if he kept his hand on her.

He stood up. She peeked at him as he picked up the chamber pot. His attention was away from her. He shifted the newspapers, holding them awkwardly under his arm. He went into the bathroom area. She tensed, ready to leap and run. She heard a muffled crash of china. He had dropped the chamber pot!

What should she do? She sat up, ready for anything, tense…She heard a clink and chunk of china. He was picking up the broken chamber pot! She must act! Now! *Now!*

She jumped up, grabbed her shoes and ran to the door. It only took a few seconds, but it seemed to her that time was racing…racing! She slammed the door shut and heard him exclaim. *"What the hell!"*

Her hands were like blocks of ice as she fumbled, trying to reach the lock, close the hasp and lock him in. She shook. *Steady, Louise. Steady.* There was a dim light in the hallway. She was barely able to see, but she managed to slide the hasp closed, then carefully pushed the lock through, clicked it closed and then collapsed against the outside of the door. She was free! *Free!*

She froze! He was on the other side of the door, hammering and crying to be let out. *"Let me out! Let me out, you little bastard!"*

Louise grinned.

She got up and walked to the end of the hallway. She opened the door and screamed. She was in a huge room and in the darkness, eyes gleamed at her. Jaws gaped and tongues lolled. *"Oh, God! Please help me! Please get me out of this!"* She screamed and ran towards another door at the other side.

The door was locked! She smashed and kicked at it, and then, calmed herself down. *I'll get out. I will, I will!* She stepped back and took a deep breath. She thought she could hear him, banging and yelling from his prison. *"Yell all you want!"* she exulted.

She stooped and put her shoes on and then examined the door, trying to stay calm and not lose what success she had won. *Ah, the lock only needed to be turned.* She turned it and then stepped out into a chilly, starry night. She had no idea of where she was. She was free. She began to cry and run. She noted that her prison was a small barn or shed. A house, with light streaming through some of the windows, was ahead of her. She ran towards the street, skirting the house carefully, afraid that some other jailer might be looking for her.

The moonlight helped her to see. She ran and ran and ran. The streets were unfamiliar. Which way should she go? She stopped for a moment, panting. She decided that she would turn right at each intersection. Maybe she would find a police station or an open drugstore. She saw lights on in the houses she passed, but she was too frightened at being recaptured to stop. Once, a car passed her. She saw its headlamps in the distance and hid behind a row of bushes until it passed her by. She watched the red lights disappear and wondered if she had made an error in not stopping the car for help. Shrugging, she came to another intersection and turned right again.

She saw some lights ahead of her. She was tired and her lungs ached with the rawness of running too hard. She slowed down, pressing against the stitch in her side. Ahead of her was a large intersection, lit with several streetlamps. There were three cars stopped in the middle of the intersection. She could see that some of the car doors had been left open and the light from the interiors brightened the scene. There were several people, all bending over what seemed to be a large package or box in the middle of the road. She slowed to a walk, wary and cautious.

Oh, joy! She could read "GREENWICH POLICE" stenciled on the side of one of the cars. The *police!* They would help her! She approached slowly.

There was a yapping sound, a growl and a bark. A dog? She crept closer.

There were six men and one lady, all of them standing or stooping around the box. Two of the men were in police uniforms. She heard one say, "Cliff, let's get the puppies out of the road."

Puppies? Both policemen were big and burly and looked safe and sure. She walked to one of them and tugged on his sleeve. He turned and then jumped as he saw her. *"Wha...!"*

"Can you help me, please?" She said. "I'm Louise Lutten and I want to go home." She began to cry.

"Louise!" The policeman hugged her, then picked her up and held her tight. "Oh, Louise! Are we glad to see you, honey!" He motioned to the other

man, who went into the car and fiddled with something. She heard him talk-ing…*did the police car have a radio?*

"Are you hurt?" She knuckled the tears from her eyes.

"No. I'm scared and lonely. I was a prisoner."

The other people in the intersection all crowded around. "Is this the girl who was lost?"

"I heard she was kidnapped."

"How did she escape?'

"Oh, the poor sweetie!"

"Are you cold, Louise? Here...take my coat…"

The other policeman came back. "Chief said to take the puppies, take Louise and get her over to her house. He'll meet us there." He turned to her. He had a round, fat face with a big grin on it. "Hey, Louise! I'm Mike, your friendly policeman. We've been lookin' all over for you."

"Here I am!" She sang out, happy as can be.

The crowd around them…all total strangers…began to laugh and clap and hug one another.

***

The ride in the police car was wonderful. She sat in the back seat togther with the cardboard box that held two yappy, squirmy puppies. One was black with white spots on his face and one was mostly white with a round black patch over one eye.

"Tell us what happened, Louise. Where were you?"

"I don't know, but maybe I can find the house. I kept turning to the right, you know. I think if we go back and keep turning to the left, I can find my way back."

"Were you alone?" Mike wasn't sure what to ask her.

"I was a prisoner. I was kept locked up in a small room. My jailor fed me and gave me a…chamber pot…" she was embarrassed to talk about bathroom facilities. "I waited until he came to change the water and the chamber pot and then he dropped the pot and I ran away. I locked him in the room." Her voice was jubilant with satisfaction.

"Who was he, honey?"

"I don't know. He never talked to me. He only came at night. There were animals and eyes and teeth in the shed. I was really scared."

"Animals and teeth and eyes….Goddamn it! Alvin *Catch*pole!" Cliff pounded the steering wheel. "The bastard! Uh, excuse my language, Louise. He's a bad, bad man."

"Tsk, tsk. That doesn't excuse your swearing, Cliffy, my man." Mike shook his head in mock reproof.

They parked in front of the Lutton's house. Louise opened the back door of the car and ran to the house, yelling and crying, *"Mommy! Daddy! Oh, Mommy! Oh, Daddy!"*

Cliff lumbered out of the car. "You're sniffing, ya big mug." Mike laughed.

"I see a wee tear in your eye, you Irish bum, you!" As they approached the house, the lights snapped on. Mrs. Lutton came to the door, screamed and gathered Louise in her arms. Mr. Lutton followed more slowly, his footsteps lumbering and unsteady. He had his handkerchief out and held it to his face.

"If you ain't crying now, you're a sour faced old loon!" Mike said softly.

"I'm bawling like a baby," Cliff confessed. The two men stood, watching the reunion. "Thank God. Halleluiah and thank You, Lord."

As the Lutton's made a circle of happiness, the door opened again and a young boy ran out. "Louise! Oh, Louise!" He joined his family, all of them crying with joy.

With the siren howling and the light flashing, Chief McAndrews pulled up. "Hi! What's happening? Is she OK?"

"Take a look. She's just fine." Cliff took out his handkerchief and blew his nose.

Chief McAndrews gathered everyone into the Lutten house. Mr. Lutten sat on the couch with Louise on his lap and his son plastered to his other side. Mrs. Lutton stood, tears of happiness flowing down her face.

"Harrumph," Emerson took out his own handkerchief and blew his own nose. "She's fine? Good. Not hurt at all? Good. Louise, I need to talk with you. No, no, you can stay right where you are. After we talk, you can have a bath and something to eat, but for now, we want to hear everything you have to say. From the beginning, tell me about what happened."

"It's Alvin Catchpole who held her prisoner. Alvin, the weird guy that we talked with about the, um, ah, string of burglaries. The one with the taxidermy business."

"That odd man?"

"I think he's the one. Tell Chief McAndrews about the animals, honey."

Louise squirmed against the pillows. "When I escaped, I was in a hallway. I went into this shed and I was terrified. There were all these animals. They were in the air and on shelves and on tables. At first, I thought they were alive, with frightening eyes and open mouths and teeth that looked sharp…but now, that I've had a chance to think, I know that they were stuffed. Like at the Bruce Museum." Mrs. Lutton gasped and went to kneel in front of Louise. She cradled her daughter close. "I'm fine now, Mommy. I missed you all and was sad, but I thought of Robinson Crusoe and how he would act. I was…intelligent…"

"Harrumph," McAndrews took out his handkerchief again. "You two, go to Catchpole's house and see if he's around. Bring him in."

"He's locked in the room," Louise told them. "I locked him in."

"You are one amazing little girl, Louise." MacAndrews marveled. "You are an honest-to-goodness heroine."

294

"Thanks, Chief. Can I ask you something?" She got up and tugged on Mike's arm.

"Of course. What is it?"

"Are those puppies lost? If they are, can I have one of them?"

Mike hoisted her up in the air. "Honey, you can have my right arm, nevermind the puppies." He kissed her soundly. "You have one heck of a daughter, Mrs. Lutten." He put Louise down. "Get the box with the puppies, Cliff, and then we'll go and pay Mr. Catchpole a nice visit."

"Mommy? I'm starving. Can I have something to eat?"

"Sure, honeybun. I'll make you a nice hot bacon and egg sandwich, or maybe you'd just like some peanut butter and jelly." She didn't quite understand why Louise began to laugh and laugh.

***

They arrived at the Catchpole residence and rang the doorbell. There was one light on in what seemed to be the living room. As they waited, several more lights went on and in a few moments, Mrs. Catchpole, dressed again in her chenille bathrobe, her hair twisted up in rag curlers, answered the door. From inside the house, they could hear the dog barking. "What do you want?" Her tone was brusque and annoyed.

"We're looking for Alvin."

"Haven't you pestered him enough? He's sleeping."

"Go and wake him up." Mike's face was implacable.

Sensing that something was really wrong, she scurried up the stairs only to re-appear in a few moments. "He's...he's not in bed." Her face was grey and worried. "Where is he?"

"Where is the shed or the barn where he does those things to dead animals?"

Bewildered, she gestured towards the back. She led them through the kitchen and pointed to a small building set at the back of the lot. "Stay here, Mrs. Catchpole," Cliff told her. "We'll be back in ten minutes." The dog barked again.

"Hush, Lucky," Mrs. Catchpole hollered. "But...but, where's Alvin?" She called after them.

"We'll bring him back, never fear." Mike called back to her over his shoulder. She clutched the robe to her throat. *What was happening?*

They went into the building and found themselves in the taxidermy room. "Shit! No wonder she was frightened! Geez! Look at them eyeballs!" Cliff shuddered, thinking how scared his little Karen would have been in a room like this in the middle of the night.

They found the door to the hallway and then heard a banging. The door was locked and there didn't seem to be a key anywhere. "Catchpole!" Mike roared. "This is the police!"

"Get me out of here!"

"How? There's no key."

A sound and then a key was slid under the door. Cliff stooped, picked the key up and unlocked the door. Mike held his revolver steady. Cliff pulled the door open. Catchpole tried to rush out, but Cliff held him by his collar, up in the air, and shook him, like a terrier shakes a rat.

Mike motioned to him with the gun. 'Get back into the room, you scum." Catchpole moved backwards.

"Thank goodness you've come, officers." Catchpole tried to bluff. "I was accidentally locked in."

"Oh, you poor thing," Mike caroled in a high falsetto voice that made Catchpole's blood run cold. "Lie down on the floor, face down and put your hands behind you."

Catchpole shrugged. He'd tried. He lay down, rolled onto his stomach and put his hands back. Mike snapped heavy handcuffs on his wrists and then kicked at him. "Don't even think of moving."

Cliff found the lantern and searched the room. "Is this where you locked her up, you piece of dirt?" Catchpole dropped his head. "Is this where you beat her?"

"I never beat her! She's lying! Lying!"

"I'd like to kick your head in, but I'm going to let the jury decide what punishment a piece of shit like you merits." Cliff went into the bathroom area, then poked at the pile of bedding and looked into the brown bags. He kicked aside the pile of stones and chalk and saw the initials scratched on the wall. "Humpf. LL and AF...they were both here." His eyes narrowed. "Mike? What was the name of that little girl who went missing a few years ago? Wasn't it Alice? Alice...um...what?"

"AF. Alice Farella." He grabbed Alvin's shirt and hauled him to his feet. "What did you do with Alice?" His face was menacing and his words spit at Catchpole.

"Alice? I don't know what you're talking about!" Catchpole was sweating.

"You might as well tell us everything. You're never gonna see the light of day anymore. If you tell us what you did, maybe they'll shoot you quickly instead of hanging you."

"I don't know what you're talking about." Catchpole was truculent.

Cliff stared at him until Catchpole dropped his eyes. "We'll find out. First we'll tell your nice old mother about all of this and then we'll dig up every inch of this yard." Catchpole swallowed. "We'll find out." Catchpole began to cry.

***

In the morning, Anderson kissed her goodbye, touched her cheek and told her that he'd see her at the opera house. He went back to his apartment.

Helena was in the kitchen. When she saw Anderson, she drew herself up and hissed at him. "I'm leaving you. The girls and I are leaving here. We'll take an apartment near Hermione. I'll expect you to give me an allowance and pay for the apartment."

He looked at her. He might have argued, he might have thrown something at her. He might have. But instead, he nodded grimly. "This marriage was a great mistake, Helena. Both for you and for me. I have no animosity to you, I only feel sorry for you. I'll make arrangements."

"What are you going to do?" She was astonished that he hadn't hit her, beat her or thrown her out.

"I'm going to change and take a shower and then go to work. That's what I'm best at." He turned and walked away as his telephone rang.

"Mr. von Vogel," Marie-Ange called to him. "It is your office."

"Chief von Vogel here."

"Anderson. Good morning, Sir."

"Pedar. Good morning to you. What's up?"

"Another corpse, Chief. We found the dwarf dead last night. He was obviously making some kind of run. Had a big case filled…I think…with jewels and money. Somebody took almost all of it. Can you get in soon?"

"I'll be there in a half-hour." Anderson hung up the telephone. *The third death attributable to some goings-on at the Metropolitan Opera House. What the hell is going on there?*

…..

Chapter Twenty-Five

*"Behold a pale horse: and his name that sat upon him was
Death, and Hell followed with him…The Holy Bible, Revelation*

The soul of the man known only as Crespi left his crippled body and traveled to the place known as Hell. As it was with Vivienne du Lac and some special others, there was no tribunal. There was no balance of the journal of his life, because his journal held no pages. There was only a black void. He was shoved into a place of such utter despair and horror, that even the Devil himself rarely visited. It was difficult to inflict enough punishment on those such as Crespi, but in this particular area of Hell, they would try.

***

The New York Herald Tribune of Wednesday, October 16, 1929 warned its public that a crisis was looming. A hushed report was revealed stating that the Federal Reserve Board, which oversaw Federal Reserve Banks, monitored the economic health of the United States, set interest rates and watched the credit history on a day-to-day basis, had been meeting for two weeks behind closed doors. Many who followed the market carefully began to worry.

On that same day, The New York Times, in stark contrast, reassured the public that stocks would continue to rise. The country's foremost economist, Irving Fisher of Yale University, together with the much-respected banker, Elwood C. Miller, made a joint statement that they saw no sign of any potential slump. Many who followed the market gave a sigh of relief and called their broker to put in a bid for Belvedere Steel.

***

The police, together with several members of the Greenwich Public Works Department, and a reporter from The Greenwich Time newspaper, arrived at the Catchpole residence. The Public Works employees brought two bulldozers and lots of shovels and hoes. No one was at home. Alvin, of course, was behind bars. His mother, mortified and shriveled, packed two suitcases and took the train to Chappaqua to stay with her sister.

The Public Works people, under the leadership of Mike Murphy, began to pace and mark out the backyard. Chief McAndrews and his men, together with the reporter, went back to the little room where Louise had been imprisoned. The police took fingerprints and photos of the room, especially the wall where the initials of two little girls were scratched. On the front page of tomorrow's Greenwich Time, four photos were featured, above the front page story telling about Louise's ordeal and escape. One photo was of the smiling Lutton family. One was of the bulldozer, beginning to excavate the Catchpole backyard; the third was a close-up of the two sets of initials. The last photograph, the one which caused the most talk, was of Alvin Catchpole's animals, their staring eyes and fanged teeth frozen in death. In the spring of 1930, this story and the follow-up, would win a newspaper prize.

It only took an hour and a half. She was buried under two feet of earth, just behind a rose hedge. The photographer, the policemen and the men of the Greenwich Public Works Department – stalwart men all - wept as they realized that the body of nine-year old Alice Farella, like the animals in the shed, had been eviscerated, the skin scraped, and then stuffed, the eyeballs replaced with glass orbs.

Chapter Twenty-Six

"From Brooklyn, over the Brooklyn Bridge, on this fine morning, please come flying…" Elizabeth Bishop, Invitation to Miss Marianne Moore

Dean's stomach, usually robust and used to eating *pierogis* and *baba gahnoosh,* curled itself into a tight knot of misery. His bravado, normally flag-waving itself from on high, was silent and watchful. And the real problem was that he had to pretend that he was brave as the women he was with, delighted at the aspect of flying and that he couldn't wait to get himself up in the air in that confounded flying machine contraption. "Wow!" he enthused with an enormous effort. "What a great opportunity!"

His eyes nearly fell out of his head when he first saw Brooks in her flying outfit. She was wearing trousers! He'd never seen a woman wearing trousers, except, of course, in a circus. Once he'd gotten used to the idea, it struck him as an excellent one. Brooks' legs…well, they were long and shapely and the trousers fitted closely to her ankles. He blinked and swallowed hard. Brooks' legs. Man, oh, man.

Brooks turned to him. "We'll never forget this, right?" Brooks was bubbling over with excitement.

"Never. I know that I will never forget today, anyhow." Nearly forgetting about Brooks' legs, Dean averted his eyes from the gate to the airport at Newark, New Jersey. The car bumped over a pot-holed dirt road, past oddly shaped silvery buildings, built like giant cupcakes. Here and there, a plane dotted the ground.

"They're, uh, small, aren't they?" Dean's face was turned away from Brooks'. That way, she might not notice his panic.

"I think we'll be going up in two of them," Brooks peered ahead, trying to see. "Carey said that you'll go up with Amelia, and I'll be with her and Melanie. Imagine! You're going up in a plane with the most famous woman pilot in the whole world!"

"Imagine."

It was dusty and windy and up ahead, Brooks spotted the two planes, one yellow and one black-and-white striped. "There they are!" She lowered her window and stuck her head out, yelling, "Hi! Carey! Hi! Melanie! Where is Amelia? Here we are!" Dean was able to notice that all of the women were wearing trousers. And they all looked rather fine. He watched as one of them, perhaps this Amelia Earhart one, climbed onto the wing of the yellow plane. The plane looked only as big as a toy. *Up in the air in* that *thing?*

Dean stifled a groan. "Hot dog!" he enthused.

***

Louise had chosen the white puppy with the black spot around his eye. The other pup, the black one with the white spots, went home with Mike Murphy. "The little bugger – I'll call him Hogan after my mother-in-law - will keep me company." He ruffled the silk-soft ears and Hogan reciprocated by licking Mike's face.

Louise's mother asked her daughter, "What will you call him?" Her mother really didn't want a puppy, but…well…this was different, wasn't it?

"Friday."

"Friday?"

"Like Robinson Crusoe's best friend." She picked up the wiggly pup. "He'll be my best friend."

"A marvelous name, honey. Just the ticket."

Mrs. Lutton walked into the kitchen so that she could cry her joy in private.

***

Faced with the discovery of Alice's body, Alvin Catchpole broke down and confessed everything. He insisted that the whole of the matter was certainly not his fault. "Girls have always hated me. No one wants me to be their boyfriend. And I don't like older girls, anyway. They frighten me."

"Tell us about Alice," McAndrews asked. "How did you, um, take her?"

"I like to watch the children in the playground. The girls and their pretty dresses and their little white socks. I feel happy watching them." He gazed into space, seeing some fantasy. "Sometimes I take the dog for a walk." *The dog tag! Lucky!* McAndrews nearly slapped his own forehead. *Lucky! How stupid I have been!*

Catchpole mumbled on, "I like little girls."

McAndrews waited, castigating himself for not being as sharp as he should have been. They all should have noticed the name Lucky. *Shit, what kind of a detective am I anyway?*

"I saw this one girl a lot. She was always nicely dressed, with long brown hair. She always wore a hair ribbon. I thought that the ribbons were beautiful. I heard another girl call her 'Alice". He hung his head.

"One day, she and several other children were playing catch in the playground. She…she missed the ball and it bounced over to where I was standing. I was sort of behind a hedge. She came out and started looking for the ball. I called to her and she came near me. She wasn't afraid of me. She…she smiled at me. Then, she saw the ball lying under the bush and bent down to get it. I….I hit her with a stone that was on the ground." He sighed.

301

"I didn't mean to hurt her, but she fell down and was…well, I thought perhaps she was dead." He bit his lip.

"I was afraid that someone would yell at me or be mad at me for killing her, so I dragged her further under the bushes."

"And then?"

"I ran home. And I was afraid, but then I felt it wasn't good to leave her there, so I got my car and drove to the school. I brought a blanket for her, in case she was cold."

"So then you knew she was still alive?"

"No…well, maybe…I thought if she was still alive, I could keep her warm," his thin face was sweaty. "And if she was already dead, then I could bring her to the hospital and leave her there."

"And then?"

"She was breathing, although I had a hard time hearing her. I had to bend down and put my ear to her chest." He shivered, remembering. "I felt…I…well, I wrapped her up and carried her to the car. No one saw me. I took her home and then I didn't know what to do. My mother…I couldn't tell my mother. She wouldn't have understood." He sat, quiet, lost in his memory.

"And then?" McAndrews prodded.

"I remembered the little room off my taxidermy studio. In the old days, we used it to store coal. It was ideal to…keep her. I put her there with a blanket under her and another blanket over her. It was almost supper time and I brought a pail of water for her to drink. After supper, I came to work on my animals and then, when it was very late, I brought her bread and some peanut butter. I also gave her a chamber pot so that if she….well…." He sat forward. "I wanted her to be happy."

"Was she awake?"

"No. She had gotten up. I know that because she had used the chamber pot. I think she drank some water and then, you know, relieved herself." Alvin seemed embarrassed to talk about bodily functions. "She must have fallen asleep after that. She never woke up. I tried to chafe her hands and feet…to make her warm, you know. I tried to give her a sip or two of water, but her mouth was closed and the water dribbled out. I…I listened to her heart. It was still beating, but her face was getting paler and waxy. I…I touched her…her skin was so smooth…and then…I…" Alvin hung his head.

McAndrews held himself back. His mind grappled with an image of Alice, dazed and injured, writing her initials on the wall. He wanted to hit this foolish, deadly, miserable excuse for a human being until he bled to death. Instead, he asked, "And then what happened?"

"She stopped breathing."

McAndrews said nothing.

After a few moments, Alvin continued. "I…I…I took her dress off. It made me…she…I touched her and then I…" He began to cry. ""She was dead and it was no good. I wanted her to be *alive!"*

"What else happened?"

"She was just another dead thing to me now. I thought that it would be interesting to see if I could do her like the fox that I had just finished stuffing." McAndrews shivered. *Dear Lord, what kind of monster did you create here?*

"And so, I did what I did to the fox and the owls and the badger. Do you want to know how I do it?"

"Uh, not right now. You can go into more detail later. Tell me why you buried her."

"I knew I couldn't put her up on a shelf in my workroom. No one would understand. So, I made her as nice as I could. I tied one of her ribbons back in her hair. I kept the other one…under my pillow. I take it out sometimes…"

His eyes looked inward. "And then, one night, I dug a grave for her, so that she would be properly buried. I said a prayer over her and filled the grave up. In a few days, the grass had grown right over the scar."

"Is that all?"

"Yes. I took care of her as well as I could. Once she was dead…well…"

"Tell me about Louise?"

"Louise?"

"Yes, the other little girl. The one that escaped."

"Oh, was that her name?" Catchpole seemed indifferent. "I never knew what her name was."

McAndrews got up and walked out. He had to get up. If he had stayed one more minute, he might have strangled Catchpole with his bare hands.

***

It was an interlude of wonder for the two of them. Their little apartment, high up on the fourth floor, sparsely furnished, quiet and closed to everyone but themselves. Anderson had never known such a time in his life. He'd had women before he married Helena…women whom he had adored, fantasized about and lusted for. The sex was great, his young body had reveled in sensations that nearly transformed him. He'd wanted more, and with his good looks, inbred manners and friendly personality, he always found more.

Then there was his work, and then there was Helena. Helena hadn't turned out as he had thought. Either in their intimate life or their life together as two married people. Their love life was painful, awkward and almost unpleasant. There was no joy, no tenderness, no laughter and no passion. Anderson, a man of great principals, had never before thought of having an affair or of cheating on his wife. A man chose, and a man kept to his promises, even if they were clothed in dust, disappointment and decay.

Until he saw a young woman, playing the part of a romantic little waif, on a stage below him, knock on a door and ask to have her candle lit.

As inexperienced as she was, she opened up his world. Together, they discovered love.

He marveled at the curve of her cheek and the scent of her skin just behind her ear. He laughed at her wide-eyed delight as he awoke her early in the morning…and then again after the honey of their breakfasts together. He delighted in the stories she told him about her family and their life. He learned about opera and cooking and the rich and complex neighborhood where she grew up. His heart, closed to warmth for most of his adult life, unfurled as a rose to the sun, and he wept openly at the wonder of it all.

Antonina also blossomed in their first few days together. She had always enjoyed the delight of a loving and warm family, but the intimacy of bathing with a large and hairy man astonished her. The quick and almost furtive coupling with Peter had not prepared her for the long and lazy nights, the whispered words of love and adoration, cocooned together in a puff of a feather bed. As a young girl, she had, of course, imagined the delights of her first romance, but the reality of her feelings and the sensations that Anderson's touch were astonishing…well beyond those her vivid imagination or romantic operatic drama could have ever conjured up. He filled her heart and her soul and her body…and she, too, bloomed in the passion of their love.

Madam Joseph, attuned to the currents that eddied through her house, went about her days with a lively step. She found herself humming snatches of song here and there, and once, found herself standing in the doorway with a broom in her hand, remembering the nights that she and Joseph had shared. She giggled and remonstrated with herself. *You're regressing, Joanna! You're like a fifteen year old girl with her first beau!* It was wonderful.

***

Brooks dragged Dean to tea at her parent's brownstone. He was of two minds regarding the summons. The first was brought on by his lifelong disdain of anyone who was wealthy. As Dean had rarely become intimate with the extremely wealthy, the second was of his fear of doing something gauche and ignorant and embarrassing himself. It was a mixed-up young man, sweating with fear, apprehension and anxiety, who rang the doorbell. A butler answered, throwing Dean into a further tizzy. *She gets me up in an airplane, she forces me to meet not only her mother and father, but her grandmother and the freaking butler… and, most of all, she dragooned me into loving her! What a woman!*

Grandmamma, otherwise known as Mrs. Deuville Alexander Allgood, a woman who ate her social inferiors for lunch, immediately fell under Dean's warm, individual and voluble spell. The feeling was mutual. Brooks, who had been holding her breath, relaxed. It would all be fine. Here was Daddy offering to show Dean his collection of rare porcelains, and Mommy, forcing Dean to eat yet another scone. Dean winked at Brooks and then went, meek as a lamb, to Mr. Allgood's study to oooh and ahhh over the Allgood porcelains. Dean was no dope.

***

Barbara convened the third meeting of The Metropolitan Opera Guild, as they all decided to call their group. "I'm sorry to tell you that, due to a personal situation, Helena von Vogel and her daughters, Chloe and Clair, will not longer be able to be active in our group." She noted that Brooks Allgood and Carey Marvel Mabley, together with Dale Troy, were working hard to hide their glee at her announcement. She winked at Brooks.

"However," Barbara continued, "You will notice a new face sitting next to me. Ladies, this is Senora LaRue Lopez, who heard of our work and wanted to be a part of it." LaRue, wearing crocheted gloves on her tiny hands, waved to the assemblage, nodding her bird-like head. "Senora Lopez has told me that she and her husband will be contributing ten thousand dollars..." A pleased gasp went up from the ladies...Senora Lopez grinned... "to be used as we see fit to refurbish or repair the interior of the opera house. Welcome, Senora Lopez and thank you from all of us."

Carey waved her hand in the air. "Carey?" Barbara acknowledged her. "Miss Marvel Mabley. You have the floor."

"Ladies...thank you, Barbara...and, if no one minds much, please just call me by my first name. I'm Carey to all of you. I think, as we are going to be working so intimately together, perhaps, especially here in these meetings, first names would be good." There was a buzz of assent, even from the richest and the most elderly.

"I've been looking into, together here with Dale, doing work with some of the schools to get youngsters interested in opera. We have had enormous success. Every school, every single principal, wants to bring a class to the next matinee. They'd even like to be at a rehearsal. One of the principals," she riffled through a page in her notebook, "Professor Lawrence Graham from The Knickerbocker Academy, feels if youngsters are exposed to opera and get to understand it...well, he feels that these youngsters will become future patrons." She smiled with excitement.

"They'd like to come and have one of us...maybe me or one of us who knows the story of the next opera well...to give a short class. We'd tell the students about the composer and the lyricist and talk about this history of the opera. They'd learn that different opera houses have their own visions of what, say, as we are doing it next, *La Traviata* should look like. The students might meet one or two of the principals, and maybe even a few of the back-of-the-house people. Maybe the property man, the make-up artist or the person who paints the scenery. And then, they'd attend the opera itself. What do you all think?"

The ladies were charmed and impressed. To think that the younger ladies here…Brooks and Dale and Carey…could dream up such a wonderful educational scheme to entice a whole new generation to know and love opera…well! "Marvelous, don't you think, Dorothea?"

"I couldn't have done it better myself!"

"We could set aside a small section of every show for students."

"I can promise excellent newspaper coverage and publicity."

"Wonderful!"

"This Metropolitan Opera Guild of ours will change our opera house forever!"

"And to think, some men thought we were silly and inconsequential!"

"Rather silly of *them,* don't you think?"

"We will show them, won't we?"

***

"Boss?"

"Pedar?"

"Just wanted you to know that we got a bulletin from Sing Sing. You'll recall your old friend, Hamilton Purcell?"

"Cut-em-up Purcell? Of course I remember the man. One of my first successes. Robbed his victims, and if they didn't have as much money on them as he needed, cut their faces with a straight razor. Who could forget such a charming member of New York society?"

"Well, he's out."

"Out? He got…what? Twenty years!"

"Twelve with good behavior and the bleeding heart help of Judge Silkington." Pedar made a sound of disgust. "The criminal's friend."

"Silkington let him out?" Anderson was incredulous. "The man is an animal!"

"Yah. Well, Purcell swears that his years behind bars have shown him the path of God. He became some sort of behind-bars minister and talked Silkington into setting him free long before any other sane person would have."

"I never would have set him free. I remember one man that he cut up…an old man…ripped his face to shreds." Anderson shook his head in dismay. "Silkington should be put behind bars himself."

"Don't let anyone hear you talk like that!" Pedar dropped his voice. "Silkington's daughter married the Commissioner's son. He's high up on the Commish's list."

"Bah!" Anderson was clear on his feelings. "I pray that one day Silkington will be strolling down the street and Purcell will need a few dollars."

"Boss! What a bad thought you have!" Pedar pretended to clutch at his heart.

"I can only pray, Pedar. Ah, what justice that would be! Let Silkington know how it really is out on the streets." He made a gesture. "The fool thinks that men like Purcell are going to become saints!"

"Maybe he did get religion."

"And maybe I'll grow wings and fly."

Chapter Twenty-Seven

"Into my heart an air that kills, From yon far country blows; What are those blue remembered hills, What spires, what farms are these?"
...A. E. Houseman, A Shropshire Lad

Enzo and his wife, Sabina, had taken two trips to Clinton Corners, Duchess County, New York. For the first trip, they had taken a train ride. Don Mantaldo, their *capo-paisano* from their little town in Italy, had heard that Enzo wanted to leave Greenwich and buy a farm. He knew of a friend (Don Mantaldo always had a friend who knew something about what you wanted, whatever it was), who had a farm for sale. It was reported to be a good farm with fertile soil and a sunny location. He called Enzo.

"Enzo, I have heard of a farm for sale. I have also heard that it is a good farm." Don Mantaldo laughed. "You know that I am a city man. I know business and I know about money, but I know nothing at all about farms."

"I will know," Enzo scratched his nose. "I know dirt and manure. I have that talent."

"You certainly have the talent to make roses grow out of stones." Enzo nodded in a modest way. "This man that I know, George Ardie. He owes me a favor." Enzo grinned. Almost everyone, sooner or later, owed Don Mantaldo a favor. "He owns the mortgage on this farm. A man that he knew...a man who played cards foolishly...had to sell the farm to meet some debts. George Ardie was able to buy the farm for a song. And because you are my *paisano* and I care for you and your family as I care for my own, I told Mr. Ardie that you may want to buy the farm from him."

"Can I afford this song?"

"It will be a song and a little chorus on top of that," Don Mantaldo's laugh boomed out. "After all, Mr. Ardie has to get his own little piece of the opera."

"And how much will this piece of the opera cost me?" Enzo wanted a farm with all his yearning, but he was a shrewd man.

Don Mantaldo waved his hands in the air. "Ah, Enzo...we have known each other for many years...we have had many adventures together. We share a few secrets, no?"

"A few," Enzo thought back to the time when Carlo Rosato was still alive... "Yes, a secret or two."

"And so, the money...it is negligible. I will pay the little piece of the opera so as to make Mr. Ardie a happy man. He..." The Don's face took on a brooding look… "will be *very* pleased at the sum I will offer him." He stood up, holding out his hand. "You will pay me a few dollars here and a few dollars there. When you have a few dollars more, you can pay me more. I trust you, Enzo. You know that." His face lit up. "Ah! And you can send me some fresh *zucchini* and *cocuzza* now and then, Enzo. That would be better than money to me."

Enzo stood up. He held the blue hat with the white pom-pom in his hands. It was the hat that he wore when he delivered bread and cakes from Francesca's bakery. He made a half-bow to Don Mantaldo. "Thank you, Don Mantaldo. Sabina and I will go and see this farm. If all is well, we will make plans to move from here." He looked down. "I will miss everyone, if we move, but I have wanted to have a farm my whole life. There is dirt in the veins of my body. I am grateful that you have found a way for me to have my dream come true."

"You're a good man, Enzo. Let me know what you think of the farm, and if it is suitable, we will begin to make some music."

***

The formal Church baptism of young Frank DeSarro was held on Tuesday afternoon. Naturally, Vittoria was the *madrina* and Urbano the *padrino*. There were several guests from the DeSarro neighborhood, a few people from the New York Metropolitan Opera, and from Greenwich: Francesca, Simeon, Maria Sabatino and her constant suitor, Alfonso Fazzolini, Mina and Sal Fiorile and Monsignor Dario Sabatino. The party walked, with Vittoria pushing the elaborate baby carriage holding young Frank, to Saint Sebastian's Church on the corner of Court Street. There, Frank was duly baptized formally into the Church by the local priest. When the cold water was splashed on his face, he cried. "A sign of very good luck," Mina avowed. "It means that he will have money in his late years."

Francesca had brought several dozen loaves of bread and one of her famous orange cakes to the celebration, and Maria had baked dozens of pastries. The neighbors brought ham and beef sandwiches and Concetta had made a huge cauldron of *zuppa de pasta e fagioi*.

Antonina carried a box of Susan's Opera Chocolates to the party, and Anderson, who had also been invited on his own merit, (Francesco told him: "You've been so nice to me, Chief von Vogel. I could have been one of your suspects…") brought three bottles of champagne. Most of the people from the Met toted wine. It was a fine party and a fitting celebration for the new American baby.

***

"I'm being besieged by the Mayor and the Governor, Anderson. We need to solve this case!"

"I understand, Commissioner. We're doing everything possible." Anderson gripped the arms of the comfortable chair. "This is a wacky one."

"How far have you gotten," Commissioner Hanover Chase was a reasonable man. He had once been the Chief of Detectives of the City of New York, and knew the inherent difficulties. He liked and respected Anderson von Vogel, although, lately there had been a rumor or two about von Vogel's wife and perhaps some infidelity. *Poor sonofabitch, to have your wife parading her tuffet around town and, even worse, having the whole town know about it!*

"This is no excuse for not solving the murder, but we weren't called until several hours had passed. The opera company was fearful that if they called us right away, we might have stopped the performance from going forward."

"I heard about it all," The Commissioner offered Anderson some coffee, and the two men sat back and sipped the aromatic brew from the tiny china cups that the Commissioner's wife had brought back from a trip to Paris. "I'm going to be at the opera on Saturday to see *La Traviata*. I hear the new soprano is the best thing to hit the city. A local girl, I think. From Connecticut."

"I was very lucky to get to see her...her name is Antonina Sabatino...I saw her sing last week. She's, um, magnificent."

"And so?"

"And so, when I finally got backstage to see the scene of the murder, seventeen people had tromped all over the room. They'd grossly disturbed the body, pulling off the costume that Vivienne du Lac had been wearing. The room was filled with footprints, a dog, the head of the corpse fell off...oh, Sir, you can't image a worse scenario for any sort of detection." Anderson's head moved dolefully from side to side. "Not that this excuses us, no. But," He scratched his head. "It made it impossible to find any clues. Furthermore, there were approximately fifty or more stagehands, performers, staff members and general lookers-on backstage. Any of them had opportunity and most of them hated Vivienne du Lac so fiercely that they applauded her death as an act from God."

"It sounds terrible. What can you do?"

"We have the other two deaths, both of which most likely stemmed from du Lac's murder. One was a stagehand named Ernest Rattner. An ordinary man, no special problems with him. Not especially liked by his fellow workers, but not a man who really had any enemies. Perhaps he saw someone or something. The other was her major-domo, a dwarf named Crespi."

"A *dwarf!*" The Commissioner laughed. "The world of the opera is a crazy one! Trust a dwarf to be in this debacle!"

"I couldn't write a mystery story like this," Anderson chuckled. "No one would believe it could happen!"

"What's the dwarf's story?"

"We think he robbed Vivienne du Lac's apartment. We think he had a lot of money and jewels and gold objects on him when he was killed. It's only conjecture, though. He *may* have killed du Lac...perhaps they argued over money…and then perhaps he killed Rattner because Rattner saw him. And it is possible that someone saw him with money and the things he stole and killed *him* for that…the money and such is missing…but, this is, as I said, conjecture on our part. We just have no idea of what happened."

The Commissioner finished his coffee and set the cup down. "Do your best, Anderson. The papers are screaming that, as usual, the police are not doing their job. I'd like to see some closure on this, if you can do it." He stood up and Anderson heaved himself to his feet. The men shook hands.

Should I say anything to him about his wife? No. It's personal and he is a man I respect…

"Thank you, Anderson."

"Thank you, Sir. I'll check back with you in a day or two. Perhaps we will get lucky."

"Oh, I hear your old nemeses, Hamilton Purcell, was sprung early." The Commissioner shook his head. "Damn Judge Silkington, damn politics, even if the bastard is related to me by marriage. He made a piss-poor decision in this matter, and, incidentally, keeps making piss-poor decisions in *other* matters. Purcell should have been kept in prison until he rots, not let out to commit his own particular brand of crime again." He spread his hands out helplessly. "I know my dear, beautiful, dumb daughter married Silkington's son. The boy is a disaster. I hope they cut and run before there are any children." He made a disgusted sound.

"I wish Purcell wasn't free. He's a bad man."

"He's threatened to do you some harm, hasn't he?"

"If I was to go around worrying about all the criminals I put into prison and their threats against me, I'd never get any work done. I'll trust in the probation system to keep a good eye on Purcell's doings." Anderson waved his hands in the air.

"Nonetheless, it was a bad judicial decision."

"What did Shakespeare say? 'First kill all the lawyers'? I'm sure he meant the judges, too."

The Commissioner laughed, a booming sound. "I look forward to the opera on Saturday. Will you be there?"

"Both as a policeman and as an opera fan." Anderson put his coat over his arm.

"I didn't know that you were an opera lover."

"Yes. It's a passion of mine. A recent passion. Goodbye, Sir."

***

At the Met, Antonina and Angelique were busy with rehearsals for *La Traviata*. Antonina was to sing the part of Violetta, the part that Vivienne du Lac had been scheduled to sing. Angelique would sing the minor role of Flora, Violetta's friend. The two women were still sharing the smaller dressing room. As they were friends, and both of easy temperament, it was a successful sharing.

"You have moved to your new apartment? Alone now?" Angelique's smile was quizzical, and her eyes danced.

"I have moved. It is a beautiful place and you must come and visit. Am I alone?" Antonina blushed. "No, not alone."

"Ah? It is the handsome policeman?"

"It is." Antonina sat down. "I know he is married, but his wife has just left him."

"I heard some rumors that all was not well at his home."

"Oh! Are there any...any rumors about...me?" Antonina's face was flamed with embarrassment. "My mother...I..."

"I haven't heard anything like that...yet." Angelique sat to put on shoes. "But, if you are involved, sooner or later....This is a small world, this world of opera."

"I have nothing to be ashamed of." Antonina's chin rose. "I love him and he loves me."

"Of course, my little goose. One can see it in his face when he looks at you." She smiled at her reflection in the mirror. "And in yours, too."

"Does it show?"

"To me it does. It blazes out in huge letters."

Antonina took a huge breath. "I suppose I should feel some shame, but the women in my family have a predilection for falling in love with men who are married to others. My *Zia* Filomande, my mother..." The breath whooshed out. "I guess I am following in a long line of women who lose their hearts."

"My darling little goose, look at me! Who am I to lecture anyone on falling in love with married men. My darling David, the man of my heart of hearts...what can I say?" She spread out her expressive hands and then, after a moment, bent forward and confided to Antonina. "I shouldn't tell you this. It's supposed to be a secret between David and me...but, his wife, poor thing, is dying. She may even be dead as we speak. The dreaded cancer has taken her life, or will take it within a day or so. David has returned to be with her when the end comes...he will bury her with love and tenderness and regret for what might have been...and then, he will come back to me." A wide smile tugged at her mouth. "I think my story will have a happy ending, and perhaps yours will, too. Perhaps his wife will file for divorce. This is one of the rumors that I have heard."

"That would be wonderful." Antonina fussed with her pearls. "I am so happy for you, Angelique. You deserve a lifetime of love and happiness."

Angelique smiled again. "I have waited for this happiness for a long time. I'm afraid to believe that it may come true."

"It will. I know it."

"And you? If he should be divorced by his wife? What will you do?"

"I'll be delighted." Antonina clearly hadn't thought past her present dizzy happiness.

"And then what would happen?"

"What do you mean?"

"Would you marry him?"

Antonina's grey eyes opened wide. "I hadn't thought that far ahead. This is all so new to me...this being with a man...And besides," she gulped and then chuckled. "He hasn't even mentioned it!"

"I wonder..." Angelique brushed herself off and stood up. "What will happen when he does? Will you be with him, his wife...or will you be an opera star?"

Antonia stood up, too. "I would do both."

"Perhaps. Perhaps."

***

In Greenwich, Monsignor Dario, crossing from the Rectory to the Church, stopped in his tracks. "Oh, my good Saint Agatha! Not again!"

The statues were again dressed in gaudy clothing. Two pair of long red underwear, three nightgowns of blue calico, stockings, hats and knitted mittens festooned the little children made of stone. The donkeys and the sheep wore gaily colored scarves. The little goats had stocking caps on their heads and one carried an Indian-patterned blanket on his back. Dario began to laugh. Then, he went back into his study and called the police station.

"Not again! Who the he...heck is playing tricks?" Emerson McAndrews chuckled. "I'll be right over."

"I'll wait until you get here before I call my mother to come and undress them all." Dario laughed too. "Has no one complained that their washing has been stolen?"

"Not yet. Break out that good whisky that you keep hidden in your study. Mike and I will be there in ten minutes to, ah, discuss the matter."

"...sounds like the word love in the mouth of a courtesan..."
Ralph Waldo Emerson, February 12, 1851

SYNOPSIS OF THE OPERA *LA TRAVIATA*

La Traviata (the fallen woman), an opera in three acts by Giuseppe Verdi, after the drama La dame aux camèllias by Dumas fils.

Paris, 1850. Alfredo Germont, the handsome son of wealthy, respectable parents, falls in love with a beautiful courtesan, Violetta Valèry. The opera opens at a gay dinner party at Violetta's home. Violetta had recently been very ill, and Germont, who had come to visit her every day, hoping that her health improves, proposes a toast. Violetta responds, singing in praise of love. Their guests depart, and Violetta collapses, coughing. Germont declares his love to her. She tells him that she is dying, needs to be alone, but that he can come back to her when the camellia she gives him has faded. He convinces her to come and live with him at his country house. He will make her happy as long as he can. Both of them are blissfully happy.

Germont goes back to Paris to try to save Violetta's estate. While he is gone, his father visits Violetta, pleading with her to leave Germont as the scandal of Alfredo living with an ex-prostitute will prevent his sister from making an acceptable marriage. He begs her to go back to Paris and leave his son alone.

Aware that she has but a few weeks to live, and also aware and that life without Alfredo's love would make life not worth living, Violetta agrees and returns to Paris to live with her former lover, Baron Douphol.

Germont believes she has left him because she no longer loves him. He accuses Violetta of perfidy and flings money at her. He challenges Douphol to a duel in which Douphol is wounded.

In the last scene, one of immense beauty, his father confesses to the sacrifice he provoked Violetta into making. The lovers are reunited for a brief moment, declaring their love and joy. Violetta rises to meet her love, and, before she can clasp him to her bosom, she dies.

"So I will have to watch you die once again on stage," Anderson kissed the top of Antonina's head. "Are you ever going to be in an opera where you don't die?"

"Ah," she gathered him to her and thoughts of operas faded away for a few moments. And then, afterwards…"Operas are about powerful emotions. Life, death, jealousy, greed, revenge…out of this is the stuff from which they are fashioned." She laughed. "I will be singing *The Barber of Seville* later this year, and then *L'elisir d'amore* a few weeks after that. Both are funny, cheerful operas and my part not only lives at the end, but lives happily ever after."

He gazed at her with eyes that glazed over with adoration. He buried his face in her tresses. "We *will*, won't we, Antonina? We will live happily ever after."

"Just like Mozart wrote," She laughed again, her mouth open with delight and pulled him down onto the couch.

***

"Tell me how he died."

Dr. Dempsey riffled the page of the autopsy on the man only known as Crespi. "Well, first off, he was riddled with childhood arthritis. Probably born deformed. I understand he was from France or someplace over there. If he'd been here in America, maybe someone might have operated on him as a baby and tried to fix the worst of his physical problems," He shrugged. "However, this sort of thing gets worse and worse, with the spinal cord growing more curved, which causes all of the internal organs to mush themselves up."

"Mush themselves?" Anderson laughed. "Is that a medical term?"

"Definitely." Dempsey laughed, too. "First year in Med School, you learn medical terminology like 'mush' ".

"Poor son of a bitch. Life must have been very hard for him. I'll bet he was teased and made fun of his whole life."

"Don't feel too sorry for him. I heard rumors about him. He was supposed to be a ruthless killer back in Europe."

"Well, rumors….that's not evidence."

"No. You're right. But I have heard, and from good sources, that he's killed more than one person. There are some veiled rumors about cruelty to children, but I can't believe that any man could do such depraved things." Dempsey's mouth twisted in a sour way. "Well, anyway, he was garroted. Someone went behind him and put a wire…" Dempsey held up a thin piece of wire approximately two feet long. "And here is the wire." He looked at it and slid it through his fingers. "Most likely slipped it over his head and gave it a good twist and pull." He put his words in to action and Buddy Manger cringed at the gesture, putting his own hands up to his own throat and being glad that no one garroted *him*.

"Death was nearly instantaneous."

"Any clues at all?" Dempsey shook his head.

"Anything else? Any marks or skin under Crespi's fingernails?"

"Nope. I think this sort of death was done by someone with a lot of strength, most likely a man. The killer would be standing over Crespi...after all, the dwarf was only about four feet tall. Then he bent and dropped the wire over Crespi's head...then, *Schhhtch!*" Dempsey made a sound and Buddy shivered.

"The satchel was empty." Von Vogel stated. "Only one earring on the ground...perhaps the assailant grabbed all of the swag, but dropped the earring."

"Most likely. The girl who worked for Vivienne...Celestina...she identified the earring as being one that Vivienne often wore. Said it was very valuable. Several diamonds and a huge emerald."

"Three violent deaths. A throat cut, a head smashed in and a garroting. Our murderer, if there is only one, is a versatile fellow."

"And are we any further along in catching this versatile person?"

"Not at all. Not one inch further along, I'm ashamed to say."

* * *

"Miss Sabatino? There's a gentleman here to see you..." Hiram Goldblatt stuck his head behind the curtain. "Says he's a friend."

"Who is it?"

"A Doctor Peter Bovi. Do you want him to come in?"

Peter! Peter was here, for goodness sake! What should I say? What does he want?

"Certainly, Mr. Goldblatt. Thank you. Please show him backstage." Frantically, she pressed her hands to her cheeks. They were hot. Peter!

He pushed aside the curtain and smiled. She could see that he was embarrassed and awkward. It calmed her. "Hello, Peter. How kind of you to come to see me." She ran to him and took his hand.

"Hello, Antonina." He cleared his throat and shuffled his feet. "I, uh...I was in New York and I, uh..."

"How is your family?" Antonina took pity on him.

"Fine, uh, fine...I, uh..." Three of the chorus members walked by: Horz Bortel, Robyn Benson and Marietta Bossie. They were chattering and nearly stopped in curiosity. Who was this man visiting Antonina? Gossip and innuendo about the least little thing backstage was fodder for discussion. "Can, uh, we go somewhere...uh, private?"

"Sure, Peter. Come up to my dressing room." Antonina smiled at the trio of chorus people. "I want you all to meet a neighbor from my home town," she introduced them. "He was here on Saturday and saw the performance." She grinned, knowing that she had ruined a perfectly good juicy item of speculation.

"Nice to meet you all," Peter rose to the occasion. "I enjoyed your performances very much."

In the dressing room, Peter wandered around, touching Angelique's candlesticks and pictures, turning on the hot water faucet, clearly ill at ease.

"What is it, Peter"

"I wanted to say that I am very sorry for the way we parted." Peter stopped fussing with the items on the dressing table. "We...we go back so many years, Antonina. I do and did love you and I treated you with disrespect. I'm sorry."

"That's fine, Peter, but I thank you very much for being man enough to come and talk with me. It's not just you. I'm still rather young for all of this and I didn't know what I wanted. Perhaps I was wrong, too."

His heart lurched. She was the loveliest thing he'd every seen. Why had it all gone so wrong?

"Do you think we could, maybe start once again? Try to work it all out?" His face was wretched in its misery at losing Antonia. He beat down the thought of the woman he had been with last night. Babs was just the kind of girl he needed: rich, beautiful and racy. She wanted only a good time and some fun from him.

"No, Peter, but thank you for being so sweet. I meant what I said. The opera will be my career. I can't be your wife and be an opera star. I have to choose. It is no reflection on you or our feelings...the feelings that we had for each other....I just...I *have* to sing. And it can't be a part-time thing for me. It is my life." She bowed her head and the silken locks of her fair hair fell forward, hiding her eyes.

He felt relieved and at the same time sad. He sighed. He'd done his best. He'd asked her to be his wife. He'd come back and asked her to reconsider. Thank goodness, she refused again. Wearing a martyred expression, he bowed and left her.

He left the stage door whistling. He'd call Babs and they'd have some cocktails at The Catamint Lounge. Then...well...

***

Anderson went to the orchestral pit. "Mrs. Odams?" He approached Patricia.

"Yes? Oh, you're the police chief, aren't you?"

He smiled. She was pretty and her blue eyes danced. "Yes, I am." He held out his hand, showing her the wire that garroted Crespi. "Does this seem familiar to you?"

"Of course!" She took the wire from him without any squeamishness. Obviously, she didn't know what it had been used for. "This is the wire from the piano."

"What can you tell me about it."

"Well, the piano wasn't quite in tune after the performance. I asked Rudolph Schubin to have it checked out. He sent a piano tuner here and the tuner replaced several of the wires. This is one of the ones that he took out...see?" She showed him the end of the wire, which was crimped and bent. "This is where it hooks up to the keys and the pedal."

"What happened to it after it was replaced?" Anderson took the wire back and put it in his pocket.

"Oh, there were six or seven that were replaced. Um..." She thought back. "They were just lying on top of the piano. I think perhaps Forsythe Wicks took them. He saves all kinds of things because he thinks they'll come in handy one of these days...you know, he does the props and is always looking for peculiar stuff." She smiled at him and her blue eyes twinkled. "Who knows what he'll do with them eventually. Maybe tie up a chandelier or some such."

He thanked her profusely and made a notation to speak with Wicks.

Chapter Twenty-Nine

"A little wanton money, which burned out the bottom of his purse…"
Sir Thomas Moore, Works.

$\mathcal{S}$tocks rose sharply. The prices on RCUSA jumped nearly ten percent in just a week. Those who hadn't yet bought stock, decided that this was the time they should jump on the bandwagon. Those who had sold stock, panicked. Had they made the wrong decision?

One of the major New York newspapers urged restraint. "Bankers all over the country are alarmed at the huge volume of credit that is being employed. It is a deep concern." The other newspaper cried the opposite, "Opportunity is here as never before! Stocks soar! RCUSA tops One Hundred! Liberty Amalgam hits Two Hundred!" People dithered, afraid to miss out, afraid to plunge.

One man, who was employed at the New York Stock Exchange, told of a typical day: "They roar like lions, they holler and scream and claw at each other's collars. Then they cheer and clap. They throw more money into the air. They are all crazy. Up and down! This boom will never stop!"

***

The economic news was plastered all over the front pages. That, coupled with the news and photos of U.S. aviator Richard E. Byrd's successful flight over the South Pole, drove the unsolved murder of Vivienne du Lac to page 5 in the New York Herald, and page 6 of the New York Times.

***

"Should we have held on longer?" Alex asked his family at dinner. "The RCUSA stock seems to be surging."

"Daddy," Rachel lectured him. "Grandfather says, 'Make your best and educated guess and stick with it'. We've made a very fine profit already. Accept that and be satisfied." Alex looked suitably abashed and Dale laughed at his hangdog expression.

"We have gotten the plans for the new hospital nursing school," Ariel Sarah told them. "Look, see what they are planning." The family spread out the architectural drawings and leaned over the table. Dale winked at Alex. What terrific daughters they were raising. Alex's smile told her that he thought that the girls were smarter than he was.

Abby sighed. "This hospital is real to me. I like being a part of it. That old RCUSA stock was just a piece of paper. This is much better." Her gap-toothed grin echoed her pleasure.

"You watch," Rachel warned. "The stock market is going to fall apart. I guarantee it."

"You are right!" Her twin sister agreed. "We'll be fat and happy and others will be crying."

***

Antonina and Anderson dined together at Delmonico's restaurant. Their waiter, Lorenzo, recognizing Antonina, went into raptures about her performances. "I have my place, Miss Sabatino, in the standing room area. I have stood there, every week that the opera is open, for seven years."

"You *stand?*" Anderson was thunderstruck. "Don't you get tired?"

"You don't understand, Sir. We take pride in standing. Many men and women, too, have their own spot. We are there by virtue of the fact that we are *there!* Each week, every week. I stand next to men who are doctors…men who own large companies, rich men, poor men. Women who work in factories, women who were born to great wealth. We are the standing room *aficionados*. We meet at least once a week and we all know one another."

"I'm humbled and grateful for your praise," Antonina blushed with modesty. "Wouldn't you prefer to sit, or is it too costly?"

"It *is* costly. But I wouldn't trade my spot for the best seat in the house." He bowed and took their order, then came rushing back out with a portly gentleman dressed in white tails. "This is my boss. This is Mr. Delmonico, himself!"

Mr. Delmonico bowed low and kissed Antonina's hand. "Ah! Miss Sabatino! Such an honor for you to dine with us!" He fussed with the glasses and snapped his fingers. Three waiters with a silver champagne holder, glasses and a bottle, wrapped lovingly, ran out, set up the stand and reverently placed their swaddled treasure into the ice.

"Champagne…on the house!" Mr. Delmonico spun the bottle himself, chilling it to a proper temperature. "And when you are finished…we have a surprise for you!" His eyes twinkled and he backed away, bowing and bowing and bowing.

"And I…am a no-body with the famous Miss Sabatino," Anderson laughed. "You, my darling are the prize!"

"Hush and drink your champagne!" She laughed with him and slipped her hand under the table, finding his.

At the end of the perfect meal, Mr. Delmonico came out again, this time with a huge silver salver, held by Lorenzo, following. The lights of the restaurant flickered as Mr. Delmonico made an announcement. The entire restaurant…all of the diners and all of the waiters were still…awaiting what was to follow…

"Ladies and gentlemen…my customers…my dear friends…As we all know, Delmonico's is the premier restaurant in all of New York, and perhaps in all of this fair country. This young lady is Antonina Sabatino, the most beautiful star and most wonderful opera singer who has ever lived!"

The customers and staff burst into excited applause. Antonina Sabatino! The *diva!*

"Gee whiz, she's so pretty!"

"I've never heard of her. Who is she?"

"Dummy! She sings opera."

"Oh, opera…well…"

"She's really famous. Came onto the stage when that other lady was killed."

"Well, she is rather pretty, but I don't know anything about opera. A lot of squalling fat ladies, isn't it?"

"I think there's more to it than that."

"Can't convince me to go. A nice vaudeville. Now, that's what I like. A lot of girls and a few prat-falls. A few laughs."

Antonina blushed, bit her lip in embarrassed delight, and bowed her head right and left, acknowledging the adulation. Anderson glowed. *I love it when they applaud her! I bask in her limelight!*

"And tonight, to honor her, Delmonico's presents our latest dessert…" Lorenzo knelt, holding the silver dish aloft. Mr. Delmonico whipped off the cover, exposing a cloud of whipped cream and hazelnuts. "I give you….Ladies and gentlemen…*Daquoise Antonina!"*

It rested on a doily of gold, three layers high. A puff of hazelnut meringue, divided by vanilla butter cream, hazelnut butter cream, and mocha butter cream… And crowned with swirls of whipped crème anglaise, dusted with gold leaf and chopped, candied hazlenuts. A poem, nay, a rapture, on a plate. [6] Antonina ate a huge portion. Anderson ate two.

"Does all of this nonsense bother you?" She wondered, modestly, if he was annoyed by the attention she was getting.

"My darling, I revel in it. You are the most wonderful woman in all of the world. And, you are mine, all mine. I smile inside. None of these people know how much I love you."

"And none of them know how much I love you, my darling man."

Actually, in the kitchen, Lorenzo and Mr. Delmonico were speculating on exactly that matter. "She loves him!" Delmonico declared, his hands clasped dramatically.

"He adores her!" Lorenzo confided. "Watch his face. He never takes his eyes off her."

"Who would, you oaf?"

---

[6] Recipe for this remarkable confection at the back. You, too, if you wish to utilize every pan and pot in your kitchen, can replicate this Daquoise Antonina.

"She is so beautiful…I cried when she died playing Mimi."

"I would die for her, myself!"

"See him…" Lorenzo nudged his boss. "Watch his hand! Ah! Such tenderness!"

"Move it!" Another waiter, Sam, who was less romantic, pushed past them. "I have to serve table six, you know."

***

On Friday, October 18th, the dress rehearsal for *La Traviata* began. Massimo Orsini, himself, was late, an almost unheard of situation. Dean, sitting in his seat next to Tom, speculated. "Maybe the old geezer got bumped off, too. Shoot, everyone else around here has been killed."

Rudolph Schubin stepped up to the podium. "The *Maestro* is late today. I will be conducting until he gets here." He tapped his utilitarian baton, one made of plain walnut, on the top of the podium. "Before the actors get onstage, please, gentlemen and ladies, let's run through the overture….And now…"

Behind the curtain, Act One was being set. The scene was the banquet hall of the house of Vittoria Valèry, Paris' most infamous courtesan. In the center of the stage, a huge dining table was set lavishly with china and crystal. Small gilt chairs were scattered around the stage and, on the left wall was a gigantic mirror hung over a marble mantelpiece. On a stepladder, Urbano was working furiously to get the stage set up properly. Johnston Redmond was fighting with the glittering chandelier that hung over the table. The lights on the chandelier would not go on, no matter how he twisted the wires or clicked the switches. Tim Weaver was on his back, legs sprawled, trying to stabilize the center leg of the huge dining room table. "God forbid, Timmy!" shrieked Forsythe Wicks, "God forbid that it should tip over and have all my lovely china smashed! I'd simply cry, I would!"

"Hold your panties on, Forsythe. The table will be fine."

Finally, everything on stage seemed to be fixed and in working order. Calle gave the signal to have the props scattered and Forsythe Wicks himself trotted onto the stage, carefully setting the expensive china and the glasses on to the tabletop. The cat, Figaro, followed along with him, winding through his legs as he placed things here and there, precisely in the correct place.

Calle checked his watch…the *Maestro* still wasn't in the building. "We've got to start, with him or without him. I'm a little worried, what with all that's been going on…maybe I should send James over to his hotel…?"

"He'll be here. He'd never miss a rehearsal. After all, this will be his last opera. Tomorrow night's performance and then Monday night…his finale and the huge birthday celebration for his eightieth…he'd never miss a moment of the whole shebang." Urbano soothed his friend.

THE METROPOLITAN OPERA HOUSE PRESENTS

SATURDAY EVENING, OCTOBER 18, 1929

LA TRAVIATA

Music by Giuseppi Verdi, Libretto By Francesco Maria Piave

PREMIER GUEST CONDUCTOR – MASSIMO ORSINI

Gaston de Letorieres, a young man about town......Claudia Vizzi

Violetta Valèry, a courtesan............Antonina Sabatino

Alfredo Germont, lover of Violetta...............Sergei Andreyi

Baron Douphol, rival of Alfredo..................Philip Perri

The Marquis d'Obigny ....Josef Mercurio

Flora Bervoix, Violetta's friend ....Angelique Orloff

Annina, Violetta's confidente and Maid......Sue Shigeoka

Giuseppi, servant to Violetta .... Simon Forest

Giorgio Germont, Alfredo's father .... Dante Lazzarelli

Doctor Grenville...Sandor Calli-Curri

<u>Friends at the Banquet:</u> Gay Ann Fay, Karen Heffernan, Ralph Bochetta, Muriel Durgin, Elizabeth Newhouse, Roque Nunez, Robyn Benson, Peter Curry, Craig Newhouse

<u>Street Singers and Revelers:</u> Morgan McCurdy, Dana Foster, Joanetta Grasser, Michael Merriman, Ruby Stevens, Annie Curry, Louis Kochanek, Boon Bryce, Cynthia Kochanek

<u>Orchestra in Act One:</u> James Fay, Leon Venedicktou, William Ferdinand, Joy Anderson, Rose Nunn, Ruth Walsh, Marlene Littlefield

<u>UNDERSTUDIES:</u> Pyter Omerosa, Korol Petroff, Zizanne Fond, Patricia Salzillo

THE METROPOLITAN OPERA COMPANY

<u>BOARD OF DIRECTORS</u>

Baron F. David Wessel, Chairman

Alex Troy, Chief Financial Officer

Rawlins J. Cottinet

T. deWitt Hollister

Sir Dennis Staer, B.P.O.O.N.

Commodore John Carson

W. K. Vandersmythe-Winthrop

Sir Eustace Maltravers-Goffe

Chalmers von Vogel

Ambassador Charles Mabley

Cornelius Marvel-Mabley

Sir Richard Dillworth D'Allee

Horatio Cooperstyne

The Honorable Athol Wolf III

<u>EXECUTIVE STAFF</u>

Arturo Calle, Executive General Manager

Urbano Valeria, Master Stage Manager

Sigrid Chalmers, Asst. Stage manager

Anatole Goodman, Choral Director

Lucien Bolte, Ballet Corps

Rudolph Schubin. Orchestral Assistant

Henry Wu, Make Up Director

Victor Calligari, Wig and Hair Stylist

Fausta Cleva, Costume Wardrobe Mistress

Forsythe Wicks, Properties

Johnston Redmond, Master Electrician

Timothy Weaver, Master Carpenter

Janet Connelly, Dresser to the Ladies

Peter Pawlowski, Prompter

Metropolitan Opera Chorus
Lillian Quimby, Michael Connors, Nancy Connors, Maria-Pia Assoluta, Charlotte Ryan, Horz Bortel, Patricia Flynn, Marietta Bossie, Lorraine Carpentier, Juliana Patten, George Patten, Jan Lawrence, Sandra Starr, Valerie Lewis, Emily Brown Shields, Caroleah Kotch, John Murphy, Elaine Neale, Jennifer Stevens, Ellen Kingsbury, Ardenia Wood, George Lamonica, James Brunetti, Curtis Neel, Harold Moran, Paul Giggi, Elizabeth Newhouse, Rita Pomerleau

Metropolitan Orchestra
Garvin McCurdy, 1st Violin, Alice Mary McCurdy, 2nd Violin, Patricia Odams, Eileen Boyle, Dean Armandroff, Thomas Zeranski, Mary Frangiamore, Wendy Littman, Kathie Hess, Arthur Littman, Sandra Marks, Joanna Farman, Carol Barnes, Judith Pedersen, William Ferdinand, Harriet Grannick, Milton Bickle, Audrey Brogden, Dorothy Jill Cleveland, Vas Hubert Brogden, James Fay, Leon Venedicktou, Joy Anderson, Janet Merriman, Marion Craig, Barbara Upton, Pat Laulette, Virginia Gerstung, Lynn Parker, Donna Vreeland, Rose Nunn, Ruth Walsh, Marlene Littlefield, Babette Vermeiren, Ann Curry

"If you say so." Calle shrugged. "For me…" He made a Sign of the Cross with his hand facing the curtains. "May this all work out well. Jesus Christ! May it all be fine! Let no one die today, Lord!" He turned, half-sheepish, half-serious, to see Urbano also bless the stage. *Good, between the two of them, perhaps the devil would be warded off.*

"Everyone, take your places on stage or back stage! Audience, please take your seats and be quiet!" Sigrid Chalmers hollered to everyone in the theater.

Clemons, holding Figaro, meandered to the back seats. Barbara, Judi, Brooks and Carey, went to seat themselves in Barbara's box. The back seats were again filled with the administrative members of the Met who could spare a few hours away from their jobs, a few of the ushers and several opera fans who had been able to wrangle an invitation to see the rehearsal. David Wessel, Troy, Athol Wolf and Commodore John Carson and his wife, Jan sat in the third row together with Anderson von Vogel, Pedar Pedersen and Buddy Manger. Anderson's heart was beating. *I wonder if I'll fall in love all over with this new character she's playing. Probably, I will. I wonder if I'll cry when her character dies. Probably, I will.*

The back doors crashed open just as Calle was giving the final signal. It was the *Maestro*, rushing down the carpet, his opera cape flying behind him, looking as if he might…just might…lift off and fly the rest of the way down. The cast, the workers and the performers gave a cheer. Massimo Orsini doffed his top hat and waved to everyone. "So sorry I am late. It is unforgivable for me to do this to you, my dear friends and colleagues. I am desolate." He waved his baton. This time it was the one given to him by Lord Halifax, Viceroy of India. It was a slender wand of rare *randa* wood, with an emerald the size of an egg on the top.

Orsini threw off his cape, landing it in the second row. He bent sharply at the waist, holding onto his stomach. Garvin started out of his seat, but the *Maestro* waved him back. "It is only a bit of gastric disaster. I ate too heavily last night. Perhaps, Garvin, my dear man, you can get me a glass of *Brisochi?*"

Garvin leaped out of his seat and found one of the pages. "Have Schubin bring the Maestro some *Brioschi,* please." The page nodded and sped on his errand.

In a twinkling, Schubin brought a foaming glass. Orsini drained it and burped softly. "Thank you, my good friend. Now I am better."

Orsini then stepped up to the podium, patting Rudolph Schubin's shoulder. He spoke softly again to Schubin, shook his hand, and then bent to speak with Garvin. They both nodded and Orsini announced that he was ready to begin. Everyone noticed that there was no score on the podium. Orsini winked at his colleagues in the orchestra. He didn't need the score.

He brought the baton down and the orchestra slammed into the overture. Anderson leaned forward, trying to notice everything. Last time, when he was first at the opera, he'd been bored. He'd noticed nothing until Antonina had appeared, and then he'd noticed nothing but her. This time, he vowed, he'd try to see the entire opera. How it worked, how it flowed, how the music blended with the voices, how the people on stage melded together with the orchestra.

Next to him, David Wessel was explaining the story of *La Traviata*. "You may not believe it nowadays, but in 1853, an opera about a fallen woman…a whore with a heart of gold, so to speak… was shocking to the audience. Violetta's death from consumption, a dread disease of the time, rather tragic and touching to us, was a very uncomfortable slice of realism then. Something that no one ever talked about, much less sang an opera about. As a matter of fact, the opera was to have been set contemporarily, in 1853. Verdi had to change the time…take the opera back to the year 1700, so that the audience could distance itself from the horrors of consumption."

"Really!" Troy was fascinated. "I had no idea. I'm just learning about opera and opera history."

"Think of it this way, suppose someone wrote an opera now about a person dying from cancer. We'd all be horrified, wouldn't we? Cancer is such an untouchable subject!"

"It would be difficult to watch people singing and falling in love when the heroine was dying of cancer. I'll agree with that!"

"It was, similar to the way Puccini portrayed *La Bohème*…also an unusual opera. It wasn't about kings and queens and dukes or giants or monsters. No. It was about three people, rather ordinary people for their times, caught up in love and torment. These characters could be us." His handsome and aristocratic face was thoughtful. "Caught up in every-day drama." He turned to Anderson. "You may not know it, Anderson, but this opera was a solid flop when it opened. Maybe because the singers they chose were bad. Maybe because the woman who sang Violetta weighed four hundred pounds and no one could imagine her as a consumptive…hee, hee." He laughed at the notion of a huge, fat woman who tried to convince her audience that she was dying from a wasting disease. "It took a year, and then, *Traviata* was a triumph and it has continued this way ever since."

"And how do you think this new little child will sing?" Troy asked, unaware that Anderson's temper nearly got the best of him at the idle question. *How do you think she will sing? You nincompoop! She will sing magnificently!*

"We shall see." David settled back in his chair.

An imp of doubt entered into Anderson's head. *Could she really sing this opera well? Was* La Bohème *a one time fluke? Would her voice crack and would she not be able to reach the high notes? Would the audience – always fickle – laugh at her?* He, too, sat back, nibbling at his fingernails in anguish.

The overture set the tone and there was an air of expectancy as the curtain rose. The guests sang to the chorus, "Why are you so late coming to this party?"

The chorus told that they were at Flora's house, playing cards. Flora had been worried that Violetta was too ill to hold a party. The cast on the stage were all dressed magnificently. Angelique, as Flora, wore a deep pink dress, embellished with silver beading. She looked beautiful.

But Violetta appeared...Antonina was dressed in a gold and green striped gown. It was heavy with panniers, sumptuous in velvet and satin, and she and the gown were glittering like a human candle of magnificent light...She was incandescent. The audience at once understood that she was like the candle...aglow, but underneath, wretchedly vulnerable...her illness made her glow even brighter. Her cheeks were pink...almost too pink...her eyes nearly feverish with the monster of consumption that writhed within, consuming her internally...and yet she sang... Sang that although she was ill, she will make the most of the rest of her life and even of this night...she will burn the candle brightly while she can.

When she came on stage, Anderson's heart leaped. Once again, he fell in love with a performer. A role on a stage. He watched and listened as Violetta danced and swayed, making the most of what was left of her life.

She meets Alfredo and learns that he has loved her from afar, coming to the front of her house every day with flowers, hoping that her recent illness has passed. She is touched and finds herself very attracted to this handsome young man who seems to adore her, even though she's a fallen woman.

Alfredo proposes a toast and then bursts into the rollicking *Libiamo*, his singing echoed by the guests and the chorus. They sing of goblets bright with gold and wine, love and lips that kiss. Anderson found his body swaying in time with the aria, and the sparse audience cheered and clapped when the song was done.

Violetta and Alfredo fall in love before the little audience, and the fears... Anderson's fears were put to rest. *My God! What a voice this child-woman has!*

Violetta began the first of two wonderful arias...what more could a soprano wish for? The first aria, *Ah, for' e lui?* (Could it really be?) tells of her wonder that someone could love her despite her background and follies. Could she, a woman who sells herself, be loved as other women are loved? Is it possible for her? And then, Violetta looks reality in the face. The naked truth is that she is a courtesan, a woman who lies with men for money, and she is dying. How can love and happiness be hers? Trying to shrug off her grief for something that cannot be, she sings *Sempre libera* (Always free), a wild expression of her feverish health and feverish life. In the background, Alfredo interrupts with his passionate, tender melody. She listens for a moment, nearly convinced, but then, with a cry of *"What folly!"* she sings her song to the pleasures of love that is purely physical. Their two voices blend, his tender and yearning, hers feverish and wild.

As the act ends and Violetta collapses, Anderson felt tears flowing down his cheeks. His throat was choked. He looked around to see if anyone noticed his grief and joy. David was openly sniffing, dabbing at his eyes with a white handkerchief, Troy was wiping his eyes with a knuckled hand. Athol Wolf blew his nose with a trumpeting sound. They were all greatly affected by Antonina's superb performance. Anderson exulted; *This woman is magnificent. Her voice is a gift from the gods. She is indeed divine. And she is mine! Mine!*

The sparse audience is on its feet, clapping wildly. "She's the best – ever!" Carey cried. *"Brava,* Antonina!"

Antonina got up and waved to Carey. "Thank you," she mouthed. The stage crew was still clapping their approval as the first act moved off stage.

***

As the stagehands wrestled the set for Act One off the stage, Anderson told Pedar about the piano wire. "Let's get little Forsythe in the office after he's set the properties for Act Two."

Act Two was a less-complicated set, a country house living room in the outskirts of Paris. The room was tastefully furnished in a casually elegant way, with chairs and small tables placed here and there. There was large writing desk set to the left, and books and cushions were scattered in comfortable haphazardness. On one wall, a glass door leads into a garden. Tim checked a few of the chairs to be sure they were secured, rocked the tables, and, happy that all would be well, dusted off his hands and sat down. Forsythe fluffed up pillows, straightened the books and brought out a large arrangement of flowers, which he placed on one of the larger tables. He stood back, his hands clasped under his chin, his head cocked to one side, checking to see how the arrangement looked. Dissatisfied, he pushed the arrangement a few inches to the right. He nodded his head. "Finished," he caroled out.

"Forsythe, can I see you for a few moments?" Anderson called in a soft voice.

"Why, certainly." Forsythe turned, pirouetting. "Here I come!"

Anderson shut the door to the office. Forsythe's eyes looked wide. *What was happening?*

Anderson pulled out the piano wire and raised his eyebrows. Forsythe looked puzzled and almost relieved. Anderson wondered if he was on the wrong track. He decided to try anyway. "What do you have to say?"

"About what?" Forsythe seemed to breathe a sigh of relief. He shrugged and raised his own eyebrows.

Anderson looked at the man sitting before him. A slight man, barely five and a half feet tall, slender hands, slender wrists, tiny, almost feminine feet. Could this man summon the strength to garrote a wily street urchin like Crespi? Probably not. Then what about the wire? He asked, "Did you use the piano wire to strangle Crespi?"

"Me?" The startled outrage was real. "Me? Strangle the little peculiar thug? *Never!"*

"Then what do you have to confess to me?" Anderson stood up, towering over Forsythe's chair and his voice thundered the question. Forsythe cowered back.

"I...I..." he squeaked.

"Tell me, *now!"* Forsythe ducked back, raising his hands up in defense.

"The dog...I...the dog!" He nearly cried. "I hated her! She was going to fight with Figaro and I hit her with the broom."

"The dog...the dog." Anderson sat down. Pedar had his hand over his mouth and pretended to cough. "The dog. Aha. Tell me what happened." He sat back, listening.

"Well, I was working late. Most everyone had already left, but you know me. I have to have every single item in apple-pie order or I wouldn't be able to sleep." His voice was almost gossipy. He seemed relieved to have confessed. "I saw the cat fly by me, pursued by that hell-hound of a dog. I hated that dog! It bit me, it bit most of the cast and it was going to bite or kill Figaro. I chased them both. They ran up three flights of stairs. Let me tell you, I was huffing and puffing and it was only my fear for Figaro that kept me from collapsing." He crossed his hands over his heart and his breathing became a gasp.

"Yes?"

"Well, I got to the fifth floor and *Poupette*...what a stupid name for a dog, I'll tell you! *Poupette* had cornered Figaro and was trying to pounce on him. There was a broom there, leaning against the wall. I picked it up and whammed the dog over the head." His face took on a look of dread. "I really didn't mean to harm the little bitch, but I guess I hit her with all of my strength." There was another wheezing sound from Pedar's chair. Anderson didn't dare to look at his companion. "Maybe two times..." Forsythe's last words were whispers.

"Figaro yowled and the dog lay still. I tiptoed over to see what was what, and the dog wasn't breathing. My heart...I'm very sensitive, you all know...my heart nearly gave out on me. I felt faint and dizzy and I didn't know what to do. Figaro ran downstairs, leaving me and the...body." His eyes rolled. "I was in a panic...I pushed the dog with the tip of my shoe...ugh! I pushed it ... the dog ... into the closet." He shuddered. "I'm sorry that I fibbed and didn't own up to it." He hung his head on his slender neck. "Are you going to arrest me?"

"No." Anderson stood up. Their conjecture that Wicks might have killed Crespi was evidently all wrong. "It's a terrible thing to kill an animal, but it seems as if you were doing it to protect the cat. We don't have laws that arrest a man for killing a dog that is attacking another animal." Forsythe looked up. There were tears in his eyes. "But, please...don't ever do this again." Anderson's voice was stern.

"Oh, no! I'll never, never be mean to a dog again." Forsythe shuddered once more. "But I do so hate them. Little yapping creatures."

"Why did you want the piano wire?"

"Oh, that. Well, I save everything. One of these days, I might be able to use it for some prop."

"Where did you store it?"

"There were maybe six wires. I just left them in a heap in a cardboard box outside the properties closet. I didn't realize that someone took one and...used it." He gulped and made a gesture with his hands, fluttering them around his neck. "Can I go now? I have to check and then re-check the props for Act Three."

"You can go. Thank you, Forsythe." Anderson opened the door.

"I'll do anything...and I do mean anything...to help you, Chief. I'm really a law-abiding man. A gentle person." His bit his lip as he got up to leave. "I just lost my head for a moment." He sidled out the door. Anderson and Pedar looked at one another.

"Well, congratulations, Boss. You solved one of the mysteries." Pedar chuckled.

"Thanks. Why do I feel so foolish, then?"

"Perhaps because this whole thing is so foolish, ya?"

"Ya."

***

Act Two of the dress rehearsal went moderately well. Two of the freshly-replaced piano strings broke during the orchestral accompaniment for the Third Act and only one piece of scenery teetered downward, causing the chorus to run for cover. The lights refused to work in the Third Act, causing many ripe, strong curses from Johnston Redmond. He finally shut off every light in the opera house, plunging everyone into total darkness. "Don't anybody move!" He hollered. There were tiny arcs of his flashlight and a lantern, and then, a crackle of a wire, followed by a leaping flame. The flame was doused, followed by even louder cursing, causing most of the audience and cast to break into nervous giggles. After all, the entire building had once burned to the ground in years gone by.

The lights flashed, went out and then came back on again. Redmond appeared at center stage and took a deep bow to frenzied and relieved applause.

"What was all that?" Calle called out.

"Don't ask!" Redmond thundered.

"I know a dress rehearsal is supposed to have some glitches, but this was scary," Carey whispered, clutching Brooks' hand.

"The performance tomorrow ought to be a whiz-bang!" Brooks marveled. "By jingo! It had better be the best opera in the world. I was frightened."

Calle called out, "All ready for Act Three! Let's get this over so we can go home and have nervous breakdowns!"

***

Act Three takes place in the sparsely furnished bedroom where Violetta is living out the last few days of her life. There, in the shuttered dimness, as the golden curtain opened, she lay asleep in her small bed, her thin hands resting on top of a worn and frayed blanket. Her maid, Annina rests in a chair and a meager fire burns in the grate.

The mournful notes of Tom and Dean's bassoons warned the audience that this scene was not to be a happy one. Anderson, sitting in row three, was almost physically assaulted when he saw Antonina as Violetta in full make up. She looked ghastly...ill and wan, almost at death's door. And listening to the singing, he realized that his beloved, once again was going to die onstage. A great melancholy overcame him as he watched and he wrestled with his common sense. *That isn't Antonina on stage! She's only playing a part! She's fine. She's healthy and she will live fifty years longer than I will.*

He heard a curse and noticed that the small fire had extinguished itself. Urbano ran on stage and re-lit the sticks of wood. The fire sullenly came to life. Arturo Calle scribbled a note to himself.

Violetta's stage business was to pull a letter from the pocket of her dressing gown. "Alas!" Antonina called out in her own voice. "The letter has disappeared!" To titters, a red-faced Forsythe ran onto the stage, holding the missing letter in his hand.

"I'm so sorry, my dear," he scrabbled, nearly on all fours, off stage. Calle scribbled another note to himself.

"Christ! I hope the damn locket is in the drawer," Calle muttered. As the opera drew to its end, Violetta took out the locket, which was where it should be, and Calle heaved a sigh of relief.

As the curtain shut down, the audience was openly weeping. Antonina had been magnificent. There wasn't a dry eye.

Calle gathered his cast and employees on the stage. "You've done moderately well. I hope you all go home, relax, come back here tomorrow at six o'clock sharp, and break all of your legs and arms."

A cheer went up, and the weary cast and crew left the stage.

***

Angelique and Antonina, with Janet's expert help, removed their costumes, washed and creamed their faces, dressed themselves in their street clothes and were in the process of finishing their hairdressing when there was a knock at their door.

Anderson peeked in. "Are you decent?"

"No one in here is decent!" Angelique quipped. "We're opera singers, after all!"

"Please come on in."

Anderson entered. Angelique was lovely in a yellow suit trimmed with some kind of fur at the cuffs and collar. But he had eyes only for Antonina, who wore a simple pale blue shirtwaist dress and a coat with matching trim. "You ladies look wonderful." He came in and sat on the extra chair.

"Are you all done?" Antonina asked him.

"I suppose so," He seemed a little disconsolate.

"What's wrong?"

"Oh, I just re-searched the dressing room. I was hoping against all hope that a second search would surprise us with some sort of clue that we'd missed. But alas, as you said on stage. It wasn't there."

"Can we have the dressing room back?"

"Yes. I've given orders to have it cleaned and repainted tonight. You can use it tomorrow, if you wish."

"What made you think you might have missed a clue?" Angelique asked in idle curiosity. "I would think you fellows are expert searchers. After all, you have so much experience."

"We're pretty infallible," Anderson made smug face. "When we search a room, we rarely miss anything."

"Shall we make a small wager?" Antonina's smile was impish.

"What do you mean?"

"I say that I can fool you...keep you from finding...something...oh, here! My pearl necklace."

"Huh?"

"Here's the necklace," She held it up. "You give me ten minutes alone in here...with the toolkit from Francesco, the stagehand. Then you and your men can come in...I will leave the room. You'll have ten minutes to try to figure out where the necklace is." She started to laugh. "If you find it, well...I'll do whatever you want as a forfeit. If you cannot figure out what happened to it, you'll have to be my slave and do whatever I want you to do." She winked at Angelique. "Angelique will be the referee. Are you game?"

"You can't be serious!" Anderson laughed. "You can't hide something from us. You're not a professional sneak thief!"

"No, but I am a woman. I can beat you. Are you afraid?"

"Pah! Let the game begin!" Anderson called Pedar and Buddy into the room. He explained the bet to them. Both of them shook their heads at Antonina.

"You're gonna loose, little lady."

"Ya. We will find your necklace in a twinkling."

Buddy went out and found Francesco. "Can I borrow your toolkit for ten minutes?"

"Sure. Why for?" Buddy explained the bet to him. "Ha! This I will have to watch!"

Antonina took the heavy toolkit and pawed through it, pulling out a hammer, a screwdriver and a wrench. "Fine. I am all ready." In her hand was the necklace. "Ten minutes," she announced. She shooed everyone out of the room and locked the door.

There were banging sounds from behind the door. The silence. Ten minutes passed. The men and Angelique paced around, suddenly nervous and apprehensive. *Where would she hide the necklace? Why did she need the tools?*

She opened the door. "I'm ready for you." The men filed in, followed by Angelique. "I'll just step outside and leave you to your task." She smiled with demure humor and exited, closing the door after herself.

Anderson rapped out the orders. "I'll take the furniture. Buddy, you do the drapes, the walls, the lighting fixtures. Pedar, you are in charge of the floors, the baseboards, doors and hardware."

Angelique stood in the middle of the room, touching nothing, her eyes darting here and there as she watched the men go over the room, inch by inch. She couldn't decide who she was rooting for. Did she want the men to find the necklace? Or, would she be delighted if Antonina managed to win?

Anderson quickly riffled through all of the drawers, taking out each one, turning it upside down and examining every crevice of the dressing table, the chests and the assorted tables and chairs. He then examined each jar of make up and cream, sticking his fingers into the goo and greasepaint. He then nearly tore apart every cushion and chair covering. He checked the dresses, the costumes and the two black velvet robes that hung on hooks. Nothing.

Buddy took off every drapery rod, unscrewed the light fixtures, felt every inch of drapery hem. He unplugged every light, took off the mirror and sconces and removed every painting. Nothing.

Pedar crawled along the floor, checking each inch of molding. He tapped the walls, hoping to find a secret panel. He unscrewed all of the door hardware, checking inside every doorknob and lock. He then turned up very carpet, every portrait, every photograph and frame. He checked the top and the bottom of each door, and tapped the panels to see if there was a hidden piece that might be removable. Nothing.

The three men looked helplessly at one another. Nothing. Nothing at all. Or, rather there were many things: hairpins, dust balls, a dead mouse that had desiccated into near mummification, a rubber ball (with nothing inside), two ribbons, a tube of lip paint, two earrings, neither one matching the other, and a half-eaten cookie that had probably been resting under the dressing table since last year. But no necklace.

Angelique held her two hands up to her face, biting at her bottom lip, delighted and astonished that her dear friend had bamboozled New York's finest.

"She wins. Where is the damn thing?" Pedar wailed.

"We've looked *every*where!"

"Not exactly everywhere," Angelique taunted them gently. "She's won."

***

Later that night, four groups discussed the contest. Angelique told the story to Janine and Anna, who listened, openmouthed. "Where did she hide them?" Anna asked. Angelique shrugged her pretty shoulders.

"Maybe under a cushion?" Janine suggested.

"They looked and poked and felt every cushion," Angelique countered.

"Well, where, then?"

"I have no idea and the little minx won't tell me!" Angelique laughed in rueful admiration. "Perhaps we can try to re-create a problem like this when David comes back."

"He's really smart," Anna boasted, warming Angelique's heart. "He'll be able to solve the puzzle."

***

And over an inexpensive spaghetti dinner, Buddy and Janet tried to figure out where Buddy and the boys had gone wrong. "Where did she hide them?" He shook his head. "We looked *every*where!"

"Was there another necklace there?"

"Sure. There were several. We checked each one."

"Perhaps one was large and she slipped the pearls down inside." Janet tried to line up her meatballs, pretending that they were pearls.

Buddy reached over with his fork and stabbed one of her pearls. "Mmmm.," he enthused. "If there was a necklace that was large enough to hide the pearls, I didn't see it."

"Well, she hid them somewhere." Janet, new to the intricacies of winding spaghetti onto her fork, immersed herself in her dinner.

***

Millie Pedersen ladled out the goulash soup. "How could a little slip of a girl fool the best detectives in New York?"

Pedar shrugged. He couldn't figure out how she had bested them. He spooned up some of the soup and buttered a slice of rye bread. "She's a cutie, that one. Ya."

"Your boss, how is the wife-thing going?" Millie sat herself down, more interested in the problems of Anderson's marriage than the pearls. She had always disliked Helena von Vogel. She felt that Helena looked down upon her (which was absolutely true) and felt superior to her and to Pedar (which was also absolutely true).

"Boss got a long, thick envelope delivered to him yesterday. From some lawyers for her." He sniffed. "I think she is now living with some man already."

"In sin?" Millie sat forward, her soup forgotten. "How will she go about getting a divorce?"

"I don't know." Pedar felt somewhat disloyal gossiping about his beloved boss and his love life.

"He likes this young singer, you think?"

"I think he likes her, but she is a likeable young lady. I like her, too." Pedar took another slice of bread.

"You'd better not like her too much!" Millie waved her knife at him. Pedar reached over and kissed Millie's nose.

***

"How in blazes did you do that?" Anderson had taken Antonina to a small restaurant that he frequented. ""You ought to be in police work."

Antonina grinned. "Think of *The Purloined Letter*."

"The what?"

"The story. Edgar Allen Poe's best mystery story. You know, *The Purloined Letter.*"

"OK, I know the story, but what has that to do with this? Come, on. Tell me."

"I'm not going to tell you. All your life, you'll wonder, now and then, how the heck did she fool me?"[7] Antonina ate her steak with gusto. She was starving.

"What time is your mother coming tomorrow?" Anderson changed the subject. He couldn't help it; he was slightly miffed at being bested at his own game.

"They'll all...all of them...be here to inspect my apartment about three o'clock. I'll give them coffee and pastries and then, at about five, I'll leave for the theater. Mamma and *Nonna* Sabatino are sleeping with me tomorrow night." She swallowed a mouthful of creamed spinach. "Where will *you* be tomorrow night?"

"Not with you," his tone was glum. "I'll stop at my club...whatever..."

"You owe me a forfeit, Anderson. You have to make my wish come true." She pointed at him with her fork.

"And what will my forfeit be?"

"Something we both are going to enjoy." She grinned lasciviously.

---

[7] How *did* she fool them? If you think you know, please send a postcard to: Antonina's Secret, PO Box 243, Kittery Point, Maine 03905. All correct answers will receive a small prize.

Chapter Thirty

"When constabulary duty's to be done, to be done, a policeman's lot is not a happy one...happy one." W. S. Gilbert, The Pirates of Penzance

"Oh, the farm, Antonina, my pet. The farm!" Auntie Sabina rhapsodized. "You must see it! There are cows and chickens and goats and we will bring the donkeys up there with us."

"Everyone will miss you if you move." Antonina adored Uncle Enzo and Auntie Sabina. They had cared for her since she was a baby in Italy. They were both funny-looking, odd people with hearts of gold. She had told Anderson, "They are the happiest human beings I know, always smiling, always a kiss to each other." She had wanted to tell him that if she and he ever married, she'd want to be just like Sabina and Enzo...in love as much after twenty years as the day they set eyes upon one another. However, she prudently didn't tell him that. Not yet.

"Everyone misses *you* now that *you* have moved," Sabina winked at her. "You are still with us, even though you are a little bit farther away. It will be the same with me and Enzo and the boys."

"Have another chocolate, Mamma." Antonina handed the bon-bon dish to Francesca. "A lady named Susan makes them for the people who go to the opera. She was nice enough to send me a box of violet and caramel creams."

It was the first time that Antonina was entertaining at her new apartment. There were dozens of relatives and friends, mostly from Greenwich, although, Antonina had invited Angelique, her daughter and her companion, too.

Madam Joseph was in her element, reveling in being entertained not only by Antonina Sabatino, but also being charmed by the rest of her family. Francesca had brought several hampers of food...fresh loaves of bread, a rum-soaked cake and two of *Zia* Filomande's famous apricot brioches. She pressed a white box in Madam Joseph's hands. "This is just for you. A brioche and a dozen of my best pastries." Madam Joseph was now putty in the hands of any and all of the Sabatinos.

Mina regaled Madam Joseph with the story of Louise Lutton. "You have the power? My mother, God rest her soul, also had a power. Not like yours, but somewhat similar. She could find lost objects using a statue of Saint Anthony."

"Ah, such a power." Mina was always gracious.

"People came from all over our town for her help. Whether it was a lost cat, a lost piece of gold, a deed or important piece of paper, Mother could pray to Saint Anthony and he would tell her where the lost thing was." Mina shook her head in wonderment.

Zio Enzo entertained Anna with some of his conjuring tricks and the little girl was under his spell, ready to follow him to the ends of the earth.

"And you will be on one farm, and *Zia* Sabina…you must learn to talk Italian, of course…and I will be on the very next farm. We will visit one another every day. You can ride on my donkeys. They are very gentle and love little girls who feed them carrots and apples."

"I can come very day?"

"Every day. I promise. Cross my heart." Solemnly, Enzo made a sign. "And your Mamma, too. She can ride in the wagon."

"Mims, will you ride on a donkey or in a wagon?"

"I'll take the wagon," Angelique chuckled. "I think I'm too old for a donkey ride."

"And as for the farm that your Daddy will buy. You tell him to get in touch with me. I'll bring him to the farm with me, and he will be convinced to purchase it. You and I will be good friends and good neighbors." He winked at her again, his funny-shaped face aglow with happiness.

Anna paused for a moment. She didn't quite know what to say. "He…David isn't my Daddy," she explained. "He's a friend."

"Ah," said Enzo. "It is good to have a fine friend like David."

***

Antonia and Angelique left early to get to the opera in plenty of time to dress and prepare themselves. "You have a wonderful family." Angelique said. "My daughter wants to be adopted by all of you."

"Are you and David really going to buy the farm near *Zio* Enzo?"

"I told you, all my life I have always wanted some very simple things. A child to love, a man to love and a farm." She spread her well-manicured hands in front of her. "You think of me as a city woman, a fragile and rather pampered person, but underneath, there is dirt also growing in my veins. I love to dig and garden. I love to milk cows. I really *am* a country girl at heart."

"That's how *Zio* is. He can make a lavish garden in a teacup. He has the gift of growing." She laughed and bent to confide; "When I was growing up, my step-father, Carlo, was also a gardener. He worked only for the very wealthy and loved to grow prize roses. He was given thousands of dollars by his wealthy employers to grow the finest roses in all of Connecticut. He had imported seeds and cuttings, the best of soils, the most expensive fertilizers and all the help he needed. His roses were wonderful, magnificent, actually." She giggled. "But *Zio* Enzo, with only horse and mule manure and the little plot in the back yard of my mother's house, grew better roses than Carlo did.

Enzo brought his own roses to the big rose shows. They were the most beautiful roses in the shows and he beat Carlo out of the blue ribbons…every time."

"Carlo must have been furious."

"Beyond furious. I think he would have killed Enzo, if he thought he could." Her eyes looked inward. "As a matter of fact, I think he may have tried to kill *Zia* Sabina and her little boy…"

"What?"

"It's a long story. When we get some time to ourselves and you feel like listening, I'll tell you about him." She shivered. "He was not a good man and I was thrilled to find that he really wasn't my father, although he *is* the father of the twins and Johnny."

"How could your mother…she seems so delightful and yet practical…marry someone like Carlo?"

Antonina shrugged. "She was passionately in love. Love can do funny things, no?"

"It certainly can."

***

Once again, the Troy family took the train into New York to see *La Traviata*. Rachel grumbled all the way because her father had forbidden her to bring the dogs along. "No dogs. No dogs at the opera."

Rachel's lip stuck out. "That other lady brings *her* dog."

"Other people do many things. We Troys leave our animals at home when we go out to the opera. And that's final."

***

Concetta and baby Frank stayed home. Francesco kissed the tops of their heads and joined Urbano on the subway. He spent the entire trip regaling Urbano with stories of Frank's incredible early-childhood deeds. "He's a very intelligent baby, Urbano. He understands both Italian and English already." Urbano, the father of three, listened with grave courtesy, interjecting an amazed gasp as suitable intervals.

***

The opera house glittered and basked in the sharp night air, like a queen who was welcoming her loyal subjects. The patrons poured in, some by carriages pulled by teams of immaculately groomed horses, some driven in long, elegant limousines, some by cab and some on foot. All were anxious to hear the new sensation sing.

Anderson met Buddy at the stage door. Pedar had begged a night off. "Mollie wants to play mah-jongg at a neighbor's house."

Anderson was stunned to find that Buddy had splurged and was wearing a tuxedo instead of his usual business suit. "What is all this splendor, Bud?"

Buddy blushed. I thought, well…you said we'd be sitting in the box with the Baron and Baroness, and I thought…I'd try to look nice." He stuck his finger into the tight stand-up collar and tried to give himself a bit more breathing room. "These things look good, Boss, but they're damned uncomfortable."

"Whew! You look like Lord Manger himself." Anderson was complimentary. "Little Janet is going to faint with delight when she sees you." He stood Buddy in front of him and prowled around him, flicking imaginary pieces of lint away. Indeed, with his dark curly hair and engaging grin, Buddy was simply resplendent.

"I'm taking her out after for dinner. We're going to splurge at Delmonico's. I even made a reservation."

"I'll be there, too. I'll be with the Sabatino family." Buddy gave his boss a searching look.

"None of my business, Boss, but you seem to be with that group a lot."

"Yes, well..." Anderson was ruffled. "Yes. They are a fine family and they are assisting me with the investigation." Buddy's eyebrows told Anderson what he thought of this remark, but Buddy was intelligent enough to leave the touchy subject alone. He'd probably already said too much.

***

Backstage, the pandemonium gradually subsided into the pattern of a successful show's preparation mode. Subdued shouting, the smells of greasepaint and sweat, an occasional swear word, and the subtle aroma that seeped from the very walls of the Metropolitan Opera House itself permeated the air and added to the sense of expectation and excitement. The members of the cast went about, getting dressed and made-up, doing those things that they did to ward off bad luck, and wishing each other *"in boca lupo"*, *"merde"*, or *"break a leg."*

The orchestra gathered itself into the pit, and toots and trills of their tune-ups floated over the audience. Tommy, Mary, and Dean, together with Brooks looked forward to an evening of *oompah* music at the local beer hall afterward. Garvin and Alice Mary wanted nothing more than to go home and relax after the show. Patricia tried to spot Neil in the standing room area, but the people were milling and crowded, and she failed to see him anywhere.

She might have seen him had she looked towards one of the best boxes in the opera house. He was seated behind David, a glass of champagne in his hand and a look of amazement in his eyes. Barbara had spotted him in the lobby. "Neil! Oh, Mr., Odams! Here! Here! It's me...Barbara!" She excitedly introduced him to her David and mentioned that Neil had been in the standing room section for several years.

"My good man, you must spend at least one opera sitting down!" David, for all of his money and breeding, was horrified that this man stood...*actually stood up*...for the whole performance. "Come." Davis urged with great sincerity. "We have an extra chair and plenty of room. We'd be delighted to have you join us."

Anderson greeted Francesca, Simeon, Vittoria, Maria and Signor Fazzolini, and the rest of the crowd from Greenwich. He bowed low over the hand of Madam Joseph, who was using the ticket that Antonina had given her to join Antonina's family, and waggled his fingers at Gia and Lucia. As he stood, talking, he felt that he was being stared at. He raised his eyes to see Helena sitting in a box with Count Smirnoff. He smiled at her and tipped his head. She gave him a flat stare and the turned to her companion, putting her hand intimately on his arm. Anderson turned away as the houselights blinked their five minute warning.

The tiny door under the stage opened and Urbano came out to kiss his wife and greet his friends. "How is everything?" Anderson asked.

"Fine. Fine." Urbano looked upwards, toward the heavens, and made a Sign of the Cross. "My only small worry is that Orsini's stomach is giving him trouble again."

"Do you think he's ill, or is it just last minute nerves."

Urbano shrugged in his best Italian fashion. "He has always had gastric distress, especially before a performance. And remember, my friend, this is his next-to-the-last performance. Monday is his swan song and his 80th birthday celebration. Perhaps a man like the *Maestro* is unable to cope with never performing anymore."

"He's a legend." The lights blinked again and Urbano rushed backstage. Anderson waved goodbye and went to join Baron Wessel and the entourage in his parterre box.

As he entered the box, he was introduced to Neil. "Why I know your wife well," Anderson shook Neil's hand. "She's a brilliant pianist." Neil agreed and allowed David to pour him "the other half" of his glass of champagne. *If this was how the swells lived*, Neil thought, *I like it!* Barbara further honored Neil by letting him hold Teddy on his lap.

The lights dimmed and Arturo Calle stepped out from behind the gold curtain to greet his audience. They roared their applause. "Ladies and gentlemen, welcome to tonight's performance of *La Traviata,* an opera in three acts, written by the incomparable Giuseppe Verdi." The audience cheered their approval.

Calle waited until the applause died down and then continued. "Tonight, I have spoken with our newest star, Antonina Sabatino..." the crowd murmured its worry...was Sabatino not going to sing?... Calle's hands were out in supplication. "Have no worry, our Antonina will be singing Violetta tonight as planned..." Again, a huge burst of applause erupted. They had come to be entertained by Antonina and nothing else would do. "As I said, I have conferred with Miss Sabatino and with Beniamino Gigli..." the crowd again exploded...Sabatino *and* Gigli? What was coming?... "Yes, both of them." Arturo made a half-bow. "They have agreed to put on a once-in-a-lifetime performance here at the Metropolitan Opera House...wait...wait, let me finish before you applaud, and I know you will applaud once you hear…And you, my dear friends, are the first to hear about this. On Wednesday night, October 30th, we will present a night of operatic duets with Sabatino and Gigli singing all of your favorites!" The crowd went wild.

Such an event!

How can we be there?

Oh, joy!

Let's get our tickets right away!

"The evening will be a benefit gala, with all proceeds after expenses to go to the Verdi Home for Aged Opera Singers here in New York City." A huge burst of applause. "Tickets will be on sale in our box office tonight. We expect a sell-out, so, please, if you wish to join us in a week and a half, kindly get your tickets quickly so that you will not miss this exciting event." He bowed. "And now, on with the show!" He melted, as he always did, into the wall of gold.

The spotlight lit the center aisle. *Crash, Bam*, the *Maestro,* again dressed in spotless white, strode down to the podium. Tonight, he wore a cape of scarlet silk, and it billowed behind him like a bright storm cloud. Anderson watched him carefully. Orsini's face was calm. There didn't seem to be any sign of distress or illness. *Good.* Relaxing, Anderson leaned back, determined not to miss one note or gesture from his beloved.

The overture began and the crowd sat back, expectant…Teddy was transferred to the cushion on Barbara's lap and Neil sat back, hoping that all of his buddies way up in the standing room area were able to see him.

As the curtain opened, Barbara leaned over and whispered to David, "Everyone has forgotten poor Vivienne."

"The Queen is dead, long live the Queen," David replied.

"I hated her, but I still feel terrible that she was murdered. And to think, David, you were most likely one of the last people to talk with her before she was killed." Barbara propped Teddy up on the cushion so that he could see Antonina and the action on stage better. She murmured, "Teddy loves Antonia. He's so happy that she's singing tonight."

***

The performance was fantastic, one that was talked about for years to come. Antonina's interpretation of Violetta was a new benchmark. Her tenderness, her yearning, her desire to just be loved…she had the audience eating out of her hand. When she sang *"dite alla giovane si bella e pura"* (tell your daughter…she who is so beautiful and pure), the phrase, in her golden tones, seemed to float in the air and the audience understood Violetta's yearning to go back and live her own life differently…but, alas, that could never be…

Violetta's death scene was uncanny. *"Ah! I am too young to die!"* was sung with a fierce intensity that electrified every patron. As she gave her beloved the locket, sobbing could be herd from various parts of the audience. Her last gasp… *"e strano"*…was so emotional that it was nearly horrific. Her voice was unearthly as she tried to rise, as if seeing some vision of a new life, and then, a glaze came over her eyes as she stood for a moment, a living corpse, and then collapsed in death.

Anderson held tight to the arms of his chair. Had he let go, he would have rushed onto the stage and carried her off in his arms. His beloved!

The audience refused to stop applauding. They would not let her off the stage, screaming and stomping, crying and cheering. She was truly a star. Anderson had a moment of worry. Did Antonina belong to him or did she belong to the audience's adulation?

Chapter Thirty-One

"There is only one illness and one cure…" Franz Anton Mesmer, Aphorismes

Anderson spent the night alone at his home. He'd gone to gather some clothing, but found the apartment dark and empty. He checked the closets and dressers…Helena had removed all of her clothes and personal trinkets and so had the girls. No one was there anymore. He sighed, wistful for what might have been, but excited at what was to come.

He climbed the stairs. The housekeeper had stripped all of the beds, leaving only coverlets on. Anderson found an empty suitcase and gathered three bundles of clothing. He dusted off his hands and snapped the suitcase shut. He carried it downstairs and set it next to the front door.

He went to the kitchen and found some tea and a kettle. He boiled some water and made himself a huge cup of hot tea, carried it into the den and set it on the table next to the sofa. He plopped himself on the sofa and gazed around at the treasures and folderols that Helena had bought and collected throughout their empty years of marriage. What a waste. His head lolled back and he smiled, thinking of Antonina, her mother and grandmother, enjoying a ladies night together. *Wish I were a fly on the wall*, he thought. His eyes shut and he slept. The tea, untouched, cooled in the chilly night air of the empty house.

***

On Sunday morning, Francesca and Maria cooked a huge breakfast for Antonina and invited Madam Joseph upstairs to join in. "We are going to see the elephants at the zoo today. Then, we plan to have lunch in the park and catch a mid-afternoon train back to Greenwich. Would you care to join us at the zoo?"

Madam Joseph, filling herself full with a French toast made with the leftover apricot brioche, demurred. "I have a weekly card game with one of my beaus."

"A beau?" Maria asked. "Is it a serious romance?"

"It might be if I were a less contented woman." Madam Joseph blushed. "He was a good friend when Joseph was alive. His wife also died many years ago. We keep one another company, but I don't think I want to wash out any man's socks any more." The women giggled. "And may I ask about your beau?"

"My beau?" Maria pretended bewilderment.

"Yes, your faithful Alfonso. What a man! I would wash *his* socks if he asked!"

Maria blushed and Antonina busied herself clearing the dishes off the table, bending her ears backwards to hear what her grandmother was going to say.

"He is wonderful. I just don't know....we have such good times together. We like the same things, he's kind and funny and romantic. A woman could do worse..."Maria smiled. "He has asked me many times. I am still thinking about it."

From the kitchen, Antonina called out, "Don't wait too long, *Nonna.* He's too good to lose."

"Get away with you, child!"

***

The crying wail of an ambulance disturbed their lunch. Anderson had come to get the ladies and they had taken a taxi to the zoo. They ordered hot dogs from a street vendor and sat on a bench, watching the antics of a group of orangutans who climbed and scratched, swinging from limb to limb in a cage that pretended to be a corner of their jungle. Antonina purchased a packet of peanuts and she and Anderson wandered close to the cage, feeding themselves and passing a peanut to any orangutan who stretched a hand out through the bars.

"I was like that, caged up," Anderson mused.

"You are still quite an ape, you know," Antonina teased.

"You have set me free, my darling. I can now eat my bananas and swing from trees in freedom." He tossed a peanut into the air and caught it in his mouth. Antonina applauded, delighted in his skill. "I'm a happy monkey."

"She loves him fiercely," Maria observed.

"Vittoria tells me that his wife is living with another man and is going to divorce him."

"And then?"

"And then we will see. Will she become his wife, or will she remain an opera star?"

"Could she be both?"

Francesca shook her head. "I fear that it would really be impossible. The two of them...look at them!...They are so much in love...they cannot see the pitfalls."

"Can you speak with her? Advise her?"

"Mamma! Could you speak with me? Advise me when I was besotted with Carlo? No. I will not interfere. I will watch and answer her if she comes to me, but, other than that, I can only love her and pray that she will be happy all of her life."

"You are a good mother, Francesca."

"And *you* are a good mother, Mamma."

"Have some roasted chestnuts."

"Thank you. What is it about roasted chestnuts? They bring back such wonderful memories."

***

At Belleview Hospital, the wailing ambulance disgorged the doubled-up body of Massimo Orsini. A nurse ran to his side and guided his stretcher carefully into a cubicle. "Hurry, he's hemorrhaging! Get me some ether and call Doctor Blessington! Hurry!

***

Anderson and Antonina walked to the subway with Maria and Francesca. "Take care and have a safe trip home. Give everyone a hug from me." Antonina kissed her grandmother and mother. Anderson bent and kissed them both, too. They waved as the train chugged off.

"Alone, at last! I missed you like crazy last night. Somehow, having my mother next to me in bed was not the same! Let's go back to the apartment and catch up." She grabbed his hand and they began to run like truant children. At the corner, they stopped, both panting hard.

They crossed the street, holding hands. "I keep thinking of Vivienne," Antonina mused. "Someone, by killing her, gave me the biggest gift I could ever ask for. What do you think happened?"

Anderson shrugged, then stopped dead in his tracks. *"David!"* He cried aloud.

"David?"

"Yes...it has been sitting in the back of my brain...something that Barbara said last night. I heard her, but the opera was just starting and all I could think of was you...but, David!"

"What about David?" She tugged at his hand.

"She said that he...She being Barbara...said that David was probably the last person to see Vivienne alive! What did she *mean?*"

"You'll have to ask her," Antonina shrugged. 'Don't they live somewhere near here?"

"Yes. Over across the street. Let's go and see if they are at home." He pulled her along, nearly forgetting that she was attached to him. His mind was whirling. Could this be the break he was hoping for?

***

"No, you cannot get up!" The diminutive nurse pressed Massimo Orsini back onto the bed. "Doctor! He's trying to leave!"

Doctor Schlomo Blessington came into the cubicle. "Dear Sir, are you nuts?" he said. "You have a very serious problem. You're lucky to be alive. Stay still and let us help you," he pushed Orsini back onto the pillows. His expressive face, generally so lively, was ashen, his cheeks sunken in.

"I want to get home. I am fine now. Just fine. Let me up." Orsini tried to rise, but the tiny nurse was able to keep him pinned down. *What is wrong with me? I am like a kitten with no strength!*

"You cannot go anywhere. You have a serious problem, my dear man. Now relax and let us care for you." Doctor Blessington fussed with a hypodermic needle, swabbed Orsini's arm, and plunged the needle into his vein.

"I just have indigestion. I have it all the time. I need some soda crystals...have you any *Brisochi?*" He grunted and tried again to sit up. "They will make me feel better."

"Not this time, my dear man."

"I am *not* your dear man! I am Massimo Orsini. I conduct orchestras and I have a final concert tomorrow night at the Met. I refuse to lay down and play dead!"

"You will not be *playing* dead, if you don't lay still. Look at the blood you have coughed up! You *will* be dead, if you do not cooperate!"

"I don't care if I die, but I want to live for two more days! I must finish my career! What is wrong with me anyway?" His worry made him brusque.

Doctor Blessington touched Orsini's stomach with a delicate finger. Orsini swore and nearly leaped off the gurney. "*Santa Maria!*"

"Delicate there, yes?" He touched him again. "And here? Hmmm?"

Ready this time, Orsini merely winced and said, "Ow."

The nurse took a vial of blood from Orsini's arm. "Have it checked immediately and bring the results here yourself." He draped himself on the foot of the bed. "You are a brave man, no? You want the opinion?"

"Certainly. What is wrong? An ulcer, perhaps?" He had been dreading this. For months now, his stomach had gotten worse. Not mere indigestion, no. Perhaps an ulcer. He'd have to give up some wine and rich foods. Ah, well. He could deal with that.

"No, not an ulcer, I think. The test will confirm it, but, my dear Massimo Orsini, famous conductor, I think it is worse than that." His myopic eyes blinked from behind the thick glasses that he wore. "I think you have stomach cancer."

"*Cancer!*" Orsini's pale face went ashen. "*Nonsense!*"

"I fear not." A gleam of sympathy showed. "I think it is very serious and I think you are very sick."

"I cannot be sick until after the performance on Monday. Help me."

"I have heard of you. My wife is a fanatical opera follower. She tells me that you are a gift to the opera world." He stood back, biting his lip. "Monday, you say? You need until Monday to be on your feet?" He rubbed his hands together. "We will see what we can do."

***

"Oh, how wonderful to see you both!" Barbara greeted Anderson and Antonina. "Come in. We're having our second or maybe third cup of coffee and David is swearing at the crossword puzzle."

Seated at the table, Anderson plunged right in. "Barbara, at the opera last night, you said something...something like David had been the last person to see or to speak with Vivienne before she died..."

"Yes, he probably was, weren't you, darling?"

"Most likely," David reluctantly laid the newspaper down.

"When did you see her?"

"Hmmm. Let's see....when was it, my pet?"

"Calle came out before the performance...he said that du Lac was causing a rumpus or something like that, and he asked you, as an old friend, to go back and try to talk some sense into her...wasn't that how it happened, David?"

"Harrumph. Like that, yes."

"What then?" Anderson nearly jumped over the table.

"I went backstage, you know. I didn't really want to get into a fracas with her, but I was trying to be a good soldier. I trotted back...went to her room and she was putting on her make-up or some such primping."

"Was anyone else in the room?"

"No. Only our star." David's expressive eyebrows climbed. "What's all this about?"

"I had no idea that you'd seen her. Why didn't you mention it?"

"No one asked, dear boy."

Anderson groaned and pulled at his hair. "What did you say to her? What happened?"

"I told her the usual, you know...best foot forward...the whole show is depending on you...that sort of tommyrot. She's...she was a...what do you call it? A melagomaniac...loved only herself...she ate that sort of thing up like Bird's Custard. She was sulky, but I made her laugh. Reminded her of one time in Vienna when she was very drunk and a group of us went out to tango. She was in a decent mood when I left. She promised to be a good girl and not make any fuss. That sort of thing."

"She was alive when you left?'

"My good man! Of *course* she was alive! What do you think!" he sputtered his indignation.

"Did you kill her?"

"*Moi?* Oh, you are joshing around. Why would I kill her?"

"Because she was ruining the production."

David shrugged. "She loved the drama of it all. She would have been fine when she got on stage. She was getting a bit long in the tooth...her voice, you know, it wasn't the top anymore. But she would have given a magnificent performance. She was a trouper of the old school."

Anderson slumped. Here he had thought it might have been a breakthrough, but David was obviously not the killer. Only the man who had been there a few moments before the killer had been.

Antonina chimed in; "Did you see anyone go into her room as you were leaving?"

David shook his head regretfully. "No one, really, except for Massimo, of course."

"Massimo?" Orsini?" Anderson stood up. "You saw Massimo Orsini go into her *room?"*

"Quite. But it was Massimo, you know. Not some crazed maniac."

"But...but...he never said...he..."

"And then there was that other chap. He saw Massimo go in, too."

"What other chap?" Anderson nearly screamed.

"That stagehand man, the one who was killed later on."

Anderson sagged in his chair. "Tell me, slowly and clearly, just what you saw and did after you went out of her dressing room." He snapped his fingers at Barbara. "Can you find me a pen and a piece of paper?"

"Dear chap, of course I can. Let' see..." Anderson snatched the paper and pen from Barbara's hands and began to write feverishly. "I shut the door behind me and went down the corridor. I was at the corner...nearly around the corner...when the little cat came to me. He wound himself around my ankles. Cute little devil, he is...what's the cat's name, Barbs? Ah, yes, Figaro. I bent down to pet him and scratch him. They love to be scratched behind the ears, just like Teddy does." At the sound of his name, Teddy came bounding into the room. David bent and began to scratch the dog's ears. "Come to Daddy, Teddykins. See how he loves it?"

Anderson cleared his throat. "If we can get back to the story, please."

"Why naturally. As I said, I bent to pet the cat and I sort of looked under my arm, like this..." David stood up and pretended to pet a cat, His head was down and, with a little twist, he demonstrated how he could see what was behind him. He stood up. "I saw Massimo go into her room. Behind Massimo, was this other chap. He saw Massimo go in, too. Neither of them saw me, I don't believe, as I was sort of crouched over."

"What else? Did you stay and watch? Was there any noise?"

David scratched his head. "No, don't believe so. Massimo was wearing one of those big black capes. Nearly covered him from head to toe. He went in and the cat walked away. I walked away too."

"I'll be damned. *Massimo!"* Anderson slumped down. "Did he kill her?"

"I haven't the faintest," David eyed the crossword hungrily.

"But, you knew we were looking for a murderer! Why didn't you mention this?"

"As I said, my dear fellow, no one asked me."

***

Anderson called Pedar to meet him at Massimo Orsini's hotel. The concierge informed that Maestro Orsini had been taken to the hospital about two hours ago. "I hope the dear man is feeling better," the concierge worried. "He's had such a stomach ache for the past few days."

Anderson and Pedar went to the Bellevue Emergency area and went in. "Yes," the nurse on duty told them when they had shown her their identification cards and badges, "A Mister Orsini has been admitted." She pointed down the hallway.

"You have cornered me," Massimo lay flat, tubes snaking in and out of his body. His strong features were grey with fatigue. "You have found out my sins." He sighed from deep within. "It is too late for you and it is too late for me." He waved towards the machine that pumped liquid in and out of his system. "I am a dead man already. The good doctor who has already pronounced me dead has promised me that he will stuff enough good blood into me so that I can conduct tomorrow night and then no more. I will die in a few weeks, so what can you do to me that matters?" He made a futile motion with his hand, pretending to lead a phantom orchestra. "My music and my life are over, my dear policeman."

Doctor Blessington came roaring into the room. "What are you doing bothering my patient? Get out...*out, out, out!*"

"I'm afraid it isn't going to be the way you'd like. Your patient, I believe, murdered three people."

"What? It is obvious that you are delusional! This is Massimo Orsini...the famous conductor! Not some homicidal maniac, you fools!"

Massimo's expressive face drooped. "It is true, Doctor. Not only am I famous, but I am about to become infamous. I have to confess, for I am soon to meet my maker and I need all the help I can get. I did kill three people." He lay back on the bed, a shell of himself. Suddenly, however, he reared up. "But they all deserved to be killed! I did the world a great favor!"

Anderson asked that chairs be brought. A nurse lugged three chairs and they all sat down, circled around the man in the bed. Pedar, Anderson and the Doctor. Pedar took out a notebook and began to write.

"Tell me what happened?" Anderson asked. "From the beginning."

"Ah, the beginning...it goes back so many years. This world of opera. You live and breathe the drama and the pathos of the great stories and sometimes, your own life becomes a drama. We have always been adversaries, Vivienne du Lac and myself. She considered herself to be above the opera, and I was so egotistical that I couldn't bear the fact that she thought nothing of ruining a performance, a future singer's life, the audience...she only thought of herself and not the whole of the opera. If she was in a bad mood, she would walk out of a performance, leaving everyone to pick up her pieces. She was mean and venal and hurtful and she was getting old and losing her talents." He propped himself up and asked for another pillow. "So I can talk better to these gentlemen."

A nurse brought him the pillow and placed it under his head. She also brought him a cup of tea. "You should try to get liquids into you," the Doctor instructed him.

"I'd prefer a glass of wine." The doctor looked horrified. Massimo waved his hand in the air. "All right, I'll drink the tea." He sipped and his expressive face told them what he thought of drinking tea.

He coughed, held onto his stomach and continued his story: "So, one night, she was so angry at me that she walked off the stage. Made a fool of me and ruined the opera for the rest of the cast and for all the people who had saved and scrimped to come to see her sing. But did she care? Not at all. She had spit in my eye successfully and I never would forget it or forgive her. Had I known that she was going to be singing for my last set of performances, I never would have contracted to come here. I hated her and she hated me." He tried to shrug, but the effort cost him pain. He sipped at the tea and continued.

"I tried to overlook her tantrums. I tried to make the performance a good one, but I knew, because she told me, that she was going to make some kind of scene at *La Bohème's* opening night. I thought that perhaps I could beg her to be good for one night. To cooperate. I went to her dressing room. I had on one of the old opera capes so that I would not soil my evening clothes…a black velvet one that was hanging on the back of my door… and I carried my baton…the lovely one with the hidden stiletto in the top. I swear I had no premeditated plan to kill her. I only wanted to plead with her."

"And what happened?" Anderson prodded.

"She laughed at me. She had several drinks. She'd been breathing ether and she was wild and crazy. She told me that she would ruin me and the entire opera. And then she laughed and laughed again. She was seated at her mirror and her throat was white and long. I took the top off my baton. The blade was long and glittered in the lights. She didn't even notice, she was so enamored of her own reflection in the mirror. I went behind her and grabbed her by her hair. I yanked her head up and cut her long, white throat from side to side. I was surprised at how easy it was to cut her. The knife in the baton sliced her throat like a piece of cheese." There was a gasp from the doctor. Massimo looked over at him.

"It was easy, you know, and I felt nothing but gladness. But the blood, my dear Doctor. You must know what I say is true…there was so much blood. It came out like a red fountain, rose into the air and covered the walls and the floor and my cape. I backed away as she fell and her head flopped down. I knew she was dead. There was no going back. I felt a delicious warmth going through me. There! Now she wouldn't ruin my opera."

He sat up further and drained the teacup. "Ah, that was good. May I have another cup? Thank you. Now, where was I? Ah, yes. And all the time, her damned dog was barking and yapping. I should have killed the dog, too. But someone else did that for me later on. Ah, well. I took the cape off and pushed it under a chair. Underneath, I was spotless, except for one or two drops of blood on one of my cuffs. I tucked them underneath and then I was clean. I opened the door and left. I didn't think that anyone saw me, but at that moment, I didn't care. I had killed her and she was gone and I was glad." He wiggled into a more comfortable position. "Then, events started to happen that were unforeseen by me. The understudy broke her leg and this young child had to sing the part of Mimi. I wondered if I had made a big mistake. But, luck was with me and the child could sing like an angel. That was all good. Splendid, as a matter of fact."

He began to cough, groaning, as he held his hand over his tender midsection. The doctor leapt up. "Enough! He has to rest if there is to be any chance of him getting out of here for a day."

"I'm sorry, Doctor. This is a triple murder investigation. We have to speak with him."

Orsini waved his hands in the air. "I must tell you. It is getting late for me and I must confess to you and then to a priest. I have sinned grievously and I am worried about my afterlife."

"Take your time. We will get you a priest, if you want. Now, please continue. You killed Vivienne and you went away. Then what happened?"

"I gave the best performance of my career. This young angel…this orchestra…this cast of performers. Without that bitch's evil machinations, we were all in harmony and presented the audience with an opera that will never be forgotten. This is what my entire life is about!" He reached out and drank some tea. "I had no remorse at all. I was triumphant both in my conducting and in my mind and spirit. She was an evil woman and a bad influence on the world of opera. I am delighted that I killed her." He wiped his mouth. "I then forgot all about her and all that she had poisoned with her touch. I was a happy man."

"And then?"

"And then that odious man…I don't even remember his name…he sent me a piece of paper, a dirty, filthy piece of paper. He said he had seen me and knew that I cut her throat. He said that he wanted a one-time payment of ten thousand dollars and he would keep his mouth closed. Ten thousand dollars! Ha! Did he think I was a *bambino* in my basket? Did he think that I'd believe that he would keep a promise? A man like that? Ha! We set up a meeting at the back of the stage. I was to bring the money and he would give me his word. I hid myself beforehand in the folds of the drapery. I waited for him to come, the little worm. I wasn't about to pay him or pay anyone. I will pay for this with God, but not to any man. He stood there, after most of the crew had gone, waiting for me. I picked up one of the discarded sandbags…there was a pile of them on the floor… and hit him hard over the head. He dropped like a stone, falling on his face. I drooped the bag back, dusted off my hands and left the building. I understand that he was found sometime later."

He moved restlessly in the bed. "I now felt safe, but I was still wrong." He looked up at Anderson. "It never stops, does it? When you kill some-one...it never stops."

"Sometimes. There is a chain that follows actions such as murder. When evil is done...when one man takes another man's life, it sets something else in motion. Something that is beyond our understanding. Murder, itself becomes a living thing. It changes us and takes on a life of its own."

"I discovered that. I thought I had killed and gotten rid of my problem, and then, another problem came, and then another....The murder part, the kill-ing, that was easy. I just hit him hard. I had no more uneasiness than if I'd killed a rat or an insect. But I was again seen."

"By Crespi?"

"Yes. Like some sort of night creature, he was hiding himself in the dark crevasse of the opera house. He saw me kill Rattner...that was the man's name. Rattner, like the rodent that he was."

"And then?" Out of the corner of his eye, Anderson saw Pedar shake his head. He thought of the old writers and philosophers...they understood evil back then... Who had said it? Shakespeare? Chaucer? *Murder will out.* Mur-der will scream and cry and make itself known. *Murder will out.*

"Crespi sent me a note, just like Rattner. A crude, misspelled missive. He told me to come backstage the next night, when all was quiet. I came. I was ready to kill once more. I had a knife in my pocket." Orsini sighed. "I am damned. I have sinned, but by Christ! They all deserved to die!" He tried to sit up, but began to cough, bright blood and sputum. The doctor jumped up and waved his arms. The little nurse ran to the bed and bathed Orsini's mouth and chin, cleaning him. Orsini waved her off.

"I have to speak. I must!" He pushed the doctor away and glared at him. "Let me speak!" Defeated, Doctor Blessington sat down, glaring and impo-tent.

Orsini covered his eyes and then lay back. "He was back up above me...in the rafters again." His voice was weak and Anderson and edar leaned close to hear his words. "He...that animal... made a inhuman sound...like some beast...I looked up. He was hiding up in the rafters, like a bat...a creature of darkness...He began to laugh and told me that he wanted money, too. He swung himself down, like a monkey. I panicked. Had I killed two people to be threatened by this creature? I saw the box of odds and ends that Forsythe Wicks had left on the floor. The wires were tangled on top. As Crespi climbed down, his attention was not on my movements. After all, what had he to fear from me, he thought, an old man? He jumped the last few feet and bent at the knees, recovering his balance. He had a heavy satchel in his hand and it made him careless. Before he could stand up, I whipped the wire around him and pulled tight. He tried to struggle. The little man was strong and agile, but I held on tight. My desperation made me as a madman. I just kept pulling and twisting and he finally succumbed. I knew he was dead because his vitals voided. The smell was horrible. His face, never pretty, was distorted, with his tongue purple and swollen and his eyes popped from their sockets. It was a disgusting death and I should be ashamed, but I am not."

"And?"

"The rest? Hell, must you have every detail? Yes? Well, I took the satchel and upended it onto a cloth. All of Vivienne's jewels were heaped there, rings and brooches and necklaces. There were many pieces of gold. I didn't want any of it!" Orsini's shaky voice held misplaced pride.

"I gathered it all up, although I understand that I missed one earring." Anderson nodded. "I put them all into the large *epergne* that sits on the mantelpiece in Act One of *La Traviata*. Perhaps the jewels can be sold to fund the home for old opera singers. The treasure is tainted. I would not touch it." His profile, against the stark whiteness of the pillows, showed his disdain.

"And that is all?"

"Isn't that enough? The two sheep killed after the lamb. What is the difference if I killed only du Lac or also the others? It doesn't matter any more. Now leave me, please." He closed his eyes, utterly exhausted.

"It doesn't go like that, *Maestro*. We'll have to arrest you and take you to prison. You'll most likely hang for these murders."

"Ha!" Orsini's eyes sprang open, glaring. "I will be dead in a week, isn't that right, my good Doctor?"

"Most likely. No more than two or three weeks at the best. I have the reports back from your testing. You are riddled with cancer." He turned to Anderson. "The cancer will rob you of the justice of a trial and imprisonment or worse. But justice will be done, nonetheless." He shrugged, a man used to death.

"A stricter justice than we mortals can mete out." Anderson sighed. "For today, you must stay here at the hospital. I will have a guard posted while I speak with my superiors about the case." He stood up and Pedar followed suit.

"And tomorrow night's performance? I want to finish my life with *La Traviata.*"

Anderson looked thoughtful. "I will see what can be done. This is strictly against everything I stand for, but....let me see what can be done."

Chapter Thirty-Two

*"Your eyes shall be opened, and ye shall be as gods,
knowing good and evil..." The Holy Bible, Genesis*

"You want me to *what?*" The Commissioner's eyes bulged. "Let a man who killed three people conduct an *opera?* Are you mad?"

"Yes, probably. Ever since I have come into contact with the opera, I have discovered that I get more and more mad. Everyone concerned with the opera is crazy, so why not me?" Anderson muttered. "What can he do? Escape? Pah! He is a dead man standing. He has only a few days to live. In fact, I'm not quite sure, nor is the doctor, that he can even be well enough to conduct for three hours. 'He might bleed to death right there on the podium', was how the doctor put it. What do you think, Sir? Can we do this without harm to ourselves?"

"This is a conundrum, Anderson. What shall I say?" The Commissioner stood up and began to pace back and forth. "On the one hand, we have a confessed murderer. On the other, a man...a legend in his field... who asks for a few hours of mercy."

"We will have him guarded at every moment. He's in no condition to flee, nor to do much else but see if he can get through the performance. They are holding a birthday celebration honoring him afterwards, but I think he'll be too ill to attend."

"Do we have a bonafide confession, signed and airtight?"

"We do."

"My wife has tickets for this affair." The Commissioner sat down and began to fiddle with a cigar. "If she knew that I held Orsini's fate in my hand, she'd beg to hear him conduct just one more time." He waggled his head from side to side. "What can be the hurt? We can charge him right after the performance and take him to the prison hospital. Ah! The newspapers will have a field day with this!"

"But we will have solved the crimes. He will be in captivity for the balance of his life, but he'll never live long enough to be tried. Never. I think we should do it."

"You and I, Anderson, we are now making a solemn pact to make this decision and fool the public as to what we are doing. It is against all regulations." He stood up and crushed out his cigar. "Let's do it!"

***

It was a night of operatic triumph. Orsini was brilliant. The music soared, perfectly blending the orchestration and the voices into one of the most memorable performances in history. All who attended felt that they had participated in the finest performance ever heard and seen.

Orsini stood, his head thrown back and his eyes closed, standing tall amidst the waves and waves of adulation that flowed over him. At last, with a sigh, he addressed the audience.

"Thank you all for a lifetime of listening to opera. For many complex reasons, I will never conduct again. I am weary and will not be attending the birthday celebration here." The crowd groaned and complained. "No, no, my dear friends and colleagues. I am saying goodbye here and now. I hope, in the very near future, all of you have some pity and compassion for me and my deeds. I bless all of you, my musicians, the cast, the staff and workers of the Met, and most of all, you, my audience. Farewell and may God bless all of you."

With that, he bowed, and assisted by Buddy Manger's strong arm, walked back up the aisle, assaulted by good wishes and applause all the way to the doorway. He looked back just once and then disappeared.

The party was a great one. There were many speeches and declarations lauding Massimo Orsini, his talent and his contribution to opera. Only Anderson's men, Urbano, Calle and Antonina knew the bombshell that would hit the newspapers the next day.

.....

Chapter Thirty-Three

One can relish the varied idiocy of human action during a panic to the full,
for, while it is a time of great tragedy, nothing is being lost but money."
John Kenneth Galbraith, The Great Crash

The panic really began on Thursday, October 24th, 1929, when nearly thirteen million shares changed hands on the New York Stock Exchange. There was a torrent of sell orders. There was no way that the ticker tape could handle such a flood and selling issues were held up for hours as the machines tried in vain to keep up.

Crowds of worried investors began to gather in front of the Exchange, hoping to obtain the latest news. The police were called to keep order as men pushed and shoved, trying to learn if they were completely wiped out of money or if there was some chance that the market would rally and they would once again be rich.

After noontime, the market seemed to make a comeback and many of the better known companies thought that the worst was over. But by the end of the day, the New York Stock Exchange had lost more than four billion dollars. Clerks and managers worked all night to clear all of the transactions, and the Stock Exchange felt a sigh of relief. They thought that the storm had passed.

President Herbert Hoover, trying to restore sanity and confidence, told his people that "the fundamental business of the country, that is, production and distribution of commodities is on a sound and prosperous basis."[8] Many felt that his words were too little and too late.

On Friday and Saturday, some relief came to investors. The two days gave them some time to plan their strategy for the upcoming week. Everyone conceded that this week would be a difficult and crucial one. Many tried to keep selling, but there were those who thought this was the time to pick up bargains, and those investors shoveled money into shares of railroads, steel mills and other once-lucrative stocks.

On Monday, October 28th, more than nine million shares were traded, but, unlike the previous Thursday, there was no cushion left...no recovery possible...to offset the enormous losses.

---

[8] The Crash and Its Aftermath, A History of Security Markets in the United States, Barry A. Wigmore

On Tuesday, October 29th, the market came crashing to near death-throes. In the first few hours, stock prices fell so dramatically and so fast, that all of the gains of the previous year were wiped out. Frantic stockbrokers tried to call in the margins, panic-stricken investors…doctors, lawyers and the man on the street…tried to liquidate their stocks. This hysteria caused even further pressure on the dying market.

At the close of the New York Stock Exchange on Black Tuesday, 16 million 383 thousand, 700 shares were sold. That number translated, on the New York Exchange alone, to more than a ten billion dollar loss. Ten billion dollars was exactly twice the total amount of currency in the entire country at that time. The market had died.

Many bankers and speculators were ruined permanently. They became bankrupt overnight, forced to sell their belongings and their homes to meet their debts. Many were not able to come up with the money to cover their losses. Some of these people, faced with shame and despair, actually jumped from buildings or shot themselves, feeling that death was preferable to ruination.

The reverberations following the crash echoed for many years, setting off the end of an era. The values and mores of the Nineteenth century crumbled, and the heroes of the era with them. Financial speculators, who had long been revered for their rugged optimism and financial acumen, were now held up as masters of corruption and greed. Overcome with despair, many Americans reluctantly discarded their deeply held beliefs in self-reliance, and with shame, turned to the federal government for help. The world of America changed.

In the aftermath, economists and historians tried to explain this disaster. When the stock market crashed, individuals tried to find a scapegoat, but John Kenneth Galbraith found:

"No one was responsible for the great Wall Street crash. No one engineered the speculation that preceded it. Both were the product of the free choice and decisions of hundreds of thousands of individuals. The latter were not led to the slaughter. They were impelled by the seminal lunacy which has always seized people who are seized in turn with the notion that they can become very rich."[9]

***

The ray of brightness that the performance at the opera on Wednesday gave to the people of New York cannot be minimized. Reeling from the blow of financial defeat, the concert gave people a moment of pleasure and delight. The voices of Gigli and Sabatino, singing the greatest love duets, did more to gladden hearts than did all of the specious discussions of sputtering politicians, who, as always, were only trying to save or advance their own hides.

---

[9] John Kenneth Galbraith, The Great Crash 1929

Had the public known in advance that they were going to be poorer on Black Tuesday, the concert might have been a financial disaster. But, as tickets were coveted and fought-over, the show was completely sold out days before the Crash.

"Thank goodness, Myra, for this concert." Mrs. Vanderhoof exclaimed. "This was a bit of fun in a gloomy week!" As Mrs. Vanderhoof's huge personal fortune had barely been nicked, she was entitled to her opinion.

And as for the people involved within, the Troys and the Odams, Anderson and the Wessels...those who had sold their holdings a few weeks ago, they secretly reveled in their good fortune, quietly gleeful that they had the sense to get out while the going was good...or even excellent.

And David della Cuore, returning to America after his wife's funeral, was cheered by the fact that the bank that had recently decided that they no longer needed his ability, had suffered great financial losses, while he, selling a month ago at a great profit, was sitting pretty, able easily to purchase a farm for Angelique and live comfortably for the rest of their lives on his new, safely invested fortune.

***

On Friday, November 2nd, 1929, the pervading cancer that was consuming Massimo Orsini's body, bloomed into his death. He died at the Prison Hospital, New York City, and saved the City of Manhattan the expense of a trial and a hanging.

The entire opera world, still agog at the incredible story that Orsini had nearly beheaded Vivienne du Lac, not to mention killing two others, mourned his death. In death, as in life, Orsini was a legend.

Death whisked Orsini's soul to the Area of Judgment. He wondered what God was going to do with this matter, a perplexing and unusual one.

God, Himself, had a difficult time. He greatly admired Orsini and his talents, but, after all, the Ten Commandments were the Ten Commandments.

Chapter Thirty-Four

"Sleep, sleep, beauty bright, Dreaming o'er the joys of night. Sleep, sleep, in thy sleep, Little sorrows sit and weep." William Blake, A Cradle Song

May, 1930

Boston, Massachusetts. It was in the middle of Act One, *Turandot*, when Antonina felt faint. She was singing the role of Liù, the little slave girl who is in love with Calef, the son of the King of Tartery. She began her plaintive aria: *Signor, ascolta!* A wave of nausea nearly made her stop singing. Only her rigorous training saw her voice through the pain and biliousness.

"Antonina!" Angelique, who was singing the title role of the Ice Princess, Turandot, grabbed her as soon as the curtain call was over. "Are you ill?"

Antonina gulped a glass of cold water and then gently blotted her mouth, careful not to disturb the make-up that turned her face into the face of a Chinese peasant. "I'm better now. Gee whiz, I felt so sick there for a moment." She reached for one of the chairs back stage and sat, fanning her face. "Is it hot in here, or is it me?"

Angelique, always an astute woman, scrutinized her friend and colleague in a new light. "I think it may be you, my little goose."

"Me?" Antonina laughed. "I'm never sick, darling Angel. It was just a passing thing."

"Hmmm, perhaps something that is passing through for nine months or so." Angelique saw the surprise and then delight that suffused Antonina's face.

"Nine months? Nine *months?* Do you think…? Oh! Oh, sweet joy." Her painted mouth was open in stupefaction. She did some mental arithmetic, counting back. "Sweet mother of Christ!" She leaped up, twirling around. "Oh, joy!" And then a doubt crept in. "Do you think he'll be happy?" Her voice rose up to a wail. "Will he want…?"

"He's going to be crazy with happiness. Trust me."

***

In the few months since the start of the Metropolitan Opera's 1929-1930 season, Angelique and Antonina had grown to be great friends, trusting one another, helping one another, reveling in their shared joys and performances.

After a two-month wait, David della Cuore and Angelique Orloff had married quietly, with only Anna and Janine attending the bride, and Antonina and Anderson providing an intimate supper afterwards to celebrate. David and Angelique had purchased the farm in Clinton Corners, the farm that lay adjacent to the farm of Enzo and Sabina Uccelli. Angelique sold her expensive apartment house and now rented one of Madam Joseph's second floor apartments.

Anderson and Antonina lived quietly together on the top floor apartment.

Anderson's wife had filed for divorce, and although Anderson had begged her to marry him the moment the divorce was decreed, Antonina staved off a permanent decision. "When you are free, we'll make a decision. I love you so much, Anderson. We'll be so happy together."

And now, the decision seemed to be made for her. "Are you sure you are happy about the baby?"

"I'm the happiest man alive. I'll be a different kind of father than I was before. Our house will be filled with love and laughter and joy. I have yearned for a life like that, my sweet." He bent and nuzzled her stomach. "I can't believe that our child is growing in there! You don't look pregnant. You look as if you are still a child yourself."

"I'm not going to tell anyone yet." Antonina crossed her hands over her stomach. "Not my mother nor anyone. I daren't even go to Greenwich."

"Why?"

"Because my Auntie Mina will see me and know that I am having a baby. Remember how she was? She knows…she'll know right away and I want to hug this happiness for a few more weeks to myself and to you. It's our secret."

"Angelique knows." Anderson wanted to shout it to the world.

"She is trustworthy. She'll tell David, but that's as far as she will talk." Her face grew distant. "When will he be born?"

"He?…How do you know it's a boy?" He teased her. You may be holding a tiny little Antonina in there."

"No. I have some powers, too. It is a boy." She counted on her fingers. "He'll be born in September. Clever little one, he is already. I can take a few months off in the slow season and be ready to get back to work in October."

"Are you sure you'll want to go back to work, darling? Maybe you'll want to stay at home with the baby." Anderson yearned for a son. A little superstitious at the happiness he'd found, he was afraid to call the baby a boy yet.

"Oh, no, Anderson. I'll find a good nurse and nanny and I can sing and still care for him. I'll stay in New York, however. I'll give up the travel."

"Perhaps you should think of taking it easy now. How are you going to manage your…your…you know…" He sketched a huge belly with his hands. "It might be hard to be a starving heroine when your stomach balloons out on stage."

"Silly. I'm not even showing. I'll finish up in Boston in two weeks and then two weeks in Philadelphia. Maybe by that time, I can stop for a few months."

"We'll get married as soon as the divorce decree is delivered."

"Of course, Anderson. The next day."

***

"It's not that I don't want to get married, Angelique. I do. I love Anderson more than I love singing. But I feel as if I am forcing him into marriage because of the baby. Is that silly?"

"This is going to be difficult for you, my little goose. He doesn't seem too anxious to have you work."

"No, he'd really like me to be at home." She sighed. "Can I do it all, dear one? Can I be a good wife and mother and a *diva* at the same time?"

"If that is your heart's desire, it will all work out." Angelique sat down and pushed off her shoes. "Ooofa! My feet hurt. I thought I could keep going, singing small parts, but I think David also wants more of me at home. He gets grumpy when I'm away for a week or more. And Anna…she needs more and more of my attention. It isn't easy to be a wife and mother and a singing sensation, let me tell you!"

"Are you thinking of retiring?"

"Maybe. I'm getting older and I'm getting more and more tired of the stress and the travel. I may pick two roles a year at the Met. Stop traveling and cut down drastically on how much I sing."

"I want it all, Angelique. Every bit of it all!"

"As they say on stage, *'in boca lupo'*, my pet. *In boca lupo.*"

***

As the weeks passed, Antonina's belly grew. The season was over, and thus, she was able to hide her condition from Arturo Calle and the people at the theater. It was more and more difficult to stave off her mother's visits. 'Why don't you want her to know? She's your mother, for goodness' sake! She'll be delighted!" Anderson didn't understand this suddenly broody woman. "I almost feel as if you're ashamed of your pregnancy."

Stung by this sensible criticism, she whirled at him. "I'm not ashamed! I love holding your baby!"

"Then why the secrecy?" Anderson was puzzled. "Let's go to Greenwich for the picnic that your mother is begging you to come to and make our announcement. What do you say, darling?"

Antonina shrugged. "I suppose we'll have to tell them one of these days, otherwise, they'll wonder who the new child I am carrying is!" She laughed and Anderson was delighted to welcome back the sunny woman that he knew so well. "We'll go on Sunday."

***

"How about a walk in the park and an ice-cream at the zoo?" Anderson had come home from a stressful day at work. There had been a robbery at the Bowery Bank three days ago. Not only had the robbers gotten away with a huge sum of money, but they had killed three customers and a security guard. Anderson and his men had been working around the clock to try to get a lead on the perpetrators.

"I'd love nothing better. I'm so hot and sticky." She waved her arms in a windmill motion. "This carrying of babies gets a girl very warm. My body isn't my own any more. I share it with a heavy, squirmy friend." He bent to kiss her and felt the heaviness of her breasts against his chest. Stirred, he wondered if they might make love. Maybe not. He didn't want to take any chances. They'd go out and if the night cooled off and they were careful and somewhat re-strained...perhaps. With that thought to buoy him, he took her hand in his.

"And we have to find a larger place to live. I don't want to live in my old house. I'm going to sell it and split the proceeds with Helena. Let's go looking for a new house next week. They have some beautiful new brownstones along the south end of Central Park."

"That would be fun. Imagine me, a brownstone owner! Me? Who could believe it?"

They crossed the street and entered the leafy bower of the carriage road into Central park, heading toward the zoo and the ice cream stand. As they passed a clump of rhododendrons, a man stepped out and grabbed Antonina by the arm, pulling her away from Anderson. *"What?"* Antonina cried.

Anderson, a few steps ahead of her, whirled. The man held a knife to Antonina's throat. "Hello, Chief von Vogel. It's been a long time coming."

"Hamilton Purcell!" The years had not been kind to him. His pallor was grey and his suit hung off his rangy frame. "How...?"

Antonina began to struggle, "Stop wiggling, honey. I'll slice your throat without even looking. Tell her, von Vogel. Tell her what I do to little girls who annoy me."

"Stay still, Antonina. Don't move. Let her go, Purcell. Your business is with me, not her." Anderson's heart was hammering.

"While I was in prison, I hated you every day. Every day I planned how I'd get even, von Vogel. At first, I thought I'd kill you, but now, I see that wouldn't be enough. I'm gonna slice you to ribbons, but let you stay alive. It's your sweetie here who is going to die. That would be the best revenge, don't you think so?" He pressed the blade against Antonina's throat. She choked and held her head rigid. A tiny line of red appeared as the knife caressed her. She gasped and Purcell smiled.

"Purcell! Let her go! Take me...she's not a part of any of this." Anderson tried to move closer. He heard a soft whimper from his beloved. Her eyes moved frantically.

"You know me...I just love to cut people..." Purcell's unearthly chuckle made Anderson's heart stop beating. *He'd kill her. He'd kill her for sure. Her and their baby.* He inched closer.

"Stop moving!" Purcell moved the knife away from Antonina's throat and made a menacing gesture towards Anderson.

Now! Anderson launched himself through the air, his hands held out like claws. Antonina pushed at her assailant at the same moment. She twisted her ungainly body and fell to the ground.

Anderson slammed against Purcell, shoving him off his feet and falling on top of him. Antonina screamed. Three men, walking their dogs, heard her. They ran toward the scene of the altercation.

"Hey! Stop this!"

"Police! Help! *Police!*"

Purcell scrambled to his feet and began to run. His hands were empty. Two of the men tackled him, dragging him to the ground. Another passer by, seeing trouble, ran to help. He went first to Antonina and helped her to her feet.

"Are you hurt, Ma'am?"

"No. No..." She turned and bent to help Anderson and stopped. "Oh my God! Anderson!" she screamed. "Oh, my *God!*"

Chapter Thirty-Five

"Do you hear the children weeping, O my brothers, Ere the sorrow comes with years..." Elizabeth Barret Browning, The Cry of the Children.

Death took Anderson's soul to Heaven. What a waste, Death mused. It is my job to do what I have to do, but I am sad about this one.

***

She spent the rest of the summer on the farm with Enzo, Sabina and the animals. Her weeping was done at night. In the day-time, she appeared dazed and confused. Francesca spent time with her and so did *Nonna* Sabatino. She didn't want anyone else to know that she was going to deliver a baby. Because they loved her and pitied her beyond reason, they did as she asked.

At the beginning of September, Auntie Mina came to see her. "You are nearly ready, my sweet child. I'm going to stay with you for the next few days. The baby will be born tomorrow or the next day. He'll be strong and healthy. This much I can promise you."

"What shall I do, Auntie Mina? I can't bear this."

"You are a strong woman, Antonina. You can bear what you have to bear. God will help you."

"I'm not too sure about God. Where was He when I needed Him?"

Mina shrugged. "Who are we to question God? Even when things seem to go wrong, He has a pattern for all of us." She rubbed Antonina's back.

"Thank you. I'll try to be good."

"You *are* good. Now tell me, what are you going to do afterward?"

"You understand, don't you?" Mina nodded. "I can't...I can't keep this baby. It needs a better mother than I can be. I only want to sing. To perform. There will be no room for this child in my life. I'm bad, Auntie Mina. Devoid of feelings. That's why God made me lose Anderson." Her face was woebegone.

"No. You're wrong. Not everyone has maternal feelings. Not everyone wants to be a wife. I think you always had doubts about being Anderson's wife, just as you had doubts about being Peter's wife. I think you have been created to bring pleasure to people. Your voice is your gift to them and to the world." Antonina turned to Mina and began to cry. "Weep, darling. The tears are good for you. Would you like to hear my idea?"

Antonina sniffed and nodded, her face red and blotchy.

"Your Cousin Marco and his wife Mary are starving for a child of their own. They have been married for six years, and I know that she is barren. Can you find it in your heart to give them a son?"

"What would Mamma think of me? She'd think I was a monster!"

"No. She would understand and pray for your happiness and peace of mind. You have been through a terrible ordeal. You are forgiven."

"I could see him, couldn't I?"

"You would be his beloved cousin. He would be happy and secure, well-loved and well-brought up. Marco and Mary are good people and they yearn for a child to hold. You do not."

"You are blunt, Auntie Mina."

"Sometimes, I have to be. I am a woman who knows babies. I care for them and bring them into this world, and often…you might be surprised at how often…I move them to where they will grow best."

"Can I name him?" Her voice was wistful.

"Of course. It would be a good idea." Mina patted Antonina's shoulder.

"I want him to be called Anton."

"Anton." Mina smiled. "A good name. It honors several people who should be honored. He will be called Anton Sabatino. You will be proud of him."

"Oh, Mina! I pray I am doing the right thing! Am I being selfish? Am I putting my career too far ahead of anything else?"

"You are doing what you think is right. For Anton and for yourself. In the end, all will be well." She soothed the feverish young girl and later that night, delivered her of a nine pound son.

Chapter Thirty-Six

"We poets are (upon a poet's word), Of all mankind the creatures most absurd: The season when to come and when to go, To sing, or cease to sing, we never know." Alexander Pope, Epistle

October, 1930

The new, glittering chandelier was extinguished. The house lights dimmed. Arturo Calle stepped out from behind the brand new golden curtain and stood in the spotlight. When the applause died down, he spoke: "Ladies and gentlemen, welcome to opening night at the Metropolitan Opera House. Tonight, we are presenting *Tosca,* an opera in three acts written by Giacomo Puccini. We salute our esteemed conductor, *Maestro* Eugene Dimitroff!" The crowd whistled and applauded. Dimitroff had been hired from The Royal Opera House. When the applause died down, Calle continued. "Thank you, my friends. The title role of Tosca will be sung by our own Antonina Sabatino."

The audience roared their approval, stamping and whistling. Ah, how they loved Sabatino. Calle waited until the din had subsided. "Thank you for your support, as always. And now, ladies and gentlemen, *Tosca!"*

***

She stood backstage, always ready ahead of time. She wore a magnificent gown of rose, and the wig on her head showed off the beauty of her slender neck. You'd have to look very closely to see the thin scar that marred her neck's perfection.

It was her cue. She strode onto the stage to confront her lover. Everyone in the audience stood up, clapping and cheering. Shouts of *Brava! Brava!* echoed throughout the theater. Antonina paused, silhouetted against the backdrop of the Attavani Chapel, waiting for the applause to die down. She was incandescent, even before she opened her mouth to sing. She truly was their *diva.*

"Mario!" she called, her voice throbbing. She was no longer Antonina Sabatino, but Flora Tosca, the great diva, as passionate in love as in her art.

In their seats, Mina, Maria and Francesca wept.

In their box, David della Cuore, Angelique and her daughter, Anna, watched with affection. "She's just wonderful, Mims. She's beautiful, she has great talent…she has everything anyone could want."

David took Angelique's hand. "Almost everything. Almost."

Chapter Thirty-Seven

"The future can be promised to no one..." Pierre Trudeau in 1968

October, 1934

*I*n 1932, Amelia Earhart became the first woman to fly solo over the Atlantic Ocean, Newfoundland to Londonderry, Ireland, in thirteen and a half hours. In 1934, Carey Marvel Mabley also accomplished this feat in thirteen hours, ten minutes.

***

Neil and Patricia Odams left New York City to move to a small fishing village – Kittery Point, Maine. Patricia taught piano, and Neil purchased a new working lobster boat, which he named "The Captain and Patty". When not lobstering, the Odams use the boat to ferry passengers to and from New Hampshire to Maine.

***

Marco and Mary Sabatino also moved to Kittery Point, Maine together with their 3-year old adopted son, Anton. Marco, who was a gardener by trade, opened a plant nursery in Kittery Point. Mary was content to stay at home and care for her young son.

***

Henry Torrence, from Newark, New Jersey, was appointed Chief of Police for the Borough of Manhattan, New York. He was heartily despised by all who knew him and worked for him and after two years, was convicted of fraud. After Torrence's conviction, Pedar Pedersen was appointed Chief of Police.

***

Buddy Manger and Janet Connolly were wed in 1931. Buddy was also promoted to Detective First Class. Janet and he have three children, Teresa, Sarah and Joseph.

***

Francesco DeSarro is still employed at The Metropolitan Opera House. He and Concetta gave birth to a second American baby, Joan, in 1932.

***

Charlie Presto married Mary Xander at Saint Catherine's Church in Greenwich, Connecticut. Monsignor Dario Sabatino was the officiator.

***

Tom Zeranski and Susan Frangiamore were married at Saint Christopher's Chapel. Brooks Allgood and Dean Armandroff were married at Saint Peter's Cathedral.

***

Maria Sabatino and Signor Fazzolini are still courting.

***

Francesca Rosato's cookbook was a smashing success, as was her new and enlarged bakery on Greenwich Avenue. She and Simeon Meade were married at Saint Catherine's Church in Greenwich, Connecticut, with her brother, Dario, officiating.

***

Antonina Sabatino became the most beloved and most famous soprano in the history of the Metropolitan Opera. Her performances, no matter where in the world they took place, were always sold out. She is adored by all who hear her sing. She is wealthy and successful beyond her wildest dreams.

There were many nights, however, when Antonina's spirit troubled her so much that she was unable to fall asleep.

FINIS

The Bread of Angels

For those of you who follow my books, I hope you were happy with "more", as you had requested, about the Sabatino family and the little band of Italians who came to America to settle. For new readers, you are introduced to the Sabatinos and all of their friends, neighbors, and family in *The Tears of San Antonio*. This book, *Murder at the Metropolitan Opera*, follows *The Tears* chronologically.

The third Sabatino book is *Cherubini*, and, in October of 2009, *The Bread of Angels* will follow.

The Bread of Angels, or *Panis Angelicus*, said musically and in Latin, will take place during World War II (1943-1944) in Greenwich, Connecticut and Kittery, Maine. As are most of my books, it will be a mystery-romance, and in it you will again greet many of your old literary friends.

Thank you all.

J. Tracksler

Angelique's Kiss

Ingredients
2 tsp. unsalted butter to grease the pan
10 egg whites
½ tsp salt
1 tsp cream of tartar
1 cup cake flour, plus more for dusting the pan
1 cup pure maple syrup
1 tsp. pure vanilla extract

Preheat oven to 350 degrees. Generously butter and flour Angel Food Tube pan

1. In large mixing bowl, using an electric mixer set on HIGH, whip the egg whites, salt and cream of tartar until the egg whites form soft peaks…about 5 minutes.
2. Reduce the mixer speed to MEDIUM and slowly add the cake flour and maple syrup until just combined.
3. Blend in the vanilla
4. Pour the batter into the prepared pan and bake until golden, about 35 minutes
5. Carefully invert the pan onto a wire rack and allow it to cool upside down, which prevents the cake from falling
6. Run a sharp thin knife carefully around the edges to remove the cake.

At Delmonico's Restaurant, this cake is served with spun sugar filling the middle. It makes the cake seem as if it is aflame. You might want to try it plain, or with fresh strawberries or raspberries.

Pasta alla Norma

This simple and delicious dish is named for Vincenzo Bellini's opera heroine, "Norma", of the opera of the same name.

Most superb Italian dishes are simple ones; dishes that depend on fresh ingredients to spark appetites. This dish comes from the area around Naples, an area known for prodigious tomatoes and eggplants.

It is said that Bellini created this opera with a certain Soprano in mind. This Soprano's name was Giuditta Pasta, a superstar in her own time. Perhaps this is why the dish is called Pasta alla Norma. In the world of opera, anything is possible.

Ingredients
1 large eggplant, peeled and cut into ¾ inch cubes
2 tsp salt
5 tbsp. olive oil
2 cloves of garlic, minced
1 medium onion, chopped fine
2 – 28 oz cans of crushed tomatoes, OR
3 pounds of fresh tomatoes, crushed
1- 6 oz can of tomato paste
A large handful of fresh, chopped basil leaves
(do NOT bother to make this dish if you only have dried basil)
Freshly ground black pepper to taste

1 pound of thick, tubular pasta. Ziti, rigatoni or farfalle are all fine

1. Place eggplant cubes into a colander, sprinkle with salt and let drain for 1 hour
2. Heat olive oil in heavy skillet over medium heat
3. Add eggplant and sauté, flipping the eggplant over and over, for approximately 3-4 minutes, or until eggplant cubes are browned
4. Remove eggplant from skillet and drain on paper towels...do not clean out skillet
5. Brown garlic and onion in the same skillet, using the oil that is left. Be careful not to burn
6. Add tomatoes, tomato paste, basil and pepper, bring to a simmer, lower the heat, and cook, uncovered for 10 minutes more
7. Add the eggplant cubes and simmer for 10 more minutes
8. Serve over hot, drained pasta

Piccata De Vitello

This sauce should have a really good tang of lemon. Just ask our son, Adam how much!

Ingredients
¾ cup vegetable oil
12 veal escallops, about 1 ¾ to 2 pounds
1 cup flour
3 tbsp. butter
1 cup dry white wine
½ cup chicken broth
Juice of one lemon or more, if desired
Salt and pepper to taste

1. Heat oil in a large sauté pan over medium high heat
2. When oil is very hot, quickly dredge the escallops in flour and carefully place them flat in the oil
3. Brown each side, turning one
4. As they are done, set them aside on a warmed platter
5. When all escallops have been browned and removed, drain the oil from the pan.
6. Return pan to heat and add butter
7. When butter is melted, return the veal and any juices to the pan
8. Simmer and add chicken broth and lemon juice
9. Swirl to coat escallops, then fork them onto a lipped serving platter
10. Bring sauce to a boil, scraping all the browned bits from the bottom of the pan, until sauce is slightly thickened. Taste and adjust salt and pepper
11. Pour over veal slices and serve

This is good with noodles or rice and a serving of braised broccoli raab.

Cannoli alla Gemelli
The Sabatino Twins' Cannoli

Ingredients
2 cups flour
1/3 cup sugar
½ tsp. salt
3 Tbsp. melted butter
2 eggs, well-beaten
4 Tbsp dry white wine
2 Tbsp brandy extract
Apprx. 4 cups vegetable oil for frying
Egg white for sealing

Pastry Filling
2 pounds ricotta cheese
1 ½ cups sugar
2 tsp vanilla extract
2 tsp orange flower water
½ cup candied citron, chopped (optional)
¼ cup semisweet chocolate (optional)

Here in modern America, one can buy very good pre-made cannolli shells. Ferraro makes excellent ones, so if you want to skip this part, buy some shells If you do, then proceed right to the filling. However, these were always hand made in Italy and many Italian housewives would hit you with their rolling pin if you *bought* them, perhaps you may want to give it a try.

For the tubes:

1. You will need 8 to 10 wooden dowels or aluminum cannolli tubes, about 7/8" in diameter and 5-6 inches long
2. In a large mixing bowl, combine flour, salt, sugar, butter and eggs. Stir in wine and brandy extract until the mixture holds together. If a bit dry, add a drop or two more brandy extract until the dough is pliable. Knead into a ball and refrigerate for a half-hour.
3. Roll the dough until it is thin. Use an empty 2-pound coffee can to cut out six circles, each about 5 ½ inches around. With a rolling pin, slightly elongate the circles into oval shapes.
4. Use a deep-fat fryer and heat the oil (which should be about 3" deep) to 375 degrees.
5. Lay each of the dowels across each of the dough ovals. Fold the dough over to form a tube. Seal with egg white to hold.
6. Gently drop dowels and dough into hot oil When golden brown and crackly, remove carefully and drain on paper towels.
7. When cool, slip the dowel off.
8. Stuff tubes with filling. Sprinkle, if desired, with powdered sugar
9. OPTIONAL: Ends of the cannolli can also be dipped in chopped pistachio nuts for a very festive look.

Instructions for Filling:

1   Combine all of filling ingredients in mixing bowl and whip into a smooth paste.
2   Chill.
3   Use a small teaspoon or a large, plain pastry tube to fill.
4   Serve at once. The cannolli are best when FRESHLY filled.

Dacquoise Antonina

Ingredients

Daquoise Rings (3)
1 cup sugar
2 Tbsp cornstarch
¾ cup hazelnuts
¾ cup almonds
9 egg whites, stiffly beaten

Rich, Rich Buttercream
1 ½ cups sugar
¾ cups water
8 egg yolks, beaten
¾ cups butter, softened
2 tsp vanilla extract
(for vanilla cream)
2 tsp coffee liquor (for coffee)
2 tsp Frangelico (for hazelnut)

4 cups rich, rich buttercream
(I cup of each flavor – 1 cup of coffee flavor for decoration)

For decoration: Heavy cream, whipped and slightly sweetened
Chopped hazelnuts, almonds, pistachio nuts
Very expensively optional: gold flakes
Confectioner's sugar, for dusting

For the Daquoise Rings – make three

1. Butter and flour three baking sheets. On each sheet, place the ring rim from a 9 inch flan pan. Butter and flour the ring rim.
2. Mix the sugar and cornstarch together. Grind the almonds and the hazelnuts and add to sugar mix
3. Fold nut mixture into stiffly beaten egg whites
4. Divide the mixture evenly into the three ring rims.
5. Bake in a preheated 390-400 degree oven for 20 minutes. The meringues should bake to a golden brown. Let the meringues cool in their ring rim molds.
6. Carefully, remove the discs of meringues. One side of each will be very flat. This is the bottom side (for assembly)
7. Place one meringue disc, flat side down, on a large, round serving platter.
8. Spoon the cup of vanilla buttercream on top, smooth carefully
9. Place disc #2 on top, pressing slightly, very lightly, just to adhere.
10. Spoon the cup of coffee buttercream on top, smooth carefully
11. Place disc #3 on top, but this time, place it flat side up. Press lightly just to adhere
12. Spoon the hazelnut buttercream on top.
13. With the remaining cup of buttercream and a spatula, smooth the remaining buttercream around the dacquoise.
14. Sprinkle chopped nuts around the sides

15. Pipe whipped cream around the top edge in decorative swirls. Decorate top with chopped nuts, then sift a dainty amount of powdered sugar over the cake.
16. Refrigerate. Serve cold, cut into small wedges, as this is a very, very rich cake.
17. Mmmmmm!

For the buttercream:

1. Stir sugar and water together in a saucepan over medium heat until sugar dissolves and mixture comes to a boil
2. Let syrup boil, without stirring, until the temperature comes to 240 degrees, the soft-ball stage.
3. Remove from heat. Whisking vigorously, pour the hot syrup over the egg yolks and continue to beat until the mixture is cool, light and fluffy
4. Cream butter until it is very soft.
5. Beat the butter and the sugar/egg mixture together until shiny and firm.
6. Divide the buttercream to flavor as you wish. Add flavorings to each small batch.

Books by J. Tracksler:

The Tears of San' Antonio

The Botticelli Journey

Murder at Malafortuna

The Ice Floe

Deceit

Cherubini

Worse Than A Thief

A Fat Virgin Death

And coming soon: The Bread of Angels (Panis Angelicus)